Praise fo

"In Dr. Teresa Van Woy's memoir, *Wildflower*, a que⸺ ⸺ hapter of her journey from destitute child with a maniacal mother to successful physician with a loving family. Reading about her *dreaming of a happier life* when it seemed like there was no way out of the cycle of abuse brought to mind a quote I'd like to contribute from the classic song, The Quest:

> *To dream the impossible dream,*
> *To fight the unbeatable foe,*
> *To bear with unbearable sorrow,*
> *To run where the brave dare not go.*

As a little girl facing struggles most of us can never imagine, Teresa bravely allowed herself to dream when dreams seemed impossible. In doing so, she created a path to a life that's now a testament to choosing positivity and envisioning possibilities. Today, the little girl from the streets of San Francisco lives a loving, fulfilled life close to the very city where she once wandered alone and lost.

Dr. Teresa Van Woy's *Wildflower* is a gripping account of triumph over adversity, and may inspire you to dream an impossible dream!"

— Martha Quinn, original MTV VJ, host of the Martha Quinn Morning Show on iHeart80s @ 103.7, San Francisco

—

"Teresa Van Woy is a writer with extraordinary emotional range. She conveys the darkest realities of her childhood experiences yet somehow takes me with her on a heroic journey that is hopeful. Everyone who loves great literature should read this heart wrenching memoir that proves you are not saddled with your past. You can decide to reinvent yourself and flourish as you travel to adulthood."

— Sean McNamara: Director, Producer: "Soul Surfer,"
"The Miracle Season," "Spare Parts," "Reagan"

Wildflower

A Tale of Transcendence

Wildflower

A Tale of Transcendence

by

Dr. Teresa Van Woy

ISBN 978-1-7343827-0-1

Published by Canyon Rose Press
Benicia, California 94510
info@canyonrosepress.com

Cover Design: Olivia@oliviaprodesigns
Book Design: Jan Malin, info@canyonrosepress.com

Publisher's Cataloging-in-Publication Data

Names: Van Woy, Teresa, author.
Title: Wildflower : a tale of transcendence / Dr. Teresa Van Woy.
Description: Benicia, CA : Canyon Rose Press, 2020. | Also available in ebook and audiobook formats.
Identifiers: LCCN ISBN 978-1-734-3827-2-3 (paperback)
Subjects: LCSH: Abused children--Biography. | Homeless persons--Biography. | San Francisco (Calif.)--Biography. | Perseverance (Ethics) | Homelessness. | Autobiography. | BISAC: BIOGRAPHY & AUTOBIOGRAPHY / Personal Memoirs. | BIOGRAPHY & AUTOBIOGRAPHY / Survival. | BIOGRAPHY & AUTOBIOGRAPHY / Women. | SOCIAL SCIENCE / Poverty & Homelessness.
Classification: LCC HV883.C2 V36 2020 (print) | LCC HV883.C2 (ebook) | DDC 362.76092--dc23.

Printed in the United States of America

For my brothers and sisters.
I'm glad we all came out on top.

Table of Contents

Part Three - Dixieland

Prologue

*"You are never too old to set another goal or to
dream a new dream." — C. S. Lewis*

One of the greatest gifts my mother gave to me is my love for the outdoors. While hiking with a good friend of mine, David Ross, we were admiring wildflowers along the trail when the topic of resiliency came up.

"Isn't it amazing how these flowers survive such harsh conditions, yet still come back year after year? Look at that one." David pointed to a single purple iris. "It appears to be growing right out of the rock. How does it do that?" He stopped walking and looked at me. "You know, Teresa, you're like these wildflowers. With all the adversity you've been through, you still stand tall and shine your beauty for all to see."

Part One

—

Treedy

The Thompson family.

− 1 −

Greyhound

Let me tell you the secret that has led me to my goals:
my strength lies solely in my tenacity. — Louis Pasteur

August 27, 1974
San Francisco Greyhound Bus Station

I don't wanna stay here!" I screamed. "I wanna go home, too!" I pounded on the glass panels of the door, but the bus driver didn't look at me. Not even a flinch. He got impatient with all our crying and clinging. The only thing that concerned him was his stupid schedule. He couldn't care less Mama was stealing me, Rache, and the twins from Daddy.

The sound of the tires crunching on the pavement was all I could hear as the bus began backing out of the lot. Well, that and the thumping of my heart in my ears, that is. My other five five siblings were pressed against the windows inside the bus, shouting silent words while tears streamed down their faces.

"Stop! Y'all can't leave me!" I hunched over, sucking breaths between sobs.

My knees began to buckle under me as the bus pulled onto the street. I didn't know what to do. Mama, Rachael, and the twins huddled together with their arms wrapped around each other, wailing and bawling. I couldn't stay in San Francisco with them. I had to get back home to Florida with everyone else.

One last glimpse as the bus turned out of the lot, then, without another thought, I tore after it. The driver had to stop if he saw me. He had to let me on. He had gained a half a block, but I could still catch it if I ran faster. Pushing hard into the pavement, I bolted past bums lying along the buildings, jumped over pieces of newspaper blowing in the breeze, and dodged all kinds of other trash as I sprinted after it. My lungs burned from the early morning chill, but that didn't stop me. Nothing was going to stop me.

A shout from the other side of the street broke my concentration. One of the bums, the scary kind who screams cuss words out loud. I shouldn't have looked. As I turned my head back toward the bus, my shoe caught the lip of buckled concrete and sent me catapulting forward. The bus was the last thing I saw as my knees crashed hard onto the pavement. My hands skidded in front of me as it disappeared out of sight.

"Noooooo!" I screamed. "Nooooo!"

I couldn't move. I pushed at the ground to get up, but it felt as if I had a heavy cinder block tied to my back. Every breath became a stuttered gasp. More shouting from across the street, but I didn't care. I didn't care about the stream of blood trickling down my knee either. Half my siblings had just left me.

Our new camper. From left, with Deborah missing: Brother, Rachael, Petesy, Gregory, Jon Eric, me, Jonas and Josh.

—2—

The Camper

*The world is a book and those who do not travel
read only one page.* — St. Augustine

June 5, 1974: Jacksonville, Florida.
Two and a half months earlier

*W*hat the hell is all that racket?" Daddy asked. He folded
his newspaper, placed it on the couch, then pulled open
the curtains in the living room to see where the noise was coming from. Outside, Mama stood next to a camper with her arm
reaching into the truck, honking the horn over and over again
until all nine of us kids crammed in the window next to Daddy.

"Come out, everybody! Look what I got!"

Mama jumped up and down, flailing her arms in the air like
one of the big winners on the *Price is Right* or something. She
adjusted her halter top while waiting for us to gather, then scooped
up Jonas and held him on her hip. The top of his behind peeked

from a saggy cloth diaper, but at least he had one on. He and his twin Josh usually just ran around naked. We called them the naked jaybirds. All the neighbors did, too. Mama pinched Jonas' nose and squeezed out thick yellowish-green snot, then flung it to the ground.

"Look what I got for us!" she said in her thick southern accent. "We're gonna take this on our trip this summer. It's gonna be the best vacation ever!"

"Where are we going?" Jon Eric was unable to hide his excitement behind his toothy grin.

He's nine, only two years older than me, and his real name is Jon. We mostly called him by both his first and middle names together, though, since Mama thought the name Jon was way too boring. She wanted to name him Jonathan, but Daddy said only sissies had names like that.

"Who knows?" Mama said. "We'll just have to see where the road takes us. Maybe we'll make it to Texas. All I know is I wanna get as far away from Jacksonville as possible this summer."

As Mama went on talking about how we'd have to use a can to pee in since there's no toilet and boring stuff like what we're allowed to pack in the limited space, something much more exciting caught my eye. In the shadows of the shrubs, a small, bright green tree frog hobbled along the grass. I snuck toward it, got on my knees, and reached my hand out to catch it.

"Little girl. What do you think you're doin'? Get over here when I'm talkin'. You hear me?"

Everyone looked at me, but Mama's eyes were the ones I felt the most. Her cold stare could freeze a Florida pond in the summer. Heat rushed to my face, causing my cheeks to burn. I didn't mean to make her mad. I just wanted a frog to take with me on the trip, that's all. I lowered my head and bit on the end of one of my pigtails as I headed back toward the camper.

Deborah noticed my eyes filled with tears, so she held onto my hand and whispered, "It's okay, Treedy."

Deborah was sixteen, the oldest of us kids, and the one who took care of me most of the time since birth. She'd joke and say she never needed a doll to play with since she had her very own baby sister to take care of. She called me Treedy, so now everybody else does, too. Treedy came from Tree, a shortened version of Teresa.

* * *

The camper was far from being new, but it was new to us, and that's all that mattered. It sat on the back of an old Ford pick-up truck, the kind with two tones of color—sky blue under midnight blue—and was so small that the tailgate jutted out from under it, creating the perfect platform for us to stand on.

"How the hell you think you're paying for this trip?" Daddy asked. "Gas costs money, ya know."

"You mean you're not coming with us, Daddy?" Deborah asked.

Daddy looked down and scratched at one of his long, bushy sideburns while cicadas filled the silence with their chirping and buzzing.

"No. Your father's staying here," Mama said. She turned back to Daddy and raised her voice. "What do you think I've been sewin' all those damn ties for all this time? And all that typin' into the wee hours of the night, transcribin' those documents? You think I did that for my health or somethin'?"

"Is this thing even anchored down?" Daddy asked.

"That's none of your damn business," Mama snapped. "You think I'd put these kids in harm's way?"

We always scattered like mice, searching for a hole to hide in whenever they started their bickering, so that was our clue to escape into the camper.

Brother, the oldest of the six boys, climbed to the upper bunk as the rest of us squeezed in. His real name is Leigh, Leigh Arthur Thompson, III, but we all called him Brother. I don't know why. He spread from one side of the bed to the other so no one else could join him, then announced, "I call this bed!"

"You can't call that," Deborah said. "I'm the oldest. I should get it. Me and Rache."

"Yeah. What makes you think you get it?" Rachael asked, placing her hand on her hip. It didn't take long for everyone else to chime in, causing one loud uproar of commotion.

"Nobody's callin' nothin'," Mama shouted above the ruckus. She heaved herself up and took a seat on the couch. "That bed's already taken. Me and the twins are gonna sleep up there." She held her hands out. "Well, what do y'all think?"

"It's groovy!" Deborah said, running her fingers through her straight blondish-brown hair. "I love it!"

"Yeah, it's so cool," Rachael agreed.

"Wait till y'all see this." Mama tugged under the edge of the couch cushion and pulled out a wooden platform. "Check it out. This turns into a bed."

We gathered around her as she laid the back cushions out to fill the empty spaces. Then she lifted the table from its stand and placed it in the center to complete the puzzle.

"At least four of y'all can sleep here," she said. "We can put two sleeping bags underneath it on the floor, and someone else can sleep up there in the truck." She pointed through a sheet of plexiglass that looked into the back window of the pickup.

"I call the truck seat," Rachael shouted, raising her hand as if she were still in school.

"Okay," Mama said. "You get the truck."

"Hey! That's not fair! You just said nobody's calling anything. Why does she get the front?" Brother asked.

"Because she does. That's why. Please don't start with me."

"Ugh!" Brother jumped from the bed and stormed out the door. "Of course, she does! She's such a queen bee!" he shouted.

It's true. Rachael was a queen bee. That's what we all called her,

DR. TERESA VAN WOY

at least, since she's Mama's absolute favorite of the bunch. Well, she wasn't the only one. Petesy and Jonas were, too. Mama said it's because they're special with learning disabilities and dyslexia and all. But even I knew that wasn't true. How could she possibly know that about Jonas since he's only two? There's no way she could know if he had a hard time reading or not. Brother said it's only because they looked like her and not Daddy like the rest of us, otherwise she would have said the same thing about Josh since he's Jonas' twin.

* * *

That night, when I finally drifted to sleep after all the excitement, I had a dream. I dreamt I was in a beautiful meadow with wildflowers covering the ground for as far as I could see. Birds chirped in the distance, but there wasn't a single other sound. No screaming and yelling. No racket from the other kids. No fighting between Mama and Daddy. I wasn't alone though. Mama was with me. Just the two of us.

I reached out to hand her a bouquet of flowers I had picked, when, all of a sudden, the sound of thunder cracked the air above us. Bolts of lightning lit the sky as the flowers wilted in her hands. Her face turned cold as stone and her eyes began to glow. Dark clouds swirled above us like the tornado from *The Wizard of Oz*.

Mama raised her hands in the air and began cursing the heavens with a loud, piercing shriek. One-by-one, the nails on her fingers grew into long, pointed spikes.

Huh! Drenched in sweat, I pulled my teddy bear close to my chest as my legs kicked to unravel the knotted sheets from my feet. No matter how many times I had that dream, I always woke up trembling.

I wish Daddy was coming with us.

Mama, photo taken at Mr. Sy's
Casino of Fun, Las Vegas.

– 3 –

Mama

You have to go on and be crazy.
Craziness is like Heaven. — Jimi Hendrix

addy stayed out of sight while we filled the camper with clothes, dishes, and canned goods. He wanted absolutely nothing to do with our trip. And with the excitement of our vacation buzzing around me like a swarm of honeybees, I had forgotten all about the bad dream I had.

I have to admit though, it wasn't easy saying bye to Daddy. I wished he could come with us. I really did. Especially after seeing the tears in his eyes when I hugged him goodbye. But even at the age of seven, I knew it was probably best that he stayed behind. Ever since Mama brought that camper home, their arguing and fighting had escalated so high, I actually couldn't wait for them to be apart. Besides, we were only going away for the summer. I'd see him again soon enough, anyway.

The good thing about being tiny is I fit perfectly on the upper bunk, so that's where I rode most of the time. Jon Eric joined me up there sometimes, too. We were becoming more like friends and our two-year age difference didn't seem like such a big deal any-more. Not like in school, at least, when two grades apart are huge.

Mama pulled into a rest area for a bathroom break and began yelling at us for sitting in the camper doing nothing.

"You knew we'd be stoppin' to eat at some point," she hollered. "Now we all have to wait. And I'm starvin'. Do I have to tell you fuckin' kids every single little thing to do?"

* * *

When we made it to Louisiana, Mama zig-zagged all through the state, making it a point to visit her long lost relatives along the way. The summer before, we took the station wagon and saw a few cousins before spending the rest of the time camping at Lake D'arbonne. But not now.

Daigles were all over the place in Louisiana—Lafayette, Baton Rouge, West Monroe, Shreveport, and towns all around New Orleans—and Mama wanted to see them all. Daigle is grandma-ma's last name, and with twelve sisters and brothers, we had a lot of stops to make.

People we barely knew opened their doors to Mama's unan-nounced surprise visits. Cousins I've never met before, and aunts and uncles Mama hadn't seen in years welcomed us with open arms. I guess that's how it is with family, or maybe it's just a Louisiana thing, but whatever the case, we didn't mind it at all—especially with all the food they made for us. Dishes like collard greens with black-eyed peas and ham with a side of cornbread, or fried okra with barbecued ribs, baked beans, and coleslaw. Shoot, at that point, even if they had only given us a bowl of plain white rice, it would have been better than the canned goods or the Velveeta cheese sandwiches we had become accustomed to eating.

It wasn't only the food, either. The best part was how Mama completely changed around others. Not only them, she did it to everyone, and to be honest, I normally couldn't stand it—the way she used her fake smile and changed her voice to make herself seem so nice and all. But now, at least, it gave us a break from how she usually treated us.

In front of them, she acted as if we were her trophies. That's the weird thing about her, the way she loved to show us off. You'd think with how mean she was, there'd be nothing to show, but in front of others, we were her pride and joy. She loved nothing more than being a mother, and always bragged about how healthy and beautiful we all were, taking full credit, of course.

* * *

Mama saved New Orleans for last—the Big Easy, a place with Voodoo, witches and magic spells. The same place she lived as a kid. She parked the camper in the French Quarter and treated us to beignets at an outside café called Café du Monde. Then we sat under the shadows of the great St. Louis Cathedral as she told us the history of our Cajun roots. She explained how long ago, French immigrants moved from France to an area in Nova Scotia, Canada called Acadia.

"When the British took over Canada, the French people refused to accept the king's Protestant religion, so they were kicked out of the country," she said. "Most of them, like your great-great-grandmother, moved to Looziana. When they got here, the Acadians called themselves *Cadians* for short, but with their heavy French accent, the D sounded more like a J, and that's where the word Cajun came from."

That's another thing about Mama. She loved feeding us tidbits of knowledge any chance she got.

When we hit the road again, it didn't take long for our excitement about the trip to fade, then disappear altogether. Laughter turned to boredom, conversations to bickering, and any playfulness we had before turned to absolute grumpiness. I guess you'd expect that with ten of us crammed into a small furnace. That's what the camper felt like, at least—a hot, scorching oven.

As the days went on, my clothes became so ratty and filthy Mama said I looked more like a ragamuffin than a little girl. Layers of dirt had settled into the creases of my neck, causing two crusty lines to form from one side to the other. Rachael said I looked gross. "You should wash your face at the rest areas," she said, but I never remembered to.

The underside of my hair became so matted, it formed into one huge dreadlock. I wasn't like my two older sisters. I hated brushing my hair. I wanted to take a pair of scissors and cut it all off, but there was no way Mama would let me. She'd have an absolute fit, since she hated short hair on girls. She said Grandmama always butchered her hair, so she'd never do anything that cruel to us.

That's another thing about her. She despised Grandmama, and in all her stories, she never once called her Mom or Mama. She only referred to her as "the witch" or "the hag", or something like that. Then she'd go on telling us how lucky we were.

Lucky we didn't have to live with such a witch for a mother. Lucky we had color in our lives, instead of the dark, depressing environment *she* had to live in. Lucky we had toys to play with instead of only being allowed to look at them in a box on a shelf. Lucky she let us have long hair so we didn't look like boys, and lucky we didn't have a mother who beat us all the time, as Grandmama did to her.

Lucky? I guess in some ways we were. She did take us on neat trips and stuff. Everything could always be worse. I know my life was definitely better than the one she had as a kid, but like her, I also felt very unlucky most of the time. I just didn't get it. Every time she said things about her mother, I wondered how she couldn't see that she did some of the same exact things to us. We all wondered that.

Mama honked the horn as we crossed the state line into Texas, but with nothing to see for miles, my eyes grew heavy. Sleeping had become my way to fight the monotony and boredom of the long trip. A sudden jerk woke me up. Mama swerved into the exit lane at the last second, causing a bowl to plummet from the counter onto the floor. We had become used to that, the shaking and rattling with each turn, and stuff flying all over the place. We tried to keep the camper tidy at first–well, mostly Deborah–but after a while, even she knew it was pointless. Things were just going to fall and get messed up again, anyway.

Mama slammed the truck door closed, then stomped her way back to the camper. She let out a deep grunting sound as she heaved herself onto the tailgate which was a sure sign of something bad to come. Everyone closed their eyes to pretend they were sound asleep as the door opened.

"What the hell is this dump? Look at this filth! What have y'all been doing back here this whole time?"

She raised her hand toward an overhead cabinet where a shirt sleeve dangled down, causing Gregory to flinch at her sudden movement. It wasn't our fault the latches didn't stay shut.

"You're nothing but a bunch of lazy heathens! Don't think for even one second I'm takin' Florida Trash with me to San Francisco. I'll leave y'all right here! And don't think that I won't!"

She bent over, grabbed an armful of clutter from the floor, and threw it toward Deborah and Brother.

"I come back here to relax and this is what I get? Get out of here!" she screamed. "Get out you filthy, rotten tramps!"

Brother pushed through the door, almost landing on Rache on the way out. She and the twins always rode up front with Mama. Everyone else rushed after him, even Jon Eric. My body stiffened at the sight of him. I thought Jon Eric was on the upper bed with me.

"How the hell did I raise such lazy kids?" Mama asked herself.

She picked up a broom and began cursing as she swept. The monster had arrived, and I was trapped on the upper bed with her between me and the door. My ears pounded with each beat of my heart. I didn't know what to do. Squeezing my muscles tight,

I hoped she wouldn't see me if I didn't move. There was no way I could walk by her while she's in that mood. She spun around as if she could hear my every thought. Her cold gaze stabbed through me like a sword.

"What are you still doing here? You think I wanna look at your ugly face?" Her clenched teeth caused the veins over her temples to bulge. "Get the hell out!" She raised the broom and screamed louder. "Get out!"

Scooting to the edge of the bed, I gripped the corner of the cabinet to lower myself down. I couldn't take my eyes off her. I had to know her next move. My foot blindly reached for the step below.

"Hurry!"

Mama propelled the broom forward like a pool cue, thrusting the bristles into my face. Its sharp quills hit me in the eye, causing me to lose hold and tumble to the floor.

"Ouch!" I yelped.

I pressed my hand against my eye to lessen the pain, but it didn't stop the tears from pouring down my cheek. Mama towered over me with eyes as wide and wild as a crazed maniac. I tucked my legs close to my body, squeezing myself tight into a ball.

"Get up," she seethed.

She reached down, pulled me up by the hair, then let go. My body crashed back to the floor, like a piece of discarded trash. I scrambled to get my feet under me, but before I had a chance to move, she thrust her foot to the side of my ribs.

Pain shot through my body as another kick pelted me.

"Ow, Mama. Stop. I'm leaving," I cried.

I looked away as long spikes grew from her fingertips. Her eyes began to glow. She was way too scary to look at. I had to get out. I pushed myself up, knocked past her, and stumbled out the door. A pot flew out after me, crashing onto the pavement below with a loud gong.

Strangers all around the rest area stopped in their tracks and stared while Mama used both the broom and her foot to shove and kick everything out until a huge heap was piled on the ground.

"Little girl, you better get those kids to come clean up this damn mess," she yelled. "Unless you wanna sit here and clean it all up yourself."

Quit calling me little girl! My name is Teresa!

"Come back, everybody!" I shouted, keeping my head low to avoid the onlookers. "Come back!"

One-by-one, my brothers and sisters eased their way from an alcove, and together we began sorting through the mess.

"I wish those stupid people would stop staring at us," I whispered.

"I know. Just don't look at 'em. They'll lose interest soon enough," Greg said.

"Did y'all hear Mama mention San Francisco?" Deborah asked.

"Yeah. I wonder what that's all about," Brother said.

Mama appeared at the door with a plastic pitcher in her hands. "Go fill this with water," she said, then slung it in my direction. The edge caught me on the back of the head and toppled to the ground.

"Geez! You didn't have to throw it at me!"

I felt brave. Always brave around others. I could never say that to her if I were alone. I rubbed my hand against the back of my head to feel for blood.

"You could've just handed it to her like a decent human being," Brother said.

"I wasn't aiming it at her. I didn't mean for it to hit 'er."

She looked around the rest area—at all the eyes glued on us and quickly changed her tone. "Will you *please* fill it with water, so I can make some milk?"

I snatched the pitcher from the ground and headed toward the water spigot. Each step felt like a dance between my brain and my heartbeat.

"Owah!" I said under my breath while trying to hold in my tears.

I hated powdered milk, and the mere thought of it made my stomach churn. It reminded me of a time Mama forced me to drink a cup of clabbered milk she found sitting on the windowsill in my room. *Yuck!* That thick, white glob floating on top of clear yellow liquid. *Uck!*

I clutched the handle of the pitcher so tight, it left a deep indentation on my palm, but I needed that to distract me from the throbbing on the back of my head, the pain in my side, and the stinging in my eye.

"I didn't mean for it to hit you," I mumbled under my breath as I filled the pitcher with water. "Yeah, right! What a liar!"

By the time I made it back to the camper, Mama's mood had already shifted back to her normal, as if sweeping everything onto the ground, screaming like a maniac, and causing a scene was all she needed to release her anger. The monster had tucked itself back inside her.

"Here's your water." I handed her the pitcher.

"Thank you, sweetie!"

Ugh! That syrupy voice.

She could have been Mrs. Cleaver from *Leave it to Beaver* by the way she sounded, so sweet and loving. *How can she act like that? I don't get it. She acts as if everything is just fine and dandy. Doesn't she even remember how mean she was just a few minutes ago?*

After mixing in the milk, Mama handed us each a cup. No matter how much she stirred it, thick globs of clumped powder always floated to the top. It was the grossest thing ever, like drinking puke itself. I wanted to sneak away and dump it out, but her eyes never left me. She knew I despised it and had to watch me until it was all gone. I pinched my nose to block the smell, then took in a small sip. Chunks of powder swished by my tongue causing me to bend over and gag.

"Drink it," Mama said through clenched teeth.

Her beady eyes narrowed, and I could tell the monster yearned to come out again. I took in a few more drops, but my stomach wouldn't have anything to do with it. Dry heaves bellowed from deep within my throat.

"If you throw that up, I'll make you lick it off the ground, so help me God," she said. "Drink it NOW! We don't have all day to wait here for you."

Please don't throw up! Pleeeease don't throw up! God, please help me! I closed my eyes to block out her evil glare. I knew she'd push my face into it. There was no question about that. It's probably what she was waiting for. *God, please help me!* I put the cup back up to my lips and pretended to take another sip to buy time. *Stop watching me!*

"I'm not waiting all fucking day for you! We could already be through Texas by now. You have exactly two seconds, or I'm leaving you right here."

Shoot! Pretend it's something else. Hurry! What's warm and chunky? Hurry! God! Tomato soup! Pretend it's tomato soup. I held the cup back to my mouth, plugged my nose, and chugged it down. *Please don't throw up!*

"Now, that wasn't so difficult, was it? Come on. Let's go."

I ran to the camper, praying the milk wouldn't come back up, then threw myself on the upper bed and began sobbing. "Why does Mama hate me so much?"

Deborah joined me on the bed and placed her hand on my shoulder. "She doesn't hate you, Treedy. She just wants to make sure we stay healthy, that's all."

"But she's so mean! I don't know how Daddy ever even married her."

"Well, she didn't used to always be like that, you know. Believe it or not, she used to be nice. I mean, she used to be kinda *normal.*

"What happened to her then?" I wiped my eyes and looked up at Deborah.

"Nobody knows. She just went crazy, that's all. When she became pregnant with you, something really wicked happened to her." Deborah tucked a strand of my hair behind my ear as she spoke.

"Like she became possessed or something. Maybe because she already had six of us running around the house driving her crazy. Who knows? But she locked herself in her bedroom and stayed there all day. Every day. She kept her room pitch black with the curtains closed and the lights off, and hardly ever left her room for months. She only came out a couple of times each day to use the bathroom, but that was it. And she became so mean that me and the rest of the kids ran and hid whenever we heard the door to her room open."

Deborah covered her face with her hands, then peeked over the tips of her fingers to recreate the scene.

"Really?" I asked.

"Yeah, then right before you were born, she finally went to the hospital. I think Daddy made her go. The doctors said she had a nervous breakdown and put her on a bunch of pills to try and fix her. They didn't work, though. She was never the same again after that."

"But why? What did I do to cause that?"

"You didn't do anything, Teresa. She just went crazy, that's all."

"Yeah, and luckily you came out with all ten of your fingers and toes from all those pills she took," Brother added from down below.

I rolled over and closed my eyes. "I guess that's why she hates me so much, then."

"No, Teresa. She only hates you because you look like Daddy," Brother said.

I inhaled a stuttered breath as tears poured down my face.

⌒

Cleaning up in the motel pool.

– 4 –

Enchantment

Never underestimate the importance of having fun.
— *Randy Pausch*

*I*t seemed like the drive through Texas would never end. It just kept going on and on with nothing to see for miles but cacti and tumbleweed. And the heat. At least in Louisiana we had relatives to visit with air conditioning and swimming pools, but there was absolutely no escaping this.

My shirt clung to me like a suction cup, and my body felt so sluggish that I didn't want to move at all, which was kind of weird since I wasn't doing anything but resting. To top it off, my lips became so dry I couldn't even smile if I wanted to without them cracking and bleeding. The worst was the back of my neck, though. Mama said I had a heat rash, but whatever it was, it felt like a thousand hot needles poking into my skin.

My stomach hurt from being hungry all the time because food had become a huge issue for us. Even though our cabinets were packed with canned goods at the beginning of our trip, we devoured them way faster than Mama had expected. The problem was, she didn't have enough food stamps to last the whole summer, so we were down to splitting one measly can between the ten of us. Don't get me wrong, we had yummy things like chili, Chef Boyardee, pork-n-beans, Vienna sausages, and stuff like that. It just wasn't enough.

Every time we thought the trip was almost over, Mama would say she wanted to keep on driving. She reminded me of the signs on the wheel flaps of semi-trucks that read, "Keep on truckin'", the way she'd pull out the map and say, "Look, we're so close to so-and-so, it would be a shame to miss it. Let's keep goin'." She did that over-and-over again, and now she tells us she wants to go all the way to San Francisco.

"You'll love it there," she said. "We'll finally be out of this miserable heat. You know Mark Twain said that the coldest winter he ever spent was the summer he spent in San Francisco?"

She had the map spread out on the picnic table of a rest area and began tracing her finger west from Texas for all of us to see.

"Check this out. When we get to El Paso, look how close we are to Mexico. Maybe we should go down here to Juarez." She slid her finger down, then continued gliding it along Interstate-10 all the way to California.

"Shoot," she tapped her finger on the crinkled paper, then moved it down toward the bottom of the map. "Well, I don't wanna skip San Diego. I've always wanted to go there, so we'll dip down a little before heading up to San Francisco."

She looked up from the map for a moment, then placed her finger back onto Southern California.

"See how close San Diego is to Mexico? Maybe instead of Juarez, we'll go to Tijuana."

I wanted the trip to be over so badly, but the thought of California and Mexico gave me an unexpected burst of energy, especially with the promise of cooler weather. When we started moving again, I climbed to the upper bunk and thought back to the beginning of summer when Mama first showed up with the camper. I was so excited and couldn't wait for the adventure to begin.

I had no idea how hot, hungry, and irritable we'd all become. Sure, we sang songs, and played games and stuff, but mostly, we fought about everything. Stupid things, too, like taking up too much space on the couch, or who's turn it would be to heat a can of food for supper, or who's going to be the one to empty the pee-can before it gets too full.

I thought about Daddy and the way his eyelashes were clumped with tears when we said our goodbyes. Back then, I couldn't understand what made him so sad, since we were only going away for the summer. But now I got it. I missed him terribly.

"I want you to know something," he said before I climbed into the camper that day. "I want you to know how much I love you. I'll always love you. Remember that."

It was such a weird thing for him to say. Why would I ever forget that? A stream of tears ran down his cheeks.

"You're my little Peanut, you know. And, don't forget, you Ute!"

"You Ute" was our thing. No one else's. Something that went way back to when I was just learning to speak. Daddy would hold me in the air and say, "You're so cute," and I'd say, "No, you Ute," so it stuck. My eyelids grew heavy as I reminisced of that day. For some reason, sadness always made me sleepy.

* * *

The camper slowed, then rocked side-to-side.

"Damn it!" Brother said. "Why does she always have to hit the curb?"

A wave of urine splashed over the rim of the pee-can right on the area where I slept under the couch.

"I'm not cleaning that this time." Brother folded his arms across his chest.

The floor always smelled so bad, no matter how much we cleaned it up. Deborah said I could scent out anything with my wolf nose, but that's only because she didn't have to sleep under there.

I peeked out the window as Mama pulled into a parking spot of a motel, then jumped up so fast, my forehead bumped against the ceiling.

"Ouch!" I rubbed my palm against my head. "We get to stay in a motel tonight!" I couldn't believe it! Finally, a real bed and air conditioning.

"What?" Gregory asked.

Mama tapped along the windows as she made her way to the camper. By then, I could tell her mood just by the way she walked from the truck. A slammed door and fast, heavy footsteps were never a good sign. Light tapping on the side windows beat the heck out of a hard thump, and any groaning at all meant I had better jump from the bed as fast as I could to camouflage myself with everyone else.

"Everybody out. We're goin' swimmin' here," she said. "And somebody grab that bottle of shampoo."

Of course. I should've known better. We weren't staying at a motel. That's how we took our baths. That bottle of shampoo went everywhere with us. From lakes and rivers, to truck-stop showers, and rest area faucets. In cities, we'd bathe in a fountain or a motel swimming pool, and sure enough, in the middle of the asphalt lot, a chain-linked fence circled around a glistening blue pool.

"Yeah," Brother said. "Last one in is a rotten egg!" You didn't have to ask him twice. He pushed through the door before anybody could say anything.

Even with lukewarm temperature, the water still felt amazing. We washed up, then played Marco Polo, had chicken fights, and cannonball competitions. We were splashing around and laughing like kids again. That's what the pool did for us. It was like magic. Not only did the dirt and grime wash away, but it took the bad moods, boredom and grumpiness as well. Even the stinging on the back of my neck disappeared when the water brushed against it.

I held my breath and went under to escape the noise and heat, then kicked off from the bottom, shooting myself in the air like a rocket taking off into outer space.

In the distance, an old woman was making a beeline toward us. As she reached her hand out to unlatch the gate, her eyes fixated on the bottle of shampoo sitting at the edge of the pool. The creases of her wrinkled skin deepened with her frown.

Hoping Mama wouldn't do anything too embarrassing, I sunk back under as the lady asked her to show a room key. I wanted to stay under to experience the lightness of my body as it floated, but at the same time, I didn't want to miss out on any of the action, so I came back up.

"Oh, please." Mama's upper lip curled like that of an angry dog. "Can't you see these kids are havin' fun? Let loose and live a little."

Come on, Mama. Don't be mean. My heart pounded as I bit on a rough patch of skin on my inner lip, an area worn from weeks of nervous gnawing.

"I'm sorry, ma'am. Rule is rule. You can't be in the pool unless you're staying here," the lady said. She patted her frizzy yellow hair which didn't move an inch from all the hairspray in it.

"Just let them cool off a little, for Christ's sake."

"I'm sor…"

"You're a hag straight from Hell, aren't you?" Mama interrupted.

The lady put her bony fingers to her mouth and took a long drag of her cigarette. Then, in one exaggerated motion, she pursed her lips to a circle and blew a steady stream of the grey smoke toward Mama. *No! Why did she do that?* Mama hated cigarettes more than anything in the world, well—except for Daddy.

"You fuckin' whore," Mama yelled. Her eyes narrowed and lips pursed.

The lady had woken the monster. Mama brought her arms behind her and scooped the water forward, drenching the lady from head to toe. The frown on Mama's face lessened, then turned to a smile as she continued splashing. The cigarette broke in half, landing on the deck as the lady retreated. Her hands covered her face as Mama began laughing hysterically.

"That's it. I'm calling the police," the lady sputtered, then stormed out the gate.

"Come on kids. Everybody out!" Mama shouted.

Before the lady even reached the office, we were back in the camper with Mama speeding down the road. More pee splashed from the can, but no one grumbled about it this time. That's the magic of the pool.

I loved swimming and bathing at motels. We were always asked to leave at some point, so I really don't know why Mama had to make such a big deal about it. It wasn't like she paid for a room or anything. They probably just didn't like all the soap bubbles floating on the water.

* * *

Mama pulled into the parking lot of a shopping center, parked between a grocery store and a five-and-dime, then came around back to let us know we'd be there for the night. Sleeping in a town was both good and bad. Good because we were able to explore around the area, and bad because we all had to cram in the camper to sleep. At least at rest areas we were able to spread out on picnic tables or lay our sleeping bags in the grass. Not in a parking lot, though. I was always stuck on the floor with Jon Eric, under the pull-out couch, surrounded by the smell of urine.

Brother heated some chili on the small gas stove, then carefully divvied the beans into ten bowls. He'd take some from one, add it to the other, then hold them in the air to compare. The whole process was really annoying because no matter how hard he pretended to make them even, his bowl always had way more than everyone else's. By the time I got mine, it was practically empty.

I tried to make the meal last as long as possible by sucking off the sauce, then smashing each bean against the roof of my mouth to squeeze out its soft innards, but after only a couple bites, it was all gone. I licked my bowl so clean you'd think I had washed it with hot water and soap.

Brother nudged Petesy and the two of them went outside. Everyone but Mama and the twins followed. They took off running toward a large green dumpster in the corner of the parking lot, leaving Jon Eric and I in the dust. By the time we caught up to them, they were already scouring through the garbage eating scraps of wasted food.

"Go somewhere else," Brother shouted. "There's not enough room in here for y'all."

"Yeah, there is." I dug my toes in a small ledge on the side of the dumpster and hoisted myself up.

"No. Wait, Teresa. Don't go in there," Jon Eric said. "Come back down. I've got an idea."

Yeah, right. He was probably lying so he could get in there before me, but I could never resist when he tilted his head to the side and pleaded with his big brown eyes. I let out a sigh, then lowered my leg and jumped down.

"What?"

He leaned toward me and whispered. "Let's see if we can get anything from inside that Kentucky Fried Chicken."

"Huh? What do ya mean?"

"I don't know. Let's knock on the back door and ask if they have any food they could give us."

"What?"

"Come on."

He grabbed my arm and pulled me to the back of the restaurant, but we just stood there staring at the door that separated us from the irresistible smells inside, too scared to do anything.

"Well? You're gonna have to be the one to ask," I said.

Jon Eric took a deep breath, cracked his knuckles, and gently tapped on the door. Then, he crossed his fingers and held them in the air for good luck.

"Someone, please answer," he whispered.

"I don't think anybody's gonna just hand us free food." *I think Jon Eric's going a little cuckoo.* I held my lower lip between my teeth and put my ear to the door to listen for footsteps.

"I don't hear anything. Knock harder. I don't think anyone heard you."

The smell was starting to get to me. We shouldn't have gone there. It was only making me feel worse. Not only did my stomach hurt, but my head did as well, and I was beginning to feel a little dizzy. I hunched over to ease the pain while the smell of chicken continued to haunt me. I could taste it and could only imagine biting into its crispy skin with its grease coating my dry lips like Vaseline. My mouth began to salivate.

"Let's forget it," Jon Eric said.

"No, let's not give up yet." My taste buds had gone beyond the point of no return, exploding in my mouth like a Zots fizzing candy. Nothing would be able to get the thought of eating that food out of my head. "They're still open, so somebody's gotta be in there. Maybe they just can't hear us."

Waiting was torture, but we couldn't give up. Not until we had food in our bellies. The other kids probably already ate everything in the dumpster, anyway. I pounded my fist on the door and didn't stop until it jerked open. A man with an unshaven face and a scowl that could only rival Mamas' stood in the doorway, glaring down at us.

Oh, crap! What are we doing? I grabbed ahold of Jon Eric's hand and gave it a tight squeeze. Neither of us said anything. We stood there frozen, as if we'd just been caught stealing, or something. The man's face softened as he looked down at us, two barefooted kids with clothes and hair still damp from the pool. We must have looked pathetic.

"Can I help you?" He scratched the side of his head.

"Uh... Uh." Jon Eric and I looked at each other.

"Do you have any leftover scraps?" I mumbled. The drool disappeared from my mouth, leaving it dry as the desert.

Oh, my gosh. I am so embarrassed. I can't believe we're doing this.

"What?" The man scrunched his face like a shrunken apple.

"Do you have any leftover food you could give us?" Jon Eric asked.

"Leftover food?" He raised his brows and stared at us like he couldn't believe his eyes—or his ears.

"Yeah, like food people didn't eat. Or food that was burnt that you're gonna be throwing away, or somethin'," I explained. "Anything."

"Uh." He looked to Jon Eric, then back at me. "Hold on a minute." Then he took a step back and closed the door on us.

"Shoot! He probably won't come back," Jon Eric said. His voice had a soft tremble, and I could tell he was fighting back tears.

"I don't know. He might. Let's just wait a little while and see."

I burst out one of the television commercial jingles, then repeated the song over and over again while we waited. "Kentucky Fried Chicken, it's really finger-lickin'...Good chicken!" But too much time had passed. He wasn't coming back.

"Ok. Let's go," I sighed. "I feel so stupid. I can't believe we just begged for food." I kicked at the pavement with each step as we walked away.

"Well, what should we do now?" Jon Eric asked.

"I don't know. My stomach's killing me from smelling all that stupid food. Maybe there's more garbage cans we can check if the other kids didn't get to 'em already."

"Hey, you two! Wait!" a voice called from behind us.

We stopped in our tracks and spun around. I couldn't believe it. The man had returned.

"Here you go," he shouted.

Chills ran through my body when I saw him standing outside the door holding up a large, round, red and white bucket.

Our feet couldn't have moved any faster as we raced back to him. "You can have these," he said when we approached. "I'm really sorry it's not much. It's all I could find."

"Thank you so much! Thank you!" Our words overlapped.

I grabbed the box and took off running with Jon Eric close behind. It was way too embarrassing to let that man see us any longer.

"Give it to me," Jon Eric said after we took a seat on the curb. He snatched the container and tore it open. Inside, stuffed to the gills was a mountain of warm dinner rolls.

"Oh, my gosh. I can't believe he gave all these to us. That guy was so nice." I grabbed one and sank my teeth into its soft dough. "Mmmm. These are the best rolls I've ever had in my whole entire life."

"I know," Jon Eric agreed through a mouthful of bread. "Finger-lickin' good!"

Teresa, age seven, photo taken at
Mr. Sy's Casino of Fun, Las Vegas.

— 5 —

Juvie

Hunger, love, pain, fear are some of those inner forces which rule the individual's instinct for self-preservation. — Albert Einstein

*M*ama said we were going to take a detour up to Las Vegas, but I didn't expect anything like this. Glitz and glamour arose from the desert as if a magic wand was waved across it. One minute we were driving through the tan, cracked earth, and the next we were in something that looked like it came straight from the Land of Oz. Only, this place wasn't green. Even through the blazing heat of the day, I could see the lights shine every color of the rainbow.

I watched in amazement as we passed by all of the flashing signs and lit-up buildings—a neon cowboy, Caesar's Palace, Flamingos, and genie lamps. It reminded me of an amusement park, but Brother said it was mostly for adults. When we finally stopped, it was in front of a place called Mr. Sy's Casino of Fun, a place not nearly as fancy as the other buildings since it was just part of a strip-mall. Mama skipped back to the camper, pulled herself up, and waved around the stack of coupon books she had raided from the visitor's center earlier that day.

"Here. Tear out the page that says free photos." She tossed a couple booklets to each of us. "We can go in there to have our pictures taken." She pulled out a brush and ran it through her long black hair.

"Can I use that when you're done?" Rachael asked after joining us in the camper.

"Then me," Deborah called out.

Rachael brushed through her hair, parting it in the middle, then began weaving it into two long braids.

"Just hurry," I said. "You don't have to get all fancied up. It's just a picture."

I didn't want to waste a single second. Flipping through the pages of each book, I tore out the ones with a picture of a camera on it.

"Come on," Mama said when Rache finished braiding her hair. "Everybody got their coupons?"

"I got mine," I said.

"Yep," Petesy said, then everyone else held theirs up to show her.

"Okay, just follow behind me. I'll find out where to go."

Like a trail of ducklings, we followed mother goose into the casino. I'd never seen or heard or smelled anything like it before. Bells and chimes echoed from slot machines, coins clanked into metal trays, cheering and shouting went on in the distance, and way too many people were talking at once. Swirls of cigarette smoke floated through the air like a blanket of grey clouds hovering after a summer storm. I wasn't sure whether to cover my ears or my nose as I walked through.

I thought back to a field trip I had taken with my second-grade class only a few months earlier. We went to a museum in downtown Jacksonville to see an exhibit about health and the human body. Inside one of the display cases there were two sets of lungs—real lungs taken from dead people. One was normal and pink, right next to a pair of black lungs from someone who had smoked. It was so gross.

That's all it took. I pinched my fingers tight to my nostrils to protect my lungs as we made our way to the photo booth. We took picture after picture, then traded in our free coupons for black-and-white photos framed in a fake hundred-dollar bill.

After Mr. Sy's, Mama drove down the strip a little further, then pulled into the parking lot of another casino, one that had a sign shaped into an enormous clown with a swirled lollipop in its hand. Attached to the building was a huge pink and white striped circus tent.

"The sign says Circus Circus!" I squealed from the upper bed.

We went in and followed Mama through the lights, noise, and smoke to a large carnival section made for kids.

"Y'all can stay here and play," she shouted above the noise. "There's supposed to be a circus show on that stage about every half hour or so." She pointed to a large trapeze net hanging over a black platform stage.

"Deborah and Brother, y'all are in charge of the twins," she continued. "I'll be back a little later."

"What? Why do we have to be in charge?" Brother asked.

"Because you two are the oldest." Before anyone could argue, Mama turned and walked away.

"What?" Deborah's eyes trailed her as she disappeared into the crowd. "Well, let's try to meet here each time there's a performance so we don't all get lost."

As everyone wandered off, I spun in a circle to catch sight of all the games surrounding me: a balloon blast game, a dart throw, stacked milk bottles, Skee-Ball, even one of those ping-pong toss games where you can win a goldfish if your ball lands in the right fishbowl. The one that caught my eye the most, though, was the camel racing game.

"This is so cool! It's way better than the carnivals we have at school," I said to Jon Eric. "Let's go play that camel game."

I tugged on his sleeve to lead him to the metal camels, then we waited and watched as the players rolled a little ball into a hole that determined the number of steps the camel would take. Just like a real race, the announcer spoke into the microphone to get the crowd excited.

"Camel number two is in the lead, followed closely by camel

number five. Number six is coming in at a close third. Oh, wait, number six has taken the lead. Number six is racing to the finish line!"

"Shoot, you have to pay for these," Jon Eric said. He pointed to a sign on the wall with big red letters that read 25 cents.

"Of course! That sucks." I let out a long sigh.

"Well, we'll have to find some money, I guess," Jon Eric said.

We kept our eyes peeled to the floor as we walked around the loop, searching each nook and cranny for any semblance of a coin. Sometimes we'd get lucky, but not enough to keep us entertained for long.

"We should look underneath those games over there." Jon Eric pointed to an arcade area with games like *Shark Jaws, Speed Race, and Dungeon.* "There's probably a lot of money that rolled underneath them."

"No way. Kids are everywhere. I'm not getting on the floor."

"I know. Don't worry about it. We'll never see these people again."

That wasn't the first time I heard those words that summer. I thought about the people staring at us at the rest area where Mama threw her last fit, then folded my arms across my chest.

"Come on. Unless you just want to stand here watching everybody else have fun."

He was right. We could only play the games if we had money, but even if we'd never see these people again, it didn't make it any less embarrassing.

"Okay." I shrugged my shoulders. "I guess."

I followed him to the arcade area, glanced around to make sure no one was watching, then got on my hands and knees in front of one of the video games. Through the dirt and grime, I spotted a quarter hidden under a large dust ball. It was too far back, though, and there was no way I could reach it. Jon Eric had his arm buried to his shoulder under one of the other machines, reaching with all his might to get something.

I got up and casually walked by a nearby trash can. After

making sure no one was watching, I pulled out a white paper cone with sticky bits of pink cotton candy attached to it. I brought it to Jon Eric who was still straining to reach a coin.

"Here. Use this," I said.

He pushed the cone under the game, swiped it back-and-forth, then pulled out a couple of coins.

"Perfect!"

We worked as a team, switching between pretending to play the video game, and laying on the floor reaching for coins. As Deborah suggested, we met at the stage each time we heard the announcement for a circus performance. The shows were all amazing, just like being at a real circus, but nothing beat the ponytail lady. She had long, blonde hair pulled up in a ponytail and wore a silver, sequined bodysuit that reflected light like a shiny disco ball. She danced her way to a ribbon that hung from the ceiling, then attached it to her hair.

The spotlight narrowed as her feet left the ground. Lifted by only her hair, she performed all sorts of acrobatics in the air. I rubbed the top of my head as I watched, thinking back to the scaring pain I felt each time Mama dragged me by my hair.

"Gosh, that has to hurt so bad. She must have had a head of steel, or something," I said.

"I know. Let's go find something to eat after this," Jon Eric said. "I'm starving!"

We walked through one of the cafés surrounding the carnival area, but the tables didn't have any of the usual jelly or ketchup packets as we had hoped. Jon Eric grabbed a handful of powdered Coffee-mate creamer packets from the counter on the way out, but I left empty-handed.

"Why didn't you get anything?" His brows forced into a frown.

"No way. I hate powdered milk. I don't care how hungry I am."

"This isn't powdered milk. It's different. You just have to try it."

He tore open the packet and reached it toward me.

"You sure?"

"Yeah."

After sprinkling some of the fine white powder onto my palm, he watched as I touched my tongue to it.

"Whoa! You're right! This is delicious! It tastes like malted ice cream. Way better than those Miracle Whip packets we got last time."

"I know. Let's finish these and go get some more."

After wiping the café clean of creamers, we tucked behind one of the video games and poured each packet into our mouths.

"Did you hear that?" I asked.

"What?"

"Nothin'. I just thought I heard 'em say Thompson over the loud-speaker. Let's go see what we can get from the other restaurants."

"Treedy! Jon Eric!" Deborah shouted. She had her finger pointing at us as she ran in our direction with a police officer and the rest of the kids trailing behind her.

"Come on! We have to go," she shouted.

"Come on, kids. Let's go find your mother," the cop said when he caught up to us.

Oh, my gosh! We're in so much trouble. I grabbed onto Jon Eric's arm as the policeman led us through the busy casino. People all around stopped what they were doing to watch. Maybe because the twins were only in diapers. Or maybe because they'd never seen nine kids getting escorted out of a casino before. Who knows?

A black and white car sat double-parked outside the main entrance with flashing yellow lights lighting the pavement around it.

"Okay, kids. You're all gonna have to pile in," the cop said. He gave an uncomfortable smile as he opened the back door. He seemed friendly enough, but kind of stiff, like he didn't know how to deal with us, or something. He probably didn't have any children of his own.

"Some of you guys can squeeze up front with me," he offered.

Rachael and Petesy jumped at the chance. Petesy held Jonas on his lap, while in the backseat, Deborah took Josh on hers, and I sat on Brother's, between Gregory and Jon Eric.

"Are we goin' to jail?" I asked Deborah while biting on the edge of my fingernail. "I'm scared!"

"I don't think so. The cops just wanna know where Mama is," she whispered.

Oh, my gosh! This is all my fault. I put my hand to my forehead and looked over at Jon Eric. *Well, mine and his. He did it, too!* My stomach knotted into a tight ball, wringing out every bit of the sweet cream I had stolen.

"We're in trouble for stealing all that creamer," I whispered to Jon Eric. "Mama's gonna kill us!"

"I know." He looked down and twiddled his thumbs.

"It's not because of y'all," Deborah said. "It's 'cuz Brother was supposed to be watchin' the twins." Her voice sounded angry. "But he fell asleep in the camper. Jonas and Josh were just wandering around the parking lot in their diapers, and a lady almost hit 'em with her car, so she called the police."

Even through all my fear, I couldn't help feeling amazed as the officer drove down the strip. Everything looked way different than when we had arrived earlier that day.

Signs all around us flashed and lit up the whole street as if we were going through a drive-in movie theatre with a different screen on each building. The city looked like it was draped in jewels and diamonds.

The police officer picked up his radio. "We're not finding their mother anywhere," he said. "I'm gonna go ahead and take 'em in. It's after midnight and these poor kids have to be tired and hungry."

"No!" Deborah shouted. "It's okay. Mama's gonna come back to the camper to get us. You can just bring us back there."

The officer put down his radio and continued driving. "I'm sorry, but I can't bring you kids back to that camper. Not without adult supervision. The two little ones could have been run over by a car... or something worse."

"Please, just take us back to the camper," Deborah begged. "We'll be fine. I'll watch 'em. I promise. I'm old enough. I'm sixteen. They won't get out again."

"No, honey," he said. "I'm taking you guys to juvenile detention until we find your mother. Don't worry, you'll be perfectly safe there."

"Juvenile detention?" Gregory sat straight in the seat. "That's like jail for kids! We didn't do anything wrong!"

Jon Eric and I looked at each other. *Not only is Mama gonna kill us, everybody else is, too!*

* * *

When we arrived at Juvie, we clumped close together like a scene from *Scooby-Doo* as we entered the building.

"Crap! Mom's gonna be so mad," Brother said. He exhaled a long breath, then wiped his hand across his forehead.

"Don't worry, kids. You didn't do anything wrong. You're not in trouble. It's just not safe to be in a casino by yourselves. There's a lot of bad people in this world, and anything could happen to you," the officer said. "Your mother shouldn't have left you there alone."

I exhaled a sigh of relief.

"But how will she know where we are?" Gregory asked. By the look on his face, I could tell he was just as scared as me. "Is *she* gonna be in trouble when you find 'er?"

"I'm sixteen!" Deborah repeated. "I was the one in charge. I'm so sorry. Please don't do anything to our mother." Tears raced down her cheeks as she spoke.

"Well, the important thing is that you're safe," he said. "We left a note on the camper, so your mother'll know where you are." He gave a soft, comforting smile. "Are you guys hungry?"

"Yes!" We all answered at once.

"Ok, let's see what kind of food they have here. It's the middle of the night, so the kitchen'll be closed, but we'll see what we can do."

He turned to a lady who had frazzled hair and black mascara smeared under her eyes as if she had just woken up.

"In the meantime, can you find these kids a place to sleep for the night?"

She let out a loud sigh as if he were asking too much of her. Her cold frown sent chills down my body. Another sigh, this time ending with a click of her tongue to shame us. She picked up the phone to call security.

"We'll have to split you guys up," she said once the guards arrived.

Split us up? I felt my heart leap to my throat. I wasn't the only one scared. We all looked at each other with panic in our eyes.

"You four boys follow him." She pointed to Brother, Petesy, Gregory, and Jon Eric, then instructed one of the security guards where to take them. "You two girls follow him." She pointed to the other guard. "Take 'em to the girl's ward. I'll find a place for these three little ones."

"Can't we all stay together?" Deborah sobbed.

"No!" The lady glared as if to say, "How dare you question me?"

My heart raced even faster as everyone but the twins and I was escorted down the long corridor. After a few minutes, the two security guards came back carrying cots and blankets.

"Put 'em in that office over there," the lady said. "This is ridiculous!"

I grabbed the twins' hands as we followed the lady to the room. *It's not our fault we're here, lady. Would you rather we were criminals, or something?*

After she closed the door behind her, I plopped on one of the cots, and hugged my knees to my chest as I looked around. We were in a small office with nothing but a desk and a couple of chairs and a small window. There wasn't even a single picture on the walls.

"This isn't so bad," I said, not sure if I was trying to comfort myself or the twins. "Sure beats the floor of the camper."

Thank God the twins are with me. I'd be so scared to be here by myself. I hope Mama's okay. I wonder what happened to her, anyway?

I got up to wrap a blanket around the twins when the police officer came back holding a small bag in his hands.

"The kitchen was closed, but I managed to scrounge something up for ya," he said.

He placed a ham sandwich, a bag of chips, a cookie, and a carton of milk in front of each of us.

"Don't worry, kids. We'll find your mother. You'll be safe here," he said.

"Thank you," I said as he turned to leave. All my fears melted away as I picked up the sandwich in front of me. "Oh, my gosh! This is heaven!" I said as I scarfed the food.

When we were done eating, I pushed the three cots together to make one big bed, then turned off the lights, and took the one in the center between the twins.

It's so comfortable here! This is awesome! Cool enough to use a blanket with the AC running, I pulled it over my face and closed my eyes. *I hope Mama's okay. I wonder why she never came back to get us. What if she's hurt?* I rolled over, hugging the blanket close to my chest. *This is so nice. So good to be out of the scorching camper.* I took in a long, deep breath and let it out slowly. *I'm so glad I don't have to smell pee tonight. What if they put Mama in jail?* The thought made my stomach tighten again. *Well, if they do, maybe they'll let us stay here longer.*

I felt guilty as my thoughts went back and forth between worrying about Mama and enjoying juvie so much. My eyes eventually grew heavy, and my body melted into the cot as I drifted to sleep.

* * *

"Come on. Get up!" Mama's harsh voice shouted above us.

Huh? I peeked from the covers to see the dark, night sky through the open slits of the blinds.

Down the hall, I heard the other kids grumbling. *What's going on?*
"Let's go. Get up," Mama said again, this time pushing the side of
the cot with her foot to jerk it back-and-forth. "It's time to leave."
"I don't wanna go," Jonas said, rubbing his eyes.
Josh smacked his lips, then rolled onto his belly, still sound asleep.
"No. We're leavin' now. Come on. Wake up, Josh." She kicked
harder on the end of his cot.
The chill of the air conditioning hit me as I dragged myself
off the small makeshift bed. With my arms wrapped around
my chest, I waited for the twins, then followed Mama out of
the room. Everyone else, including the mean lady, was already
waiting for us in the foyer with their eyes half-closed and groggy.
"She could've at least let us just spend the night," Petesy mumbled.
"I'm so tired," Gregory said. He stretched his arms out and yawned.
"Miss, you have to report to the police station first thing tomorrow," the lady said. "I'm only letting you take the kids because we
need that office in the morning."
"You already told me that," Mama snapped. "What do ya think?
I'm deaf or somethin'?"
Mama was in a mood and the last thing we wanted was a face-
off between those two, so no one said a word as we made our way
out the door.
"Can't even do one simple thing, can you?" she turned to Deborah.
"What the hell happened? I come back to a note on the camper. You
think this is what I want to deal with in the middle of the night?
And then to have to listen to that hag lecture me before she went
to get y'all? Now we have to leave Las Vegas, and it's all your fault!"
Mama brought Deborah back to tears. "It's not my fault. Me
and Brother were taking turns watching the twins."
"I don't want to hear a word. You're the oldest. You were
in charge. Y'all can sleep in the fuckin' camper while I drive.
I'm not going to no damn police station in the morning.
They can kiss my ass."

I held my head down and moped as I climbed into the hot camper and onto the couch. "I wish they *did* arrest her. She's such a meanie," I said, thinking how she'd probably scream at the nice cop if she went to the station in the morning.

"Don't say that, Treedy. You don't mean it," Deborah said.

"Yes, I do."

She didn't drive far out of the city limits before pulling to the side of the road to sleep.

* * *

"What happened last night, Mama?" Gregory asked in the morning.

"What do you mean, what happened?" Mama scowled.

Gregory must have thought she was in a better mood to ask such a question, but now he had to continue. His voice softened to almost a whisper. "I mean, where were you?"

"What the hell kind of question is that? I was in the damn casino. Where do you think I was?"

No one said anything. Deborah would have probably wanted to explain that the cop took her all around Circus Circus to look for Mama. But when they couldn't find her anywhere, that's when he gathered all the rest of us up. She wouldn't dare say that now, though. No way.

"Then I went to an empty camper, and you know what I found? I found a fucking note saying that my children were in juvenile detention. I don't even know what the hell y'all did to put yourself there, and I don't even want to hear about it. My own kids, going to jail. Now I've heard everything. You know what I had to do then? As tired as I was, I had to go back in that fucking casino and look through the goddamn telephone book for juvenile hall. How the hell was I supposed to find it? You think I know my way around this town? You're damn lucky one of those whore cocktail waitresses told me how to find it."

Josh, age two, squatting under our camper at
Coit Tower.

– 6 –

Coit Tower

If you don't know where you want to go, then it doesn't matter which path you take. — *Lewis Carroll, Alice in Wonderland*

*M*ama honked the horn as we drove across the Bay Bridge. I could only imagine *her* excitement since every cell in my body buzzed as the city skyline approached in the distance. The buildings, the hills, the bay—everything I had become so familiar with from all the pictures Mama showed us was now right there, getting closer and closer. The triangular building, the tall brown one, the ferry building with its large round clock. There they were, right on the other side of the bridge.

My mind raced to remember the names of each structure, but before I could recall them, Gregory shouted, "There's the Transamerica Pyramid, and there's the Bank of America building."

Below us, the water swarmed with barges, large cargo ships, and sailboats.

"Look, that must be Alcatraz," Petesy said, pointing to an island with a tower and large pale yellow buildings.

"And there's the Golden Gate Bridge," Gregory motioned to a bridge in the distance with its top buried in a sea of fog.

"Wow, it looks even more beautiful in person," Deborah said.

"I wonder why they call it the Golden Gate if it's red?" I asked, but no one answered.

Skyscrapers dwarfed us as Mama pulled off the exit as if the camper were nothing more than a small ant navigating through a concrete forest. I had to crane my neck in order to see the tops of the buildings we passed. Statues, spires and intricately laced window frames of the older grey buildings stood next to the more modern ones with their sharp edges and mirrored panels.

"I can't believe we finally made it here." Deborah's eyes welled with emotion. "Mama's so brave for taking us all this way. It's been such a great trip." She wiped her tears on her arm. "I mean, really, we got to see so much. I don't know of any other mother who would've been brave enough to do all this."

Everyone became quiet as we pondered her words.

"Yeah," Gregory said, then more silence and nods of agreement.

The camper tilted back, causing us to lean into one another as Mama drove up one of the huge hills.

"Whoa!" Brother said. "Shit! I hope we don't flip backward."

He got off the couch, stood on the floor with knees slightly bent, and held out his arms as if riding a wave on his surfboard. At the top of the hill, he opened the back door to see what we had just climbed.

"What in the heck are you doing?" Deborah asked, but before she could discourage him, he grabbed onto the handle outside the camper and stood on the tailgate.

"This is far out," he said, then began singing, "Rice-A-Roni, the San Fran-cisco treat."

Petesy joined him on the tailgate, and together they clung to the metal hand grip as the door bounced back and forth off Petesy's shoulder. Through the open windows of the camper, the rest of us belted out the song, singing it over and over again as we drove up and down the hilly streets.

After driving around a while, Mama found a place to park, then she, Rache, and the twins joined us in the back. She stopped at a plaza near the Civic Center, an area someone directed her to when asking for directions to the Main Library.

"We made it!" Mama's smile lit up her face. "I can see why Tony Bennett said he left his heart here. It's beautiful!" She let out a long sigh. "Now, how can we celebrate?"

Celebrate?

"I know, I'll cook y'all up a nice pot of spaghetti with that hamburger meat Gregory found."

She got up and shuffled through one of the cabinets for the noodles she had stashed after our last shopping trip.

"See these white buildings 'round here?" she asked, pointing out the window. "They're made from real granite. Can you believe that? I read all about it, so I wanted to show y'all. The style's called Beaux-Arts, taught from an architect school all the way in Paris. We can go check 'em out once we're done eatin'."

We waited along the sidewalk outside the camper while Mama cooked the spaghetti. Brother held his fingers in a circle and whispered, "Yeah! Mama's finally doing the cooking!"

Across the street, the plaza buzzed with people, but most of them were scary-looking street people with long scraggly hair and beards. A flock of pigeons flew overhead in large circles, then scattered amongst the statues, park benches, and the windows of buildings. Then, as if someone rang a dinner bell, they all flew to the ground together, pecking at invisible scraps on the concrete.

Brother patted Gregory on the shoulder. "Yeah, Greg," he said, then leaned his head back and took in a long sniff to savor the smell of hamburger.

Gregory was our hero that day. The one who found a half package of hamburger meat in a garbage can earlier that morning. He was the reason we got to have spaghetti, and the reason why Mama bought the noodles and sauce. He smiled, then looked down at the pavement. He never liked being the center of attention.

"Spaghetti's ready," Mama shouted.

She piled our plates high, almost overflowing, then we brought them to the sidewalk to eat. We hadn't seen that much food since we left Louisiana. I closed my eyes as I slurped each noodle, taking in every bit of the delicious beef and tomato flavor. *Mmmm! Real-cooked-food! Not from a can. I loooove spaghetti.*

"Stop!" Gregory shouted.

I nearly choked on my noodle at the sound of his voice. One of the bums, wearing a long, dark trench coat squatted next to him. He loaded Gregory's fork with spaghetti, shoved it into his mouth, then stabbed it back onto the plate for more.

"Get out of here," Mama shouted. She pushed her plate aside, and charged toward the man, but he ran before she could get anywhere near him.

"Eww. He ate from my fork," Gregory's lips curled in disgust as he pushed his plate away.

"Just wipe it off. It should be fine," Mama said. "That guy's lucky I didn't get my hands on him. Y'all need to keep a closer eye on your food around here. These people are like rats."

Using two fingers, Gregory held the fork away from his body as his eyes began to well with tears.

"Give me that," Mama snatched the fork from him, and wiped it on the inside of her shirt. "Here. You can have mine."

Poor Gregory. He cut the noodles where the man took a bite and scraped them onto the ground. "That was so gross," he said.

* * *

After eating, we walked around the Civic Center, then checked out all the granite buildings along Van Ness Street.

"Looks like they show a free movie here each day at three,"

Mama said after reading the bulletin board at one of the Federal buildings. "If we hurry, we should be able to catch one today." We rushed up the stairs and took a seat in folding chairs next to some other kids, just as the movie *Pippi Longstocking* began. I sat upright in my chair watching the strongest girl in the world beat up a crew of pirates while fantasizing I was her—strong, brave, independent and funny.

I walked from the movie with a skip in my step, ready to beat up anyone who bothered us. *Where's that bum who took Gregory's fork? I'll show him!* I held my fists up and punched at the air as I walked.

Once the sun began to set, we piled back in the camper so Mama could look for a place to sleep for the night. Only to me, it wasn't the camper. I was in Villa Villekulla, Pippi's pink and yellow home with a bright green roof overhead.

Mama drove around, circling each block over and over again, then wound her way up a hill, and parked the camper.

"We'll stay here tonight," she said when she climbed in the back. "It's a perfect place. That's Coit Tower right there." She pointed to the concrete column we were parked next to. "A really rich lady had that built as a dedication to the firefighters after the big 1906 earthquake."

"I saw it while we were crossing the bridge," Rachael said.

"Come check out the view outside. It's amazing," Mama said.

We sat on a stone ledge watching the sunset fade to the glimmering lights of the city below. It felt as if we were on the top of the world and could see so much from up there. I couldn't wait to explore everything Mama had told us about. I wanted to run down the hill as fast as I could and leap into the air to see if I'd be able to fly. With the cooler weather and excitement of being in a big city, I finally had energy in my body again. Mama was right, San Francisco isn't hot like Florida. Not at all.

Since we weren't at a rest area, we couldn't spread our sleeping bags outside, so back under the pullout couch I went. I was awakened in the middle of the night by someone moaning above me. I couldn't tell who it came from, but it got louder. Footsteps crashed on the couch-bed, the back door flung open, and someone ran out.

My stomach began to grumble, which reminded me of a can of rotten pineapple Jon Eric and I snuck out of the camper one night. The thought made me feel sick. *Ugh!* More noise overhead, and someone else left the camper. Mama groaned from the top bed, then she too trampled along the couch above me. I pushed my hands against the wooden frame to make sure the whole thing wouldn't collapse from all the stomping.

More rumbles in my stomach. Something brewed inside me. I felt suffocated under the couch with Jon Eric's nasty feet pressed against my head. *Ugh! I'm trapped. I need to get out.* With the door open, I inched my sleeping bag, like a caterpillar, out the back.

My stomach felt like it was going to explode as I scrambled out of the tangled bag. I didn't have time to make it to a bush like everyone else, so I pulled down my pants and squatted next to the camper. It didn't take long before all of us were scattered around the parking lot, squatting and moaning. Under the truck, I caught a glimpse of Josh crouched down with his diaper laying on the ground next to him.

This went on all night–everyone running in and out, moaning and groaning. The next morning, we woke to a loud pounding on the back door.

"What the hell? Am I the only one who hears that? Can someone please open the door?" Mama asked.

Deborah mumbled something under her breath, then reached from the couch-bed to the door. A man in a dark blue uniform with a peaked cap on his head stood outside. Covering his nose with the side of his hand, he said, "You guys can't park here. You're gonna have to leave."

"Can't you see these kids are sick?" Mama barked. She didn't care that he was a police officer while using that tone.

"Yes. I can see that. You made a big mess in this parking lot. You're gonna have to do some cleaning before you go."

"The hell I am," she snapped. "We'll leave your precious tower if you don't even care that I have a camper full of sick children. Where's the humanity?"

She made her way from the bed, then snatched the keys from the counter. She shoved by the policeman, slammed the door, and started the engine. Winding down the hill, each curve and tilt made me feel even sicker. She stopped near a park, then pulled herself back into the camper.

"I don't know how we're gonna get rid of this nasty smell," she said as she crawled up to her bed.

Brother jumped out and ran behind a tree. When he came back, he grabbed his sleeping bag and brought it to the grass for fresh air. One by one, we followed him. All of us. Even Mama.

"At least this park has a bathroom," Mama said. "And make sure y'all drink some water from that fountain over there."

I felt weak, like my body didn't want to move, or anything. No more strong Pippi, no running down hills to see if I could fly or walking through fog to see if I'd turn invisible. I just wanted to sleep. And poop.

* * *

We slept most of the day, ten sleeping bags sprawled about the city park, until the chill in the air woke us all up. What started as a clear blue sky had turned white with fog.

"Let's go back to the Civic Center," Mama said. "Y'all go in the library and wash up in the sink. They have warm water and soap in there. And I want you to bring all your dirty underwear and clean those, too. Once you wash 'em out, you can use a pair as a washrag to clean your body."

We trudged across the plaza, into the library, then headed straight to the bathroom. Luckily, no one else was in there as I used the pink powdered soap from the dispenser to wash my dirty underwear.

When we were done, the wind had calmed enough for us to hang our wet underwear along the outside of the camper. They hung from the truck window, the side mirrors, the hood, and all along the tailgate.

"It's almost time to watch the free movie," Mama said. "I'm gonna read my book and take another nap. I'm wiped out. When the movie's done, y'all can hang around here and play with the pigeons, or something. I'm sure y'all can find something to do. After I relax a while, we can start looking for a place to park for the night."

I wished I felt like Pippi again, then I'd do all kinds of fun stuff. I'd go on the back of one of the park benches and jump off, I'd climb one of the funny knobby looking trees, and run around chasing pigeons. But I didn't feel like doing anything fun like that now.

"Come on," Jon Eric pulled on my arm once the movie let out. "Let's go check out that cool building with the dome on the top."

"Do you think this is where the President of San Francisco lives?" I asked.

"No, Stupid. It's City Hall. San Francisco doesn't have its own president."

I hated when he talked to me like that, like he's so much older and smarter than me. I hung my head low and plopped down on a patch of grass. "I'm still not feeling so great. How 'bout you?" I asked.

"I'm okay now."

"I think I just want to stay here for a little while. Can you come get me when it's time to go?"

Jon Eric looked at the crowds of people walking along Van Ness—hippies and homeless mixed with men in nice suits. "Nah, I'll just stay here with you."

He began picking small flowers from the grass as I drifted back to sleep.

"Treedy," he nudged me on the shoulder, waking me from a dream. "I think we'd better go check on Mom and everybody else now. It's getting really late."

I sat up and rubbed goosebumps from my arms. "Whoa! Check out the sky!" Pink and orange clouds surrounded City Hall, and the dome on the top of the building lit up a brilliant blue color, like a globe of the world. "That's so neat! Man, how long did I sleep?"

"Not too long. Here, I made this for you." He placed a daisy chain around my neck, and gave me a hand to pull me up. "Thanks!"

I felt a lot better than I did earlier that day. Maybe it was the necklace that put the skip back in my step, or my bath in the library restroom. I don't know. All I know is I felt good enough to race Jon Eric back to the camper.

"You're just in time," Mama said. "We have to move the truck. Damn meter maid's kicking us out. Go find your brothers and sisters, and tell 'em to hurry. She's giving me five minutes before she writes a ticket."

Jon Eric and I ran back to the library, searching each floor until we found Brother, Petesy, and Gregory sitting at a round table with a stack of magazines in front of them.

"We have to hurry back," I said. "Help us find Rachael and Deborah."

I peeked my head into the bathroom and shouted their names. "Rachael! Deborah!"

"What?" Rachael asked from one of the stalls.

"Oh, thank God! We have to go back to the camper. Now! Mama's about to leave!"

We ran back, piled in, then drove off to find a park to camp for the night.

* * *

I was searching for a sweater when Mama pulled herself into the camper. Everyone else had already jumped out to go to the playground, so it was just me and her. I hated being alone with her. She scared me.

"Let's figure out something to eat," she said.

Let's? Huh. She means me!

I opened a can of Chef Boyardee, then dumped it in a pot to heat on the stove. Once it started bubbling, I divided it among the ten bowls, then shouted out the door for everyone to come. One-by-one, everyone grabbed their bowl and brought it back out to the grass.

"Why are there still two bowls sitting here?" Mama asked as she took hers into her hand.

"One's mine," I said.

"I know that, Stupid. Who's the other one for? Go see who didn't get one yet."

I rolled my eyes. "Who didn't get food?" I shouted out the door.

"Nobody. We all have some," Gregory said.

"I must've served an extra one," I said to Mama.

"No. You couldn't've. We only have ten bowls."

Mama jumped out of the camper and headed to where everyone was sitting. "What the hell? Where's your sister?"

"Oh, my gosh. Where's Deborah?" Rachael asked.

"That's just great. You know how long it took me to find this damn park?" Mama asked.

Is that all she cares about?

"Why didn't anybody say she wasn't here before we took off?" No one said a word. "You're a bunch of damn imbeciles. That's why. Get these dishes washed so we can go find her."

* * *

Mama made a sharp U-turn at the corner so fast it almost caused the camper to tip on its side. She honked the horn and shouted Deborah's name as we drove by the plaza at the Civic Center. The men we saw earlier were now tucked under dirty blankets, asleep on the benches. Some of them stirred from the disruption, and one shouted, "Shut the fuck up," but Deborah was nowhere in sight. Mama turned onto Van Ness Street, still honking the horn while Brother hung out the back door, calling out her name.

What if we can't find her? What if she's gone?

I thought of all the times Deborah smoothed my hair with her palm while telling me stories. *What if something happened to her?* I thought of the man with his brown teeth and scraggly hair who took a bite of Greg's spaghetti.

"Deborah!" I joined everyone, calling her name out the window.

Mama pulled up to City Hall where I had napped on the grass earlier that day. Nothing. Then she drove by one of the Federal buildings where three people were standing out front—two men and someone much smaller. As she pulled closer, we saw Deborah hunched between a cop and a man in a shirt and tie.

Brother quickly got off the tailgate and climbed back in the camper. The man's suit coat draped over Deborah's loose cotton top and shorts, but it didn't stop her from shivering. Mama came to a screeching halt in front of them.

"Mama!" Deborah shouted. She handed the jacket to the man, then ran toward the camper. "I'm so glad y'all found me. I was so scared."

"Get in the back," Mama said. "I don't want to hear a word from you."

As the cop walked to the driver's door, we huddled near the window in the camper to hear what he had to say.

"Ma'am, your daughter was left here all alone," he said.

"We need showers. We're filthy." Mama said, disregarding him completely. "Do you know where we can take one?"

"Ma'am, you left your daughter by herself." His voice sounded stern.

"I said, we're filthy and cold. We've been sick all day. Do you know where we can take a shower?"

The officer looked dumbfounded. "Shower?" He crossed his arms over his chest, then looked away from her, as if he couldn't stand seeing such a hateful woman. His gaze moved to the back window, to where all of our faces were crammed in. We quickly ducked down to hide as he took a step toward us.

"What's going on?" Petesy whispered. Brother peeked out and waved for us to come back up. After seeing us, the officer's tone had softened.

"There's a place called Raphael House where you guys can take a shower. It's ten o'clock, so I'm not sure if anyone'll answer this late, but I'll show you where it is," he said. "Follow me." He got in his car and pulled onto Van Ness Street.

"Holy crap! Can you believe we're getting a police escort?" Brother asked.

"I believe it," Deborah said. "That guy was so nice. Y'all wouldn't believe how scared I was. I ran everywhere looking for y'all." She wiped her tears on her shirt. "That man in the suit was going to take me home. Who knows what he would've done with me." Her whole body shook as she spoke.

HELEN THOMPSON, LEFT, AND FAMILY ENJOY THEIR DINNER
'St. Anthony's helped me stand on my feet'

Newspaper article about St.
Anthony's Dining Room.
From left, Mama, Jonas, Josh,
Rachael, & me.

_7_

Raphael House

He prays best who does not know that he is praying.
— *St. Anthony of Padua*

*M*ama double-parked next to the cop car in front of a large tan building, then came back to the camper, peeked her head in, and told us to hang tight while the officer rang the bell. A few minutes later, a lady appeared at the door, cupping her hand over her eyes to block them from the porch light she had just turned on. Her other hand held a sweater closed over her nightgown.

The three of them talked back-and-forth, and the next thing I knew, Mama had her arms wrapped around the cop, giving him one of her big kisses on the cheek. She hugged the lady, then turned toward the camper, and waved for us to come.

"This is Sister Margaret," Mama said as we gathered.

"Come on in. Let's get you out of this cold," Sister Margaret said. Even though it appeared we had woken her up, she still put on a pleasant smile, and counted each of us on her fingers as we walked in. "One, two, three, four, five, six, seven, eight, and nine. Wow! What a big beautiful family you have."

Mama grinned. She loved when others complimented her on her children, especially a nun or a priest. To her, having nine kids only proved her devotion to the Catholic church.

"You children must be tired," Sister Margaret said. "Let me go find a nice room for you."

We didn't have to wait long before she came back and led us down a long corridor decorated with children's artwork on the walls.

"You can have this room." She opened the door and stepped aside for us to enter. "There's just enough beds in here so you can all stay together."

Five bunk beds lined the walls of the large dormitory style room. Each with light-blue, polka-dotted comforters and a fluffy white pillow. Ruffled curtains with the same polka-dotted fabric hung over the windows, and a small table with a vase of fake flowers sat next to an open bathroom door.

Being there felt like Christmas, and the bed was my present. Never could I have ever imagined that having a real bed to sleep on would cause my body to buzz with such excitement. The older kids snatched the upper bunks right away, but that didn't bother me one bit. Sleeping on a lower bed still beat the heck out of staying on the floor of the camper.

The room seemed like a slumber party as everyone began hooting and hollering. Brother started a pillow fight, and the twins were small enough to jump on the mattress of one of the bottom bunks. Sister Margaret cleared her throat from where she stood in the doorway.

"Okay, children. You need to settle down now." She shouted above the noise, but with all the ruckus, no one heard a word. She flicked the lights on and off to get our attention, then said, "Lights out is at 10:00 p.m. and we're way beyond that now. You need to keep it down in here. I'll be back in the morning to wake you up."

At 8:00 a.m., a knock on the door woke me from the best sleep I'd had all summer. "Rise and shine, everyone. It's time for breakfast."

Sister Margaret peeked her head into the room. "Time to get up!" She clapped her hands. "Once you get dressed, I'll show you to the dining room."

She had the same warm smile on her face as the night before, and if it weren't for the wooden cross pinned to her top, I would have never known she was a nun. She certainly didn't look like the sisters we had at San Jose Catholic in Florida. She didn't wear the black dress, or habit, or anything. Just a simple, straight skirt, with a buttoned-up blouse, and short, brown hair neatly pulled back in bobby pins. I had always wondered what the nuns hair looked like under their veil.

In the dining room, a large pot of oatmeal sat next to bowls of brown sugar, honey, sliced apples, cinnamon, and a carton of milk. I never thought I'd want to see oatmeal again after our trip in the camper, but having all those toppings was another story altogether. It reminded me of times when Mama set up a sundae station for us at home. On her good days, when she was happy, she'd put out a half-gallon of ice-cream surrounded by whipped cream, Maraschino cherries, chopped nuts, and chocolate sauce.

Like those sundaes, we piled our oatmeal high with toppings, then took a seat as Sister Margaret and one of the other nuns strummed on guitars and began singing the Cat Steven's song, "Morning Has Broken."

Mama and Deborah sang along that first morning, and after about a week of hearing that same song every day, the rest of us joined in as well.

* * *

Our routine became pretty consistent. We'd sing grace, have our oatmeal, then we'd have to pack everything and leave for the day. That was the bad thing about Raphael House. It was only a place to sleep for the night. Once we cleared our bowls from the table, we'd have to be out by 9:00 a.m., and weren't allowed to return again until after dark.

From Raphael House, we'd go to Mass at St. Boniface Church,

then have lunch at St. Anthony's Dining Room*, a place that fed the poor and homeless. For the first few weeks, we had to wait in a long line to get into St. Anthony's—one that went down the street, and around the corner with the smell of body odor, bad breath, alcohol, and pee following us each and every step of the way.

It was scary being around so many people. Especially since a lot of them seemed to be even more crazy than Mama. Mama was mainly just mean, but those people had full-on conversations with themselves. Some even screamed out cuss words. Mama said they couldn't help it because they probably had something called Tourette Syndrome that made them have no control over what they said. It didn't stop me from being scared though, especially when an argument or fight really did break out.

Not only that, I'd have to keep my eyes glued to the pavement and stand as close to my brothers as possible as we made our way toward the entrance. I learned after the first couple of days not to look at anyone, since eye contact always caused some sort of reaction. The first day we stood in that line, the man behind us pushed his false teeth out of his mouth at me, then roared with laughter when I let out a yelp. Another man opened his eyes so wide, it looked like they were going to pop right out of his head. Keeping my eyes down was hard, for sure. I liked people watching, but it was way too scary whenever I did.

The thing about the Dining Room, once we made it through the door and walked down the ramp under a statue of St. Anthony, all the chaos and scariness from the street disappeared altogether. The bad odors, the grumpiness, and the arguments stayed outside, replaced with the mouth-watering smells of dishes such as Chicken à la King, or turkey with mashed potatoes and gravy, chicken and dumplings, and pot pies. The meals were so delicious everything else faded into the background as if some sort of magical power took over.

"Look around," Mama said. "When people come here, they know they aren't alone in their hardships. Really, take a look. It's like Thanksgiving here. Like a family. Look at all these people sharing a meal together."

She was right. It's true. The magic didn't only happen for me. The whole room became hypnotized under its spell. Strangers sat next to one another at the long tables, eating their meals quietly, or having peaceful conversations with each other. Peaceful! No yelling. No arguing. No fighting. All of that was kicked to the curb once they came in.

* * *

We didn't have to wait in those lines at St. Anthony's for very long. Each day, once we finished eating, Mama did what she does best. She'd wear her disgusting short-shorts, the ones that showed the bottom of her butt cheeks when she leaned over, then she'd sashay into the back office where men sat at their big desks, smoking cigars, shuffling through stacks of paper. She'd smile, twirl her hair around her finger, shift her body back and forth, and use her fake sing-song voice to flirt with them. It was so gross, but it worked—and soon we were able to march right to the front of the line and head straight in.

That wasn't the only thing we got from her flirting, either. It also brought John Chaney into our lives, one of the men who worked in the office. A man who became a great friend to our family for years to come.

* * *

After staying at Raphael House for a few weeks, as we were finishing our breakfast one morning, Mama said, "Once y'all clear the table, I want everybody to meet in the living room for a few minutes while I go over somethin'."

In the room, I grabbed a National Geographic magazine from the bookshelf, and took a seat in a big, overstuffed chair near the window. As Mama spoke, I flipped through pictures of wild animals in the Namib Desert of Africa, pretending I was on safari as photos of lions, giraffes, elephants and water buffalo jumped out of the pages at me.

"What are you talking about?" Deborah shouted. "You have to bring us back. All of us!" Her voice caught me by surprise. I never heard Deborah scream at Mama before. "The lawyer said you weren't even allowed to leave the state with us. I was there! I heard him!"

Deborah stood in front of Mama with her arms folded over her chest. "You planned this all along, didn't you? You never planned on going back home. Did you?"

What's she talking about? The magazine dropped to my lap. I wished I had listened to what Mama had been saying the whole time.

"I'm never going back to that hot hellhole you call Florida," Mama snapped. "You can tell your precious father that, too!"

"You lied to us! You said this was just a vacation," Brother said.

Mama slapped her hand on the coffee table. "I don't have time for this. Y'all need to hurry so we're not late for the bus."

"Why can't Teresa come back with us?" Jon Eric asked while rubbing his eyes along the length of his arm.

Teresa? Is he crying? What the heck is going on?

"I went over that already," Mama said. "Rachael and the three little ones are staying here with me, and I don't want to hear another word about it!"

Her words sucked the air right out of my chest. *Staying here? In San Francisco?*

⌒

* *"Founded by Fr. Alfred Boedekker, St Anthony's is the only free food program in San Francisco. It's open 365 days a year and serves an average of 2700 meals a day to homeless and low-income San Franciscans."*

— *stanthonysf.org*

Part Two

—

Wildflower

Forgiveness is the fragrance the violet sheds
on the heel that has crushed it. — *Mark Twain*

Petesy, Brother, Deborah, Jon Eric and Gregory before heading
back to Florida, 1974.

– 8 –

Greyhound

(Continued from chapter one)

Grief is like the ocean: it comes in waves, ebbing and flowing.
Sometimes the water is calm, and sometimes
it is overwhelming. All we can do is learn to swim.
— *Vicki Harrison*

The Greyhound bus had faded out of sight, taking with it any hope of ever returning back home to Florida.

"Come baaaaaack!" The words forced their way from my throat. My heart felt as if it had been pulled out of my chest and crushed on the filthy sidewalk, leaving me feeling empty. I crawled into the entryway of a nearby building and belted out throaty howls as a stream of snot mixed with the tears on my face. A dirty piece of newspaper blew against my leg, but I couldn't even feel it. I didn't feel anything. The bus was long gone with half of my family on it.

The sound of footsteps approached, but I didn't look up. *Let the creepy men take me away. I don't care.*

"Come on, Teresa. It's time to go." Mama said my name in an unusually soft voice. She rubbed her cold fingers across my shoulder, then grasped onto my arm. "Here, let me help you up."

"Don't touch me!" I yanked my arm out of her grip. "Don't ever touch me!"

"Well, you're gonna have to come back sooner or later. They won't let me stay parked in front of that station for too long."

She headed back toward the camper, but I didn't bother getting up. Instead, I leaned my head against the wall, closed my eyes, and cried more tears.

"Everything okay?"

A deep voice caused me to open my eyes. A man held his hand out to me with dirt caked under his fingernails. The sight of him and the other scary looking people scattered around the area shocked my body to life again—the cold wind, the stinging on my knee from the fall on the concrete, the smell of urine, my racing heart. All those sensations hit me at once. *I have to get back to the camper! What if Mama left me? I've gotta get out of here!*

"Yeah, I'm okay." I pushed myself up and ran back toward the station. *Please let the camper be there. Please be there! Please don't leave me here, Mama! Please, God.*

I never thought I'd be so happy to see Mama and that camper again. I wanted to run up and throw my arms around them. All of them. Mama, Rachael, and the twins. I wanted to. I really did. Instead, I waved and continued around back.

When I opened the door, the emptiness hit me like a black hole, sucking every bit of air from my lungs. I threw myself face-down on the couch, and let out a howl like that of a wild animal, then punched at the couch cushions like a young child throwing a tantrum. I cried loud and hard, hoping the tears would wash away my pain. With no one else in the camper, I felt so alone, as if I were banished from the outside world—from my family.

Mama drove out of the station, pulled up to our usual park

and stopped. Beyond the playground, eucalyptus trees swayed in the wind, and next to the camper, orange and yellow nasturtiums spilled onto the sidewalk. Everything I loved was right there—the trees, the flowers we'd suck nectar from, the playground... but I had no interest in any of that now.

The twins sprinted to the seesaw, hoping to get there before anyone else. The poor things. They had no clue they didn't have to race anymore. It's just us now.

Walking at a snail's pace, Mama and Rachael also made their way out of the truck, headed to the playground. Rachael hugged her arms tight to her body as wind blew through her long, wavy-brown hair. She went to the swingset, grabbed a hold of one of the chains, then sat on the black rubber seat with her gaze never leaving the ground. Her feet stayed anchored as she swayed side to side.

Mama plopped herself close to where the twins were on the seesaw, and hunched over to rest her head in her hands. Her body trembled, but it wasn't from the cold. I could tell she was crying. She blew her nose into her hand, wiped her fingers on the grass, then raised her head, and stared off into nowhere. She looked different. Sad. Like she lost more than just half of her children that day.

My tears began to flow again. I lay back down on the couch, and as I watched the fog pass under the puffy clouds, I pictured my brothers and Deborah waving to me from the back row of the bus, cheering me on as I chased after them.

Cooking supper on the fire at a park. That's me in the background carrying a large pot.

— 9 —

Homeless

Start by doing what's necessary; then do what's possible,
and suddenly you are doing The Impossible.
— St. Francis of Assisi

I heard Mama call me, then the sound of tapping on the camper window. I must have fallen asleep. Except for a faint beam of light seeping through the fog, the camper was pitch black. "Little girl, come out. We're here! We're at Raphael House." *

I blinked my eyes to adjust to the darkness, as I got up to search for a sweater, but something stopped me in my tracks. An eyeball. A yellow, glowing eyeball stared right at me. "Huh! The rat's eyeball!" I threw myself back onto the couch, and buried my head into my arms. *No, no, no. It followed me here.*

"Little girl!"

Last Christmas, I had begged Mama and Daddy to buy me a Baby Love Light doll. All the rave on the television commercials was that futuristic doll whose eyes lit up when you squeezed one of her hands. Daddy always gave the same response, though. "She's way too expensive. We just can't afford her." Christmas morning, all my hopes and excitement dwindled, then disappeared altogether, as the last present under the tree was unwrapped.

"Teresa, there's still something under here with your name on it," Daddy said after breakfast.

"What? There can't be. I searched everywhere."

I dove under the tree to see what he was talking about. Tucked in the corner, behind the nativity scene, lay a single box wrapped in gold paper with a large yellow ribbon around it. I grabbed the present, and looked up at the big smiles on Mama and Daddy's faces.

"Well, go on. It has your name on it, doesn't it?" Mama said.

Sure enough, a small tag taped to the package read, *To Teresa, From Santa Claus*. I tore off the wrapping paper, pulled out the Baby Love Light doll, and danced around the room with her.

"This is the best Christmas ever," I said, then gave them both a big hug. "Thank you!"

I named the doll Sally, and she became my absolute favorite toy. She slept with me each night and went everywhere I went, but my love and excitement for her came to an abrupt end the day Brother snuck her out of my room.

"These are the rat's eyeballs!" he chanted as he held Sally's hand to make her eyes glow. His deep voice dragged out the words, singing them in a scary way. "They're going to get you!" I ran from the room while Brother roared with laughter.

It didn't stop there, either. Brother ended up liking Sally way more than I did. Not that he liked dolls, or anything, he just loved tormenting me. He'd force me in a closet, hold the door shut while lighting up her eyes and chanting about rat's eyeballs.

* * *

"Little girl. You better come out. We're freezing out here," Mama said.

I peeked through my fingers and realized it was only the street lamp reflecting off one of the pots. *Oh, thank God.* It didn't matter, though. Fear had already taken over. I jumped off the couch, ran to the door and fumbled with the handle. *Come on.* My heart pounded. *Get me out of here!* I flung the door open and jumped to the street.

Mama, Rachael, and the twins were waiting outside, standing unusually close to one another. I'm not sure if it was because of the cold or from fear that any distance could tear them apart forever, but whatever the case, I joined in as we made our way toward Raphael House clustered tight as grapes on a vine.

Specks of water could be seen through the thick fog with each passing headlight, like the city mourned with me—shedding its own tears—feeling my pain. At that moment, through my sadness and grief, I felt an odd sort of connection to San Francisco.

* * *

There wasn't the usual ruckus and horseplay as when we were all together outside Raphael House. Instead, we stood in complete silence waiting for one of the nuns to let us in. Sister Margaret gasped when she opened the door. I wondered what her reaction would be when only five of us showed up that night. I guess I expected something like that. I just wasn't ready for it.

Tears slowly built in her eyes, which caused a lump to swell in the back of my throat. I lowered my head so she couldn't see my swollen, red eyes, then ran past her to the bedroom, threw myself onto one of the bunk beds, and buried my head under the covers until I cried myself back to sleep.

* * *

"Rise and shine." Sister Margaret tapped on the door to our room. "Breakfast is ready."

I pulled the covers off and eased myself out of the bed. My body felt heavy and weighed down, as if a lead balloon had been shackled to my ankle. I slowly made my way down the hallway, toward the dining room.

The aroma in the air was the only thing that brought any

sense of comfort to my sadness. The smells were familiar, something I could rely on each day. They filled my nose as the rest of my world collapsed around me. I closed my eyes, and leaned against the wall to take in the scents of oatmeal with maple brown sugar, and the remnants of apple-flavored tobacco from the pipe the priest smoked. It smelled like heaven.

As I sat at the large table in the dining room, I sensed the weight of Sister Margaret's eyes on me. *Please don't look at me.* Glancing down to avoid her gaze, I moved the sticky oats around with my spoon, watching the steam rise in swirls above my bowl. For once, I didn't feel like eating. My body quivered each time I took a deep breath. *Please don't cry, Teresa.*

The strum of a guitar echoed throughout the dining room, then the singing began. None of us sang along. Not even Mama, and she's the one who usually sang the loudest. Instead, we sat in complete silence.

"Mine is the sunlight, mine is the mor-or-orr-ning…" I glanced at the sisters and smiled. They looked happy singing, and I felt bad for not joining in. I loved that song and the routine of our mornings.

Tears dripped down my face. I couldn't hold them back anymore. They fell into my bowl, forming shallow puddles on top of my oatmeal.

* * *

After being at Raphael House a few more weeks, the nuns started bringing Mama the classified ads so she could search for a place to work. Sister Margaret explained that Raphael House was only a temporary place to stay until we got our feet back on the ground, but each time they brought her the paper, Mama threw it in the trash the second they walked out of the room.

Day in and day out, they tried to encourage her to find a job. I lay on the upper bunk one night, listening as Sister Margaret explained to Mama how much nicer it would be to have our own apartment.

"You don't want to be homeless forever," she said. "These kids would do much better with a place of their own."

I nearly dropped to the floor. *Homeless? We're homeless?* Up until that moment, I had no idea. I thought homeless people lived on the street like the bums we see. We didn't live on the street. We lived at Raphael House, and it wasn't anything I would have expected from a homeless shelter. Other families came and went, but we had our own room with bunk beds and warm, soft blankets. It felt like home to me.

"If you find a job, then you could get an apartment," Sister Margaret continued.

"Enough about getting a job, already. I'm not going to waste my time looking for a job until I find a school for these kids. Catholic schools have to provide for low-income families." Mama stormed out of the room and slammed the door shut behind her.

My body cringed. It was one thing for her to talk to us like that, but I hated it when she used that tone with others, especially Sister Margaret.

⸱⟶

* *"Raphael House was the first homeless shelter for families in Northern California. Since its inception, it has provided over 20,000 families with personalized family-centered solutions to build brighter, independent futures."*

— *Raphaelhouse.org*

Rachael, age 12, in sixth grade at NDV and me, age seven, in third grade at Morning Star.

– 10 –

Third Grade

Prejudice is the child of ignorance. — William Hazlitt

*M*ama finally found schools for me and Rache. Rachael went to Notre Dame des Victoires, otherwise known as NDV, a quaint little French Catholic school right up the block from Chinatown and Union Square.

Unfortunately for me, NDV's third-grade class was full and not accepting new students, so we weren't able to go to the same school together.

I was excited to start school again. Don't get me wrong, I liked going to the park every day, but it did get a little old after a while, and I really did want to meet new friends.

At Raphael House that morning, Rachael sat across the dining table from me, piddling with her oatmeal while the sisters sang grace. She didn't look up or join in on the singing. She stared at her bowl, skimming the top back and forth with her spoon. I felt bad for her when Mama said she had to repeat the 6th grade again. Something about moving from Florida to California. It didn't make any sense, though, especially since Mama had already held her back a few years earlier. But Rachael didn't fight it, or argue, or anything. She just kept her mouth shut as she usually did.

I squeezed up front in the truck as we hurried to our new schools. I have to admit, I felt a little envious of the navy blue school uniform Rachael got to wear. It was designed to look like a French sailor's, and had a red tie and collar with red stripes that flapped over her shoulders onto her back. Her's was cool. Mine was plain and basic, kind of like the one I wore at San Jose Catholic in Jacksonville—a plaid skirt with a white button-up blouse.

After dropping Rachael off, Mama made a U-turn and headed back up the hill toward St. Dominic's. I wished Rachael and I were going to the same school together. Not because of the uniform or the fact that Mama hyped NDV up so much since Mayor Moscone's kids also went there, but because I was scared to go to a new school alone. Every little tiny bit of excitement I had up until that moment turned straight to fear.

"I'm not ready yet." I licked my lips and clenched onto my book-bag as panic began to set in. "Can I please start tomorrow instead?"

"Don't be silly. You'll be fine. Besides, you keep saying how much you wanna meet some friends," Mama said.

Her words spun through my head like paper in a tornado.

"Please, Mama. I'm too scared."

"You'll be fine. If you don't go today, tomorrow'll be no different. You have to take that first step sooner or later." She pulled into the school parking lot, shut off the engine, and opened her door. "Come on. You're already late."

I plodded after her to the office. Normally, I would have been horrified to have Mama tag along, but not then. Her presence brought comfort.

The secretary led us to my classroom, introduced my teacher, Mrs. Taylor, then Mrs. Taylor showed me where to hang my bookbag, and which desk I'd be using.

All eyes were on me as I placed my bag on the hook. When I got settled in my seat, I was surprised to see Mama still lingering at the front of the room. Her greasy hair and tight pink pants turned any comfort I had before into complete humiliation. *What's she still doing here? Please leave, Mama.* But she just stood there, eyeing one student to the next.

"She'll be fine," Mrs. Taylor put a hand on Mama's shoulder, then opened the classroom door and stepped aside for her to leave. "We'll take good care of her. Don't worry."

At recess, several of my classmates came up to me. Talking all at once, they asked about Florida, and offered games of hopscotch, jump rope and tag like they were fighting over me, or something. I couldn't believe it! I never imagined my first day could be that easy.

When school let out, I waited on the corner by St. Dominic's church as instructed. Mama said the enormous grey church was built in the gothic style, but to me, it looked more like a castle from the Dracula movie. Two large beams reached from the top like the legs of an insect, making it both beautiful and eerie at the same time.

I waited while kids bustled around the schoolyard, and continued waiting long after everyone had left. I waited and waited until my eyes welled with tears. *What if Mama forgot me? What am I gonna do?* I tried to remember the words she told me that morning but couldn't think of them. *What if I didn't hear her right? What if I was supposed to go somewhere else?* I set my book bag down and paced back-and-forth from one side of the corner to the other.

My body shivered as more thoughts raced through my mind. *What if she got in an accident? Or what if she fell off a cliff? I hope she's okay!*

All my fear melted as fast as it came when I saw the camper approaching in the distance. "Thank you, God!"

She pulled to the curb next to me and had Rachael roll down her window.

"Don't go in the back," Mama said in a sharp tone. "Come sit up here with us!"

Rachael scooted over for me to squeeze between her and the

door, which was kind of weird since she never gave up the window seat. She must have felt sorry for me.

"I thought you forgot about me," my voice quivered as more tears filled my eyes.

"I didn't forget you! I had to get Rachael first then drive all the way over here. Plus, I spent all day looking for a new school for you," she said.

"What? What do you mean a new school?" I asked.

"You're not going to school with a bunch of niggers," she said.

"What?" I snarled my upper lip.

"There's no way that any daughter of mine is going to a school with a bunch of niggers. You're gonna go to a school called Morning Star—starting tomorrow!"

"But I don't wanna go to another school. I like this one. I already made friends, and everything."

"I don't want to hear another word about this. Have some appreciation for once. I spent the entire day looking out for you so you don't have to be stuck with those people every day. I'm not going to raise my own daughter to be like no nigger."

"What are you talking about? Quit saying that! There's nothing wrong with those kids. They liked me. Which is way more than I can say about you."

Mama reached her hand across Rachael and the twins to dig her fingernails into my arm, pinching deep into my flesh. *What is wrong with her? I hate her!* Tears ran down my cheeks, dripping on my white uniform blouse.

The next morning I couldn't even look at Mama. I kept my head turned toward the window as she dropped Rachael at NDV, then drove toward my new school.

"See those?" she asked, pointing to a row of trees lining the sidewalk. "Those'll be loaded with beautiful pink flowers come spring. They're cherry blossoms. You're lucky to be near Japantown, you know. There's only three Japantowns in the whole United States."

100

Her effort to comfort me didn't work. Not this time. I didn't care what she had to say. She pulled the camper in front of a pale yellow building with dark green ceramic tiles on the roof and put it in park.

"Well, here we are," she said.

I clung to the armrest and slid my back down the seat, thinking of how all the kids stared at me at me when I first walked in the room the day before. Fiddling with the small pigtail I put in my hair, I pictured the girls at St. Dominics with their fancy hairdos—braids, colorful barrettes and ponytails. I thought of how friendly they were when they came up to me at recess, and how lucky I was to make friends so fast.

"See how the roof is curved up like that on the corners?" Mama asked.

I didn't answer, so Josh said, "Yeah?"

"Well, those curves are thought to ward off evil spirits in the Buddhist religion. They believe spirits only follow straight lines, so you'll be safe in there. No evil spirits'll go on a roof that's curved like that."

"Wait. What?" I sat up straight. "This school's not Catholic?"

"No, silly. Don't be stupid. I just wanted to point out the Japanese architecture. Of course, I'm sending you to a Catholic school. Come on."

Like the day before, I followed her to the office, then we were led to my new classroom. Fear gripped me as soon as we walked in the door. My eyes darted from one side of the room to the next, then back to Mama. I tried to swallow, but my spit went dry.

There's no way Mama's gonna let me stay here.

Mama smiled as the secretary introduced her to Ms. Takahashi, my new teacher, a look quite different from the ugly glowering she had at St. Dominic's.

Ms. Takahashi shook Mama's hand, then led her back out the door. She looked me up and down as she pointed out my desk. I tried to force a smile, but my cheeks felt frozen in place. Like the day before, everyone stared as I made my way to my seat.

"Okay, class, eyes back up here," Ms. Takahashi said. She scooped some papers from her desk and handed a small stack to the first person in each row. "Take one and pass back," she said in broken English.

I couldn't take my eyes off her—the most beautiful lady I had ever seen in my whole entire life. I had never even seen an Asian person before coming to San Francisco. I ran my hand down my hair, feeling the lumps of tangles as I looked at her long, black, silky hair. Her pale skin reminded me of one of the porcelain dolls my aunt kept on a shelf in her apartment in Florida.

As I sat alone at recess watching the other kids run around and play, I wished I was back at St. Dominic's. No one at Morning Star came up to ask about Florida, or invite me to play with them, or anything. No one. Not until lunch, that is. Then a boy and girl walked over and introduced themselves as Stephen and Tina.

"You can hang out with us," Stephen said as he nervously patted the side of his light brown afro.

"Yeah. We're the rejects," Tina laughed. "And don't expect any of the other kids to talk to you, either. If you're not Japanese, you're toast." She scratched at some crusty scabs on the inside of her elbow. "Psoriasis," she said when she saw me looking at her arms.

"Huh?"

"I have psoriasis. It's a skin condition. It makes me itch."

* * *

As the weeks went on, Ms. Takahashi couldn't stand the daily disruptions I made by showing up tardy each morning, and she always made a big deal about it in front of the whole class.

Opening the door to my third-grade classroom became even scarier than standing in line at St. Anthony's.

"Is it okay to continue teaching now?" she'd ask as my classmates roared with laughter.

I could tell that she didn't like me, and it wasn't only because I showed up late, either—or because I wasn't Japanese. For one, she hated that I didn't always do my homework. I tried to remember to do it each day, I really did. But after school, we'd have to go to the park while waiting for Raphael House to open, so a lot of the time I'd forget.

Still, that wasn't the main reason she didn't like me. She didn't like me because I was poor, and she acted as if I had some sort of disease or something. Sometimes, she'd even take a little step back as I walked by, not on purpose or in an exaggerated way for others to see, or anything, but I could tell she thought I was gross.

Her favorite word for me was "Messy." Messy work, messy uniform, messy hair. You name it, I was Messy.

"Why is your paper so messy?" she asked, holding it between two fingers for the whole class to see. "How am I supposed to read this with all these wrinkles?" She reached into a bin and pulled out someone else's work. "See this one? No wrinkles! Your work is always such a disgrace. Messy, messy, messy! Take pride in what you do." I sunk in my chair while a kid behind me called me *baka*, a word that meant stupid in Japanese.

Even though Ms. Takahashi liked to embarrass me, I always tried my best to win her affection. John Chaney, the friend we met from St. Anthony's, sometimes gave our family a whole case of goodies if they had too much of something in the Dining Room. Those treats were my ticket to get Ms. Takahashi to like me. I'd bring her a box of Cracker Jacks, or a frosted cookie on a stick, thinking, *now she's gonna like me for sure.*

After a few weeks of receiving treats, she said loud enough for the whole class to hear, "Why you bring me these? I don't even like them." She picked up the frosted cookie, held it over the trash, and dropped it with a loud thud. "You think I give you better grade if you give me this?"

The kids roared with laughter. "Yeah, baka. You think you'll get an "A" from a cookie?" Haha haha!　　⌒⌒

Our apartment on Eddie and Hyde, across the street from the Brown Jug Saloon.

– 11 –

Solo

The brave man is not he who does not feel afraid,
but he who conquers that fear. — *Nelson Mandela*

Once we had settled into school, Mama began her search for a place to call home—and that was no easy task. Not with four kids and an adult, at least. There were just too many of us to fit in the tiny places she could afford. That wasn't the only thing either. No one would rent to her without proof of a job and a steady income. But after weeks of searching, she finally found somewhere that accepted us.

"The apartment's in the Tenderloin District," she explained. "They call it the Tenderloin because it's in the middle of downtown, just like the tenderloin of beef is in the middle of a cow."

I later learned there are several stories as to why it's called *the Tenderloin*. Some say it's named after the red light district in New York City, while others argue that it's the *soft underbelly of vice* in San Francisco, or the cops get paid more for working in such a dangerous area so they can afford *beef tenderloin* for dinner. Others claim it's a reference to *the loins of a prostitute*. Whatever the case may be, it was now our home. And if the Tenderloin is the heart of downtown, our new place had to be the heart of the Tenderloin.

Mama pulled up to a large, white building on the corner of Eddie and Hyde Streets. "Well, here we are," she said, then turned on the hazard lights and double-parked.

The whole area looked scary, bustling with people, mostly drunks and bums, hanging out in doorways, or gathered outside a bar across the street called the Brown Jug Saloon.

The thought of the man who stole a bite of Gregory's spaghetti made me cling tight to my armload of clothes as we made our way toward the front door. Trash blew around us in swirls as if to welcome us to our new neighborhood.

A couple stood outside a liquor store that shared the bottom of our building, swaying back-and-forth as they argued in slurred words. Half naked ladies with heels as high as stilts paced back and forth on each of the four corners.

We dodged a group of men passing around a bottle wrapped in a brown paper bag as we followed Mama up the marble steps that lead to the front door of the apartment.

"Sheesh. They didn't even make room for us to get by," I whispered once we entered the lobby.

Mama ignored my comment as the corners of her mouth slid upwards in a proud smile. Happy as a puppy, she clapped her hands in front of her face, then pointed toward the back wall.

"Y'all see that gate over there?" she asked. "That's an elevator! Can you believe it? We have an elevator in our apartment!"

She skipped toward the black iron gate and slid it open by squeezing the metal bars together like an accordion.

"Isn't this neat?"

"Yeah!" Rachael said.

It barely fit the five of us, especially with our arms loaded with clothes. Mama pulled the gate closed and pushed the number six button, then the small cage began to shake and rattle its way upward. We could've walked faster, but it *was* fun to have a ride.

"I think I can! I think I can!" I teased.

Jonas stuck his hand through one of the slots in the gate to touch the number three as we passed by the third floor. Mama jerked him away so fast, some of her clothes toppled to the floor.

"What are you, crazy?" she shouted. "You wanna get your arm cut off, or somethin'?"

After scooping up her clothes, she rattled a set of keys in the air. The sound brought me back to Florida—to Daddy sifting through the coins and keys in his pockets after a long day of work to find a shiny penny for me. And just like that, I became weighed down with sadness. As if a ghost came on the elevator with us, like the one from *A Christmas Carol*, to remind me of the life I had in the past.

"Our apartment is in the corner. Number 606," Mama interrupted my thoughts as we approached the sixth floor. "We're so lucky it came furnished. But I have to warn you, it's not very big. It's only a studio."

Studio? Whatever that is.

We raced in the direction she pointed, then waited by a black door at the end of the hall with brass numbers 606 nailed to it.

"Why is the door black? It's so creepy," Rachael whispered.

Mama put the key in, pushed the door open, and reached inside to flip the light switch.

"Here it is," she said.

She stepped aside, and as we pushed our way in, brown bugs scurried all over the place—the floors, the walls, even upside down on the ceiling.

"Roaches!" I shrieked as I backed out of the apartment.

"Seriously? Someone who loves bugs so much, and you're worried about some little roaches?" Mama asked.

"Yeah, they're not the same. Roaches scare me to death." I backed a few more steps into the hallway.

"Come back in and quit bein' a baby. They're all hidden now."

"Yeah, but they're not gone. They're just hiding. They're still in there." I checked the walls next to where I stood to make sure there weren't any near me.

"Well, if you don't want to be in here, then make yourself useful and get more stuff out of the camper."

"No. I can't walk by those bums by myself."

"Bums! Roaches! If you think you can do any better than this, then be my guest. Otherwise, come in and quit your damn complainin'."

"I'm not complaining. It's just scary."

"Scary, schmary. You'll have to get used to it, sooner or later, so it might as well be now."

I peeked in the apartment, scanned the walls and ceiling for roaches, then went in and sat on a brown and yellow tweed couch to have a look around. The seat sunk so low, it felt like I was falling into a hole with the springs hitting against my bottom. A tiny television sat on a small, wobbly table across from the couch with tinfoil wrapped around the tips of its bunny-eared antennas. It rattled with Mama's heavy footsteps as she walked by. Three windows overlooked the Brown Jug Saloon six floors below, and the one and only bed was pushed next to the wall in the corner.

I got up and followed Rachael into the kitchen. Grey concrete peeked through the worn-out linoleum in a trail that ran from the door to the sink, and an old refrigerator, the kind with rounded edges and a long, horizontal handle, stood next to a small card table with two yellow, swivel chairs.

"Look at all these disgusting flea-jays," Mama said. She pointed to pieces of lint on the green shag carpet of the main room. "They could've at least vacuumed the place before we moved in."

I agreed, but definitely did not want to say anything to make Mama think I was still complaining.

"Can someone please rattle the toilet handle so it'll stop makin' all that damn noise?" she asked.

The bathroom had a small sink attached to the wall with rust stains running from both the hot and cold faucets down to the drain. Next to it, a ring of brown showed through the worn out toilet seat, and the shower was so close, you'd practically be standing over the toilet to bathe.

And that was our apartment. Nothing more. Nothing less. One room with a dirty shag carpet, a single bed, and TV, a kitchen with a small table, and a teeny-tiny bathroom.

"We're lucky to have our own bathroom, you know. A lot of the places I looked didn't even have one. You'd have to go down the hall and share one with everybody else. We got really lucky with this place," Mama said.

"Where's everybody gonna sleep?" I forced a smile on my face, trying to sound as upbeat as possible.

"Well, me and the twins'll take the bed. You and Rache can just put your sleeping bags on the floor 'til I can get y'all a mattress to share."

The floor? What about all the roaches?

* * *

After unloading everything, I found the perfect spot in the middle of the room—as far from the walls as possible so no bugs could crawl on me. I cuddled my teddy bear in my arms and snuggled into my sleeping bag to watch TV while Mama parked the camper. My teddy bear and sleeping bag were the only bits of comfort I had left from Jacksonville. The same bag I used when we'd go camping at Lake Gold Head in Florida, and the one I slept in all summer when all nine of us kids were still together.

Rachael shuffled through the channels until she found a *Tom and Jerry* cartoon, but it was so staticky, we could barely see the picture. Mama adjusted the antennas for us when she came back, then tore a piece of paper from a brown bag, and sat at the table in the kitchen. She loved to journal and wrote about everything we did. Whenever she couldn't find her book, she would use whatever scrap of paper she could get her hands on to write her thoughts.

But those weren't thoughts she was writing. She came back into the room and stood over me with the paper in her hands.

"I'm starvin'," she said. "We need to get some food in this place."

Why is she telling me? My cheeks burned like the hot Texas desert as she continued. "You need to go to the store for us."

"What?" I swallowed hard. "I don't know where a store is." I looked to Rachael for help, but her eyes didn't leave the television.

"There's a little grocery store down the street somewhere. I think it's called *Solo* if I'm not mistaken. I saw it as I was drivin' by."

"What? Where? I can't go by myself."

I pulled my sleeping bag close, tucking it under my chin. "This neighborhood's way too scary."

"Go with her, Rachael." A huge wave of relief flushed through me like air leaving a balloon.

"I don't know where it is, either," Rachael snarled.

"Well, we passed a store somewhere a few blocks that way." She pointed out the window. "It shouldn't be that hard to find."

She dug through her pocketbook and handed me a book of food stamps.

"Why do I have to go? She can go by herself," Rachael said.

"Go with her this time. Please."

This time?

Mama turned back to me. "Make sure you look at all the prices and compare them before buying anything, and get whichever brand is cheapest. And don't get anything that's not written here." She handed me the crinkled piece of paper. "We don't have money to throw away on junk."

I read over the list: 2 gallons of nonfat milk, Velveeta cheese, a jar of mayonnaise, bread, a large can of Pork 'n Beans, eggs, margarine, oatmeal, hamburger, salt, spaghetti noodles, 2 boxes of Hamburger

Helper, 3 cans of tuna fish, 2 cans of tomato sauce, and a can of tomato paste.

* * *

It felt weird being alone with Rachael since the two of us hardly ever did anything together. I guess, with our five year age difference, we really didn't have much in common. Or maybe because she just liked to keep to herself. Either way, I was glad Mama made her come with me.

We tiptoed over the same men who were now sound asleep on the front steps. The mouth of their empty bottle peeked from its brown paper bag as it lay at the bottom of the stairs. As I stepped over one of their legs, my foot slipped on a yellow puddle, causing me to almost fall.

"Ayyy." I quickly covered my mouth with my hand, so my outburst wouldn't wake them. "Ugh. That was awful. Did you see me almost fall?" I asked Rachael once we were out of earshot.

"No. I was too busy making sure I didn't step on one of them myself." She snarled, making it obvious she was still mad Mama made her come.

"I was so scared one of them would wake up and grab me by the leg," I said.

I stopped in front of a store in the middle of our block to admire some round, shiny coins displayed in the window. It seemed so out of place in the Tenderloin neighborhood.

"I wonder who can afford to shop here?" I asked.

Rachael didn't stop, or even look at me, so I skipped to catch up with her. As I walked by her side I wondered what made her so special? What was it that made Mama like her so much more than everyone else? I thought about what Brother said. The way her, Jonas, and Petesy looked more like Mama than the rest of us, but I couldn't see what he was talking about.

Rachael's long, wavy, brown hair wasn't at all like Mama's straight black hair, and Rachael's chin came to a soft, rounded point, not like Mama's square jaw. *What is it about her?* I kept peeking as we walked, hoping she wouldn't catch me. Then it hit me. It was her eyes. Her eyes looked just like Mama's, slightly sunken and olive-shaped, not big and round like the rest of ours. Her nose was a lot more narrow and straighter than mine as well. *I guess Brother's right. She does kind of look like Mama.*

She edged her scrawny body closer to me as we passed a group of men in a doorway, then we continued walking in silence for a few more blocks.

"We should probably ask somebody where the store is," Rachael mumbled. Her words were so meek I had to strain my ears to hear them. "Maybe we can ask one of those ladies."

She pointed to two half-naked ladies walking back and forth on the next corner.

"Okay. I'll ask," I said, trying to act brave to impress her.

My courage disappeared as we got closer, and all of a sudden, it felt so cold outside, my body began to shiver. I looked to Rache, wishing she'd ask instead, but she shrugged her shoulders and looked away.

I knew I had to do it. Not only to get directions, but to prove myself to Rachael. It was my chance to show her that I'm not just a little imp, but I'm brave and fearless, worthy of her friendship.

Clenching my hands into fists to control the shaking, I approached one of the ladies. She towered above me, and had what Daddy called a five o'clock shadow peeking through her caked-on makeup. I bit the inside corner of my lower lip, and took a small step back. *Just ask her, Teresa! Do it!*

"Uh. Excuse me." I looked from her face, to my feet, then back up again. "Uh, do you know where a grocery store is?"

"Oh, honey. I think there's a store a few blocks up and to the left," she said in a deep, husky voice. "Just keep walking. You should find it."

"Oh. Okay. Thanks."

I stumbled on my feet as I hurried away. The chill in my body turned to fire as my face flushed red as the stoplight. When we crossed to the other side of the street, I took a deep breath, then let it out slowly.

"I think that lady might have been a man," I whispered. Rachael looked at me as if I had lost my mind. "I wonder why those ladies don't wear warmer clothes? They must be freezing out here."

"They're hookers, Stupid," Rachael said. "They dress like that so men'll like 'em."

"What?"

Rachael didn't say anything else. That's all I got.

"Well, I sure wouldn't want to be freezing in the cold just so a boy'll like me," I said. "Poor ladies. There has to be an easier way to get men to like 'em."

Rachael let out a deep sigh, then opened her mouth to say something, but kept it to herself instead.

Two more blocks, then around the corner, we found the Solo Supermarket. I have to say, I felt a little proud that Mama gave *me* the shopping list and the food stamps and not Rachael. It made me feel more grown up and important.

* * *

We didn't even make it two blocks before a handle on one of my bags broke, causing everything to fall to the ground and scatter.

"Ugh! These are way too heavy," I whined. "Look at this." I placed the other bag on the sidewalk and ran my fingers over the indentations it left on my arms. "I don't know how Mama expected *me* to carry all this all by myself. She's crazy. She must think I'm Stretch Armstrong or somethin'."

"I guess we can just keep takin' breaks 'til we get home," Rachael said. She placed her bags down and took a seat next to me on the sidewalk as I gathered the spilled items.

"Whatcha got there, girls? Anything for me?"

A bum appeared out of nowhere. He smacked his sunken lips together in a loud exaggerated way, then exposed his toothless gums with a big smile. My eyes widened. He looked like the witch from Snow White, only he was a man. He reached one of his dirty hands toward my bag.

"Stop!" I shouted.

I scooped the groceries in my arms, then ran to the end of the block with Rachael following close behind. I couldn't cross the street, though. The light had turned red. Trapped by a steady flow of traffic, my body tensed. *Hurry, light, hurry. The man's gonna grab my bags.* I expected him to be behind me, reaching his hands out for me. *Hurry.* I turned my head to look over my shoulder, but he was gone. Vanished back to the same hole he crawled from. *Thank you, God!*

* * *

That night, I tossed and turned in my sleeping bag for hours. The soothing orchestra of cicadas and crickets was replaced with wailing sirens, honking horns, screeching tires, and shouting voices. The later it got, the noisier it became. To make matters worse, each time I'd start to drift to sleep, I'd feel a tickle on my skin and think a roach was crawling on me.

Waiting for the cable car at Powell and Market Street to go to church. Back row from left: me, Mama and Rachel. Front row from left, Josh and Jonas.

– 12 –

Routines

A man with outward courage dares to die;
a man with inward courage dares to live. — Lao Tzu

"Get up, little girl," Mama said in a raspy, tired voice. She stood over my sleeping bag, tapping my leg with her foot. "What? What time is it?"

It felt as if I had just fallen asleep. I rubbed my eyes and looked around the dark apartment. No movement. Rachael and the twins were still tucked in, sound asleep.

"It's time to make breakfast. That's what time it is." Mama said as she stumbled back to her bed to snuggle next to the twins. "And make a cheese sandwich for you and Rachael, too. Y'all need to get ready for school soon."

"What?" I asked. "Why do I have to?"

"Because. I've been cooking for nine kids way too long. I'm done with that. It's your turn now."

"But, why me? Why not Rachael?" I looked at the lump sleeping next to me on the floor, then back to Mama.

She pushed her blanket off and sat up. "Make the goddamn fuckin' eggs and sandwiches right now before I have to get up from here!"

Goosebumps piled high on my arms and legs from the frigid apartment, and my teeth began to chatter out of control. When I flipped the light switch on in the kitchen, nasty brown bugs scurried all over the place. I ran back to the room and stood on my sleeping bag.

"I can't go in there. Roaches are everywhere."

Rachael rolled over and mumbled something in her sleep.

"Go make the eggs and quit worrying about those damn roaches. They couldn't hurt a flea," Mama said.

"But some ran under the stove. They might crawl on me while I'm cooking."

"Trust me. Those roaches are way more scared of you than you are of them. They're not gonna crawl on your feet." She let out an annoyed sigh and pulled her blanket over her face.

I got out a dish and pan from the cabinet and mumbled under my breath. "There's no way those roaches are more scared of me. How would she even know that? She doesn't know how I feel."

I cracked eggs in the bowl, popped the yolks and mixed them together with a little salt and pepper.

What a liar! She didn't cook for us all her life. We all took turns making stuff.

I scooped a glob of margarine into a pan and brought it to the stove, but the burner was eye level to me.

"Great!" I shouted. "How am I supposed to cook these when I can't even see into the stupid pot?"

"What is wrong with you? You wanna wake everybody up? Quit being so dumb. You have a brain in your head, don't you? I'm sure you can figure somethin' out."

Ugh! You have a brain in your head, don't you? And, yes, I do wanna wake everybody up. Why do they get to stay sleeping?

I slid one of the yellow chairs next to the stove, grabbed the bowl of eggs, then, as I climbed on, the seat swiveled side-ways, causing the eggs to spill over the side in one large glob. I quickly grabbed onto the stove so I wouldn't fall myself. "Crap!"

I wanted to scream, but couldn't let Mama know I wasted eggs. Using a dishrag, I went back-and-forth to the sink, over and over again until all the gooey slime was gone.

Ugh! You have a brain in your head. Why doesn't she cook these stu-pid eggs?

I looked around for something else to stand on, but there wasn't anything. Not a single chair or stool. Not even in the other room.

"You have a brain in your head," I mocked.

I pulled the oven door open, hoping it wouldn't collapse under me, then climbed on and cooked the breakfast.

* * *

That became my routine, my life. Now that Mama wasn't under the watchful eyes of the nuns at Raphael House, she didn't have to pretend to be nice anymore, and she certainly didn't have to pretend to like me.

Each morning I stood on the oven door to make break-fast, then made our lunches while everyone else slept. I also got the jobs of cooking supper each night, washing the dish-es, and cleaning the kitchen once everyone had finished eating.

I really didn't mind cooking, though. I liked being in the kitchen. And even though I hated that everyone else got to sleep in, it was the only time I had any peace and quiet in that small apartment. I used the early morning time to be creative, experimenting with different ways to cook eggs. Plain scrambled, scrambled with cheese, scrambled with chopped peppers or green onions, sunny side up, and over medium.

I enjoyed it, but I also hated it. Hated it with a passion. I hat-ed that I *had* to do it. That I had no choice. And hated that I had to feed her, my mother, and Queen Bee, Rachael. If it were just the twins I had to feed, I wouldn't have minded as much.

Grocery shopping was also my job, and my job alone. Well, sometimes Rachael came with me, but mostly I went on my own. Shopping may not seem like such a big deal to anyone else, but it was to me. For one, Mama and the twins drank milk as if we owned our own cow, and a gallon of milk was way heavy, especially with all the other items I had to carry.

I also had to make sure I had enough food stamps to buy everything on the list, so I'd have to count and recount how much everything cost before loading it on the grocery belt. That also might not seem like such a big deal, but it is when you get to the counter and don't have enough money to buy things. It didn't even matter that I was only seven at Solo Market either. The cashier still got annoyed that she had to call the manager to have items removed whenever that happened. After a few times, you'd better believe that I never had to experience that again. But, even with counting and recounting the costs of each item, my heart still raced when I went to the checkout stand.

Going to the store in the Tenderloin was scary and an adventure all mixed into one. Even so, those trips were my golden ticket to freedom. My chance to escape the screaming, and the chaos, and never-ending chores. Even when creepy men followed me and I'd have to run and hide—even then I preferred being away from our tiny apartment. Besides, I knew I could outrun every one of those bums.

⌒

Me, age seven, in third grade at Morning Star.

– 13 –

19 Polk

*Lots of people want to ride with you in the limo,
but what you want is someone who will take the bus with you
when the limo breaks down.* — Oprah Winfrey

*M*ama drove me and Rache to school in the camper, as
she did when we lived at Raphael House, dropping
Rachael off first, then me, but the second week at the apartment
was a different story altogether.

As we were finishing the scrambled eggs I made for breakfast,
Mama pushed her plate aside and said, "I'm gonna have y'all start
taking Muni to school from now on."

Rache and I looked at each other.

"What's Muni?" Rachael asked.

"It's the city bus. There's no reason why I need to lug the twins
out in this cold every morning when San Francisco has one of the
best bus systems in the country."

Mama rode with us for the first couple of days, only this time,
we went to my school first, because she wanted Rachael to know

the route. After that, Rachael had to escort me since Van Ness was too busy to cross by myself. That street had so many cars speeding by, it was more like a highway.

Of course, that made Rachael furious, and the tension between us grew even stronger. I resented Rachael for sleeping in while I had to make her breakfast and lunch, and now she hated me for making her late to school every day. At least she only had to take me in the mornings. I never had to cross Van Ness Street after school. After school, I just walked to a nearby park for Mama and the twins to pick me up in the camper.

* * *

The following week, Mama woke up in one of her moods and complained about every single little thing I did. The eggs were over-cooked, I forgot to turn the light off in the bathroom, and she tripped over my sleeping bag since I didn't roll it up before I began cooking.

Days like those made everyone feel uneasy. We just kept to ourselves, not saying a word as we ate our eggs. After breakfast, Mama stayed in the kitchen with her brows bumped together in a tight scowl, waiting for a reason to explode. My body was so tense, I could barely lift the frying pan to the dish strainer after I washed it, knowing she was in the kitchen, right behind me, watching and waiting for the slightest mistake.

"You're on your own today, little girl."

Her words startled me, causing my heart to jump to my throat.

"Here's two nickels for the bus." She held out her hand with the coins staring at me like the eyes of an owl.

What's she talking about? "What?"

"One for the way there, and the other for the way home."

"What?" My stomach tightened as if her words punched a hole in my gut. "I have to go by myself? You mean, Rachael's not coming with me?"

I wondered what I had done to make her become so mad.

"Teresa, you're seven years old. You're not a baby anymore."

"And I'm late every day because of you," Rachael butted in.

"But I don't know how to get to school by myself." I wiped my soapy hands on my uniform skirt as I looked from Mama to Rachael. "I never paid attention."

"Well, there's lesson number one for you. You should always pay attention to everything! How else do you think you'll ever get ahead in this world?" Mama asked.

"Okay. I will from now on. I promise. Please, come with me." I clasped my hands together in a desperate prayer and held them toward Rachael. "Pleeease?"

"Take her one more time, Rachael, and show her how to get back home while you're at it. I'm not taking the twins all the way to that park to wait for her anymore."

"Thank you!" I took a deep breath and sighed it out slowly. Rachael pushed by me, knocking into my shoulder, and stormed out of the kitchen.

"Come on! Tomorrow you're on your own." She snatched her book bag from the wall so fast, she almost pulled the hook out right along with it.

I had to skip to keep up with her as we headed toward the bus stop, but after the first block, her anger seemed to fade. The glare on her face softened, and her pace slowed as we approached Polk Street. I think she felt sorry for me. She must have sensed my panic, or maybe it was because she knew she'd never have to go with me again. Either way, I did feel bad for making her late every day, but it really wasn't my fault.

She sat on a fire hydrant and began explaining how to get to Morning Star.

"We're gonna get off on Pine Street, then you cross the street, and walk up four or five blocks like you usually do. After school, all you have to do is walk back down to Polk Street and catch the 19 Polk bus back home. It's as easy as that. Easy peasy. You could even ask the driver to let you know when you get to your stop if you want."

It sounded simple enough, but it didn't stop my stomach from hurting all day. I had never taken the bus home before. Mama always picked me up. And I definitely never took it by myself. When the bus arrived, I grabbed a seat by the window, but instead of people watching as I usually did, I tried to pay attention to everything I could.

"Look around and get your bearings," Rache said once we got off. "As long as you remember everything here, you'll be fine. Just hop back on the 19 Polk, put your money in the slot, and go back home."

Squeezing the nickel in one hand, I pulled at my uniform blouse with the other. Even though it was nowhere near my neck, it still felt tight and constricting as if it were choking me. I looked at the buildings—a café, a small store, the Polk Street sign, and the bus stop.

"You'll be fine," Rachael said as she crossed the street with me.

"Thanks, Rache. I'm sorry you're gonna be late for school."

"It's okay. Starting tomorrow I'll always be on time."

Heading up the hill, I repeated the words 19 Polk over and over again, then throughout the day in class. *19 Polk. 19 Polk.* The sick feeling in my stomach never eased, and I thought I was going to have to run to the bathroom to throw up several different times.

I barely heard a single word Ms. Takahashi said, either. She might as well have been one of the teachers from a Charlie Brown cartoon. *Wa wa wa wa wa.*

My mind kept flashing to the small store on Polk Street, but the more I thought about it, the more my memory faded. *19 Polk. Take the 19 Polk.*

After school, I raced down the hill to Polk Street. The knot in my stomach unraveled as soon as I recognized the bus stop where I got off earlier that morning.

The tense feeling I held on to all day melted away, right there on that street corner. *What was I so worried about?* The café, the small store, the Muni bus stop sign. They were all there. *I did it!* I wanted to throw my arms in the air, spin in circles and scream out to the world, *Yes, I did it!*, but there was no time. The bus arrived as soon as I made it across the street.

"Do you go to 19 Polk?" I asked the driver. I didn't have to ask. I knew it was the 19 Polk. It said so on the sign. I just wanted to say it, to celebrate.

The bus driver chuckled. He was a middle-aged man with a large round belly and friendly face. "This is the 19 Polk, Kiddo. Where do ya wanna go?"

"19 Polk," I repeated proudly. *What does he mean where do I want to go? I wanna go to 19 Polk.*

He furrowed his bushy eyebrows, causing a deep crease to form between his eyes. "Sweetie, you're on the 19 Polk bus. What street do you want to go to?"

"19 Polk." I drew in my lower lip and held it between my teeth.

"Where are you headed?"

"Home." *Why is he asking me that?*

"Ok. Where do you live?"

My chest tightened. Words had a hard time forming in my mouth as reality hit me. *19 Polk is the bus. I don't know where I live. All Rachael told me was 'remember 19 Polk'.*

"Do you know what street you live on?" he asked, as if rephrasing his question would make it any easier for me to answer. I looked down at my feet, at the lump on top of my shoes where my toes curled inside.

"Honey, tell the bus driver where you live, and he can take you to the right stop," an old lady with a scarf covering her hair butted in. I kept looking down and didn't say a word.

"Where is it you live?" the driver asked again, bringing his fist to his chin. The creases on his forehead sunk deeper as he looked at me.

"I... I don't know," I managed to stutter. My hand felt clammy against the cool metal as I clung to the stainless steel bar that separated him from where I stood. "I just moved here."

"Oh." He took his fist from his chin and began tapping his fingers on the steering wheel. "Hmmm. Well, I'll tell ya what. I'll take you to the end of the line," he said, then reached for something that looked like a walkie talkie. "And I'll radio the police to help you find your way home. Have a seat right there next to me," he pointed to the sideways facing bench that's normally reserved for the elderly and handicapped.

I sat down and kept my gaze out the window so no one could see the tears streaming down my face. A hand on my back caused my body to stiffen.

"Don't worry. They'll help you find your way home," a lady reassured as she patted me.

When we got to the end of the line at Fisherman's Wharf, a police car was already waiting for us.

"Stay in here a minute," the driver told me. He walked out to talk to the officer, and after a few minutes, both men came on the bus.

"Hi. My name is Officer McLaughlin," the policeman said. "You can call me Officer Mike."

He was a good-looking man. Tall like Brother, and had the same black hair and dimple on his chin, only he had blue eyes, not brown, and he looked older, too. He held out his hand for me to shake.

"What's your name?"

"Teresa."

"Teresa. That's a very pretty name. What's your last name?"

"Thompson." *Why does he need to know my last name? Am I gonna be in trouble?*

"Are you lost?"

I looked down at my hands and didn't say anything. *I'm not lost. I'm on the 19 Polk, just like I'm supposed to be.*

"Here, come with me and sit in my car," he said. I followed him down the steps of the bus, then he opened the passenger door for me to get in. I couldn't believe it, my second time in a cop car in only a few months. *Is he gonna take me back to juvie?*

"Well, let's start here...Do you know your phone number?" he asked.

"No, we don't have a phone."

"Ok, what school do you go to?"

"Morning Star."

"Oh, that's great. We'll call the school and ask them for your address." His eyes sparkled with confidence as he picked up the radio in his car to call the dispatcher. "Can you try and get a hold of someone at Morning Star school and ask where Teresa Thompson lives?" He nodded his head as he spoke, then gave a half-smile and winked at me.

"We'll get you home in no time," he said as we waited to hear back from the lady on the other end of the CB.

"No one's picking up the phone," she said after a few minutes. "It just keeps ringing and ringing."

"Okay. Well keep trying," he said. "While she's doing that, can you think of any landmarks near your apartment?"

"Landmarks?"

"Yeah, like a store, or a restaurant, or something like that. Something that can help us narrow our search."

"Yes! There's a little store on one corner of my block. It's right under our apartment! And there's a laundry-mat on the other corner."

"Ah, a little store and laundromat. That's a great start. Can you think of anything else? There's a lot of little stores and laundromats in the area, so if there's anything else you can remember, it would be very helpful."

I tried to think, but my mind went blank. 19 Polk seemed to erase all other memories. "Um. No. That's all I can think of," I mumbled.

He spoke into the radio again. "Any luck with Morning Star?"

"Still no answer."

"Okay, look for streets along the 19 Polk line with a small store on one corner and a laundromat on the other."

Within a minute, she came back with the location. I exhaled a sigh of relief that deflated all the fear I held on to the entire day in one single breath. I couldn't believe how easy it was. Rachael's words rang through my mind, *Easy peasy! Thank you, God!*

Officer Mike drove a few blocks, then pulled next to the curb in front of a laundromat. Nothing looked familiar, though. Not even a single person hung out on the sidewalk. It was way too quiet for my street. "This isn't it," I said before he could say anything.

We drove up and down, crisscrossing, street after street, stopping each time he found a laundromat and liquor store. But he was right. There seemed to be one about every four or five blocks, or so. I craned my head sideways as tears rolled down my cheeks. I didn't want him to see me crying, but he caught on when he heard my sniffles.

"Oh, Darlin', it's okay. We'll find your family. Don't worry." He put his hand on my shoulder. "I've got all night. I'm working a double."

Aw, Darlin'. It made me think of a song Brother used to blare out of his bedroom. He'd hold an album cover between his fingers, flipping it in circles while the music played. Something like, "Oh darlin', darlin', darlin'." I pictured the album cover with little naked figures on some rocks. It was a weird cover, but it made me think of the twins, and how we'd call them naked jaybirds. *I wonder if I'll ever see them again?*

No matter how hard he tried to hide it, I could tell Officer Mike was worried, too. I heard it in the way his voice changed. Not as loud. Not as reassuring. And his face lost its smile, at least the one he started with. He tried to cover his disappointment with upturned lips, but I knew it wasn't real. I had become the master of hiding the way I feel.

Thinly scattered clouds began to glow like wisps of colorful cotton candy. The setting sun swirled and danced like magic, transforming the sky to a masterpiece of yellows, pinks, and oranges, as if God suddenly appeared to calm me and make me feel at ease.

I closed my eyes and pretended I had the power to make the apartment appear. As if I could summon the heavens above to guide our way. *Please, dear God. Help him find our place.*

I pictured the big, white apartment building with the small store under it and thought about the hookers standing on the corner, and the bums who hang out on our front steps. I saw the coin store in the middle of our block that I'd pass on the way to the market, and imagined the –

"Huh," I gasped. "Wait!" Officer Mike jumped from my sudden outburst. "I remember somethin' else! There's a coin store in the middle of our block, too."

"A coin store?" He scratched the side of his head. "A coin store?" Then lifted the radio to give the new information to the operator.

"Okie Dokie. A liquor store, a laundromat, and a pawn shop. Here we go." The lady blurted out directions.

"Yes!" Officer Mike beamed. He gave me a thumbs up, then turned the car around.

I sat on my knees so I could see better out the front window as he followed the dispatcher's instructions. He turned a corner and double-parked his car.

"Ta-da!" he said, holding his arms out to present the street to me. "Here we are. Which building is yours?"

"This isn't it," I cried. "This isn't my street." I buried my head in the crease of my arm. "I wanna go home."

My shoulders bounced up and down as I gasped for air between sobs. I didn't want to cry. I hated that Officer Mike had to see me like that, like a baby.

"This isn't her street," he said into the radio, then put his hand back on my shoulder for comfort. I felt bad he had to waste his whole night dealing with me.

"Wait! Here's another one," the dispatcher said. "Try Eddy and Hyde Streets. There's an actual coin store on that block."

"Okay," he said. "Let's give it a go."

He turned the car around and drove without stopping for what seemed like miles. As soon as he pulled onto Eddy Street, I almost jumped out of my seat.

"This is it!" I shouted. "You found it. I live in that big white building on the corner." I looked across the street at the Brown Jug Saloon with its nightly crowd already gathered on the sidewalks. *How stupid! How in the world could I have forgotten about that noisy bar?*

Me, age seven, climbing walls near
St. Anthony's Dining Room.

– 14 –

Imagine

*You have an awesome power that most of us have never been
taught to use effectively. Elite athletes use it. The super-rich
use it. And peak performers in all fields now use it.
That power is called visualization.* — Jack Canfield

*D*riving around all day, in and out of different neighborhoods, Officer Mike never once came to this
part of town. He probably couldn't fathom me living in such
an area, or maybe it was because I got on the bus headed in the wrong direction—either way, we finally found it.

He double-parked his car in front of the apartment, just as
Mama had done a couple weeks earlier, and turned on the siren
for a quick second, causing the bums on the stairs to scurry as fast
as the roaches in our kitchen.

I ran my finger down the long row of doorbells, feeling the
bump of each one as it glided along my fingertip, then hesitated at number 606. Glancing at Officer Mike, I paused before
pushing the button. He looked intimidating now. More like
a cop than the friend who I just spent hours with in the car.

He towered over me in his dark blue uniform with the shiny star pinned to his chest. I didn't even notice the long billy club or the handcuffs and gun while we were in the car together.

"That better be you, little girl," Mama's shrill voice snapped on the other end of the intercom.

"It's me," I said, hoping Officer Mike wouldn't pick up on her hateful tone.

When the door buzzed to release the lock, Officer Mike pushed it open and stood aside for me to walk in. "After you," he said.

"Thanks for taking me home. You don't have to come up with me. I know which apartment is mine now. I just have to go to the sixth floor. I'll be fine."

"I know. But, I'd like to speak to your mother," he said.

Shoot! What's he going to say?

I led him to the elevator, slid the gate closed once we were inside, then pushed the button for the sixth floor. This time, I welcomed the slow struggle as the small cage crept its way upward.

Officer Mike winked at me. "We did it," he said, then nudged me with his elbow.

Yes, we did it, only I wasn't happy and excited as I should have been. Instead, my body felt heavier with each passing floor, as if that ghost from *A Christmas Carol* hopped back on to remind me of the dread that awaited in 606.

The playful look on Officer Mike's face made me feel even worse. I wanted to cling to him—to keep him, as my protector and friend. *Why did I want to come home so badly, anyway?* As we got closer to the sixth floor, my heart pounded with the sound of Mama's footsteps thundering down the hallway. Before the door even opened, she began shouting.

"Where in the hell were you?"

No! Dear God, Please let her be nice. Please. Please. Please! I slowly pulled open the black iron gate as she swung the outer door open.

"Don't you know..."

Her screaming stopped as she looked from me to the tall man in uniform. She froze.

The shock didn't last for more than a couple of seconds before her intuition kicked in. She shifted her body back-and-forth, side-to-side in a disgusting dance to exaggerate her curves. It was so gross. It was like she took lessons from the ladies on the corner. I was getting used to it, though. She did it to all the men.

"Sweetie. You made it home," she said in her slow Southern accent, while twirling a strand of her long hair around her finger. "I was so worried."

Shut up! You're so fake. That voice makes me wanna puke.

"Teresa didn't know her address, or even what street she lives on," Officer Mike explained.

"What? How could you forget your address?" she asked. "She had it memorized this morning."

Liar!

"Well, I'm sure she won't forget it after this, will you, Teresa?" Officer Mike asked.

"No sir."

From down below, we heard someone walking up the stairs so Mama said, "Well, let's get out of this hallway."

Office Mike followed us to 606. "Looks like you're safe and sound now, sweetie," he patted my head as he glanced around the apartment.

Sleeping bags, toys, and clothes spread across the unvacuumed floor. The twins didn't have anything but underwear on. At least they weren't in diapers anymore.

As he looked at the small, lumpy bed, I hoped that he thought our place was bigger with more bedrooms. *For all he knows the kitchen could be mine and Rache's room.* I wrapped my arms across my chest. *It's freezing in here.*

Jonas slid his fingers along the billy club dangling by Officer Mike's side.

"Don't touch that," I scolded.

"Oh, it's okay." Officer Mike squatted next to him. "What's your name?"

"Jonas."

Josh and Rachael also inched closer. The smiles on their faces lit up the room as if having a real live policeman in our apartment was the coolest thing they had ever seen.

Go away. He's not here for y'all. He's my friend.

The twins took turns touching gadgets along his belt, while Officer Mike explained what each item was used for.

"Okay, I gotta get back to work," he said. "Make sure you write down your address and put it in Teresa's bookbag in case she forgets it again," he said to Mama, then turned to me. "Get some rest. You've had a rough day today."

"Okay."

Don't leave. Please, don't leave me. I could tell Mama was furious, even through her fake smile. I walked him to the elevator and waited as he slid the gate closed and disappeared out of sight.

"Do you plan on staying out there all night?" Mama shouted.

My nose crinkled at her words. She didn't even care how scared I was all day. "Do you plan on staying out there all night?" I mocked.

That's it. That's all it took. The moment she waited for. She stormed out of the apartment and charged toward me. Like the Incredible Hulk, each pounding step transformed her into an ugly monster. Muscles bulged and buttons popped as she rushed toward me. Only she was no superhero. She became the villain when she changed, with the sole mission of attacking her own child.

I dropped to the floor and covered my head with my arms, but as always, she found a way in. I think that was the reason she loved long hair so much. Holding as close to the roots as possible, she dragged me toward the apartment with my legs kicking in all directions. I couldn't scream, though. I couldn't do anything. Officer Mike may have still been in the building, and that would have been the most embarrassing thing ever if he saw how Mama really was. Then he'd know I wasn't normal because I had a crazy mother. I kicked until I got my feet under me to lessen the pain, but as soon as I did, she flicked her wrist to give it a tighter pull.

"Ow," I shrieked once we were in the apartment. "Please let go! I didn't mean to say that."

But her hand only gripped tighter. Tears poured down my cheeks as if a sprinkler system had turned on to put out the burning fire on the side of my head.

I pried at her fingers, trying to pull each one off to free my hair. Mama was shocked by my confrontation. She let go, glared in my eyes, then shoved so hard, I stumbled back to the floor again.

"How dare you humiliate me like that, you little whore."

Rachael and the twins ran to the kitchen to hide behind the door frame.

"Don't you know I was worried sick about you? You think it's funny to come up here with a cop? What were you thinking?"

"It's not my fault!" I cried.

"Not your fault, huh?" She kicked at my side. "Whose fault is it then?" She kicked again, this time taking my breath. "I bet you hoped he'd take me away, didn't you?" She gritted her teeth, lifted her leg and stomped her heel to my thigh.

"Ow! Mama. Stop. Please." I kept my head covered with my arms as I tucked my legs closer to my body.

"I asked you a question." Her jaw clenched tight. I could tell by the way she sounded.

"What?"

"I said, I bet you wished he would take me away, didn't you?"

"No, I didn't wish that." I gasped for air. "But I do now."

I don't know why I said that. I couldn't help it. It just came out. She leaned over, grabbed my arm and squeezed with all her might, wiggling each of her fingers until her razor-sharp nails dug into my flesh.

"Ow! Let go!" I shrieked.

She scowled and squeezed harder.

"Let go, you crazy witch!" I grasped her fingers, but they were locked tight into a vice-grip.

With her other hand, she reached in and grabbed a hold of my hair again, then yanked me back to my feet.

"You better learn where you live now, you little tramp." She let go, and shoved me backward. This time I didn't fall.

"Rachael even took you to school today to show you. You're so fucking stupid..."

Dadadadadadadadada... I can't hear you! I mocked her words inside my head. I wished I could cover my ears, but I had to pretend to listen.

"Don't even know where you live..."

Dadadadadadadadada! I'm not listening.

"What's the one thing I always tell y'all?"

Shut up!

"Always know your surroundings so you don't get lost."

"Always know your surroundings!" *Shoot! I didn't mean to say that out loud!*

I took a small step back, then another. Never losing eye contact with her, I raised my arms over my head. Like the dance of two wild animals before an attack, she stepped toward me as I shuffled backward. Her fingers stretched wide, then clenched into a fist. *No!*

Something dropped in the kitchen. I turned my head toward the sound just as the side of Mom's fist pummeled my face. A searing pain shot through the side of my mouth as I spun sideways and stumbled forward, almost falling to the floor again.

Mom took a step toward me. Her eyes wild and crazy, fixed on mine like magnets. Even though I had to know her next move, she was too scary to look at. I looked away, searching the kitchen for Rachael and the twins, but they were hidden out of sight.

"Get in the corner and stay there till you learn not to smart off with that filthy mouth of yours," she screamed. Her trembling finger pointed toward the wall. "Move, I said."

I sneered at her with a look of disgust—the same look Ms. Takahashi had when she threw my cookie into the trash. I moved in the direction of her finger but didn't get far before her foot thrust into my ribs. The wall shot toward me as my body slammed against it.

"Stop it," I wailed. "Stop!"

Collapsing into the dirty drywall, I slid down, hugging my knees tight to my chest. *Dear God, Please don't let her kill me.*

She looked possessed, like the monster had taken complete control of her. She stood over me with her hand raised in the air to hit me again.

"Stop, Mama," Josh shouted from the kitchen. Enraged, with his eyes wide and unblinking, he stormed toward her with a plastic cup handle gripped in his hands. *No, Josh. Don't do anything.* He threw the cup at her, but it fell short.

"Josh. Don't. I'm ok."

Mom turned toward him. Her three-year-old son who came to my defense.

"Don't touch him," I said.

His cup had broken the spell, shattering the veil of hatred like shards of glass crumbling around her. She unraveled her fist, but didn't bother with Josh. She didn't bother with me anymore either. She snatched up her paperback and threw herself on her bed. Reading was her way of escaping. Her way to calm down and pretend nothing happened. Within minutes, that book could transform her to another place while I lay damaged against the cold wall.

I buried my head on my thighs and slid my tongue over my upper lip. It didn't hurt much, not like the rest of me. That pain turned to numbness. Tears pooled in my eyes—tears of pain, tears for Josh, tears for my time with Officer Mike. It didn't matter though. My face was hidden. Mom couldn't see me.

My arm stung from the four half-mooned-shaped blood spots. *What a witch!* I smeared the blood from one claw mark to the other, painting them to mask the ugly shape of her fingernails, then leaned my head against the wall and closed my eyes. *I wish we had never found this stupid apartment today. I wish he had taken me to juvie instead.*

* * *

The apartment was dark and quiet except for the distant sound of sirens and some loud chatter outside the Brown Jug. *Where did everybody go?* Panic set in. *They left me.* My eyes felt scratchy from all the crying as I scanned the apartment. *Please, no! Please be here.* Not far from me, on the floor, I noticed a familiar lump. *Oh, thank God.*

"Rache," I whispered.

Nothing. Then movement and the sound of breathing. *Is she sleeping?* Through the faint glow of the streetlamp outside, I made out the forms of Mom and the twins in their small bed by the window. *I can't believe they're sleeping. What time is it? Did they even have supper?* I glanced at the clock just as the numbers flipped from 1:49 to 1:50. *1:50? Why is it dark? Is it the middle of the night?*

The taste of copper inside my mouth reminded me of Mom's fist. I rolled my tongue over the lump on my upper lip as I fought back tears. *What if somebody notices this at school? Oh no. School! I didn't even do my homework. Ms. Takahashi's gonna be so mad at me again.* The thought sent a burning pain from my belly to my throat, as if a wick had been ignited, fizzling and ready to explode. I placed my hand on my chest as the intensity grew. *I don't wanna go to school. The kids are gonna make fun of me.*

Moving my lower jaw back and forth, it hurt to open my mouth. *I hate Mama.* I rolled onto my hands and knees and crawled toward my sleeping bag. Every jostle sent waves of pain throughout my body—my ribs, my thigh, my side, my arm, my jaw, my scalp. They all hurt now. Everything did.

As I slipped into my bag, I felt what was sure to become a large bruise on my thigh. I lay down and stared at the ceiling. *At least it'll be hidden under my skirt.* Tears ran down the side of my face, soaking into my hair like a sponge. I couldn't stop them. *I wonder why Mama hates me so much?*

Rachael's breathing became heavy. She must have been dreaming. *Why doesn't Mama make her do anything? Why only me?* My whole body quivered as I took a deep breath. *I wish I could run away.* The thought made me shiver. *Ouch! I wish I didn't live here with her.* Mama rolled over and mumbled something in her sleep. *I hate, hate, hate, hate her! I wanna live with Daddy!*

I closed my eyes to try and sleep, but the crazed look on Mama's face kept haunting me. *Stop! Don't think of that!*

Holding my palms over my ears, I squeezed my eyes closed to try to erase the memory, but the thought kept popping back into my head. Her mouth. Her tight lips. Her face. It changed from pink, to red, to a darker red, to almost black. Horns grew from her head as she took a step toward me. *Huh! The Devil. Stop! God help me! Please! In the name of the Father, and of the Son, and of the Holy Spirit God, please protect me. Please. Amen.*

The Florida Gang returns for a summer vacation. Front row from left: Jonas, Josh, Jon Eric, Petesy. Back row from left: me, Gregory, Rachael and Brother.

– 15 –

The Florida Gang

*Like branches on a tree, our lives may grow in different
directions, yet our roots remain as one. — Unknown*

Summer of '75

I counted down the days till summer break by putting
hash marks on a small piece of paper I had taped to the
wall of the apartment. The Florida Gang were coming back
for the summer. The Florida Gang! That's what we called my
other siblings now. There wasn't a special name for us that I
knew of. We weren't the San Franciscans, or Californians, or
anything like that. We were just the ones stuck with Mama.

As the time got nearer, I began to have a recurring dream. My
siblings would be walking down the stairs of the Greyhound
bus with their hair blowing in the breeze. I guess that part was
included since it was windy the day they left, and that's how
I remembered them. Anyway, Brother would always be the
last one off. He'd have a large duffle bag on his shoulder, and

when he'd take a step down, I'd see Daddy standing behind him. Daddy! He'd run toward me, pick me up and swing me around in circles. "*I'm gonna take you back home with me,*" he'd say.

But when I'd wake up and look at the growing number of hash marks on the wall, reality always sank back in. No one knew how Mama treated me. How could they? I never said anything about it in my letters, and I knew Rachael and Mama wouldn't tell them. I wondered if they would even care if they *did* know? *Would Daddy come back to get me? What if they don't even like us anymore?*

The thought of the Florida Gang seeing our tiny roach-infested apartment horrified me. Especially after reading the letters Jon Eric sent me. He wrote about all the changes that happened once Dad's girlfriend, Joye moved into the house. He explained how she ran a tight ship and kept everything in tip-top condition. "No more messes, no more yelling, and no more hot nights," he wrote. He described the new furniture, and carpet, and how the air conditioning ran day and night. I wasn't sure if he was bragging or not, but it sure sounded like it. *They probably think they're better than us now.*

* * *

Mama had been planning our trip for weeks. When I'd get home from school, she'd always be in the same spot, sitting on her bed next to a pile of library books. She'd jot down points of interest, then spread a map in front of her to mark our path with a yellow highlighter pen.

When the day finally arrived, we went back to the same Greyhound station, only this time, I barely even noticed the bums or the smell of pee as I did before.

We got there early and waited in the lot, each holding a homemade welcome poster and a metal noisemaker Mama had saved from a New Year's Eve dance. We rattled the noisemakers and held our posters high in the air, while jumping up and down, and cheering as bus after bus pulled into the station. When theirs finally arrived, all five were squeezed in the last row with their faces pressed against the window, just as they were the previous summer when they drove out of sight.

"Welcome to San Francisco!" We cheered as they made their way toward the front of the bus and down the stairs. Just like my dream, Brother was the last one off, but he didn't carry a duffle bag, and Daddy wasn't right behind him.

Everyone looked different. Older. It was strange how much they changed since all of us in San Francisco were exactly the same. Well, except maybe the twins. They were a little taller, and definitely not in diapers anymore, but that was it. I wanted the Florida Gang to be the same, too, as a way to erase all the time we had apart, as if it had never happened at all. It just wasn't fair. Too much time had gone by. The boys were taller, with longer hair. Brother even had a black mustache, and he and Petesy had deep voices like Daddy when they spoke. I don't know what was up with Gregory's. It squeaked and cracked with each word, and Deborah's breasts were now noticeable through her sweater. Jon Eric just looked different. I don't know what. His face was thinner, or something.

Just like last summer, we stood outside the door of the bus in one big clump, hugging, and clinging and crying—not wanting to let go. Only this time, they weren't tears of sadness. We were all back together, and nothing could have been better than that. Well, except if Daddy had been there.

On the way to our apartment, everyone talked at once, asking questions faster than any of us could answer. Mostly stuff about San Francisco, and school, and if we met any famous movie stars, and things like that.

As we wound our way through the Tenderloin, that's when the panic set in. *Please, don't let those bums be on the stairs!*

Mama parked the camper, and as we made our way through the smell of urine on the greasy sidewalk of Hyde Street, I kept my head down—too embarrassed to see my brothers and Deborah's reaction to our neighborhood. *Please, no bums.* Luckily, only one man sat on the marble steps as we made our way to the entrance. Just like the first time we walked through those doors, Mama showed off the elevator against the back wall with the same enthusiasm in her voice. She was so proud of that elevator.

Since there wasn't enough room for all of us to ride up, Rachael took the keys from Mama, and together, she and I bolted up the six flights of stairs. We rushed to our apartment, turned the lights on, and ran around the room waving our arms in the air to scare the roaches back to their hiding places. Rachael plopped on the old tweed couch and let out a long sigh.

"Thank God they didn't have to see those cockroaches," she said.

I couldn't believe it. Rachael and I were on the same page. I had no idea she worried what the other kids would think. Down the hall, the elevator door opened, followed by the sound of a cattle stampede as everyone approached the small apartment.

"Y'all come take a look," Mama said before they even put down their bags. "I have our whole trip outlined for you to see." She unfolded the crinkled map and placed it on her bed. "We're gonna explore the Northwest this summer."

She traced the yellow highlighted route going north from California, through Oregon and Washington, then across Canada, and back down through Idaho, letting us know of the sites we'd see along the way—the national parks and monuments, each state capital, and any other tidbits of information she could think of. I had heard it all before, and didn't want to waste my time listening again, so I watched everyone as Mama moved her finger along the map.

Deborah, Gregory and Jon Eric seemed enthralled in what she had to say, but Brother and Petesy were busy looking around the apartment. I wondered what they were thinking.

"So, after Idaho, we'll go over to Wyoming and spend some time at Yellowstone and the Grand Tetons, then we'll head to Utah. Just wait till I show y'all the pictures in this book!" She held the book up for us to see, then hid it behind her back. "It's going to be a great trip. My goal is to take y'all to every national park in the United States. The Canadian ones are just a bonus. But after seeing the pictures, there's no way we could miss out on those."

* * *

Mama laid blankets on the floor so everyone could sleep in the tiny studio, and for the next few days, we showed them all around San Francisco. To my surprise, no one said anything negative about our apartment, at all. Of course, there was the occasional screech from seeing a roach, but that was it. The excitement of being together again outweighed everything else.

The twins were a little shy from the sudden intrusion because everyone wanted to hold them. They were being passed around like ragdolls and had the same look of panic on their faces as when Mama threw one of her fits. When they could, they'd run and cling to mine or Rachael's side. I'm not sure if they remembered their other siblings, or if it was all just too overwhelming for them.

That didn't last very long though, soon they were loving all the attention, especially Josh. Even though he didn't get beaten or have to do chores like me, at his young age of three Mama was already showing favoritism toward Jonas. Josh would melt in their arms, suck his thumb, and hold their earlobe between his fingers as he always did for comfort.

Everyone had grown a little, so the camper felt more cramped than on our last voyage. Well, not as much for me and Jon Eric on the upper bed, but now even the twins wanted to ride in the back. At least we didn't have to worry about the heat. Going north wasn't nearly as hot as crossing through Texas.

Not only was I excited to see all my brothers and sisters, and have Jon Eric back, but I also didn't have to do all the work anymore. As a matter of fact, with everyone else around, I rarely had to do anything at all. I could be a little girl again, almost invisible to Mama.

Even when she threw one of her fits, I could hide behind Deborah and mostly go unnoticed. To Mama, it was like I didn't even exist.

* * *

It didn't take long for all our food to dwindle just as it had the year before.

"Ten mouths are a lot to feed," Mama said. "Y'all are smart. You figured it out before."

So we were back to begging at restaurants and digging in garbage cans before we even made it to Canada.

With so much to see, I kept my eyes peeled out the window as we crossed from British Columbia into Alberta. Mama parked the camper near a humongous castle, then we followed her out to see the jagged, snow-capped mountains surrounding a pool of turquoise water. Only it wasn't a pool. It was a lake—Lake Louise.

"Is this real?" I asked.

I had never seen anything like it before. A castle on one side of the lake and mountains all around. Puffy white clouds reflected on the water as if someone had painted them there. It had to be from a fairytale, or maybe I was dreaming. The place took my breath away. I didn't want to move. I couldn't. Nothing else in the world mattered at that moment, like I was in a trance or something.

"A bald eagle!" Petesy shouted, pointing to a large bird flying over the lake.

I held out my arms and swayed my body, pretending to fly along with it—flying over the lake and the mountains. I leaned to one side, one arm up, the other down, as I turned to take flight over the castle.

"Silt comes in with the snowmelt," Mama said.

"Huh?" I didn't even know she was standing next to me. Jon Eric, either. She pointed to the mountains surrounding the lake. "That's what makes the lake this turquoise blue color. The silt."

"Oh, cool!" I said. *Whatever that means.* "Who lives in that castle?"

"That's not a castle, sweetie. That's a hotel."

Sweetie? A smile swept across my face.

"A hotel?" Jon Eric asked, but Mama already headed toward the other kids who were taking turns skipping stones on the water, rippling out the cloud formation.

"This is the best place in the whole wide world," I said.

"Yeah. I know. It's so cool. But, Treedy, you're only eight. You haven't really seen anything in the whole world, so you can't really say that."

There he goes again. Acting like he's so much smarter than me.

"Well, I'm gonna travel the world when I'm older," I said. "And I'm gonna stay in that fancy hotel one day, too!" Before he could say anything, I stormed off to where everyone else was.

Enjoying an ice cream treat.

–16–

Xs for Lulu

I measure every grief I meet with narrow, probing eyes–
I wonder if it weighs like mine–or has an easier size.
— Emily Dickinson

When we arrived in Salt Lake City, Utah, Mama pulled in front of a small café, shut off the engine, and came back to the camper. "I'm so exhausted. I can barely see straight," she said. "I'm gonna close my eyes for a few minutes, then we can go check out that museum by the Mormon Temple."

Once we all piled out, she pulled the couch into a bed and plopped down so she and the twins could take a nap.

"Come on, Treedy," Jon Eric said. "Let's go look around."

By that point, I knew that *looking around* meant only one thing. It was time to search for food. The café we parked next to didn't have a backdoor like the fast food places we were used to, but since it was the only eating establishment in the area, we had to come up with another plan.

"I really don't want ketchup packets right now," Jon Eric said. "We should go in and one of us'll just have to ask for leftovers."

"Ask who? I'm not!"

"We'll just ask that lady up front there." He pointed in the window.

"Okay," I sighed. "Let's Roshambo for it. If I win, you ask." I held my hand up in a fist ready to play the game.

"No, wait. I got it. I have a better idea. See that table right there?" He pointed through the window. "Let's go get some sandwich baggies from the camper, then we can walk by all the tables that don't have people sitting at 'em and grab whatever scraps they left."

"Hmmm?"

"We'll split up. You go to the right, and I'll go to the left. Grab whatever you see, put it in your bag, and we'll meet back outside. Okay?"

"Yeah, I guess."

My heart pounded as we walked through the front door, but the plan worked easier than I had expected. My side had two empty tables that hadn't been cleared yet, so I looked around, stuffed everything I could into the baggie, and hauled butt back out the door. Jon Eric came out right after me, and we didn't stop walking until we made it to a nearby doorway.

"Wait till you see everything I got," he said.

Between the two of us, we had a steak bone that still had bits of meat on it, a piece of toast cut into a triangle, a couple bites of chicken fried steak, three tater tots, a few unopened packets of jelly, and a piece of a fried egg. Jon Eric split the loot between the two of us, and we devoured it in seconds.

"Did you notice all that money on the tables?" he asked as I licked the inside of the baggie.

"Yeah?"

"Well, don't you know what today is?"

"No!"

"It's Mom's birthday, Stupid! It's July 7th. We should go back in and get the money so we can buy her a present."

"No! That's way too scary."

"Well, don't ya wanna get her somethin'?"

Of course, I wanted to get her something. I loved seeing Mama happy, and she loved getting presents. I thought about it for a moment. *If we were the only ones out of the whole family to get her anything, she'd like us the most for sure!*

"Come on. We'll do exactly what we just did. You go on one side, and I'll go on the other. Just grab the money and leave. We'll meet right here again."

"Okay."

When we went back in, the two tables on my side were still loaded with dirty dishes. I kept my head down but checked that no one was watching, then grabbed the money from the first table. My heart raced so fast it made it hard to breathe. *I can't go to the other table, somebody's gonna see me.* I took a deep breath. *Okay, just do it.*

As I reached to grab the dollar bill, my hand knocked against a glass of water, sending it clanking to the plate next to it, then spilling to the floor. I grabbed it and bolted out the door. I didn't stop at the doorway as we had planned. I kept running down the block, around the corner, all the way to the end of the next street, then ducked into a doorway to hide. Jon Eric ran after me. When he heard the glass fall, he darted out the door as well.

I was way too scared to be the one holding the money if someone came around the corner, so I handed it to him to count. He didn't seem worried at all. He laid the money on the ground like it was no big deal, separated the coins into different piles, then counted it out. Twice.

"Six dollars and thirty-two cents," he said.

"Whoa! Seriously? We can buy so much with that."

We walked to a nearby souvenir shop that had all sorts of trinkets. Things like keychains, coffee mugs, pocket knives, and statuettes of the temple, but nothing Mama would really like. Jon Eric looked through the postcards, as I continued searching on the rows of shelves.

"Oh, my gosh. Jon Eric, come here. Mama'll love this!" I held up a Little Lulu paper doll for him to see. "She loves Little Lulu."

We paid for the doll with enough money to spare for a couple of Sugar Daddies for ourselves, then skipped back to the camper to give her the gift. When we got there, she and the twins were still sound asleep on the couch.

"Should we wake her up?" Jon Eric whispered.

"Yes. Mama, wake up! We got somethin' for you!" I said without pausing between words.

She rolled over and rubbed her eyes. Still a little dazed from the nap, she looked around the camper to orient herself, then back at us.

"Happy birthday, Mama!" I said.

"We got you something for your birthday," Jon Eric held up the brown paper bag, moving it from side to side as Mama pushed herself up.

"What?" Her face switched from grumpy to smiling. "What do you have here?"

Jon Eric handed her the bag.

"It's your birthday present. Open it!" I said, then climbed onto the bed to sit near Josh's feet.

"Oh, how cute! I love Little Lulu." She pulled it out of the bag. "I used to play with paper dolls when I was a little girl. Thank you!"

Her joy was contagious. She hugged the paper doll close to her chest and rocked back and forth, then placed the feet of the doll on Jonas' back to make it dance. Mama looked so innocent and happy, as if her little girl self climbed out of her to play for a while.

I imagined her as a child. A scrawny kid with the short, pageboy haircut she always talked about—wearing dirty, faded clothes, two sizes too small with her bony ankles showing from the bottom of her pant cuffs. I felt sorry for her as I thought of the horrific stories she told us of Grandmama, and pictured her hunched over, cowering in a corner as Grandmama snatched the doll from her.

Poor Mama.

When I looked back at her, the smile never left her face. Grandmama wasn't here. Mama was safe. The little girl was able to come out to have fun and play.

"Where did y'all get this?" she asked.

"At a store right down the street," Jon Eric pointed out the window.

"Oh." She looked up from the doll, right into my eyes. "How did you pay for it?"

"We got money from a restaurant," I said proudly.

"What do you mean you got money from a restaurant? How?" her tone deepened.

"There was money just sitting on the tables, so we took it," I said.

Jon Eric looked at me with big eyes.

What?

"There was money just sitting on the tables, so we took it!" Mama mimicked.

Her face hardened, and just like that, the little girl disappeared. Vanished. As if a needle on a record player scratched, the whole scene changed in an instant. That child cowered back to the dungeon Mama had trapped her in. Roped, gagged and bound.

"You took the money off the table? That money belongs to a hard-working waitress. It's not yours for the taking. You stole that money like a little thief!"

She dropped Little Lulu from her hands, and, like a falling leaf, the paper doll swayed side to side before finally hitting the floor. The joy and excitement I felt inside fell right along with it. I lowered my head in shame. I wished we would have had our own money to buy the doll with so that playful girl could have stayed longer. I knew that taking the money wasn't right, but the thought of Mama being happy outweighed everything.

Mama pushed up from the couch, pulled open a drawer, and fumbled around inside.

"I'm not raising thieving tramps," she said.

She looked at me with such disgust in her eyes I wished I could melt away and disappear. She grabbed a black magic marker out of the drawer, the permanent kind with a broad tip, and held it out in front of her.

What the heck is that for?

She had a crazed look on her face. The one that makes my heart stop before it pounds out of my chest. Her eyes burned with hatred as she pulled the lid off the marker. I didn't know what she was about to do, but I knew it couldn't be good. Without looking away from her, I reached my foot to the floor to slide away, but she grabbed hold of my hair, and yanked so hard, she had my head pinned to the couch.

"Stop! Let go!" I shouted. "What are you doing?"

I fumbled at her hand to pry her fingers off, as one of her knees thumped onto my chest. She climbed on me with the full weight of her body crushing me, suffocating. I couldn't breathe. My arms flailed about, pushing at her stomach, at her leg, anything to get her off. She moved her knee from my chest to my arm. Her other knee went to my other arm, trapping me.

"Get off of me!" I howled.

I tried to squirm and wriggle my body from under her, but she didn't budge. She was too heavy and strong. She released her grip from my hair then gouged the marker into my cheek, stabbing, as if it were a knife. Then she began scribbling like a maniac. I turned my head to the side, but she grabbed onto my hair again, and with one yank, she had control of exactly where she wanted my face.

Jon Eric froze, eyes wide and jaw open. He looked petrified, like a piece of wood stuck in the mud. He had to get past us to reach the door. His eyes moved all over the place—me, the door, the upper bed, Mom. Finally, he got up the courage to push past us, but nobody could get by Mom. Nobody. She let go of my hair and scooted off my arms. Crushing her heavy weight into my stomach, she turned and reached for him.

"Where in the hell do you think you're going, you Florida Fucking

Trash?" Her knee dug deeper into my belly as she grabbed onto his hair. I gasped for air.

"You think you're going to come here and teach my daughter how to steal like you, you Florida piece of shit?"

Her knuckles turned white as she threw him onto the couch. She pushed off my body.

That was my chance. I had to get out. I jumped from the couch, and ran out the door while plugging my ears to block Jon Eric's screams.

She better not hurt him! Panting heavily, I paced outside, feeling helpless and unsure of what to do. *I should grab that marker and scribble all over her face.*

The camper door swung open, and Jon Eric jumped down, shamefully covering his face with his arms to block me from seeing.

"You better return that damn doll and bring that poor waitress back her money," Mom shouted. The paper doll came flying out the door behind him.

I looked at my reflection in the side mirror of the truck. My face was covered in black Xs, outlined in pink welts. The Xs faded as my vision clouded with tears.

"Let those Xs be a reminder to never steal again!" she shouted.

"I can't stand her," I said. "I wish I could go back to Florida with y'all."

"I know. And we were just trying to be nice and give her a birthday present."

"Crap. Here comes everybody else. Let's hide somewhere," I said. But it was too late. Before I could even find a place to go, Deborah appeared ahead of the pack.

"What in the world happened to y'all?" she asked. She wrapped her arms around me as I began sobbing.

Jon Eric explained what had happened when they all showed up and how scared we were to have to go back to the restaurant to give back the money.

"That's one sick mother fuckin' lady," Petesy said. "Here, give me the doll. I'll bring it back for you."

* * *

I didn't want to go to the Mormon Museum, but, of course, Mama made me. Even with my head bent as we walked around, people still stared, especially the kids. They'd be with their perfect little families pointing and whispering to each other. None of them had a mother like mine. I wished they did. Even for one day, so they'd know what it was like. Maybe then, they'd keep their stupid whispers to themselves.

Jon Eric and I mostly hung out by an animated display while everyone else walked around. The exhibit had a boy sitting on a tree swing outside his home. It was really cool because his legs would actually move back and forth as he swung. It told the story of his family, a mother and father who were so nice and loving, and something called *Family Home Evening*. I watched it over and over again, each time dreaming I could have a family like his.

"I wish we could have Family Home Evening," I whispered.

* * *

No matter how hard we scrubbed at each rest stop, those Xs stayed on our faces throughout the whole state of Utah and into Nevada. Deborah said it was like we were branded and shunned with our own scarlet letters.

We made it back to San Francisco just as summer was coming to an end. What felt like a long, drawn-out trip, now seemed way too short as we drove everyone back to the Greyhound bus station. It's like we were just there with our posters and noise-makers only days before. The summer flew by in an instant, and with my siblings gone, all responsibilities were back on me again.

Me, age eight, in fourth
grade at Notre Dame des
Victoires.

– 17 –

Notre Dame des Victoires

"A fighting spirit, Konjo, cannot be taught.
It comes from within."
— Dr. James Tanaka, my judo instructor.

*T*he sound of Glen Campbell belting out "Rhinestone
Cowboy" from the clock radio startled me from a deep sleep.
It was too early. I rolled over and covered my face in my sleeping bag. *Just one more minute. That's all I ask, one more minute.*

As I listened to the words of the song, I dreamt I was at a rodeo,
decked out in a fancy white suit with sequins sparkling along the
trim of my jacket. I rode a beautiful horse, the large, powerful
kind with long hair around its ankles. I held my cowboy hat high
in the air, prancing around the corral as the crowd in the stands
cheered me on.

"Little girl, are you still sleeping?" Mama shouted.

Crap!

"Another Somebody Done Somebody Wrong Song" was playing
in the background.

A different song? How long have I been sleeping?

"You better get that breakfast going so you're not late on your first day."

I blinked my eyes a couple times to adjust to the darkness, then rubbed them with my knuckles to get rid of the hard, crusty eye coals. Sunlight peeked through the edges of the closed blinds, but I didn't dare pull them up. No way. Everyone else needed their precious sleep, and that would have been the end of me if I woke them up with sunshine. At least I knew better than that.

I couldn't wait for this day to arrive. Even when we were still on our summer trip, I couldn't stop thinking about it. The day I started Notre Dame des Victoires (NDV), the same school as Rachael. But even with all my excitement, waking up early on the first day was never easy. I made my way to the bathroom, flipped the switch, then closed the door partway, to allow a crack of light to beam through.

My uniform had been tantalizing me in the closet ever since the day Mama bought it at the St. Vincent de Paul Thrift Store. I finally got to dress like a French sailor girl like Rachael. I held up the navy blue top, admired its red tie and collar flap, then slid it over my head. After pulling on my skirt, I put my hair into two braids. I really wanted French braids, but they were impossible. I spent at least an hour the night before struggling to figure out how to do them, but each time I tried, I failed miserably. Now I looked like a dork. The pigtails looked stupid. No one was going to like me with my hair looking like that. I needed more time to figure something else out, but it was already 7:15, and I hadn't even started making breakfast yet.

On the way to the kitchen, I paused by Rachael— tucked in, all warm and cozy, sound asleep with her hair draped over her face, and mouth wide open. I wondered if a roach ever climbed in while she slept. Her sleeping bag rose and fell over her chest as she took slow, shallow breaths. My insides boiled as I watched her. I wanted to take my sock and shove it in her mouth, not to hurt her or anything, just to stop the bag from moving.

She should be the one making the stupid breakfast. It's my first day at a new school, not hers! I gritted my teeth and kicked her shoulder, then ran to the kitchen before she could see what hit her.

* * *

Breakfast time had always been a nightmare at our place. It didn't matter how early I woke up, either, we always ran late. It never failed. To make matters worse, Mama was not a morning person at all, and she certainly wasn't shy showing off her foul moods. Day in and day out the pattern repeated—screaming and chaos that ended with either a slap across my face, fingernails in my arm, or my hair being ripped from the scalp. I don't think a day went by that I didn't show up to Morning Star with red, puffy eyes from all the crying. I wasn't going to let it happen like that today, though. Not at my new school. No way.

I knew some of the madness could have been prevented if I didn't talk back so much—if I just did my work and kept quiet about it. But at the same time, I couldn't help myself anymore. Something made me scream inside, something I wasn't able to control. Things were too unfair around our apartment. Even when I purposely planned for the mornings to be peaceful, the snarky tone in Mama's voice made it hard for me not to talk back. The more the flames of hatred burned inside her, the more the fire of rebellion blazed in me.

"Breakfast is ready!" I shouted as I scooped eggs onto each of their plates.

No one budged. Not even a stir. *How dare they sleep.* I stormed in the other room and shouted at the top of my lungs.

"Get up! Breakfast is ready, your highnesses."

I couldn't believe I had done that. Not on my first day. *What was I thinking?* I ran back to the kitchen and sat at our new round table, one Mama bought before the Florida Gang arrived for the summer.

I stared at the scrambled eggs in front of me as Rache and the twins slowly meandered in. Mama followed behind them, grumbling something under her breath. I knew it couldn't be good.

"What the hell's all that mess in the sink?" She pulled her chair out and took a seat. "Those dishes were in there all night? No wonder we have roaches in this damn place."

Shoot. I wanted to knock myself on the head for being so stupid. I would have never been that brave if I had remembered those darn dishes.

"I'm talkin' to you, little girl."

"Oh, sorry. I didn't know it was a question. I forgot to do 'em, cuz I was trying to figure out how to do my hair last night."

She took a bite of her eggs and chewed with her mouth open, smacking her lips together like an animal at a trough. She didn't do it on purpose; it was the way she always ate, and sometimes it bothered me more than others. This just happened to be one of those times. It was as if someone held a small chalkboard right next to my ear and slowly scratched their fingernail from the top to the bottom just to torture me. My body cringed, and the noise made me want to jump out of my skin. I wished I could ask her to chew more quietly, and tell her how rude it was to eat with her mouth open, and how the noise grated on my nerves. But, of course, I couldn't say anything, especially when she's in *that* mood. I had to sit there and take it while each cell in my body buzzed with growing tension, ready to implode.

"Why can't Rachael wash 'em?" I didn't mean to ask that. Her smacking lips made me.

"Don't you start with me," Mama said. She took another forkful of eggs, and I could swear the smacking got louder.

"Why? What's wrong with her? She can do 'em just as easily as I can." *What's my problem? Why do I keep talking?*

"I said don't start with me with that sarcastic mouth of yours."

"I'm just sayin'..."

Before the words finished coming out, Mama pushed from the table with her plate in her hands. I figured she was going to take it to her bed to eat so she wouldn't have to look at my ugly face anymore, just as she did the other times.

"I don't know where you get that filthy mouth of yours. You're getting more sarcastic by the day. It's definitely not from me."

"Huh," I scoffed, raising the corner of my lip. *Stop, Teresa. Just stop. What are you doing?*

"Gotta be from that crumb of a man you adore so much."

"What?"

"Your father and his trash mouth."

"Tss, yeah, right. You should've just left me there with him. Then you wouldn't have to deal with me anymore."

"I wish I would've. You're the biggest mistake I've ever made in my whole entire life. You're nothin' but a piece of trash, just like your father."

She held her plate in the air, then slung it toward me like a flying saucer. It was so unexpected, I didn't have time to dodge it. It slammed onto my shoulder, causing a trail of scrambled eggs to roll down the front of my uniform like little yellow gumballs, leaving a greasy stain in their path.

"That's great! There's no way I'm going to school now." My voice quivered as I tried to hold in my tears.

"The hell you're not. Clean up this fucking mess, and those dishes better be washed by the time I come back in here." She grabbed my pigtail and yanked as she walked out of the kitchen. "That's for making me waste all that delicious food."

I slid down the chair and covered my hands over my face as tears began to flow.

"I hate her!" I cried. "I'm not going to school today. I'm gonna run away."

"Don't run away, Teresa. I'll help you," Jonas said.

Nothing could help me, though. My day was ruined, even with Jonas and Josh on the floor picking up bits of eggs for me. I held out the bottom of my uniform top to see the mess on it.

"Everybody's gonna make fun of me if I go to school now."

I imagined a group of kids surrounding me, all with their cute

French sailor uniforms, and perfect little french braids in their hair. They'd be pointing and laughing, calling me egghead, or greaseball, or something. And my teacher would probably say I was messy like Ms. Takahashi did.

I wanted the day to be perfect. A chance to make new friends and to have a new teacher—a teacher who could like me. *Nobody ever likes me.* More tears poured down my face as Rachael handed me a wet dishrag.

"Here," she said. "You can use this to clean your shirt."

* * *

Rachael walked with me in silence through the Tenderloin— all seven blocks, and we didn't say a single word to each other. We chased a cable car and jumped on mid-block to get to school, but I couldn't look at her. Not even for a second. It wasn't how I had planned for the morning to go. Not one tiny bit at all.

I wanted to ask her all sorts of questions about the school. *Did she ever meet my teacher? Is she nice? Did I tie my tie the right way? Does my hair look okay?* Instead, I walked a few steps behind her with my arms folded across my chest, seething at what a Queen Bee she was.

Of course, the hallways were empty and quiet by the time we arrived. I hated being late on the first day. I planned on getting there early so my teacher wouldn't hate me, but now all that was ruined, and couldn't be taken back.

Like Mama said before, nothing could ever change a first impression. I wished I was still at Morning Star. At least Ms. Takahashi expected me to be tardy.

Instead of going to the office, Rachael led me up the ramps to show me to my classroom. NDV had ramps, not stairs, kind of like walking on the big hills outside.

"Thanks," I said with a smile. I felt guilty for being angry at her. I always felt guilty. I knew it wasn't her fault the way Mama treated us, and I tried to like her. I really did.

"How do my eyes look? Does it look like I've been cryin'?" I asked, trying my best to rekindle the only connection I had at NDV.

"No, you look fine. Besides, if they did, everyone would just think you're nervous on your first day."

"Yeah, I guess so."

As she walked away, I put my hand on the door and hesitated, I wasn't sure if I should knock first, or just walk in. I took a few deep breaths, turned the doorknob, slid into the classroom, and stood with my back pressed firmly against the wall. *Dear God, please let my teacher be nice to me.*

"Can I help you?" the teacher asked.

I opened my mouth to speak, but nothing came out. Everyone stared. It felt as if my lips were glued to my teeth with every bit of saliva drained from me.

"You must be Teresa," she said, fingering down her roll call sheet. "Teresa Thompson?"

I stood quiet as a mouse, too humiliated to answer. *I wanna go back to Morning Star!*

"Teresa Thompson?" she asked again.

"Yes," I managed to mumble.

"Well, welcome to the fourth grade. I'm Sister Geraldine, and you're late. Take a seat over there."

She pointed to the only empty desk in the room. The one that had a rectangular card taped to the front with *Teresa Thompson* written in cursive.

"Okay, class. You'll have time to introduce yourselves at recess," Sister Geraldine said. "I was just telling everyone about the French choir, Teresa. I lead the choir, and if you like to sing, you can sign up after school."

I nodded.

As Sister Geraldine continued talking about her expectations for the year, I placed my hand to my forehead to hide my eyes as they wandered from student to student. It was okay because most of the other kids were looking at me as well. Like Morning Star, most of them had been together since kindergarten. I was the new kid.

* * *

I liked NDV, and it wasn't only for the cute uniforms, or the fact that I met two friends right off the bat, Therese and Lori, but because Mama took special pride in our learning French. It was a language she never understood as a child. One that her French mother and aunts spoke secretly in front of her. A language that kept her and her sister isolated and shut out when they were little girls was now back in her life, and she had the chance to learn it along with me as I practiced my vocabulary words each day. It was my opportunity to shine. My moment to make her like me, even if it was only for a few short minutes each day.

Since the school had a great reputation and taught French at the grammar school level, it drew families from some of the most wealthy neighborhoods in San Francisco—places like St. Francis Wood, the Marina, Pacific Heights, and Forest Hill. Tuition rates were also some of the highest in the city, but as usual, Mama found a way to finagle us in. To make up for the lower cost, she volunteered her time, mostly with yard duty work. It wasn't a problem for her since all she had was time. She didn't work anywhere else. All her money came from the state, oh, and by selling some of our food stamps for cash, because, really, who needs to eat so much? It'll only make us fat, like the slobs we see hanging around outside the apartment, she'd tell us.

She used the extra money she saved to buy herself some new clothes. She wanted to look glamorous in front of all the other rich mothers at NDV, but even more than that, she wanted to look good for the men. Mama loved getting attention from men, and she'd flaunt herself all over San Francisco. Petesy said he thought she was a hooker, like the ladies on the corner, but I didn't think so. She found a store called Frederick's of Hollywood and fell in love.

I was mortified the day she showed up for yard duty wearing her new clothes. After school that day, I told her I thought they should only be worn around the house, but she said that was nonsense.

"This is the new style. The new rave. All the fancy Hollywood stars wear clothes like these."

I wanted to tell her she was wrong. I never saw any-one on the television wear clothes that you could see under-wear through. I wanted to say something, but she was in such a good mood wearing her new tight pants, that I didn't want to jinx it. She wouldn't have listened to me anyway. She'd probably just think I was jealous of all the attention she got.

She pranced around the schoolyard, showing off her brand new clothes—lavender pants with cut-out diamonds along the outer legs, white pants with a lattice design, and yellow pants with see-through lace.

I hated that she had to do yard duty, and it wasn't only because I overheard some of the kids whispering and laughing about her out-fits. I hated it because she watched me like a hawk. No one was good enough for me to play with, except Therese and Lori. Thank God she liked them, otherwise, I would have been completely doomed.

A girl named Mercedes started to hang out with us for a little while, but Mama said I wasn't allowed to play with her since I already had a black friend. "There's no way in hell you're gonna play with two niggers," she said. She didn't even care that Lori was only half black.

I wasn't allowed to play with Bonnie either. Mama said she didn't smile enough. "I'm not having you moping around the apartment all day. It's bad enough you have a sarcastic mouth like your father," she said. I thought Bonnie smiled just fine.

Monica was too fat. Mama said it was a mortal sin to be so overweight, and Monica's mother must not have had strong faith to allow that to happen. "No way any daughter of mine is going to pick up bad eating habits and end up like one of those fat slobs we see around town."

When I told her I could play with whoever I wanted, all she had to say was, "You wanna make a bet? If I see you anywhere near those girls again, I'll go over and rip you away by your hair. So help me God."

I never messed with anything that ended in "so help me God."

* * *

I joined the French choir as Sister Geraldine had suggested. Well, Mama made me. I didn't really have a choice, but I didn't mind it at all, especially since we got to go to some really neat places. We sang at parties around the city where the rich people went. Women decked out in elegant evening gowns with their hair held in beautiful updos, and fancy jewelry dangling from their wrists and necks.

Since we dressed in uniform, I didn't stand out from the rest of the kids. I was one of them, admired and praised just as they were. I felt special, not like the imposter I was. I sang with my head held high, proud to be part of such an amazing choir, hobnobbing with the rich and famous.

I studied the way the women dressed and carried themselves—the way they socialized and laughed and moved their hands as they spoke. I wanted to be like them. I wanted what they had, but I didn't feel sad. Instead, they fired me up and gave me *Konjo*, a fighting spirit. Those people gave me something to aspire toward, to dream about. I wasn't going to be trapped in the Tenderloin forever. At least not when I 'm older, and I would do anything I could to ensure that happened.

* * *

After our lease ended on Eddy and Hyde, we moved to another place, a little nicer, but still a small studio in the Tenderloin. We didn't last long before the landlord caught me and the twins hiding in the closet during one of his unannounced inspections and were evicted after only a few short months.

Mama finally got a job. She worked as a teacher's aide in a kindergarten classroom all the way out in the Avenues. It didn't pay much, but it was enough to move us out of the Tenderloin and into the Richmond District.

No more bums or prostitutes loitering the streets in that neighborhood, and no more one-room studios. We now had a living room and two bedrooms—one for me and Rache to share, and the other for Mama and the twins. There were times when we still had to hide in the closet if the landlord visited since Mama lied and said there were only three of us living there, but at least this one gave notice before knocking on the door.

At the end of the year, Lori and her family moved back to Hawaii where they were originally from. The Florida Gang came back that summer for a bicentennial tour of America, but Deborah didn't join them. Even though she had a job as a photographer and couldn't take the time off, I still couldn't help thinking she just didn't like us anymore.

Christmas time with Santa, 1976. I was ten.

– 18 –

Freedom

Freedom's just another word for nothin' left to lose.
— Kris Kristofferson

It took about a half an hour on the bus to get to school from our new apartment, so getting there on time was even more impossible. No matter how many times I showed up late, the routine never got easier, and fifth grade was no exception. First, I had to come up with an excuse, and even though I tried to make them each a little different, they still pretty much sounded the same. I guess the story of missing the bus and running after it for blocks and blocks must have sounded pretty lame after a while, but I couldn't let the secretary know what really happened each morning. And I certainly couldn't tell her why I showed up with red, puffy eyes each day. Luckily, she didn't ask about my eyes too often, but when she did, I knew I couldn't always say that I had allergies, or got a cat hair in them, or cried from a sad movie the night before. I'd mostly tell her I cried since I missed the bus, or couldn't find my shoe, or something pathetic like that.

She'd listen, then hand over the late slip. I wish she just made it easier by having one already filled out for me when I arrived. I don't know why she had to hear a reason every single day. The morning ride on the bus would've been much more pleasant if I didn't have to spend the whole darn time coming up with another explanation.

I think the secretary thought it was always my fault, like I was lazy and didn't want to wake up early like the other students, or something. I knew she never believed my stories by the way she'd roll her eyes, so I don't know why she even bothered asking in the first place.

After leaving the office, I'd head to my classroom, which used to be a big deal. The class would stop what they were doing while my teacher held out her hand for me to give her the slip. I guess she thought if I had enough embarrassment and humiliation, that I'd be taught to show up on time. But that never happened, so eventually she quit trying, and would just go on teaching while I placed the slip on her desk.

I wish Sr. Geraldine would have warned my fifth-grade teacher, Sr. Grace, so I didn't have to go through the same darn thing all over again, but of course, she didn't.

I was beginning to believe Mama made me late on purpose. I don't know why she would've done that, but even the times I had set the alarm clock extra early and had my bookbag in my hand, heading out the door, there would always be something I had to turn around to do before leaving.

* * *

One morning, when I arrived at my desk, there was a little note waiting for me. I hunkered down in my seat and unfolded each corner as Sr. Grace continued talking about an upcoming assembly. *We don't have to go to French class today! signed, TREZ!* The note read. Happy faces, stars, and hearts surrounded the words. I looked over at her and smiled. Trez. Her new way of spelling her name was cute. I liked it. I changed it since so many of our classmates called her Teresa instead of Therese. She winked at me and gave two thumbs up.

I had phoned her the night before asking about our French homework, but Mama made me hang up before she could give me the assignment.

"What's the assembly about?" I asked her as we lined up outside the door.

"It's time for the 'Bal de Paris' again," she said as Sr. Grace led us to our seats in the auditorium. The whole school was there, kindergartners in the front, all the way to the eighth-graders in the last rows.

"I can't believe we don't have French today," I whispered, "How lucky am I?"

"Shhhhhh!" Sr. Grace held her index finger over her lips.

Mr. Bergez, our principal, went to the front of the auditorium, stood at the podium, and tapped on the mic a couple of times. Next to him was a large object draped in a sheet. He cleared his throat as he often did, then began speaking.

"As you know, the 'Bal de Paris' is our annual fundraiser, and it takes *your* help to make it happen."

He went on about selling raffle tickets, and how we could keep two dollars out of every twelve tickets we sold. The volume in the auditorium elevated to loud whispers as he stepped aside for someone else to speak.

"And we have prizes that will go to the top three sellers in the school," a lady said. "The grand prize for the student who sells the most raffle tickets is—" she looked at our principal. "Mr. Bergez, will you do the honor?"

He lifted the sheet to unveil a beautiful yellow bike. Commotion filled the auditorium again.

"The prize for the student who sells the most raffle tickets is this amazing ten-speed Schwinn bicycle!" The lady's voice went up a couple octaves as she spoke.

Mr. Bergez rolled the bike from one side of the auditorium to the other for all to see.

"Blah, blah, blah." I didn't hear another word after that. I wanted that bike so bad. *I'm gonna win that. It's mine!* I looked around the room at my competition, knowing that most of the kid's parents would probably take raffle tickets to work with them, and I wouldn't have a fighting chance. *No. I'm gonna win! I'm going to sell the heck out of those tickets!*

After school, as I sat on the Muni bus for the long ride home, I closed my eyes and fantasized about winning the bike. *And this year's winner is... Teresa Thompson! Congratulations, Teresa!* The whole auditorium cheers as I stand with my hands raised in the air, bowing my head, taking in their praise.

I envisioned hopping on my new bike, exploring the neighborhood. The cool breeze hits against my skin as I tear down the street, and the bumps in the pavement cause me to bounce in my seat. My hair blows behind me as I gain speed. I smell the delectable spices and hear the clanking of dishes as I pass an Indian restaurant. I push my feet hard on the pedals and slowly make my way up a large hill. At the top, my heart races as I look down the steep grade. *Should I do it? Should I?* I slowly release the hand brake. The bike rolls forward, slowly at first, then shoots like a rocket toward the bottom. My skin tingles and chills cover my scalp. I felt so free, as if I had wings, flying through the air. At the bottom, I squeeze the brakes so hard, the back tire spins sideways in a half-circle. I gasped, then opened my eyes, hoping no one heard me. *I'm gonna win that bike!*

As soon as I got home, I threw my bookbag on the bed and headed back toward the door.

"Wait a minute. Where do you think you're going so fast? You're not even gonna say hi?" Mama asked.

"Hi, Mama. I have to sell raffle tickets for school," I told her about the 'Bal de Paris' and about the prize for selling the most.

"Well, what are you waiting for then?"

* * *

Each day, after my chores, I'd hit the pavement to sell those tickets. I went up and down each block, selling to all the houses and apartments along the way. On Sundays, everyone helped me: Mama, the twins, and even Rachael. We took the bus to different churches and sold to the congregations as they poured out. *Would you like to buy a chance to win $1,000? Would you like to buy a chance to win $1,000?* Over and over again, we said that. It didn't matter what type of church we went to, either. Catholic churches, Greek Orthodox, Lutheran, you name it. I waited outside grocery stores and stood downtown near Union Square. Not only did I want that bike more than anything, but I was getting rich off the two dollars per book I sold.

Breakfast, lunch, supper, dishes, grocery shopping, helping with the twins, cleaning, homework—now I had a new job to add to the list. One that was fun. One that paid me and gave me hope. I felt rich and alive. That bike was going to be my ticket to freedom. With a set of wheels, I could ride anywhere.

* * *

When the day finally arrived, I shifted back and forth in my seat, anxiously waiting for the other classes to pile into the auditorium. The wait was torture.

"I hope you win, Teresa," Trez said with a delicate warmth to her voice. She took my hand into hers and leaned into me, acting as a pillar to comfort me. She knew me well, better than anyone else. The school me, that is. No one really knew me outside of school. No one. Sometimes I was sad about not having a friend at home, but most of the time, I was glad that Trez lived so far away. I would have hated it if she saw our place or how Mama treated me.

When the classes were finally seated, Mr. Bergez went on and on about how much money we raised for the school, then spoke of the upcoming "Bal de Paris".

Blah, blah, blah! Nobody cares about that. Get on with the winners.

"Now, what you've all been waiting for," he said. "Drum roll, please. The third-place winner for the student who sold the most raffle tickets goes to... Angela Giavelli" *Ugh! Who cares about third place? Who won the bike? Hurry up, Angela. Get your prize and sit down.* "The second-place winner..." *Not me. Please. Let me be first. Let me be first!* From Miss Mott's class," *Oh, thank God it's not me.* "Maria Boucher." *Please, please.*

"And finally, the grand prize winner for the student who sold the most raffle tickets, and the winner of this brand new ten-speed bicycle," he held his hand toward the bike. "From Sr. Grace's class," *Please! Please! Please!* I crossed my fingers, "Teresa Thompson!" *Oh, my gosh!* A wave of heat rushed to my face. "Come on up, Teresa, and see your new bicycle!" Trez gave my hand a squeeze.

I couldn't believe it! Every cell in my body danced with joy. Hoots, hollers, and whistles buzzed in my ears.

"Go up there, Teresa!" Trez nudged me.

My face burned as I looked around the room—at everyone staring in my direction. My insides screamed with excitement, but my outer self felt paralyzed. I stood up and plodded to the front of the auditorium. My feet were all I saw. The saddle shoes with the scuffed-up beige tips and the blue leather surrounding the laces. Right foot, left foot, right again.

I hated the attention. It wasn't like my dream. I didn't hold my hands in the air and bow as everyone cheered me on. I didn't want to be the hero anymore. I wanted to grab the bike and hide so no one could see me.

After the assembly my classmates gathered around to check out my prize. Their hands were all over the bike, touching the small black seat, squeezing the hand brakes, holding on to the handlebars. They even helped me roll it up the ramps to the classroom, which I could have done just fine by myself.

Getting home was another story all together. The bicycle was built for a giant, not a midget like me. My feet didn't even come close to reaching the pedals.

For once, I wished Rachael would've come home with me. We hardly ever took the bus together because of the different activities we had after school, not that she would have wanted to anyway. We barely said a word to each other anymore. I went looking for her anyway, but she was already in the gym for basketball practice.

Mama made us sign up for every sport the school offered, no matter how bad we were at it. And I was the absolute worst, a complete disappointment to my team. No matter how hard I tried, I never hit a volleyball over the net, I was always struck out in softball, and couldn't shoot a hoop for the life of me. I just got too nervous when it was my turn to do anything, and I hated people watching me, especially all the mothers.

Running was the only thing I had any chance at, but since we signed up for track through the Police Athletic League, and it wasn't part of the school, no one ever knew that I was decent at something. Terez didn't do sports, so I was on my own, and being the worst on the team didn't help my other classmates like me any more, either.

* * *

It took forever just to go a few blocks down to the Sutter Street bus stop. I couldn't take the stairs at the Stockton Tunnel as I usually did, so I had to go an extra block to Powell. Of all the times I've walked those hills, I never once realized how steep they were until I had a gigantic ten-speed in my hands.

I wished I didn't have to bring my book bag home. I wanted to leave it at school, but we were loaded with homework. You'd think they'd give us a break after how much money we earned for the "Bal de Paris", but no way, not NDV. I tried balancing my bag on the seat, but the books fell all over the place, and hanging it from the handlebars didn't help much either, since the front tire kept turning from all the weight.

When I finally made it to the bus stop, a man had the nerve to say, "That's an awfully big bike for someone as small as you." I nodded and clenched my jaw to prevent me from saying anything. I wanted to say, *Of course, it's a big bike for me.*

Ya think I didn't notice? But I bit my tongue. He didn't know how hard it was for me to bring it down those steep hills. I'm sure he wouldn't have said something so stupid if he did.

"Here, let me help you," he said as I struggled to get it up the steps of the bus.

"Thanks." Whew! I was glad I didn't say anything mean to him earlier.

Once he brought the bike up, I rolled it toward the back of the bus and sat in one of the sideways seats, so I could hold it in front of me. With each stop, and each start, and each turn, and each uphill and downhill, like a wild stallion, the bike tried its absolute best to get away. Even so, I loved my new yellow Schwinn ten-speed and was proud of myself for winning it.

Others on the bus looked at it with envy. I know they did. They probably wished they had a brand new bike, too. Brand new. I couldn't believe it. Other than my Baby Love Light doll, I don't think I'd ever had anything brand new in my life before. I couldn't wait to get home to show everyone else.

I made a complete fool of myself trying to get off the bus. My books fell, then the bike fell, then tears came when I scraped my shin on the jagged metal foot pedal. The man who helped me earlier was long gone, and no one else seemed too concerned with my struggles.

At home, I left my bookbag by the door as I dragged the bike up the stairs to our second-floor apartment.

"Come look, everybody! I won!"

Mama and the twins came running to see, and just like the kids at school, their hands touched every part of the bike.

"You did it!" Mama said. "See? All that hard work paid off."

"Thanks. It's a little big for me, but I'll grow into it."

"That's silly," Mama said. "Why don't we give this bike to Rachael?"

"What? No!"

"Yeah, then we can get you one that's more your size."

"No! This one's my bike. It's brand new. I don't want one from a garage sale or anything."

"Who said anything about a garage sale? I'll just get you one that's smaller.

I finally agreed, and just like that, we got two bikes for one. Rache got the ten-speed, and Mama bought me a brand new, beautiful, white 5-speed, Schwinn Stingray. The 1976 bicentennial model with red and blue decals, and a red, white and blue basket in the front. Instead of the tiny triangular seat like Rachael's, this one had a soft banana seat, long enough for me to tow the twins if I wanted. The frame was perfect for my size, too. And the handlebars reached up high, so I didn't have to bend over like Rachael did on hers. My new bike was way better.

Having a new bicycle also attracted a new friend. Her name was Courtney, and even though she was a grade younger than me, that didn't matter since we went to different schools.

We went all over the place on our bikes, riding to different neighborhoods, playing in every playground we could find, and even discovered China Beach where we could climb on the big rocks by the ocean.

We were adventurers and explorers, prowlers and spies, and I think she liked being away from her home just about as much as I liked being away from mine.

When we weren't on our bikes, we'd travel from one person's backyard to the next, carefully balancing on the small 2x4 plank that held the fences together. Dogs barked and people shouted as we made our way across the yards. We'd climb fire escapes, then hop from one rooftop to the next, peeking and tapping on skylights to scare the people inside. It was a rush, especially when the rooftops weren't connected and we had to jump from one to get to the other.

On the days Courtney couldn't play with me, I liked to go to a grove of eucalyptus trees in Lincoln Park. It was my favorite hideout, especially after Mama threw one of her fits. Even though I was in a big city, you'd never know it while hanging around those trees. It was a place where I could get lost in nature. A place near deer and squirrels where I could hide and never have to be yelled at or hit. A place where I could go to think and dream.

I often imagined the animals coming to me as they did with Snow White. They'd hear the sound of my cries and emerge from their hiding places to comfort and cuddle me. Animals were like me in a way, they didn't have anyone to protect them. Boys could use their slingshots or BB guns to shoot at birds and squirrels, birds got chased as soon as they landed on the grass, and insects were constantly being crushed by the people who walked by. Sometimes, I felt sorry for animals and wanted to protect them just as I imagined they did to me.

It wasn't only animals either. I felt that way toward kids, too. They can't help whose family they were born into. And they can't protect themselves, either. I wished I could help them and keep them safe.

Maybe one day I'll be a teacher and I'll be extra nice to kids who have a mother like mine. But, none of my teachers know Mama hurts me, so how would I know? Maybe I could become a veterinarian or a doctor. That way I could help animals or people for sure.

Mama said I was like her in that way, the way I always cared for the underdog. I didn't like her saying that because I certainly didn't like being compared to her. It wasn't true anyway. She didn't care for the underdog; otherwise she'd care for me.

The weird thing about being in solitude is that I knew I wasn't alone. And I wasn't scared. Not in nature, at least. I always knew God was with me.

Even though I couldn't understand why He didn't protect me from Mama each time she went crazy, or why He even let me be with such a mean lady in the first place, I knew that once I stepped foot out of that apartment, He was right there by my side. Not only to protect me, but He helped me forget about Mama by making sure I noticed all the beautiful things around me. That may have been from my Catholic school upbringing, but I saw God in everything—the sunsets, the chirping birds, the cute puppies, the waves splashing over the rocks in the ocean, the big trees in the park, and even in the man who helped carry my bike up the steps on the bus. God was there.

He was there for me each time I got scared, too. All I had to say was, *God, please help me,* and I knew I could count on Him. I'm just not sure why He didn't come to my apartment very much. I think Mama must have scared Him the way she scares me. Or maybe He just liked being outside like I do. I don't know.

Jon Eric and me in front of the
Washington Monument, Washington,
D.C., 1976.

– 19 –

Scavenger Hunt

Imagination is the only weapon in the war against reality.
— Lewis Carroll, Alice's Adventures in Wonderland

Summer of '77

I couldn't wait till recess to tell Trez the Florida Gang were on their way back to California. If only I had made it to school before the morning bell, I could have told her then, but now I had to wait. I don't even know why we had class. No one paid attention to a word Sr. Grace said, anyway. The schools in Florida were already out for the summer. It was stupid that we had to finish the week.

I shifted back and forth in my seat while waiting for the recess bell. There was no way I could sit still after hearing my siblings had left Florida that morning. Trez was being weird, though. I flicked a note to her desk on a small piece of paper I had folded into a triangle, but it went sailing right past her—and she didn't even bother picking it up. I don't know how she couldn't be in a good mood on the last day of school. Even when we lined up for recess, she kept quiet. I know we were supposed to, but *we* never did. We were the ones Sr. Grace always had to shush.

"Teresa, I have something to tell you," Trez said when we got to the schoolyard.

She held onto each of my arms, but kept her eyes down and didn't even look me in the face. I tucked one of my feet under the other hoping she wouldn't notice how scuffed my shoes were.

"What?" I asked.

Her grip on my arms made me nervous. Something was seriously wrong. She sniffed her nose, then parted her lips just enough to mumble, "I." That was it. Nothing else, just more sniffling. A tear landed on the tan part of my saddle shoe making a dark circle in the scuff. *How could she possibly cry on the last day of school?*

"What, Trez? What's going on?" She still had a hold of my arms so I reached for her elbows.

"I'm not gonna be coming back to NDV next year." She lifted her gaze, exposing her pink eyes to me.

"What? No! Why?"

"It's too hard for my dad to take me this far every day," she shuddered as she spoke. "I'm gonna have to go to a school closer to my house from now on."

"No! That's crazy. He has to still take you."

I knew her father complained about how the traffic kept getting worse and worse—and I knew she lived in Mill Valley, a town all the way on the other side of the Golden Gate Bridge in Marin County, but I never dreamed she'd quit coming to NDV. She couldn't. She was the only friend I had in that class. My best friend. She couldn't leave me.

I grasped her arms tighter, but she vanished from my grip—melted into the concrete of the schoolyard until only a puddle of memories remained. Just like the little girl in Frosty the Snowman, I leaned over the puddle, causing ripples to form from my tears.

The excitement I had for the last day of school and the news that the Florida Gang were already on the bus headed to California drained right out of me. I didn't want to go back to class. I wanted to spend every last second with Trez. I didn't even care that Sr. Grace promised to play the "Magical Mystery Tour" album for us after recess.

* * *

First thing when we got back from picking the kids up from the bus station, Mama gathered us around her to talk about our upcoming trip. I loved our summer adventures. Those trips were what made me most proud she was my mother. She pointed along the map from California all the way to the North Carolina Coast, then ran her finger down to Florida.

"Since we're gonna be all the way on the other side of the country, we might as well stop by to see your father," she said.

"Daddy?" I asked. I couldn't believe it. My insides swelled with happiness. It had been three long years since we left our home in Florida. Sure, he wrote us letters sometimes and called for our birthdays and Christmas, but it was hard to read his cursive writing, and the calls were always rushed since it cost so much to call long distance.

Rachael's face lit up the way it did from the candles on her fifteenth birthday cake earlier that year, only there weren't any candles in front of her now. That glow came from her smile. The twins, too. Jonas held up his thumbs and danced around the room while Josh clung to Petesy's earlobe.

When Mama finished going over the trip, Jon Eric and I hopped on my new Schwinn Stingray and took turns towing each other while I navigated us to all my favorite spots.

I showed him around like I owned the place, as if San Francisco was all mine. I took him to a playground, then we rode around the mansions in the Sea Cliff neighborhood, and finally to China Beach. We spent hours bouldering, building driftwood forts, and searching for starfish and fiddler crabs. After we left China Beach, I took him to a Cypress tree, way up on a hill overlooking the ocean in Lincoln Park. One that the wind had blown so much it grew sideways, forming a perfect bench.

"Isn't it beautiful here?" I asked.

"Yeah. Kind of scary how high up we are, though. One slip and we're toast."

"Nah, we're fine. I come here all the time."

"It's way different from our beaches in Florida, that's for sure," he said. "I love how those big rocks jut out of the water like that."

He flicked a small twig from his fingers and sent it flying over the edge of the cliff, then shuffled in the dirt for another.

"How's it been with Mom lately?" he asked.

Everything inside me shifted. The pride I felt for having it all in San Francisco, for living in the best place in the world, for being the queen of Sea Cliff. That all vanished into the wind as he spoke, causing me to shrivel back to my own pathetic reality. My gaze shifted to the crashing waves below. *Why does he have to ask about something like that?*

A whirlwind of thoughts spun through my mind, almost to the point of dizziness. I grabbed onto the bark of the cypress and squeezed tight as pictures flashed through my mind like an old-fashioned reel of film. The monster reaching out from Mama as she grabs my hair. Fingernails clawing into my flesh with trails of blood dripping from my arm. Sharp teeth biting into me, leaving round, green and yellow bruise marks. Punches and kicks and shoves. My arms over my head, cowering.

Even with the cool wind blowing, I couldn't take a breath. His question knocked the air right out of me. *I should tell him.* I scooped up a handful of dirt and sent it flying in the wind. *But I don't want to ruin our time together. I'll probably just end up crying and looking stupid, anyway.*

I kept my head down, pretending to search for something in the dirt so Jon Eric couldn't see my face. He didn't say a word, though.

He just sat there, waiting for an answer. I forced a breath, gritted my teeth, and let out a heavy sigh.

"Things are okay," I said. "You know, good and bad. You know how Mama is. She hasn't changed."

I wanted to tell him that she really *has* changed, that she gets meaner by the day and hates me more and more because I look like Daddy. I don't tell him that, though. Not even Trez or Courtney knew that. *He probably knows anyway.*

I thought of telling him about a time at the Muni bus stop when Mama began flirting with the first man she saw. And when the man told her what a beautiful girl I was, how she used that syrupy-sweet voice, the one that makes me want to puke, and said, "Her? She's nothing. You should see my Rachael," and how she reached into her pocketbook and pulled a picture out. *"A picture!"* I'd say, *"She had a picture of Rachael in her purse! Can you believe that?"*

I wanted to say that because it wasn't as bad as telling him how much she beats me up. But even that story wasn't worth wasting the time I had with him. Besides, she wasn't always mean. We *were* about to go on another cool vacation after all. And to be honest, half the time I couldn't even decide if I hated her or loved her. I guess, in some ways, I did both.

Every time I thought I hated her, she'd end up doing something good—like helping me sell the raffle tickets, or making sure I practiced my gymnastics every day so I could win competitions. After stuff like that, I'd feel really bad for hating her, but when she was mean, I'd wonder how I could ever love such a person. It was always back and forth, and no matter what, I always ended up feeling guilty for whatever thoughts I had.

"We went to Disneyland during Easter," I told him instead.

"No way! That's so cool. Lucky. Did John Chaney go with y'all?"

I know why he asked that. Since the day we met John Chaney at St. Anthony's, he had been the one who paid for most of the fun things we did. I think John Chaney liked Mama more than a friend, but I don't know why he did since she was always mean to him.

"Nope, just us. You wouldn't believe how we did it," I said. "It was awful." I sat straight up and looked him in the eyes. "Mama gave me the money to go in by myself, and I had to wait in line to buy my own ticket. I was scared to death. There was even a girl about my age in front of me who kept staring. Then, once I went inside, I had to go to the exit, get a stamp, and rub it onto the back of Rachael's hand as fast as I could."

"Huh?"

"Yeah, and after I rubbed my hand onto hers, I saw that I didn't even have a stamp anymore. I thought Mama was gonna kill me. But Mama said it was just invisible ink. I was so scared that it wasn't, even though I could still smell it. It smelled kind of like Band-Aids. After that, Rache and I went back in together. We had to stick our hands under a light to see if the stamp would glow in the dark. It was the scariest thing I'd ever done. I thought for sure there wouldn't be anything. It was there, though, even on Rachael's. It was only a smudge, but it was enough to get us in. I couldn't believe it. Then we had to do the same thing again to get Mama and the twins into the park. I thought I was gonna die." My words came out so fast they left my body shivering.

"Why did she make *you* do it? Oh, wait, that's a stupid question. Duh!"

"Yeah, well, the real reason she made me, cuz my ticket was cheaper than Rachael's since I'm only a kid. But, yeah, duh, I'm sure she would've made me do it anyway. I did get an extra E-ticket out of it though, so I got to go on the Matterhorn a second time while everyone had to wait."

We threw pebbles and sticks into the water below while I talked about Disneyland, then Jon Eric told stories of Florida.

"Why do you think Daddy never comes to visit us?" I asked. The question had been burning inside me for months.

"Because it's too expensive. He said he has to work for a living. He's not a free-loader like Mom, living off welfare."

I couldn't believe Jon Eric said that. I know he was probably just repeating what Daddy had said, but still. Mama could be pretty awful at times, but there were a lot of good things about her, too. I know the Florida kids didn't go on long vacations with Dad. *He probably thinks he's better than us now.*

I wanted to remind him how Mama makes such a big deal about every holiday, and how she throws the best birthday parties ever. I wanted to say something, but I didn't feel like I had to defend *our* mother. I mean, really, she's his mother too, or did he forget about that? Besides, I knew we had to get moving before it got too cold. In the distance, the top of the Golden Gate Bridge had already disappeared into a thick layer of fog.

"Come on. I wanna show you another cool place," I said.

I wanted to take him to Ocean Beach and show him Musée Mechanique near the Cliff House and point out Seal Rock, but as he stood up, he wrapped his arms across his chest and started shivering.

"I'm gettin' hungry," he said. "And it's freezing. We should probably start heading back."

Ugh. How stupid. Why didn't I bring any sandwiches? Mama said the free summer lunches at Cabrillo School wouldn't start till next week, but I was in such a hurry to get out of the apartment that making something didn't even cross my mind. The last thing I wanted was to go back home though. I picked up a little twig and broke it into a million tiny pieces as my mind raced.

"I have an idea," I said, "Let's go on a scavenger hunt."

"What?" He looked at me as if I were out of my mind.

"We can pretend we already have most of the items on our list. We'll go to each house and say that all we have left to find is a piece of bread and an old comb, or something like that." I explained. "They'll probably give us bread before they give us a comb. Then, at the next house, we can do the same thing, but we'll ask for some cheese, and a piece of lunch meat, and stuff like that. We can keep going until we have enough food to make a whole sandwich."

"Hmm. Doubt that'll work. But, okay. I guess it's worth a try."

It worked way better than we could have ever imagined. House after house, people shuffled through their refrigerators for us. No one even thought for a second to give us a comb. Not only did we get enough to make a Dagwood sandwich, but we got chips and cookies and even a pickle and a coke just for the heck of it, to fill our bellies one last time before taking off on our trip the next day.

Japanese tourist wanting a photo with me and
Jon Eric.

– 20 –

Key to Cherokee

Coming together is a beginning, keeping together is progress; working together is success. — *Henry Ford*

After spending time in the Great Smoky Mountains, Mama found a spot alongside the highway to "rest her weary bones." I'm not sure what made her bones so weary, but whatever it was, it meant she needed a nap. She parked next to the river for us to cool off, then decided we'd just stay there for the night.

The next morning, we gobbled down some oatmeal, then headed into Cherokee, a small town on a reservation named after the Cherokee Indians. Mama pulled into the parking lot of the Oconaluftee Indian Village and told us to hold tight near the camper while she figured things out. After speaking to a girl at the ticket counter, she called us into a huddle to go over the plans.

"In order to get in, y'all have to pretend you're under twelve," she said.

Brother rolled his eyes. "Under twelve? Seriously?"

He went along with it, since he had no other choice, and no one said a word about an eighteen-year-old pretending to be eleven when we walked in—or a seventeen-year-old, or a sixteen-year-old, or thirteen year old. Jon Eric, and the twins and I were the only ones who really didn't have to worry. Even though Jon Eric was twelve, no one would have ever suspected that he wasn't eleven.

As soon as we entered the village, we were taken back in time to the life of the American tribal people. A woman, probably about Mama's age, but more on the plump side, introduced herself as Ama, our guide. She began the tour by explaining how her outfit was the traditional way the Cherokee women dressed back in the day.

Her long black hair was pulled back in a single braid to show off her beautifully beaded earrings and necklaces. She wore a brooch made of bone, and a wraparound dress from real buckskin leather. The only thing I knew made from leather, well, other than cowboy boots, was Daddy's belt, and there was no way you could make a dress out of something hard like that. When I asked Ama about it, she let me feel how soft her skirt was, then explained the process of smoking the deerskin to prevent it from becoming stiff.

She wore suede moccasins that looked more like boots since they went all the way up to her knees, and like her earrings and belt, the tops had a pretty pattern of turquoise and maroon beads. When she finished talking about her clothing, she led us into the village.

It was kind of like a museum but way better. More like a camp with real people showing how their ancestors used to live. We watched everything from men hulling canoes, to ladies making pottery from the clay they had collected near the river. Others demonstrated how they wove yarn with their fingers, and how they made baskets, tools, and musical instruments. Ama tended the fire as she continued to speak of their primitive lifestyle. After our tour, we sat down to watch a reenactment of the Trail of Tears.

The show started with dancing, drumming, and chanting, and I quietly chanted along as I imagined myself as an Indian girl, dancing around the fire with them, singing and celebrating

Mother Earth. When they talked about how President Andrew Jackson's soldiers rushed into camp with rifles and bayonets to force them to relocate onto reservations, I was right there with them, grabbing a blowgun from my mud house, escaping to the hills, while others from my tribe followed behind me.

The explosive sound of a gunshot brought me back to the reality of the play. I wasn't a hero after all. I wasn't with them in the 1830s to save the day, or dancing around the fire in my buckskin dress. I was just one of the many tourists watching as one Indian after the other collapsed to the ground on the thousand mile walk to the reservation. Nearly a third of the Indians died before even making it there by either starving or freezing to death. That's where the name *Trail of Tears* came from.

After we left the village, Mama parked the camper in a lot near a big statue of an Indian chief. The street was lined with tourist shops, same as a lot of other places we saw along the way, only this town was cool because it was on an Indian reservation.

Everyone, except Jon Eric and I, headed into the first shop on the corner. The two of us wanted to go across the street to explore on our own.

The store we chose had every fun thing imaginable: small teepees, bows and arrows, tomahawks, suede jackets with fringe on the back, moccasins and pocket knives.

"Hey, check this out," Jon Eric said.

He put on a Daniel Boone hat made of real fur, then pointed a wooden gun at me.

"Pow!" he said as a small cork attached to a string flung in my direction.

"That's cool."

I wanted to dress up, too, but something more Indian-like, something better than his. I tried on a pair of moccasins and put on one of the fringed vests, but it still wasn't enough. Then I spotted it. Displayed high on a rack near the window, the sun lit up a fancy headdress with soft white and grey feathers—the type only a chief would wear. Using the bottom shelf as a step, I stood on my tippy-toes and pulled it down. When I put it on, the long feathers reached all the way down my back, nearly touching the floor. I knew it was only there for the tourists because Ama told us the Cherokees never wore those types of headpieces. She said theirs weren't that fancy. Their tribe only attached a single feather to a patch of long hair they kept on their otherwise shaved heads.

I spun around to model my new look, then picked up a small raw-hide tom-tom. It reminded me of the guys back home who sat on the steps at Aquatic Park playing the bongo drums on the weekends. I lifted my knees, one at a time, and began dancing in a small circle.

"Hi-ya, hi-ya, hi-ya, hi-ya," I chanted.

Jon Eric took his hat off, picked up a tomahawk, and danced around with me.

"Hi-ya, hi-ya, hi-ya, hi-ya," we both sang.

"Ah-hem!" The shop clerk cleared her throat and cinched her brows tight into a frown.

My cheeks burned like the coals of fire at the Indian village as I placed the headdress back on the shelf. I felt so ashamed. I wanted to tell her we weren't making fun of her tribe, that we were only having fun, but I was way too embarrassed. She probably wouldn't have believed me, anyway. I kept my gaze to the floor as I followed Jon Eric out.

We walked from store to store down the touristy street, still trying on outfits and playing with the souvenirs, and stuff, but we did it without the chanting, so no one seemed to mind.

"I wish I had money to buy something," I said. "Especially a pocket knife."

The store had all kinds of cool knives, really expensive ones with turquoise embedded in the handle, and some with han-dles made from real deer antlers, but all I needed was one of the tiny, cheap ones. The kind made from plastic with the word Cherokee printed on the side. A knife would've been the perfect thing to keep me from being so bored in the camper.

"I could carve little people out of wood for us to play with," I said, "and make a canoe, and things like that. Maybe I should go look for coke bottles to trade in."

Before I had time to search for bottles, something else caught my eye. Jon Eric noticed it at the same time, so we bolted across the street to a small arcade. It was like Musée Mecanique, the place I wanted to take Jon Eric while we were in San Francisco with old-time, interactive games—only this one also had live animals.

"What the heck?" I asked when I first noticed one of the cages.

In a wooden crate with two plexiglass windows, a white bunny sat near a small red fire engine with the words, "The Rabbit Fire Chief" painted above it.

We waited to see what would happen when a man slid twenty-five cents into the money slot. Once the quarter dropped, the lights on the truck turned on, and the little bunny hopped to the steering wheel to press a button with his paw. A loud siren blared as the rabbit stood on his hind legs, pretending to steer the firetruck.

"That's so cool," I said. "I wonder how they taught him to do that?"

We followed the man to "the Dancing Chicken," then the "Piano Playing Chicken" and went back and forth, over and over again, as more tourists used their quarters to give us free shows.

"I haven't seen any of the other kids or Mom in a while, have you?" Jon Eric Eric asked.

"No. Not since we saw them in that one store, but that was a long time ago."

"I guess we should go look for 'em," he said.

We walked from store to store, peeking our heads through the doors to scan the aisles for our brothers and sisters. Then we went from one end of the block to the next, and from one side of the street to the other, but there weren't any Thompsons anywhere. What started as a relaxed stroll quickly turned to panic.

"You try this side of the street again, and I'll check the other." The words raced from Jon Eric's mouth as he spoke.

This time, instead of just looking in from the sidewalk as we did on our first go around, we ran up and down each aisle of every store calling out their names, "Mom... Gregory... Rachael!" Still no Thompsons. Jon Eric and I met at the end of the block, then ran toward the parking lot where Mama had parked the camper earlier that morning. The huge statue of the Indian near the lot became blurred as salty sweat dripped into my eyes, but that didn't stop me from running. As we turned the corner, I stopped in my tracks and shrieked.

"Oh, my gosh! She left us!"

High pitched sounds came from my chest with each breath. Sounds I had never heard before, as if I had swallowed a whistle, or something. I could barely breathe. The heat, the running, and now the missing camper caused my lungs to seize. I placed my hand on my chest and hunched over as the sidewalk spun around me.

"There's no way, Teresa. She couldn't've left us," Jon Eric said. "You okay?"

I brought my head back up when the spinning and wheezing stopped. "I'm okay. I don't know what happened."

Jon Eric's wide eyes darted around the parking lot. "She probably just drove to a grocery store or somethin'. Besides, someone would've noticed that we weren't there."

"Yeah, but, even if Mama *did* drive to the grocery store, there's no way she would've taken all the kids with her."

"True. Come on. Let's go check the stores one more time."

Again, we each took a different side of the street, and went store to store, aisle to aisle, calling out their names, but no one answered us. We ran back to the parking lot again, then all the way to the Indian Village, stopping only occasionally to catch our breath. There wasn't a single Thompson anywhere.

"Maybe we should tell somebody Mama left us," I said. Tears ran down my cheeks as I looked for a spot on the hot curb to rest.

"We can't do that. They'll call the cops." Jon Eric inhaled a sharp breath and sat next to me. "Besides, Mom has to realize she left us at some point."

I couldn't believe it. We were left behind, abandoned in Cherokee, North Carolina. Jon Eric put his hand on my back as my body shuddered from sobbing.

"That's just great," he said. "What are we gonna do now?"

I didn't have an answer for him. I had no clue what we were going to do. I wanted to come up with ideas, but my mind was too foggy. Even with Jon Eric right next to me, I felt all alone and scared. I thought back to Officer Mike and the time I got lost on the 19 Polk bus when I was seven. And how—even though it took a whole day to find our apartment—at least we found it. *Dear God, please let us find Mama and the camper. Please! I promise I'll be nice to everybody. Please, God.*

"I don't care if they call the cops," I said.

Jon Eric stood up and reached his hand out to me. "Let's at least see if we can find some Coke bottles so we don't starve to death like the Indians did."

My stomach had been screaming for food all day, but now it was tied in knots. There was no way I could eat. Jon Eric was right, though. We had to eat something. What if Mama never came back for us and we were stranded on the sidewalks outside the Indian stores forever? Or worse, what if we were put in those wooden cages and had to perform each time someone put a quarter in the slot? The thought caused me to whimper even louder.

The tourists looked on as we scrounged through the garbage cans on the corner of each block. I kept my head down and repeated to myself, *don't worry about them. You'll never see 'em again. You'll never see 'em again.* We had to search the garbage cans on the main strip because that was where all the tourists were walking around with their sugary soft drinks.

We dug through all sorts of trash—melted ice cream, crumpled papers, empty cigarette packs, even some nasty diapers. Yellowjackets and ants feasted on discarded scraps of food as we rummaged through each can. Even with all of the mess, we managed to pull out a few bottles, and we knew the exact store that sold candy since we'd already been in it at least a half a dozen times that day.

"I bet that lady behind the counter is called Black Hawk since she's watching us like a hawk," I whispered.

If only she knew about the time when Jon Eric and I stole money off that table in a restaurant to buy Mama that Little LuLu paper doll, and all those stupid black Xs Mama gouged on our faces with that permanent magic marker. If she knew that, she would have known we wouldn't be stealing anything from her. We learned that lesson loud and clear.

We picked out a couple of Chick-O-Sticks and two bags of chips, then set them on the counter. The puzzled look on Black Hawk's face made me worry they didn't trade Coke bottles in North Carolina. She placed them behind the counter, then rang up our items. *Phew! She's probably just grossed out by the dead ants. Or maybe she still thinks we stole somethin'.*

Sure enough, just as I had expected, as soon as we reached the door, she called out to us.

"Hey, you two. Can you come here for a minute?"

Crap. Everyone's gonna stare and think we're thieves. Oh, no! What if Jon Eric did steal somethin'? My heart thumped in my chest as we headed back to the counter.

"Hey, I was wonderin' if y'all could help me with somethin'?" she asked.

She tapped her fingers on her chin as she waited for our reply. I knew the next thing out of her mouth was gonna be for us to turn out our pockets.

"Uh... sure, what?" I shrugged my shoulders and looked to Jon Eric. *Please don't have anything in your pockets.*

"I'm looking for the Key to Cherokee," she said as she tucked her long black hair behind her ear. "Would you mind goin' to the shop next door and ask the guy behind the counter if he has it? I'll give you each a quarter if you do that for me."

"The Key to Cherokee?" I asked.

"Yes." She opened her till, pulled out fifty cents, and placed a quarter into each of our hands.

Embarrassed by the lines of dirt on my palm, I quickly pulled my arm behind my back and squeezed my fingers tight around the coin.

"Okay!" I said.

I looked at Jon Eric and smiled before we ran out the door. At the next shop, the man behind the counter tugged at a turquoise bolo around his neck as he spoke on the phone.

"Huh? Uh-huh. Okay," he said into the receiver.

I couldn't stand still. I put my finger in the ring of a keychain and spun it around as we waited. It wasn't every day somebody handed me a quarter, especially for something so easy. I felt important and couldn't believe that lady trusted us enough to hand over fifty cents. I thought instead of Black Hawk, maybe her name was Gentle Flower, or something like that.

Jon Eric nudged my arm and gave me a wide-eyed look to stop fidgeting.

"Can I help you?" the guy asked after hanging up the phone.

"Yeah! The lady next door's looking for the Key to Cherokee," I said. "She wants to know if you have it?"

"The Key to Cherokee?" He smoothed the side of his black hair and looked from me to Jon Eric, then back to me again.

I wondered what he was thinking as he glanced at us. Did he think we were special because the lady next door trusted us with the Key to Cherokee? Or did he see us as street urchins like Mama always called us?

"No, I'm sorry. I'm not the one who has it," he said. "You might wanna try the next shop over. They might have it there." He fumbled through some coins, then handed us fifty cents to split.

"Thank you!" I said.

I tried to contain the huge smile on my face—to make it look as if we were on official business, and all, but I couldn't. No way. Not with fifty cents in my hand. I couldn't even walk to the door without skipping.

"Oh, my gosh!" I said once we were outside. "I wonder what the Key to Cherokee is for?"

"I don't know, but it must be pretty important for these people to want it so much."

We continued from shop to shop, each time with the same results. No Thompsons, no Key to Cherokee, and an extra quarter in our sweaty hands.

Try next door... try the pottery shop... here, have an ice-cream cone... ask at the Skylift, I think he was the last one to have it...

We scarfed our Chick-O-Sticks and chips, then went back to the parking lot by the big Indian to see if Mama came back for us. Even with the thrill of our new adventure, the empty lot left a burning sensation in my gut.

If she had gone to the grocery store, she would have had plenty of time to return by then. She was gone. She left us. Every feeling under the sun stirred within me—fear and excitement, worry and thrill, hungry, yet sick to my stomach.

"What if Mama never comes back for us?" I asked. The thought caused the pain in my belly to grow even more intense. "What'll we do?"

"I have no idea! I can't believe she left us."

Jon Eric flipped one of his quarters in the air then caught it in his hand. "Come on. Let's go check the Skylift for the Key."

"I wish I was home," I said.

It was so hot, my clothes were drenched in sweat. I wasn't used to that kind of heat anymore. It had been a long time since I lived in Jacksonville. I missed San Francisco and its cool breeze, and even missed the fog.

"Hey, you two," the operator at the Skylift shouted as we approached. He acted as if he were expecting us or something.

"Can I help you with anything?" He smiled from ear to ear, baring a set of tobacco-stained teeth.

"Yeah, we're looking for the Key to Cherokee," Jon Eric said.

"The Key to Cherokee?" he asked in an exaggerated way as if he were rehearsing for a part in the school play. He put his hand to his chin. "Hmmm, let's see. I'll check."

He looked around the kiosk, lifting magazines, opening drawers, and even dumped out a coffee cup filled with pens, loose coins, and other knick-knacks.

"Shoot," he said. "I'm sorry, I don't have it. I'll tell ya what, though. How would y'all like a free ride on the chairlift?"

"Really? No way!" Jon Eric nudged me with his elbow and smiled. Goosebumps tingled my scalp. I wanted to dance and jump for joy.

"Sure, step right up and I'll get you on the next chair."

The man pulled down the safety bar after we got on, then we started the slow ascent to the top of the mountain.

"What's up with this town? I've never met people like this in my whole entire life," I said.

"I know."

The higher we went, the more we could see—from the tree-lined mountains surrounding the town, to people fishing along the riverbank and tourists walking in and out of the shops. I even saw the big Indian statue near the lot where Mama had parked earlier that day.

"I don't see Mom or the camper anywhere," Jon Eric said.

My eyes began to well again. Jon Eric's did, too.

"We have to come up with a plan," he said.

"Maybe we could sleep in the woods and catch fish with our bare hands or something," I said. "And with the money we earned, we could buy a hatchet and some matches to build a campfire."

"Yeah, but what about that huge black bear we saw in the Smokies?" he asked.

"I know! Maybe we could sneak into the Indian village every night and sleep in one of those mud huts!"

"These people aren't gonna keep givin' us money, either, if we don't find the Key to Cherokee," Jon Eric said. "But I guess we could always find more Coke bottles."

When we returned to the bottom of the mountain, the lift operator chatted with us a bit. I told him I was ten and Jon Eric twelve, and he asked things like our names and where we were from. When Jon Eric said Florida as I said San Francisco, we had to explain about Mama and Daddy's divorce, and how we were only together for the summer. I wanted to tell him about the rest of the family—how they were somewhere in the camper and how we were left alone, but Jon Eric squeezed my hand tight as a warning. I don't know why he didn't want to say anything. Maybe that man could have helped us.

"Well, kiddos. You might want to check over there at the water park," the operator said. He pointed to some tube slides in the distance.

I wanted to hug him. "I love Cherokee!" I said. "Y'all are the nicest people in the world here."

"I think they must know we're lost," Jon Eric said as we headed to the other side of town. "That's why they're doing all of this for us."

"Oh? Yeah, maybe."

The water park attendant was no different than anyone else that day. When he didn't have the Key, he stepped aside to let us in, and that's where we spent the rest of the day. We were having the time of our lives going down one slide after the other and only talked about being left behind every once in a while.

"Oh, my gosh! There's the camper," I shouted, after spotting it from the top of the highest slide in the park. "Mama!" I screamed. "Mom!"

"She can't hear you. Let's hurry down!"

The smell of chlorine filled my nose for one last time as I shot down the slide. We grabbed our shoes and took off running out the gate, then continued down the street in our sopping wet clothes, shouting for Mom at the top of our lungs.

"Mom! Mom! Stop!"

The camper was already a few blocks away, but the back door was wide open with Petesy standing on the rim of the tailgate. He must have seen us because he began waving his arm in the air. The camper made a U-turn in the middle of the street, then sped back in our direction, and came to a screeching halt next to us.

"Where in the goddamn hell have you two been?" Mama shouted.

We stood on the scorching hot pavement, shifting our bare feet back and forth while water dripped down our legs.

"You left us," I said.

"I didn't leave you anywhere. You knew that we were gonna be parked at that same spot by the river as last night."

"We didn't know that," Jon Eric said. "And how would we have known where that was, anyway?"

"It was only a couple miles down the highway. All you had to do was follow the road by the river."

"Yeah, but we had no idea you'd be there," I said, "even if we *did* know how to get there."

"What do you think, I'd drive away and leave my own children behind?"

"Well, that's what you did," Jon Eric answered.

"Get in! I don't want to hear another peep from your filthy mouths."

When we got in the camper, we told everyone of our adventures with the mysterious Key to Cherokee—the Skylift ride, the free ice cream, the fun water park, and all of the quarters we earned.

No one wanted to hear it, though. They didn't want to know we were having fun while they were stuck cleaning out the camper, especially since Mama had thrown one of her fits.

* * *

We never did find the Key to Cherokee that day and never learned what it was for, or even if such a Key really existed in the first place. All I know is that town came together as a community, offered us the Key to their city, and kept us safe and secure with their love and generosity. Perhaps it was the souls of those who lost their lives on the Trail of Tears who came to protect us? Maybe they hang around to keep an eye on their ancestral homeland and protect all those who treasure it.

Josh and Jonas turn five.

– 21 –

The King

Ambition is a dream with a V8 engine. — Elvis Presley

The next day we headed east toward the Atlantic Coast, then south to Myrtle Beach. Mama parked near the harbor and came back to the camper.

"Let's go get y'all something new to put on so you don't look like a bunch of tramps when we see your father," she said.

I still couldn't believe we were gonna see Daddy again, and definitely wanted to look nice when we arrived. We went to a nearby thrift store and began searching the racks for new clothes. With eight of us kids trying on things, it didn't take long for the store to turn to a complete mess.

"Oh, dear Lord," the clerk said.

Clothes were off the shelves, toys scattered, and Greg was chasing the twins up and down the aisles.

"Dear Lord," the lady repeated, but she wasn't talking to us.

She sat behind the counter holding a black transistor radio to her ear. Mama joined her to see what was going on, so the lady held the radio out for her to hear as well.

"Oh, no. Say it isn't so." Mama brought both hands over her mouth. *What the heck?* We left toys and clothes scattered in the middle of the aisle and rushed to the counter to see what was happening.

"Elvis Presley died today," the man on the radio repeated. "He was 42. Apparently, it was a heart attack."

Mama grabbed ahold of my hand since I was standing closest to her. Tears ran down her face as she reached her other hand to the clerk. No one said anything as the announcer continued with his report.

"What's today?" Mama asked the lady.

"August 16th."

Mama bit on her lower lip while she brought her gaze to the ceiling, then tapped her fingers on the counter and whispered, "We're going to Graceland." Then she let go of my hand to wipe the tears from her face. "We have time. We'll drive the kids down to Florida, then, instead of going back the way I had planned, we'll head back through Memphis. We'll just have to cut our time in Florida a little shorter, that's all." She looked to the ground. "I can't believe Elvis is gone."

* * *

The mood stayed somber as we continued down the highway, Mama's for Elvis, mine for less time with Daddy. Don't get me wrong, I was sad Elvis Presley died. I liked his music and all, I just didn't want it to take time away from our visit. Brother tried to cheer me up by singing my favorite Elvis song, "Put Your Hand in the Hand" and after a while, we were all singing along with him.

Mama woke up early the next morning to drive to Jacksonville, so I climbed on the upper bed to sleep a little more. When we made it to the house, she laid on the truck horn to wake us up, and kept honking until Dad peeked his head through the curtains in the living room.

"Oh, my gosh! We're here!" I squealed. I climbed down and reached for the door as everyone else stirred and stretched on the pull-out couch.

"Get this piece of shit out of my driveway!" Daddy yelled. "Park it down the street somewhere."

What? What's happening? I opened the door, then paused and shut it again.

"I'm not moving anywhere! This is my house, too!"

"The hell it is. And don't think you're stepping a foot in here."

"Watch me. Half of this house belongs to me. I'll step wherever I damn well please."

Stop! Stop screaming at each other. I backed away from the door as everyone else rushed out. It wasn't how I imagined our reunion to be at all. I thought Daddy would come running down the steps with his eyes filled with tears. His arms would be wide open, and he'd be so happy to see me that he'd almost collapse to the ground as he clung to me. I didn't understand. It wasn't happening that way at all.

"Quit worrying about me and say hi to your children, you spineless louse," Mama said. "And don't expect me ever to bring them back here again."

I stood behind Rache and the twins, waiting for my turn to hug him, wishing I could turn back the time—not the three years I've been gone, but the last five minutes. I felt bad for Mama. She was just as excited to visit Jacksonville as we were, and for once, it wasn't her who started the fight.

"You Ute!" Daddy said as he leaned in to hug me.

"Huh? Oh." I lowered my head and gave a shy smile. "You Ute!"

"How are you, Peanut? I missed you so much."

"I'm good. I missed you too, Daddy."

"Have y'all eaten yet?"

I nodded.

"Well, come on in and I'll start some breakfast."

Mama took a step toward the door, so daddy held his hands across the frame to block her.

"Not so fast," he said. "You need to go park that piece of shit around the corner so I don't have to look at it. How long do you plan on staying here?"

"Don't worry. We'll be out of your hair before you know it," she said.

Jon Eric tugged at my arm. "Come on. Let me show you the house," he said as he pulled me away.

Daddy stayed by the door like a guard to make sure Mama didn't come in before heading to the kitchen to cook. My feelings were way too hurt to notice anything Jon Eric pointed out. I wanted to run and hide, but there wasn't anywhere to go. It clearly wasn't my home anymore.

* * *

At Graceland, hordes of people were gathered outside Elvis' mansion.

"I thought for sure we'd be the only ones here. It's been almost a week since he died," Mama said. She pushed our way through the crowd until we were close to the gate.

"Thank God his body isn't still here," I said. "That would've been so gross."

Mama told us that his body had been displayed in the front yard for all to see. She was hoping it would still be there.

"The King is dead," a lady next to us whimpered.

Mama held onto the lady's hand. "The King is dead," she said.

Petesy in front of the camper, with Jon Eric and Josh in back.

– 22 –

Liar Liar

Distrust and caution are the parents of security.
— Benjamin Franklin

*M*s. Blanchard, my sixth grade teacher, loved giving pop quizzes to keep us on our toes. This time, an essay on the Declaration of Independence. "Write everything you know," she said.

Thanks to Mama, I knew a lot. I learned all about our nation's history the previous summer when she took us on the bicentennial tour of the United States. We saw the Liberty Bell and Independence Hall in Philadelphia. She even bought me a funny hat in the souvenir shop of Betsy Ross' house. It looked like one of Mama's shower caps the way it cinched at the sides, and all, but I loved it just the same.

I tapped my pencil on the desk as I reminisced about that summer. Fudgsicles in New York– the taste of the cool chocolate on my tongue, and the sticky feeling it left on my fingers. It's strange what memories pop up first when asked to write about the Declaration of Independence.

We had the best time in Washington, D.C. since the National Mall

217

had all sorts of fun activities to celebrate our country's 200th birthday. Chills tingled my scalp as I remembered racing down the hill of the Washington Monument on a go-kart Brother and Petesy had built.

"Get on, Treedy," Brother said.

I clung to the sides as we raced down, laughing and squealing until I almost popped out when we hit a bump.

"I'm gonna start calling you Eety Beety Treedy from now on," he teased when we got to the bottom. "Because you're so tiny!"

A knock on the door brought my attention back to the essay. *Crap!* Everyone else was busy scribbling their pencils across the paper, while I didn't have a single sentence written. Ms. Blanchard stood at the door speaking with the school secretary, something about Mr. Bergez, but that's all I heard. She glanced at me, then headed toward my desk.

"Teresa," Ms. Blanchard whispered. She put her hand on my shoulder. "Mr. Bergez wants to see you in his office. You can put your quiz on my desk and finish when you get back."

"Huh?" *What? What did I do? I didn't do anything.*

I bit on my lower lip as everyone's eyes watched me.

"Ooo, Teresa's going to the principal's office," someone said.

"That's enough!" Ms. Blanchard snapped.

Shut up! I hated that class now that Trez was gone. Everybody was so mean.

The secretary waited for me in the hallway. It's not like I didn't know my own way, I'm there almost every morning getting a late slip. That's probably why she called me out of class. She didn't say a word, though. Not a single hint. And she walked so fast, I had to skip with every other step just to keep up with her.

When we got to his office, she knocked on the door and opened it just enough to peek her head in. "She's here," she announced, then stepped aside for me. "Go on in, Teresa."

My hands clenched at my uniform tie as a horrible thumping began in my chest. Mr. Bergez stood from his desk as I walked in. Next to him were two men, both wearing white long-sleeved, buttoned-up shirts and dress slacks. *Who in the heck are these guys?* A tall, lanky one with skin as pink as an eraser and blonde hair cut short into a crew-cut, nodded his head to me. The other reminded me of Starsky from Starsky and Hutch and was definitely the better looking of the two. He was a little shorter and had curly black hair that hung midway down his ear. That style would never fly at NDV.

What in the world do they want from me?

"Hi, Teresa," Mr. Bergez began. He cleared his throat, causing his Adam's apple to move up and down his skinny neck. "These gentlemen are from Social Services. They'd like to ask you a few questions."

"Huh? What for?" I looked down and shifted my weight to the outer edges of my feet as I always did when I got nervous or scared.

"Don't worry. You're not in trouble," Mr. Bergez said.

Shifting my gaze from my shoes, I stared blankly at the two men, then back to Mr. Bergez.

"Teresa, I'm Mr. Whitaker, and this here is Mr. DeSilva," the taller, lanky man said. "You're not in trouble. We'd just like to ask you some questions about your life at home."

"Huh?"

Mr. Bergez cleared his throat again, then gave a nod to tell me it's okay to talk. The guys went back and forth with all sorts of questions. Starting simple, they asked my name and birthday, then stuff about the apartment, where I slept, if I had enough food to eat, and stupid things like do we have lights on at night? And is there hot water when I take a bath? The lanky guy asked all about school. Do I like it? How are my grades? Do I have friends? Then they moved on to questions about Mama.

"Teresa, are you happy at home?" Lanky asked.

"Uh, yeah. I guess?"

They were making me so nervous with all their questions, I just wanted to leave. And I hated how Mr. Bergez just kept staring at me. I don't know who called the men to come talk to me either. I never told anyone about Mama. No one.

"You guess?" Starsky asked.

I didn't say anything.

"Let me ask in a different way. Do you ever feel unsafe or threatened at home?" Lanky asked.

"Uh, no." I squeezed my sweaty hands together in front of me.

"You're saying that you always feel safe at your home?"

"Yeah, I guess so."

"How does your mother discipline you?" Starsky asked.

"I don't know."

"You don't know?"

"Well, I guess I've had spankings before."

Stop asking so many questions!

"Has she ever hit you with anything other than an open hand?" he asked.

"What? No!" I lied.

"Teresa, we're here to help you. We have reasons to believe that your mother hurts you."

Never taking my eyes from my feet, I squeezed my hands tighter, causing the edges of my nails to dig into my palms.

These men are trying to get Mama in trouble. That's what they're doing. Who told them, anyway? Oh, my gosh, it must have been the Mormons.

I thought back to when the missionaries were at our house. They'd come once a week during the past few months for something called *Family Home Evening*, the thing we learned about on our trip to Utah. It took a while, but Mama finally set it up for us. We'd sit on the floor with the missionaries and play games, then they'd tell a story and say a prayer with us before leaving. It was a lot of fun since we never really did stuff like that as a family before. Even Mama enjoyed it. Of course, after they left, she'd always remind us to never listen to anything they said about Joseph Smith since that was a bunch of hogwash.

After their last visit, I asked Mama if we could have them over for supper one night. She agreed, so I prepared my favorite meal, Salisbury steak and gravy over mashed potatoes with a side of string beans and a salad. I wanted the night to be perfect, and it would have been if Mama hadn't been in such a mood.

"Why are you feeding them all of our expensive Salisbury steaks?" she asked. "And why in the hell did you peel so many potatoes? There's two boys comin', not an army. You act like you worship them or somethin'. You know, they're only here to try to convert us to that crazy religion of theirs."

Oh, my gosh. Please don't start.

She was interrupted by the doorbell, and her mood never let up after the missionaries came into the apartment. She watched them with such hatred in her eyes, it was as if each bite they took of her expensive Salisbury steak caused a hot poker to jab into her gut.

"This is delicious," one of them said.

"Of course, it is," Mama snapped. "She made the most exorbitant meal she could think of."

"Mama. Please?" I whispered.

"Mama, please, nothin'. You're wasting our good food on them. They come here with that trashy religion, feedin' y'all all kinds of bullshit, and you want to treat 'em like they're kings or somethin'?"

I cringed. *Great!* Rache and the twins didn't dare look up. They kept their eyes on their plate, fiddling with the food.

"Stop being so rude," I mumbled.

And that was it. I don't know why I couldn't keep my mouth shut when she's in a mood. I just couldn't. Especially when she's being mean to someone else. She stood up and snatched her plate from the table. *Thank, God she's leaving.* My body relaxed as if someone stuck a pin in me to deflate all the tension.

She didn't leave, though. She just stood there, staring and seething with her plate clenched between her fingers. Her eyes narrowed as her plate lifted higher. *Oh, my gosh. No!* She hurled it across the table, but it sailed right past me, hitting the wall, then clattered to the floor. A clump of mashed potatoes slowly slid its way down the slick white paint, and specks of gravy were splattered all over the place.

"Helen!" one of the missionaries called out to Mom. I couldn't look at them.

Mom was steaming. The monster had emerged from her. I raised my head and glared in her direction with as much hatred as I could muster. *Haha, bitch! You missed.* She wasn't done though. She grabbed Rachael's plate and flung it–this time hitting me square in the chest.

"Helen!"

"I can't stand you!" I screamed. "You're such a witch!"

"Look what you made me do, you little tramp! Clean up this fuckin' mess!"

"You clean it!" I don't know what came over me. Maybe because the Mormons were there, or maybe because I just couldn't take her cruelty anymore.

She pushed away from the table and charged toward me. "Okay, I'll clean it!" she said.

She grabbed my ponytails with both her hands and yanked me from the chair. I scrambled for solid ground, but my feet slipped in the slop as I tried to stand. She dragged me to the mess on the wall, then used my hair as a rag to wipe the spattered gravy, jerking my head back and forth, side to side. With my hair in her hands, she had complete control of me, as if I were nothing but a limp ragdoll.

"Ouch! Stop!" My arms flailed about, grasping and reaching until I was finally able to grab her hand. Squeezing with all my might, I tried to dig my fingernails into her just as she always did to me. Anything to get her to stop.

"You little whore! How dare you!"

She let go of my hair and slapped me across the face. My eyes filled with tears as I fell to the floor, so I quickly looked away. I wasn't about to let her witness me crying. Not anymore. No way I'd give her that satisfaction. I covered my head with my arms for protection as she reached for me, but instead of my hair, her hand squeezed onto my arm. Digging her nails deep into my flesh, she clawed from one end to the other.

The room went silent. I peeked through my arms. Mama's face looked horrified when she realized what she had just done. "Shit!" she said.

No one else was in the room. *Where did they go?* Four trails of dotted red blood ran from my elbow to my wrist. She had broken the skin. Not knowing what to do, she stormed out of the room.

She had fits of rage all the time. That wasn't anything new, but never in front of others, and even though it seemed like it, she never really got completely out of control. She always had a plan. NEVER-LEAVE-A-MARK.

By the time I stumbled out of the kitchen the missionaries were gone. I don't know when they took off or even how much they saw. I only knew they weren't there anymore. Rache and the twins must have escaped to the backyard because I couldn't hear them anywhere, either. Mom was on her bed, holding her head in her hands, rocking back and forth. I knew the routine well. It was all my fault, and she was feeling sorry for herself for what I made her do. "How could she have such a hateful daughter," she'd say. I snuck into my room, buried my head deep under my stuffed animals, and cried.

* * *

Mr. Bergez cleared his throat to bring me back to the present.

"Don't be afraid. Tell us the truth, and we can help make things better for you," Lanky explained. "We're on your side."

"Teresa. Please answer him," Mr. Bergez said.

I don't know why Mr. Bergez's even here. And why is his stupid Adam's apple so big? I hate looking at it.

"Teresa —"

"Uh, what?" I asked. *Get me out of here!*

"I was just asking if you feel happy at home?" Starsky asked.

"Happy?" I paused. "Of course! Why wouldn't I?"

"Can you show me your arm?"

My heart stopped. At least it felt like it did. I gulped, but my spit was so dry it felt like sand going down my throat. A cold sweat formed on my forehead as I realized my arms were exposed.

Dear God, please help me. What do I do? I had taken my sweater off during the quiz, but I had planned to put it right back on afterward. *How could I have forgotten to grab it? I'm so stupid!*

"Teresa—"

I tried drawing in a breath, then held out my right arm. My hand shook like leaves on the tip of a branch. I wished I could stop it. The shaking made it look like something was wrong.

"Your other arm, Teresa," Lanky said.

No! I clenched my fists tighter.

"Teresa. Your other arm, please."

I extended it, palm side up for them to see.

"Turn it over," Starsky said.

I felt my heart in my throat. *Don't cry. It's okay. Be strong.* I clenched my jaw, causing my loose molar to press hard into my raw gum. *Don't cry.* I rolled my hand around to expose four long, crusted, brown scabs. The warm sensation of tears built in my eyes. *Stop! Don't cry!* I pushed my tongue hard against the painful loose tooth to distract me from sobbing.

"What happened here, Teresa?" Starsky asked.

It's none of your business, that's what.

"Teresa?"

"Those are from my cat. My cat scratched me the other day."

Shit! They'd have to be stupid to believe that.

"Your cat?"

"Yeah." I licked under my dry lips. *Don't breathe so hard.* "My cat was laying down and I tried to pick her up, but she scratched me and ran. She hates being held, so sometimes she does that."

I'm talking too fast. Slow down or they'll know I'm lying!

"I hear that sometimes you come to school with puffy eyes like you've been crying. Why would someone your age cry before school?"

You heard? From who?

"Because I hate school!" The muscles on my lower jaw quivered. I hated saying that in front of Mr. Bergez. I wished I could take it back, and tell him that I really did like it at NDV, but I didn't know what else to say.

"Teresa, you can trust us. We're not here to interrogate you. We're here to help you. Please, is there anything you'd like to share with us?" Lanky asked. "Anything at all?"

"No. I don't think so. I'm ok. Really," I lied again. "Everything's good at home."

They glanced at each other, then over to my principal. Mr. Bergez shrugged his shoulders and gave me a pleading look. A look that begged me to tell the truth. A look of compassion mixed with heartbreak. A look that made me want to start bawling, right there, in front of them all. Lanky scribbled something onto his notepad.

"Okay. Well, if there's ever a time that you don't feel safe, or would just like someone to talk to, let Mr. Bergez know, and he can contact us," Lanky said.

"Okay. Is that it?" My voice broke. I had to get out of there before the tears came.

"Yes, you can head back to class now. Thank you for your time," Starsky said.

I couldn't get out of that office fast enough. I ran down the hall and went halfway up the first set of ramps, clinging to the railing so my body wouldn't crumble under me.

They had to know I was lying. Cat claws. Really? That was so stupid. Those marks are way too wide to come from a cat. I ran my trembling fingers along the length of them. *That was my chance. I should've said something. But not with Mr. Bergez in the room. There's no way I'd want him to know anything. How embarrassing. What would they do anyway? Would I go to Juvie? Mama can't go to jail.*

I dawdled my way toward the second floor. *Tell Mr. Bergez? Seriously? Those guys are so stupid. He's the last one I'd ever wanna tell.* I continued up the ramp. *Shoot, why didn't I say anything? I should go back.* I paused with my hand on the railing, ready to turn around. *But what if something happens to Mama? She's not always bad.* I thought back to Christmas when we loaded the camper with bags of stuffed animals from garage sales to bring to Mexico, and how fun it was standing in a plaza in Tijuana, passing them out to the children. "There's always people worse off than we are," Mama said. "Y'all should appreciate everything you have."

I let go of the railing and continued to my classroom.

* * *

Those guys also pulled Josh out of his first-grade class that day. Only Josh. Not Jonas. And they didn't go to Rachael's high school, either. Josh denied everything, just as I had.

Over the months, the missionaries must have seen how Mama treated me and Josh differently than Rachael and Jonas. That must've been why Lanky and Starsky only spoke to us. According to Deborah and Brother, Josh looked just like me, and I looked like Dad, so Mama hated us both. We never did see the Mormons again after that, but as it turns out, they tried to save us in more than one way that night. I only hope Mama didn't scar them for life, and that they were able to continue on their missions after their visit with us.

Me, age 11.

– 23 –

The Fairmont

The question is not what you look at, but what you see.
— Henry David Thoreau

*A*nother lease ended, which meant another move. This time, back downtown, but not in the Tenderloin as before. We were a block from Chinatown, two blocks from the Fairmont Hotel, and four and a half blocks from our school in an area called Nob Hill. Mama called it *Snob Hill*, but you'd never know it by our apartment. We were back in a studio, roaches and all, only this one had an extra room, kind of like a bedroom, but way too small to be considered so—just big enough to squeeze mine and Rachael's bunk bed and our worn-out dresser with the drawers that barely closed.

Outside, the sound of cable car bells chimed in the distance as gripmen (cable car drivers) practiced for their annual bell ringing contest. We were in the middle of everything, right on Powell, the same street the cable cars ran on. The street where I found a new type of freedom—hotels, Union Square, downtown, Chinatown, North Beach, and Fisherman's Wharf. You name it, I'd explore it!

I went everywhere. I knew which hotels had the best views

of the city and which had the glass elevators that rode on the outside. I knew the back alleyways of Chinatown and where the little Chinese ladies folded hot fortune cookies by hand. I knew which stores had a dish of free candy on the counter and the ones where the shop owners watched me like a hawk. I knew which cable car conductors let me ride for free and which ones gave me all-day transfers. I found the funnest hills to skateboard on and knew which ones had the dangerous areas of uneven pavement.

I knew how to be tough when I needed to be but also how to be nice. I was alert and aware of everything—every bum lurking in the doorway, every dark alley, all the drunks and crazies.

Even the creepy men who got off by exposing themselves to me. I was aware even if I didn't look. And the man who offered me five dollars to suck his thing, yeah, even with that sicko, I still felt safe in San Francisco. Safer than in my apartment, anyway.

It seemed as if the city took care of me and kept me protected. Or maybe it was St. Francis himself, the saint whom San Francisco was named after, maybe he took me under his wing and watched over me? I don't know. All I know is that city became my playground—and my new best friend.

I met a girl named Alice who lived across the hall from us in the apartment. Alice wasn't her real name. She had a Chinese name, but liked to be called Alice instead, which was okay with me since I couldn't even pronounce her other name. She'd play with me sometimes and go on adventures when her father wasn't home, but mostly she wasn't allowed to. She said her father hated white people, so he didn't want her to hang out with me. I think her brother was in a Chinese gang or something, too. But I still wondered if the real reason her family didn't like us was because of all the screaming they heard through the walls.

The Fairmont became a hideout for me, a sort of refuge where I went to escape. I knew the hotel inside and out—the glass elevators with gold trim that cruised outside the building, the Tonga

Room, the Crown Room, the Rooftop Garden, and the red velvet couches in the lobby.

Oh, those red velvet couches. I'd melt into the plush cushions and pretend I was one of the guests as I fantasized of a different life. I knew I was stuck with Mama, and there wasn't anything I could do about that, so I dreamt of my future instead. You know, the typical house with a white picket fence, a garden, and enough bedrooms to fit my whole family. A place where I'd tuck my children in at night, read stories, and give goodnight kisses.

I watched the guests at the Fairmont as they came and went, taking note of their outfits, their hair, the way they walked, and the way they looked at me. Just like at school, some were friendly while others were just rude.

I called the snotty ones *les Yeux,* or just *yeux,* using the French word for *eyes* because that's the only way they looked at me— through their eyes. They'd be so blinded by my appearance that they couldn't see beyond it. I mean, really, as if an eleven year old had a choice of what clothes she wore. I sure didn't.

They acted as if being poor were a disease, something dirty and contagious that might infect them. And you should have seen the way they sneered at me. There'd be such disgust in their eyes that I thought for sure one day they'd have the concierge kick me out. No one that worked at the Fairmont ever asked me to leave, though.

Then there were the nice ones. I called them *coeur,* French for *heart.* Overall, those people seemed to be a lot happier. They were the ones who saw the world through their hearts and were able to overlook my ratty hair and worn-out clothes to offer me a kind smile. They probably just felt sorry for me, or maybe I reminded them of their granddaughter or someone else.

Either way, those were the people I wanted to be like, friendly and nice. After a while, I shortened the names *yeux* and *coeur* to just *yux* and *kur.*

* * *

I sunk into one of the red couches to people-watch but ended up falling asleep. The night before, Mama had come home from a dance and woke me up because there wasn't any milk in the fridge. It was the middle of the night, and the cable cars had already quit running, so she made me walk all the way to Cala Foods, the 24-hour market. It wasn't quite a mile away, but with all the big hills from my apartment to the store, it might as well have been five miles, especially in the middle of the night.

I was so tired in school, all I wanted to do was sleep. But afterwards, there was no way I wanted to go home. Mama wouldn't have let me take a nap, anyway.

When I woke from dozing on the couch, the people in the lobby had changed to the nighttime crowd. No more backpacks and sweatshirts. Those people were dressed for a fancy night on the town.

Outside, the stars lit up the night sky. *Oh, crap!* I was so worried, I got up and ran out as fast as I could. *Crap, crap, crap, crap!*

When I got home, I headed straight to the kitchen, hoping Mama would think I was there all along.

"Where were you?" her harrowing voice called out as I tip-toed down the hall.

My plan had failed. Surrounded by pillows on the upper mattress of the trundle, she straightened herself on her throne like a queen. She always sat there. It never failed. I guess because there really wasn't anywhere else to sit, other than the floor or at the kitchen table, but it still bothered me just the same.

"At the Fairmont." *Shoot.*

I glanced at the clock. *Crap! 6:47.*

"Why you always at that damn hotel, anyway?"

My toes curled in my shoes from the tone in her voice. Not only was I late, but she was in a mood, and I needed to get out of there quickly.

"Sorry, Mama. I lost track of time. I'll go start supper now."

"You didn't answer my question."

"Huh? Because I like it there. It's fun," I mumbled without looking up. I slid my foot sideways to inch out of the room.

"What?"

"I like to explore there." *And it's way better than hearing your grumpy voice always screaming at me.*

"You think you're like one of those rich snobs, don't you? Walkin' around with your nose up in the air like you're better than all of us. Well, you're not, so get that through your thick skull!"

"I don't think that."

I wanted to tell her that someday I *would* be at a place like that, not crammed in a roach-infested apartment like hers. But I bit my lip and took another step toward the kitchen.

"Since you love it there so much, you should make yourself useful and *explore* in some of the bathrooms."

"What? What are you talkin' about?"

"Get us some paper towels while you're there. We can use 'em for toilet paper."

"What?"

I looked from the floor to her beady eyes. *What the heck is she talking about? Please stay calm, Teresa. Don't say anything to make her explode.*

"Do I have to spell everything out for you? Get a stack of those paper towels they leave on the bathroom counters. I can't keep buyin' toilet paper. I might as well be flushin' money straight down the toilet."

"What?" My upper lip curled. *Don't say anything. Don't get her started.*

"Toilet paper costs money, you know. And unless you have money to buy some yourself, you're gonna get it from that damn hotel you love so much!"

"You're kiddin' me, right? I'm not stealing paper towels!" *Stop! What are you doing?*

"Well, you're not going to be using any of our expensive toilet paper anymore, either."

She charged from her bed so fast, I dropped to the floor and covered my face and head with my arms. She didn't hit me, though. Or pull my hair. Her heavy footsteps stomped right past me, thundering on the floor like an earthquake as she continued to the bathroom. Just as I expected, Her Royal Highness came out clutching the roll of toilet paper in her hands.

"If you need any paper, you know where you can get it," she said. "All you have to do is wear a jacket and stuff the towels inside. It's as easy as that."

"You've gotta be kidding me!"

I stormed to my room and pushed the door shut behind me. Sweet Rachael didn't bother looking up from her small TV. She was used to ignoring what went on around her, which infuriated me even more. I was mad at Mama, but my insides boiled toward Rachael.

"You're such a Queen Bee," I mumbled.

I threw myself on the lower bunk and kicked at the boards that separated her bed from mine.

"I'm never gonna be like Mama when I grow up. Never!"

"Little girl! You better get out of that room this instant and get some supper on the table," Mama shouted.

"Ugh!" I threw one of my stuffed animals at the door and screamed with all my might. "I'm coming-ah!"

Climbing over storage boxes on the floor, I went through the small passageway that led from our room to the kitchen so I wouldn't have to pass by Mama. I got the frying pan from the dish drainer and slammed it onto the burner. *She's such a witch!* Then I ripped open a pack of frozen hamburger meat and tossed it into the pan. *She's so rotten.* I filled a pot of water, then carried it to the stove. I didn't care that it sloshed over the sides, soaking into my shoes and socks. *Crazy witch.* I paced the kitchen as I waited for the water to boil, and seethed over the thought of Mama's words, *a watched pot never boils.* When the bubbles finally appeared, I added spaghetti noodles, then went to the bathroom as they cooked.

Ugh! "Can someone *please* get me some toilet paper?" I asked.

"You know where to get it," Mama shouted.

"Forget it." I shook myself dry. "There's no way I'm stealing toilet paper!" *She's so stupid.*

"Yeah? We'll see about that."

She had a book in her hands as I walked back to the kitchen. Always reading. Another luxury reserved just for her. An escape that took her on journeys far from our reality. A pleasure I wasn't allowed. I just had to use my imagination if I wanted to escape. If I had time to read, surely there'd be something in the apartment more useful for me to do. I had to learn that the hard way. It didn't even matter if I had to read an assignment for school either. Not if there were chores to be done. And trust me, if Mama caught me just laying around reading, she'd always find a chore for me. That's okay, though. I didn't like reading, anyway. Music was my thing.

* * *

I didn't bother looking at anyone as they stuffed their faces with the meal I had just made, and nobody said a word with the mood Mama was in. Her mood always dictated how we acted at the supper table. At least we had music playing in the background. That's all I ever focused on, anyway. The twins brought their plates to the sink. Then, when Rachael got up to do the same, I quickly shoveled in my last bite so I wouldn't have to be alone with Mama.

"As soon as you get these dishes done, I want you to march over to the Fairmont and get those paper towels." She wasn't about to let up on that.

"No!" I stood up. "If you want 'em, *you* steal 'em! You're the one who taught us not to steal. Remember? Or did you forget about all those Xs on my face?"

"That was different. Quit using that word. You're not stealing. That hotel has so much money, it'll be like they're donating some of it to the poor. It's only pennies to them."

"Oh, my gosh! It's still stealing! What is wrong with you?"

"Well, either you get those towels, or you can sleep outside until you do. You're not staying here with us. The choice is yours."

"Fine! I'll sleep outside then!"

She pushed away from the table and pointed toward the door. "Get out! I'm sick of looking at—"

"That ugly face of yours!" I screamed as I bolted out of the kitchen.

I slammed the front door as hard as I could, then hoofed it down Powell toward the Fairmont. Turning up the big hill on Sacramento Street, I headed to the front of the hotel. The international flags flapped so hard above the entrance, I thought they might come undone and fly off like a runaway kite.

Through the windows, I saw the rich people in their nice clothes, talking and smiling as if they hadn't a care in the world. I wanted to sit on one of the red velvet couches and dream of a future like theirs, but I just couldn't bring myself to do it, even if it meant getting out of the cold. No way. Not then. Who was I kidding? I wasn't one of them. I was a street urchin, just as Mama always said. The girl from Powell and Clay whose mother wants her to steal. That's who I am. How could I ever step foot into that hotel again?

I kicked at the pavement as I walked to the park that separated the Fairmont from Grace Cathedral, then plopped myself on a bench. The cathedral looked beautiful with its large rose window coming to life, acting as a nightlight for the park. The church reminded me of some pictures Madame Thibault showed our French class of the Notre Dame Cathedral in Paris—only this one's not Catholic, it's Episcopalian. Like the hotel, I couldn't go in there to keep warm, either. The doors were always locked around that time.

I sat on a bench and wondered what Father Mike, the priest from NDV, would think if he knew Mama was trying to make a thief of me just so she could wipe her holy ass with paper towels from a rich hotel? What would he think of the nice lady who knelt in the front row of church each morning, clutching a rosary in her hands? The one who acts so righteous while praying for God's forgiveness? Would the priests still admire her for dragging her four ungrateful children to mass every Sunday if they knew this?

Goosebumps piled high on my arms, leaving me wishing I had been more careful with the pot of water so it didn't get my shoes and socks all wet. I don't know why it always got so chilly in San Francisco when the sun set. It was never like that in Florida. Even on the hottest days, once the fog rolled in over the bay, the temperature always dropped so cold.

I tried to think of all my possibilities. I couldn't go to Chinatown. It was way too late for that. That place scared the heck out of me once the tourists left for the night. Chinese gangs came out after dark, and even though they mostly fought amongst themselves, I wasn't about to take a chance on it, especially after the recent massacre at the Golden Dragon Restaurant.

The thought of walking to Union Square in the cold made me shiver even more, so I decided to head back home. Enough time had to have passed for Mama to be in a better mood by then, and sure enough, when I rang the doorbell, the bottom door buzzed to let me in the lobby.

"You got the toilet paper?" Mama asked through the door. She didn't even bother opening it to talk to me.

"No. I don't have your stupid toilet paper," I snapped.

"Well, you might as well make yourself comfortable out there, because you're not comin' back in until you have some."

Seriously? What a witch. I took a seat on the stairs. At least it was warmer than outside. I wished we lived on the top floor, because every single person who entered the building had to walk right past our place to get to thiers. Each time I heard the lobby door open, I pretended to be unlocking our door with a key. Some mumbled under their breath, but I was used to that by now. They were probably talking about me in Chinese. I don't think anyone in the building liked our family.

What am I gonna do? No way Mama's gonna budge.

I knocked on the door. When no one answered, I scanned the Fairmont in my mind, picturing its layout. *I'd have to use the downstairs bathroom.*

I knocked again. Still no answer. I could only imagine what Mama told Rache and the twins she'd do if they *touched that door.* I finally decided to go. I had to. I had no choice. Mama would never let me back in the apartment empty handed. I walked back to the Fairmont, this time going up California Street instead of Sacramento. I knew the hallways of the side entrance would be less traveled.

Once inside, I made a beeline to the women's restroom. My heart raced as I peeked under each stall. Voices from down the hall were getting closer by the second. I had to act quickly. I grabbed a stack of white paper towels from the counter and shoved them under my shirt. Just as I turned to leave, the door to the restroom swung open. I froze as three women walked in, chatting and laughing amongst themselves. They must have come from the Tonga Room around the corner.

My belly protruded as if an alien were trapped in it. I was caught red handed. The ladies quit talking as they walked past me toward the mirror. With my hands holding the bottom of my shirt, I ran out the door, then down the hall, looking over my shoulder to see if they were chasing me. I expected to see the ladies from the bathroom or a security guard or the hotel manager running after me, yelling, *Stop! Thief!* But no one was there.

I ran out the side door and didn't stop until I made it to the apartment. I needed to hunch over to catch my breath, but I couldn't. I didn't have time. The cops were probably on their way. My finger trembled as it hit the doorbell for apartment number two. *Maybe I should ring them all?* I couldn't stand still. The cops were sure to show up at any second. *Hurry! Before I get arrested! I'm gonna get caught!*

Just as I raised my finger to press all the doorbells, Rachael's voice came over the intercom. "Mama said you better have paper towels with you or you can't come in!"

"I have them!" I shouted. "Hurry!"

When the buzzer rang, I pushed through the door and ran up the stairs, skipping two and even three at a time. Everything I felt before, the fear, the embarrassment and shame, were now all swirled together in one fit of rage. I pushed past Rachael and rushed to Mama's bed. Propped with pillows, she had on her pink negligeé with a towel wrapped around her head like a turban. *How dare her relax in the tub while I almost got caught stealing for her.*

"Here's your stupid paper towels!"

I lifted the bottom of my shirt and let them fall to the ground. They didn't scatter as I had hoped. Instead, they landed in a single clump at my feet as if to mock me. *Ugh!* I kicked the pile, then kicked it again, flinging the paper all across the room.

"You little tramp! Pick those up this instant and put them on the back of the toilet. And they better be folded just as neatly as they were in that hotel, or you'll get it!"

"Get what? A pat on the back for stealing for you?"

"Stop, Teresa! Why do you wanna make her mad?" Jonas pleaded. He had just come out of the bathtub, still dripping wet.

"Shut up, Jonas!" I snapped, then turned back to Mom. "You wanna turn me into a thief? I can't believe how rotten you are!"

I got on my hands and knees to round up the paper towels, then brought them to the bathroom, and slammed them on the back of the toilet. *She can straighten 'em herself! I can't believe her!*

Without a single spot to hide, I stayed in the bathroom so I wouldn't have to see her face. The tub still had the scuzzy water from when she and the twins took their baths. Since we were in the middle of the worst drought in California's history, all five of us had to use the same bath water. It was so gross, but no one was sure if it would ever rain again. There were even signs posted on the walls of bathrooms that read, *If it's yellow let it mellow. If it's brown, flush it down.*

I didn't really want to get in, but it was my only choice. At least I could escape under the water. I got undressed, climbed in, plugged my nose, and submerged my head under the soap scum. *Mama's so mean to me!* I wished I could stay under forever and not have to come back up for air, but I was so angry I could barely even hold my breath for a few seconds. I came up, took a breath, then went back under. *How am I ever gonna step foot in the Fairmont again? She ruins everything!* The more I thought about the Fairmont, the angrier I got. I came back up for more air.

"Gosh, I hate Mom! She's such a crazy witch! Only somebody who's completely out of their mind would make their daughter steal like a thief!" I screamed. I couldn't help myself. It was true, anyway.

Something hit the floor in the other room—her book. Then pounding footsteps. *Oh no! I shouldn't have said that!*

Me, age 11, striking out in softball.

− 24 −

Thrown Out

*Even a happy life cannot be without a measure of darkness,
and the word happy would lose its meaning
if it were not balanced by sadness. — Carl Jung*

*P*ain would be better than giving Mama a peek at my naked body. She always tried to look. All the times she barged in while I was in the middle of taking a bath or using the toilet, she never even bothered to look away. Always so nosey. Like the time she made such a big deal in front of the whole world when we were at a swimming pool, "Look, she has hairs down there!" she shouted, pointing at the crotch of my bathing suit like a lunatic. I wanted to die, but all I could do was jump in the water and hold my breath for as long as I could.

Let her pull my hair. I don't care. I'm not going to let her see me. I scrunched into a ball with my arms around my legs to cover myself when the door flung open.

She had that crazed maniac look on her face as she charged toward me, a look that could scare anyone watching a horror film. If only she could get a glimpse of herself in the mirror when she acted like that, then she'd know how scary she looked—more like a monster than the lady with men ogling at her feet. *How ugly.* I wished they could see her now.

She reached in, grabbed two tight fistfuls of my hair, then yanked with all her might. I struggled to keep myself covered, but with another pull, she had half my body slung over the edge of the tub. Water splashed all over the place as I tried to grab anything I could get my hands on.

"Get out!" she screamed.

Another heave and she had me over the edge, causing my slippery body to flop onto the floor. I was her puppet now. With her fingers gripped around my hair, she was my master and had complete control. Wherever her hand went, my head and body followed. I managed to get my legs underneath me to stand, then I reached for the doorframe so she couldn't pull me out. Instead of the frame, my fingers slid against the lightswitch.

The warm, burning sensation of electricity jolted up my arm from my pinky finger all the way to my funny bone. My legs crumbled beneath me as if I were nothing but a glob of jelly. Mom tightened her grip as I went down, suspending me by the hair.

"I hate this place!" I screamed as I struggled to get my feet under me again. "Let go of me!"

My words added fuel to her fire, strength to her pull. She bit her lower lip and dragged me toward the front door.

"No!" I yelled. "Stop!"

With nothing to grasp, my hand slid along the slick wall of the hallway. A searing pain shot through my head as I dug my heels into the worn-out carpet, pulling with all my might against her force. I didn't care if she scalped me. I'd rather people think I had mange or leprosy than to have them see my nude body.

"Somebody help me! She's gonna throw me out naked again!" I yelled.

With her evil superpowers set in high gear, there was no stopping her. She had gone beyond the point of no return, and with each pull, the door inched closer and closer.

"Get out of this damn house! Right now, you little whore!"

She released a hand from my hair to reach for the doorknob, so I clawed at the other in an attempt to free myself. But she was way too strong for me. She opened the door and shoved so hard that I stumbled down the stairs. The walls vibrated as the door to our apartment slammed shut.

Click.

I ran up the stairs, grabbed the door handle, and frantically jiggled it back and forth. I was too late. She had locked me out. I pounded with both fists and kicked hard, hoping that at least if no one opened it, the door could come loose from its hinges. But no such luck.

"Let me in! Josh! Jonas! Rachael! Please! Somebody open the door for me! Please!"

"Shut up!" someone yelled from one of the other apartments.

You shut up!

Footsteps approached from the inside. Someone came to my rescue, to save me from the humiliation that was about to happen. I couldn't believe it. Somebody was finally brave enough to stand against Mom. *Ha ha!* The deadbolt turned. *Hallelujah!*

"Do - not - touch - that - door!" Mom said, and I could only imagine the look on her face—narrow slits for eyes, speaking through clenched jaws.

Before I could get my hand on the doorknob, the lock clicked back into position. *I'm so stupid! Why didn't I push through?*

"Open it. Please don't listen to her. Please!"

I didn't know who was on the other side, but as I heard them back away, my heart sank with each receding footstep. I guess I couldn't blame them. They'd be crazy to test Mom when she's that angry.

I had to get back in the apartment before any of the neighbors saw me. No matter what time it was, the building was always alive with tenants coming and going. And there wasn't a single place to hide. The lobby was just a large, empty waste of space. No pictures. No furniture. Nothing. I pounded on the door again, but not even the tiniest little shuffle came from inside.

My only hope was to get to the backyard. But how? I couldn't go on the street with my soaking wet, naked body. What if a cable car drove by and all the tourists saw me? And that stupid Chinese restaurant on the corner was probably jam-packed with people, all eating delicious, warm noodles and sweet and sour pork. I could see it now. They'd be holding their chopsticks, chatting about what a wonderful day they had as I zipped past them naked.

At the bottom of the narrow set of stairs, a large window opened onto the sidewalk. If anyone looked in from the street, they'd be able to see me. I had to get out of there. *I'm gonna be the laughingstock of the whole building.* I hunched over, covering as much of my body as possible with my arms and hands, then, like a crab, I hobbled sideways down the stairs. *I have to hurry.*

My heart pounded hard and fast as I reached for the doorknob. *Please, God. Don't let a cable car come. Please!* I took a deep breath, pulled the door open, and sprinted down the street. I passed in front of the Chinese restaurant—*Please, please, please, nobody look, nobody look at me*—went around the corner, then tore up the steep hill to the back of the building. I don't know who was out there, or who saw me naked. The only thing I could see was the blur of pavement in front of me.

I peeked through the gate that led to the backyard to make sure I was in the clear, then ran to the back door of our apartment. Luckily, we lived on a big hill, so even though we were on the second floor in the front of the building, around back we were ground level. Using the tip of my fingernail, I quietly tapped on one of the small glass window panes of the French door that led to mine and Rachael's bedroom.

"Please, Rachael let me in."

"No one better touch that door if you know what's good for you!" Mom said. "This'll teach her to talk to me like that."

"At least throw some clothes out to me, you crazy lady," I said in a loud whisper, careful for the neighbors not to hear. "It's freezing out here."

"I said no one touch that door!"

"I guess you want me to freeze to death, then. Or get raped." I thought the last one would get to her, for sure. The big R word. Something she always feared, especially when it came to her precious Queen Bee. But it didn't. She didn't budge.

I sat on the step that led to my room, squeezing my body tight to keep warm. The fog passed by faster than it had earlier, and each wet clump of hair felt like an icicle hanging from my head.

Even with the cold wind and the possibility of someone seeing me, all I could think about were the scary faces that lurked outside my door each night. The ones who watched me through the window panes as I tried to sleep. The ones in the same spot where I was now sitting. *They're gonna get me.*

"You have to let me in!" I said through chattering teeth. "You can't keep me out here all night." I lowered my voice. "Someone's gonna get me."

"Well, you should have thought about that before you mouthed off to me."

Gosh, I hate her!

"Rachael, please open the door. It's freezing." Something touched my back so I jerked my head around to see. It wasn't anything, though. Only the wind. "And it's so scary!"

It didn't matter how brave I was on the streets. As soon as I stepped foot into our apartment, I became scared as a mouse, or scared of my own shadow as Mom would say. She didn't even know how brave I really was, because this is all she ever saw of me, a petrified little girl, scared of the tiniest things. Everywhere— every room, every window, and under every piece of furniture, even the raised clawfoot bathtub—something was always there, lurking in the shadows, waiting to get me. An arm under the bed, a hand reaching up from the toilet, faces outside every single window of the apartment—all scarier than the scariest movies in the whole world were there to grab me and drag me away.

"I'm so scared," I whispered. "Please, Rachael."

The glowing blue light of Rachael's television filled our closet-sized room. I knew it was no use. She couldn't hear me. My body shivered from the cold, but felt hot at the same time, tensing and jerking with every sound. I didn't dare open my eyes. Not with the faces surrounding me. Ugly faces with long greasy hair, black eyes, and dirty, brown teeth. I'd probably see their whole bodies now that I was outside with them.

The wind swept my hair across my back. *They're grabbing me! Stop! Please! Please! Please! Please! God, please help me!* I tensed my muscles even tighter so their hands couldn't reach in to grab me, but my body convulsed from fear and coldness. *God! Please! They're not real! They're not real. I'm brave. Go away! You're not real. You're just my imagination.*

I pictured my body turning blue, then frozen solid with Mom kneeling next to me, crying. "How could I have done such a thing?"

Stop. Quit thinking that. The yard became darker as, one by one, lights shut off in each unit of the building. *God, please help me. In the name of the Father, and of the Son, and of the Holy Spirit, God, Please save me from the faces. Don't let me die!*

The warmth of my tears felt good as they slid down my cold cheeks. Their familiar salty taste on my lips gave me a strange sense of comfort.

Think of daylight. Think of the sun. The warm sun. Imagine a hot day. God, please help me.

I buried my head under my arms and thought of the summer trips we took in the camper—the times I'd be on the upper bed, too hot to move. I thought of the cracked earth in the Arizona desert, and the time all ten of our noses bled at a rest area from the hot, dry heat.

I imagined the sun shining down on me, so bright and warm, that I could actually feel the heat touching the back of

my head. I envisioned the icicles melting from my hair, causing warm water to drip down my shoulders and back. The
darkness under my eyelids turned yellowish-orange as the sun
worked its way along my body. One by one, I pictured the scary
faces exploding into little tiny pieces. Since they only came
out at night, sunshine had the power to make them go away.

As I imagined the yellow rays of sun wrapping around
me, swaddling me like a baby, my tense muscles softened. I
kept dreaming of the sunshine until I finally drifted to sleep.

A creak in the door caused my body to stiffen again. The invisible blanket of sunshine had disappeared like a cloud of smoke,
leaving me exposed and unprotected.

"Teresa," a whisper. "Here, take this."

I peeked through a small slit between my fingers, and saw
a large creature standing in front of me. I lost my breath,
couldn't breathe as my heart raced double-time. *No! No! No!*

"Don't tell Mama where you got this."

It was Rachael. She stood above me with a blanket spread between
her two arms. *Oh, thank you, God!*

"Sorry it took me so long. I tried waiting till Mom was sleeping
but ended up falling asleep myself."

She knelt down, covered the blanket over me, then tucked it in
around my body. Before I could register what was going on, she
disappeared back behind the closed door.

* * *

The morning light had already peeked through the clouds by
the time I woke up again. With the blanket wrapped around me,
I tapped on the window. A stirring noise came from inside, then
the sound of footsteps.

"Come in," Mom said, then pulled the door open a crack. "You've
been out there long enough."

She didn't notice the blanket, or if she did, she ignored it. 6:02

displayed on the panel of the clock radio. *Thank God, I still have time to sleep.* I put on some warm sweats, crawled onto my bed, and buried myself in stuffed animals.

Rod Stewart played in the background as I skipped through a meadow of wildflowers. Around my shoulders, a yellow blanket flapped in the wind like a cape. I was alone. Mom wasn't with me. No black skies. No lightning and thunder. Only the raspy sound of Rod Stewart singing that I'm in his heart, and in his soul.

"Ra... Jo... Little girl!" Mom shouted. "Can't you hear the alarm?"

You've gotta be kidding. It can't already be time to wake up!

"Little girl!"

"Unbelievable!" I snapped. "I can't even catch a break when I get stuck outside all night? Make somebody else cook breakfast this morning!"

"Don't start with me, little girl!"

"My name is NOT little girl! My name is Teresa!"

"I know what your name is. I'm not stupid. Now get in there and cook us some breakfast before I throw you outside again."

Rachael leaned her head down from the top bunk. "I'll make the breakfast," she whispered. "You can sleep longer. I'll make the lunches, too."

"Thanks, Rache!" I rolled over as she snuck through the closet passageway to the kitchen. When she came back in the room, the only sound in the apartment came from the clock radio, playing my favorite song, Electric Light Orchestra's "Turn to Stone." No matter what else was going on at the time, the rest of the world stopped when that song played.

That's what music did for me—my distraction from the chaos. Mom could scream her lungs out, right in front of my face, calling me all sorts of horrible names, but as long as the radio played in the background, I didn't hear a thing from her mouth. I knew every word to every song and sang along with each of them in my head to block out her hatefulness. I sang when I cooked and when I cleaned, when I cried and when I cowered. Music was my saving grace. The only time it didn't help was when I was scared. When fear took over, nothing could save me, not even ELO.

San Francisco Cable Car.

– 25 –

When One Door Closes

I can't go back to yesterday because
I was a different person then. — *Lewis Carroll*

*M*y body tensed as Ms. Blanchard approached my desk after speaking with the secretary at the door. *You've gotta be kidding me! Not again! Not today, please.* The thought of those two men with all their questions had haunted me ever since the last time they came. I had such a battle of conflicting emotions whenever I thought of them. Furious that they believed me about the cat scratches, but at the same time regret weighed on me almost every day. Whenever Mom hurt me, I'd beat myself up inside. *I should've told 'em. Why didn't I say anything? I'm so stupid!* But when she'd be nice, I'd think, *Thank God I didn't say anything.* A day didn't go by where there wasn't guilt and confusion gnawing at my stomach.

I scanned my body as I followed the secretary down the ramps to the first floor. All of Mom's recent attacks flashed through my mind. Her kicks and claws, the different objects she threw at me, all the times she ripped my hair out—*Was there anything for them to see? Did she leave a mark again?* My jaw still hurt to open wide after she threw a book at me a few days earlier, but I don't think it left a bruise.

What's gonna happen if they find something this time? Will they believe my stupid lies? At least I had my sweater on. I ran my fingers up and down the length of my arms under my sleeve to feel for any scab marks.

The secretary opened the door and stood aside for me, just as she had done the last time. Mr. Bergez sat at his desk writing something on his yellow notepad and didn't bother looking up. He was alone. No Lanky or Starsky. *What's this all about?*

"I have Teresa for you," she said.

"Thank you. Have a seat, Teresa." Mr. Bergez pointed to the chair across from his desk, then cleared his throat, and finished what he was writing before looking up at me. "Ahem. Teresa, I want to talk to you about repeating the 6th grade," he said.

"What?" That's not at all what I had expected. *What's he talkin' about? I'm flunking? There's no way! I know my grades suck, but I'm failing?*

"Your mother and I were talking and feel it's in your best interest to repeat the 6th grade again."

"What are you talkin' about? I'm flunking?" My voice came out louder than I would have wanted.

"Well, we... um... your mother asked that you repeat the 6th grade," he cleared his throat again. "With a November birthday, I agree with her. You're so much younger than everyone else in your class."

"So. You're gonna flunk me?"

"Well, you're technically not failing, but you're not excelling, either."

"What?" I asked again in disbelief. "You... she... y'all can't do that."

"Your mother and I spoke about it. She feels strongly about you staying back a year. You're going to be held back."

"No! Please don't make me. Please, Mr. Bergez!" I tilted my head to the side and folded my hands in prayer as I begged.

"I'm sorry, Teresa. It's already done," he twirled his fountain pen between his fingers. "I just wanted to let you know. Sorry. You can go back to class now."

"Those men would have been better than this."

I stormed out and slammed the door behind me. I didn't care. What was he going to do, flunk me? *Sorry nothing! He doesn't know anything. I'm gonna be the laughing stock of the whole school now.*

I kicked my feet hard into the ramp with each step I took toward the classroom. *What am I gonna say now when everybody asks what he wanted with me? I'm sick of always having to lie about everything. I just wanna run away. I hate school! I hate everything!*

I passed my room on the second floor... *There's no way I'm going back in there...* then continued up the ramps to the third floor, walked to the end of the hall, and went out a door that led to the roof. I sat on the black tarred surface and buried my face into my thighs.

As if these kids need something else to make fun of me for. I can't believe Mr. Bergez. I thought he was on my side!

The wind pushed the door shut with a loud bang. *Crap!* Within seconds, and I mean seconds, it re-opened.

"Teresa. Get off the roof and get back to your classroom. Now!" Sister Geraldine stood in the doorway. *What's she doing on the third floor? Crap! Stupid wind.*

As I went through the door, she grabbed the back flap of my uniform top and pushed me forward in front of her. "I should write you up, you know."

She escorted me all the way back to my class without saying another word. I didn't care if she wrote me up, or not. Let her. Nothing could be as bad as failing.

Everyone was busy working when I slipped back to my desk. The same paper waited me for me as well, but I couldn't think about a stupid worksheet. *Why should I anyway? What's the point? I already flunked.*

I didn't bother picking up my pen. I just watched my classmates as they worked. *Only one more week with them. None of these kids are really my friends, anyway.* I rested my forehead on my hand.

Maybe I could just go to a new school and start all over. There's no way I wanna come back here next year.

* * *

Everyone sat quietly as I slopped lasagne flavored Hamburger Helper onto their plates that night. They knew something was bothering me, but there was no way I wanted Rache and the twins to know I failed. *They'll think I'm stupid. I'm just never going back to school again, that's all.*

"This is the quietest I've ever heard y'all," Mama said. "Why isn't anyone saying anything?"

Jonas looked at me for an answer, but I just stared at my plate.

"Seriously, what's going on?" she asked.

Don't say a word. Just listen to the music. I strained my ears to hear the radio, but Mom's stupid lip-smacking polluted the air. *Ugh! That noise makes me sick!*

"Stop smacking," I snapped.

The noise didn't stop.

"How could you do this to me?" I shouted. *Stop!*

"Do what?"

"You know exactly what I'm talking about!" *As if she doesn't know. What a liar.*

"Well, if I knew, I wouldn't ask now, would I?"

"How can you hold me back in the sixth grade?"

My fork trembled in my hand as Rachael let out a gasp. I could only imagine what she was thinking. *'Haha, Miss smarty pants! You have to repeat the 6th grade, too!'* She didn't say a word, though.

"I didn't hold you back!" Mom argued. "Mr. Bergez did!"

"That's a lie! Mr. Bergez said that you were the one who wanted me to."

"Well, don't you think it would be better for you?"

"Are you kidding me? How could that possibly be any better for me?"

"Maybe you'll make some new friends. You could be with kids your own age now," she said. "I should've started you in kindergarten when you were five, not four."

"Since when do you care if I have friends, or not?" I asked as I pushed from the table. I wanted to run out, but didn't have anywhere to go. "If I have to stay in the 6th grade, I'm not going back to NDV!"

"Don't be ridiculous! Of course, you're going back to NDV. It's the best school in the city. You don't even know how lucky you are to go there."

"Not when I'm repeating the same grade again."

I couldn't eat my dinner. I stormed from the kitchen, went to my room and threw myself on my bed. *My life is ruined now.* Thank God I had Georgie, an old Scotty dog, with more grey fur than black, who I found wandering the streets a few weeks earlier. He jumped on the bed next to me, so I pulled him close and wrapped him in my arms.

"Can you believe her, Georgie?"

He had become my best friend in the whole world. I couldn't believe Mama let me keep him. She said as long as I found a way to feed him, he could stay, but she wasn't about to spend any of her money on him. I didn't think it would be a problem since I did all the grocery shopping. I could just sneak him some food, and she'd never know. It didn't work like that, though. The cashier said I couldn't use food stamps for dog food.

Luckily, the Chinese restaurant on the corner put scraps out by the trash can each night, so that's what Georgie ate—fried rice. At first I thought he was lucky to have fried rice instead of dog food, but as the weeks went on, I started feeling really sorry for him.

Footsteps approached my room. I didn't care who it was. I just wanted to be alone. I jumped out of bed and grabbed onto the doorknob so no one could open it.

"Let me in!" Rachael said.

"Go away!"

"Let me in! It's my room, too!"

I held on as tight as I could, pulling toward me as she pulled from the other side in a game of tug of war.

"Mom! Teresa won't let me in the room!"

"Open that door and quit feelin' sorry for yourself!" Mama said in an irritated voice.

I let go and sent Rachael tumbling backwards.

"You little brat!" she said. She got up and kicked me on the shin as she passed. "You know she holds us all back, don't you? What makes you think you'd be any different?"

"What?"

"I said, she holds us all back. She held me back in the third *and* sixth grade. And why do you think she made the twins go to kindergarten twice?"

"What do you mean? I thought you flunked."

"No, I didn't flunk. She told me she's scared we're growing up too fast, and that once we graduate from school, we'll all be gone, and she'll be all alone. Don't you know her biggest fear is to be all by herself?"

"Yeah. But it's not only that. She won't have her slaves around to work for her anymore, either," I said.

"Yeah, that, too."

NDV school picture of me, age 12, with my
new gold chain.

– 26 –

Good In the World

Only a life lived for others is a life worthwhile.
— Albert Einstein

The tourists looked on as I climbed onto the platform of the cable car.

"Hey, cutie pie!" Pete said.

"Hi, Pete!"

I don't know why, but it always made me feel important whenever a cable car gripman acknowledged me in front of all of the tourists. Especially when it was Pete. With his teasing smile and flirtatious ways, he'd keep the lady passengers enchanted the entire ride. He kept everyone laughing and smiling all the way from Market Street to Fisherman's Wharf.

I stood next to the row of seats on the outside as Pete pulled the long lever of the cable car's grip handle. Once its jaws grabbed onto the cable beneath the tracks, we slowly began making our way up the big hill. Pete pulled again, this time harder, using his whole body to bring the car to its maximum speed of -1/2 miles per hour.

"I got something for ya," he turned to me and winked.

I smiled. I knew what he had. He kept a five gallon bucket of roses by his feet. He'd hand one to all the pretty ladies to make them blush, and sometimes I'd get one, too. I could go onto his car blindfolded and know it was his just by the scent alone. The sweet fragrance of flowers, mixed with the pungent aroma of cable car grease and over-heated wooden brakes was a smell that could only be found on Pete's cable car in San Francisco.

This was my day to shine. The tourists were going to look at me and wonder, "Who is this girl? She must be really special for our charming cable car driver to give her a rose."

As we made our way up the hill, I wondered which color he'd pull out for me. Red? Pink? Yellow? Orange? I hoped he would pick an orange one. Those were my favorite.

At the top of the hill, he stepped on the big brake pedal, then squatted down to get something by his feet. His hand swept right past the five gallon bucket of roses as he reached further under the bench. The tourists were already engrossed in his every action, so they all watched as he came up holding a rectangular box.

What the heck?

"Here you go, Teresa."

Everyone stared as I clung to the package. I wished they'd look away.

"Go ahead, open it!" Pete said with a big smile.

I slowly pulled off the lid, keeping my gaze down to ignore the gawking eyes. Nestled under white tissue paper were a pair of blue tennis shoes with three white stripes on the sides. I didn't pull them out like I would have wanted to. I just stared as my heart thumped in my chest.

"I hope you like 'em. I'm pretty sure they're your size," Pete said.

The crowd cheered. *Why are they clapping?* I didn't know what to do. My eyes filled with tears. I'm not sure why. Tears of joy, for sure, and tears that came from his kindness, but there were also tears of embarrassment and tears of shame and humiliation. I couldn't look up. Now those people knew I wasn't anybody special. I wasn't so important that the cable car gripman knew me by name. I was just a poor girl from the neighborhood.

"Thank you," I managed to mumble while self consciously covering a hole in my shoe with my other foot.

When the cable car began rolling up the next street, I jumped off. I didn't know what else to do. As I watched it continue up the hill, I felt bad for worrying what the stupid tourists thought.

How dumb! I shouldn't have jumped. It's not like I'd ever see any of those people again. I can't believe I acted like that. I'm so stupid. Poor Pete. He's so nice. He probably thinks I don't even like the shoes now.

I squeezed the box close to my chest as I made my way home. I couldn't wait to pull them out to get a better look. They weren't the fancy leather Nike shoes like the other kids wore, and they weren't the Tretorns I'd always dreamt of having after seeing Billy Joel wearing them on the cover of *52nd Street*. I loved that album. Ever since I got eleven records for a penny from Columbia House, I played it all the time.

Even though they weren't the fancy ones, they were still the very first pair of brand new shoes I'd ever had in my whole entire life. The tops weren't scuffed, there weren't any holes in the canvas, and the white rubber sole had never even touched the pavement before.

When I got to the apartment, Georgie was the first to greet me. He jumped up and down on his hind legs with his front paws tapping my thighs. I peeked in the room to see Mama's mood, but only the twins were there.

"Come on Georgie," I said. "Jonas, Josh, come here. I wanna show y'all somethin'."

Jonas, wearing a towel draped over his shoulders to mimic a priest's vestment, held up a bowl with both hands, filled with smashed, round pieces of bread. I knew the game well. They loved to play church and switched off who got to be the priest each time.

Jonas ignored me and continued reciting the Liturgy of the Eucharist, well, as best as a first-grader could.

Josh rang the bell as Jonas held the bread in the air. "Just a minute," he said. "I want my Communion first."

"The body of Christ," Jonas held up a piece of bread.

"Amen." Josh closed his eyes and stuck out his tongue for Jonas to place the pretend wafer on.

It was a funny game they played. Ever since I became an altar girl at NDV, they couldn't wait to be one too, especially since they recently received their First Holy Communion. I wasn't sure if pretending to be a priest was sacrilege or not, but Mama never minded them doing it, so I guess it was okay.

"Hurry," I said. "Sheesh." I couldn't wait anymore. "Look what Pete got me! Can you believe it?" I tore open the box, grabbed the shoes by their laces and dangled them in the air for them to see. "I have a new pair of tennis shoes!"

"What? Pete gave you those? Lucky!" Jonas said.

"Why do people always give *you* things?" Josh asked.

Huh?

"Nobody gives me anything," I said, then placed my hand on the necklace around my neck. "Oh, yeah." My heart felt full as I held on to a shiny gold chain that a lady at the Hyatt Regency had given me.

The Hyatt Regency hotel had become our Friday night ritual. It wasn't only me who went, either; we all went as a family. Each week, the twins and I would position ourselves at the top of the enormous hill at the intersection of Powell and California Streets, then we'd sit on our skateboards and race all the way down to the Embarcadero. At the bottom of each hill, we'd put our feet out, the way Fred Flintstone did in his car, and use our heels to stop. That's probably the reason our shoes always had holes in them.

We went to the Hyatt for their weekly Tea Dance. Well, Mama did. She loved to dance and loved to show me off whenever the Charleston played. I learned that dance from a class I took at the rec center, and ever since I performed it onstage at Stern Grove, Mama would drag me out to dance with her. She loved to show us off whenever she got the chance. Luckily for me, a boy named Dallas was usually there with his dad, so I'd escape with him while Mama swayed and twirled to the big band music.

Rachael usually stayed near Mama, hanging out by the dance floor. She didn't wander around like me and the twins. At sixteen, she was becoming more beautiful by the day. Mama said Rachael reminded her of herself at that age, only she said Rache was even prettier with her wavy brown hair and slender body. Mama wasn't the only one who thought that, either. The old men at the Hyatt also adored Rachael. They'd flirt with her and ask her to dance. I think it made Mama proud, as if they were flirting with her instead. That's the way she worked. Any compliment to us, she took as a direct reflection on herself.

The men bought Rachael all kinds of fancy drinks, too. It didn't even matter that she was underage. They came with tequila sunrises, piña coladas, and strawberry daiquiris, which was great for Mama too, because most of the time, they brought one for her, as well.

Rache wasn't the only one spoiled at that hotel; the twins were also. They'd take the glass elevators to the top floor, then go to the bar at Equinox Room to get a stick of sugar candy from the bartender. He'd give them candy and skewers piled with fresh fruit—pineapple triangles, orange slices and Maraschino cherries. I guess it was because they were so cute, especially when Mama dressed them in matching outfits. They didn't look anything like twins, though. Jonas was at least a whole head taller than Josh by then, and Josh had a little more plumpness to his body. Rache said that's one of the reasons why Mama didn't like Josh, because he ate all of Jonas' food when they were in her belly together. Either way, even if Jonas had been the chunkier one, Mama wouldn't have liked Josh, anyway, since he looked like Daddy.

One Friday, I waited for Dallas and his father to arrive, but they never showed up. The twins were already off on their own, and the Charleston was bound to play at some point, so I had to get the heck out of there before Mama grabbed me to dance with her. I made my way to a set of stairs that led to the outside plaza and figured I could sneak some coins from the Quebec Libre Fountain before it got too dark.

I straddled the handrail at the top of the steps, then slid to the bottom. I shot down so fast, it felt like I was on a rocket, so I did it over and over again after that. Each time I landed on the ground floor, a lady who worked there smiled and said hi to me.

"Hi!" I'd say, then run back up to slide down another time.

I never did make it out to the fountain. I was having way too much fun riding the banister. I expected the lady working there to be mean and to make me quit playing on the railing after a while, but she didn't.

Instead, she greeted me with a smile and hello each time I passed her. She had a beautiful smile that lit up her face, and there must have been at least seven gold chains around her neck, all different lengths and types—rope chains, S chains, some with pendants, some without. Against her dark skin, they shined as bright as the setting sun, glimmering on the fountain outside. I wondered who bought them for her. A boyfriend? Or was she just rich like the kids at my school?

"Hi again! I love your necklaces," I said when I swished to the bottom for the sixth time.

"Thank you!" she said as I ran back up.

With one push at the top, I zipped down again, trying to make each descent faster than the one before.

"Hi again!"

"Here, I want you to have one of these," the lady said. She reached behind her neck to unclasp one of the gold chains. "Turn around. I'll put it on for you."

"Are you serious?" *What in the world?*

"Yes. Really. I'd like for you to have one."

I couldn't believe it. She didn't even know me and she was offering me one of her necklaces. I turned around so she could clasp it around my neck. "Oh, my gosh. Thank you!"

I ran up the steps, skipping two at a time, but didn't stop at the top to slide down again. Instead, I continued running all the way to the bathroom to have a look in the mirror. *It's so beautiful. I look rich like the other kids now.*

* * *

When I got home that night, I could barely sleep. I kept taking off the necklace to hold in my hands, then I'd put it back on and look in the mirror. I thought about the nice lady and couldn't get over the fact that she gave it to me. *Gees, she didn't even know me. How can somebody be so nice like that?* I felt bad for taking off the way I did, but after running to the bathroom, I got too scared and ashamed to go back.

Now I did the same exact thing to Pete. *How stupid I am. People must think I'm so rude. I don't know why I always run when somebody gives something to me.*

Me, Jon Eric and the twins.

– 27 –

Another Door Opens

In the middle of difficulty lies opportunity.
— Albert Einstein

I always looked forward to summer, so, of course, I joined the daily chanting on the schoolyard as the last day of sixth grade approached: "*No more pencils, no more books, no more teacher's dirty looks.*" I lived for summer vacations. No more getting in trouble for missing homework, no more trying to be goofy so kids would like me, and no more Trey.

He was a new guy at the beginning of that year who had transferred from another school. When he first came to NDV, he liked me. Not like–like, but he liked me as a friend. Maybe because I wore that beautiful gold necklace. Who knows? Well, necklace or no necklace, that friendship ended the second he found out that not only was I not one of the *cool* kids, but I happened to be the poor kid with the crazy mother.

Once he found that out, he had to make up for his mistake by making my life miserable. And that's exactly what he did.

He'd walk by me and say my name, "Teressssssssssssa," exaggerating the S like a hissing snake. Then, he'd call me "shrimp" and other stupid names to try to get my classmates to laugh. They didn't though, so I don't know why he kept doing it.

The worst was when he made fun of Mama, teasing about the way she dressed and all. That's the worst anyone could do, and boy did it ever get to me. I know. It's kind of strange since I honestly couldn't stand Mama myself, but I hated it when anyone else said anything bad about her. I could have laughed along with him or felt relieved that someone saw her as I did, or even been embarrassed that I had such a mother, but those were never the reactions I had.

Instead, I felt the need to protect her, and I started feeling sorry for her, too. I knew she was crazy, but I also saw the young, innocent girl trapped inside her, tormented and cowering from her alcoholic father and malicious mother. I knew that scared little girl stayed alongside the monster, still searching for someone to love her. So when anyone said bad things about her, I got angry, but I also felt sad and guilty. Guilty at how mean I had become to her, and even more guilty that I couldn't love her myself.

Being away from Trey wasn't the only reason I looked forward to summer. I also couldn't wait to see the rest of my family again. On the last day of school, I made a practice round of meatloaf with the words "Welcome" written on top with ketchup. It's the meal I had planned for the following week when the rest of the kids came, so I wanted it to be perfect for that big night. I danced around the kitchen with the pan of meatloaf in my hands before setting it on the table.

I couldn't wait to test it out on Mama, Rache, and the twins, especially Mama. She loved it when we were creative, and this was going to be my time to shine. My insides tingled with excitement when I called them to supper. Not only did I write on the meatloaf, but they were going to get a big surprise when they bit into it since I added bell peppers and onions.

I expected Mama to be the first to notice, but she didn't say a word when she came into the kitchen. Not that she was in one of her moods or anything. Believe me, I could feel those from a mile away. For one, her footsteps didn't sound like a stampede of elephants. I barely even heard her when she walked into the room. She also didn't mumble anything under her breath the way she often did when she was mad. She just sat at the table with her head hung low, looking very sad.

"Look at the meatloaf I made, Mama!" I said proudly. "See how I wrote 'welcome' on it?" I pointed to the red cursive writing with a butter knife. "It's kind of hard to see right now, but when the kids come next week, I'm gonna add more ketchup so it'll show up better."

"That's nice, sweetie," she said in a flat voice. "But all the kids aren't comin' this summer." Her eyes misted with tears.

"Huh?" The piece of hamburger meat I kept hidden in my hand for Georgie dropped to the floor.

"What?" Josh asked.

"I guess they just don't wanna come anymore." Mama's voice cracked as she stared at her plate.

Her pain and sadness could be felt all the way to my side of the table. I drew in a breath to say something, but no words came out. What could I possibly say to make either one of us feel any better?

I served up the meatloaf, corn, and rice, but didn't even want to eat anymore. How could I with a huge lump in my stomach? I picked up Georgie and held him close to my chest. He wasn't allowed at the table, but I didn't care. His soft fur absorbed my tears as they began to pour. The weird thing is that they weren't just tears for me. They were for Mama, too. She lived for summers just about as much as I did and always tried her best to show us everything she could on our vacations.

She said she wanted our lives to be different from the one she had as a kid. I just wished she could see how cruel she was though. It's not only because of the monster trapped inside of her, either. If it was, then she'd be hateful to everyone, not just me and Josh. That came from somewhere else completely different. Somewhere dark and evil.

But she also did good things. That's why it was hard for me to always hate her. She'd go garage-saling and shower us with toys. And she made a huge deal out of every single holiday, even the simplest ones like April Fool's Day. During those special times, I wasn't isolated from anyone. She showered me just the same as everyone else.

She showed us the beauty of the United States during our summer vacations and taught us to love the outdoors. Everything was always a comparison to how she lived as a child. "Go outside," she'd say, "instead of being crammed in this tiny space like I had to be when I was a kid. Look at all these toys y'all have. I had nothin' growin' up. You don't know how lucky you are to go to all these national parks. I didn't get to go anywhere."

She did her best to provide us with everything she never had. She brought color into our lives—and music. We went to festivals and dances and were allowed to play on our own and explore. She gave to the poor to teach us that there were others who had it worse than we did.

I've always said, "I'm never gonna be like her when I grow up. Never! And I'm never going to be poor and homeless either. Never! I'll work my butt off to ensure that."

What I said wasn't completely true. I'm never going to be homeless or mean like her, that's for sure, but I *would* be like her in other ways.

"Jon Eric's comin'," Mama finally mumbled.

In a flash, those words lightened the weight on my chest, allowing me to breathe freely again.

"Your crumb of a father said he's not payin' for Jon Eric's bus ticket both ways, so he can only come if I buy his ticket back home."

"What did you say? You're going to, right?" I asked.

"What a louse. He's swimmin' in money and can't even buy his own daughter a coat when she's freezin' to death out here."

And just like that, Mama switched back to her old self. The coat was for me, and I know she mentioned it because I often said I wanted to live with Daddy. She wrote him a few letters asking if he could send money for a jacket since mine was too small and worn out, but anything coming from her was personal. It was always about them. Never us. And even though they had been apart for four years, their hatred toward each other only grew stronger by the day.

* * *

Turns out, I didn't get singled out too much that summer even with the absence of everyone else. Rache and I were granted a free pass to go to a Girl Scout camp, called Camp Bothin, which was the funnest place ever. We both chose the horseback riding session, which meant sleeping outdoors, singing campfire songs, making S'Mores, and wearing old worn-out clothes. Yep, worn-out clothes. That's what we were asked to wear, and we fit in just like everyone else.

By the time we got home, Jon Eric was already there, and he and Mama had the camper loaded and ready for our next adventure. First, we went to Yosemite with a club she joined a few years earlier called Parents Without Partners, or PWP.

Then we went to a few other parks south of Yosemite: King's Canyon, Sequoia, and Mammoth, before camping with another group called the Folk Song Club. Mama had so much fun dancing and flirting that summer that I was able to stay under the radar the whole time.

I loved it when we did things with those clubs, because Mama rarely acted out in front of them. The people in the Folk Song Club were mostly the hippy type, and everyone was super friendly to us. The kids had holes in the knees of their pants, unbrushed hair, and ran around barefooted just like me. In front of them, I could always be myself.

When we got home from the third camping trip, it was already time for Jon Eric to make the long journey back to Florida. Unlike me, he couldn't contain his excitement. He was about to start high school—the last of the Florida gang to leave San Jose Catholic.

"You need to ask your father to buy you a ticket home," Mama said to him.

"What? No! Dad told me you were paying for my ticket," Jon Eric said.

"Well, if he wants you back, he's gonna get the ticket. Otherwise, you stay here with us. We'll figure out a way to get you home next summer."

Jon Eric pleaded with Daddy, but Daddy wasn't about to give in. No way. He and Mama had a deal, and he wasn't about to break it.

The fighting continued between them, so Jon Eric started his first year of high school in San Francisco.

* * *

You'd think it would be the best thing ever to have Jon Eric in our lives, but I'm not going to lie, it wasn't easy. With our tiny studio apartment, Jon Eric couldn't find a single comfortable place to sleep. He couldn't even fit on the floor in mine and Rache's room without the door hitting him each time we opened it. So he ended up on the floor in the main room, in a sleeping bag, next to the pull-out trundle where the twins slept below Mama's bed.

Day after day, Jon Eric cried into the phone, begging Daddy to get him a ticket back home. But Daddy wouldn't budge, and after the second week, he finally quit accepting Jon Eric's collect calls.

The weird thing about Jon Eric was that he never really had it bad with Mama. It's not like he was one of her favorites or anything. Same with Gregory. Maybe being right in the middle of the pack kept them hidden? I don't know. All I know is that those two were practically invisible to her.

At least that's how it used to be. Not anymore. Jon Eric now shared my spotlight as a constant reminder of Daddy's hatefulness and stubbornness—a piece of Florida Trash who reminded Mama of the stepmother whore who stole her house in Florida. To her, he was just another hungry, ungrateful mouth to feed.

* * *

On the first day of school, I woke up with a gnawing pain in my stomach. You'd think I'd be excited like everyone else, but I barely even slept a wink. How could I possibly go to school when I'm sure to be the laughing stock of NDV. I wished Mama had held Jon Eric back, too, so he could come with me.

From Mom's room, the clock radio blared out music from the Bee Gees. Normally, I would have been happy waking up to them, but "How Deep is Your Love" didn't do anything for me that morning. I felt sick.

"Little girl, can't you hear the damn alarm? It's time to get up! You don't wanna be late on your first day of school."

Late? That's exactly what I want. She didn't even care how I felt. At least if I showed up late, no one would see me lining up with the sixth graders again.

"I'm not feeling so great," I mumbled. "I think I'm sick!"

"Well, get up and make breakfast and see how you feel after you get somethin' in your stomach."

"Well, get up and make breakfast!" I mocked under my breath.

Of course, she wouldn't let me miss a day. She took pride in our perfect attendance record each year. It showed that her children were strong and healthy, not sickly like some of the other kids. I snailed my way into the kitchen, then cracked eggs into the pan while the scene of the schoolyard flashed through my mind—the same scenario that haunted me over and over again throughout the summer. The more I thought of it, the more my belly burned on fire.

First, my old classmates would notice me standing in the sixth-grade line next to them. They'd surround me, pointing and laughing, and like a wave at a football game, the roaring would spread until every single kid on the schoolyard joined in, even the twins. They'd spin around me chanting "Coming from slum, Teresa is dumb!" They'd spin so fast that I'd feel dizzy and nauseous. That stupid chant had been stuck in my head all summer. I couldn't believe I made it up.

Once I served breakfast, I didn't look at Rache, Jon Eric and the twins while they talked about their new school year, who their teacher was going to be and what classes Rachael and Jon Eric signed up for. Blah, blah, blah. Hot rocks were burning a hole in my intestines. I moved the eggs from one side of the plate to the other with my fork, then pushed the whole dish aside to lay my head on the table.

"Aren't you gonna eat, Teresa?" Josh asked.

"You better. You need that nutrition to stay healthy," Mama said. She took a bite of her eggs, then tilted her head to the side. "This isn't about repeating the sixth grade, is it? You know you're gonna have to show up to school sometime, so it might as well be today. Trust me, tomorrow will only be harder."

"I really am sick," I mumbled.

"It's probably just nerves. If you start throwing up, then you can come back home."

* * *

I walked as slow as I could all the way to school, but of all days, I managed to get there on time. I don't know how in the heck that happened, maybe God was playing some sort of sick joke on me or something? Time would usually bend for me in the mornings, like one of those hard, colorful ribbon candies old people kept in a dish. Up and down, climbing and sliding, impossible to make it anywhere in a timely fashion. Not now, though. It was a straight shot, and it made me want to scream.

The twins ran ahead to find their second-grade line, but hoping the bell would ring before I made it down, I hesitated at the top of the ramp. *Everybody's gonna make fun of me. Please, dear God, I don't want them to see me.*

My nose ran like a faucet and wiping it on my uniform tie only left a long wet smear. I thought of a riddle Jonas once told me, "How is it that your feet smell and your nose runs?" He always made me chuckle with his stupid jokes, but no way I could laugh now.

The first bell had rung by the time I made it to the bottom of the ramp, and the students were already standing in neat rows of single-file lines: kindergarteners nearest the building, all the way to the eighth-graders at the far side of the schoolyard. Two separate lines formed for each grade, one for boys and the other for girls, and mine had to be at least a mile away.

My ears burned as I trudged across the yard. I didn't look up. I couldn't. Why would I want to see anyone pointing and laughing at me? I planned on humming the song, "Mr. Blue Sky" as I walked in order to block their laughter, but I couldn't even think of the darn tune.

I kept my eyes on the brand new pair of tennis shoes Pete had given me. I would have never been able to wear those to school before, but the dress code had relaxed a little, and no one wore saddle shoes anymore. I had taken those shoes out of the box so many times to admire them, and couldn't wait to wear them, but now they felt like lead on my feet, anchoring me down, slowing me so the next bell would ring before I made it to my new classmates.

I thought of many different scenarios for that morning. I could line up with the seventh graders, then switch at the last second when Ms. Blanchard came, but that probably would have made it worse. At least the new sixth graders didn't know me. They never had recess or lunch with our class, since they were still with the lower classmen last year.

I walked between the fourth and fifth-grade lines to approach my row from the back as the second bell rang. All the students were talking amongst themselves, excited to be back at school, but I didn't hear anything else. Definitely no chanting.

No one in the other lines pointed or laughed, either. They were so elated to be back with their friends, they didn't even notice me. I guess I had practiced all those scenarios in my mind for nothing. What would I have done anyway? Would I have run off, crying like a baby, out the front door all the way to Union Square? Or, would I have been strong enough to hold out the sides of my skirt and curtsy the way we had to when we received our report cards. *"Merci beaucoup, mon Pére,"* we'd have to say as Father Faringo handed us each a slip of paper.

The seventh-grade teacher arrived before Ms. Blanchard, and my old classmates followed behind her like little ducklings. Those kids were okay. I hung out with a few of them once Trez left. They just never invited me to their houses or birthday parties or anything.

"Hey, shrimp fry. Whatcha doin' in that line?" All the color drained from my face as Trey turned toward me and pointed. I hated him.

No one paid attention, because just as his words were coming out, a woman with black wavy hair appeared at the front of our line. My heart raced even faster. *Please don't say anything, Ms. Blanchard. Please.*

"Good Morning, everyone. I'm Ms. Blanchard."

She smiled and tucked a strand of hair behind her ear. I followed along as she led us up the ramps to our classroom, wondering if she even knew I was going to be in her class again.

"I put your name on a desk. Once you find your seat, put everything away except for a pen." She stood at the door, smiling and nodding at each student as we filed in. *Shoot. I don't want her to see me.* I lowered my head and felt a gentle pat on my back as I walked by.

"We have two new students in the class this year," she said once we had settled into our assigned seats. "Will Teresa Thompson and Adrienne Pointeau please stand up?"

Great. She's about to tell everyone I flunked. I grasped the side of my desk with my clammy hands and slowly stood up. Queasiness inched its way from my stomach to my throat.

Ms. Blanchard, please don't tell them. Ugh! Please don't throw up.

"Take some time at recess to introduce yourselves to them," she continued. "You guys can sit back down now."

I couldn't believe it! She said I was a new student. That's all! Nothing else. I sunk in my chair and let out a long, heavy, but quiet sigh. The knots in my stomach began to unravel one thread at a time. *Thank you, Ms. Blanchard. Thank you, God!*

At recess, I didn't have to deal with the awkwardness of

who I'd walk on the ramps with since Ms. Blanchard lined us up in alphabetical order to go down in a single file line.

As the class dispersed, I took a seat on one of the long benches that lined the schoolyard, knowing the worst was yet to come. I wanted to be invisible to the seventh-graders, especially Trey.

The other new girl from my class headed in my direction. She was a lot taller than me, but, of course she was. Everybody was. That's why Trey called me shrimp fry. She wore a fuzzy, bright pink sweater that wasn't part of the uniform code, but she'd probably get away with it since it was the first day of school and all. She walked over and sat down next to me.

"Hi," she said. Her eyes sparkled when she smiled.

"Hi." I looked down at my hands folded on my lap.

"I'm glad I'm not the only new kid this year," she said. "I thought everyone would have been here since kindergarten."

"Yeah!" *Please don't ask where I went to school last year.*

"What do you like better, cats or dogs?" she asked with a nervous giggle. She bit on her lower lip, the same way I do when I'm nervous. I looked up at her.

"Cats! Definitely cats!" Another girl answered as she approached us. "Hey, my name is Teresa, too. H or no H?" She bent down to shake my hand, causing her black, shoulder-length hair to fall forward, covering part of her face.

"No H," I said. It was a Teresa thing, and every Teresa in the world knew what that meant.

"I like cats better, too!" Adrienne said. "How 'bout you, Teresa?"

"Uh, yeah, I like cats, but I really like all animals." I curled my toes in my shoes as soon as the words came out. *Shoot, why did I say that? I should've just said I liked cats.*

"That's great! We'll all be good friends, then," Teresa said. "By the way, I don't have an H either!"

Huh? Friends? This was supposed to be the worst day of my life.

Okay, Don't get too excited. As soon as they find out who I really am, they won't wanna be my friends anymore.

"Teresa?" Teresa asked.

"Yeah?"

"I was just asking if you like that song, *Come Sail Away?*"

"Huh? Yeah, the one by Styx? I love that song!" *Cool, she likes music, too!*

* * *

As the weeks went on, Teresa and Adrienne became my two best friends. The rest of my classmates were okay, too—definitely a lot friendlier than the kids in my other class. Maybe because they didn't know Mama. Her job as a teacher's aid pretty much kept her away from NDV. And as much as I'd hate to admit it, Mama was right. Holding me back a year wasn't such a bad thing after all.

Confirmation at NDV, 1981. I'm on the left, age 14, Deborah and
Rachael are on the right.

– 28 –

Supper at the Thompson's

You are the master of your destiny.
You can influence, direct, and control your own environment.
You can make your life what you want it to be.
— *Napoleon Hill*

*J*on Eric didn't even last till Christmas before Mama kicked him to the curb. Well, not exactly the curb. Her friend Billy let him stay at his place—a small trailer tucked inside the city dump in South San Francisco. As a freshman in a new city, Jon Eric had to learn his way around the bus system, just as I had in the third grade, only his commute to school took almost a full hour each way.

* * *

I grabbed the leash and headed to the front door. "Go for a walk, Georgie?" Georgie lept from under the covers and ran to me with her tail wagging so hard, it shook the back of her body right along with it. She loved her walks, and I felt bad that I didn't take her on more of them. I attached her leash, then, together we went up the hill to the park near Grace Cathedral.

The park was empty except for some pigeons rummaging near the trash can and a girl swinging on the swingset. It was the perfect time for me to practice my balance beam routine for an upcoming gymnastics competition. Georgie sat nearby on a patch of grass as I carefully put one foot in front of the other on top of a short concrete barrier. I swooped my leg behind me, balancing on one foot with my arms held out to a T, then swung it back in front to a straddle leap in the air. I swayed side-to-side, trying to hold my balance on the landing, then fell to the ground. It was horrible. I still had a lot of work ahead of me to perfect it.

The girl on the swingset jumped off mid-swing and headed in my direction. I wiped crumpled leaves from my sweater as she approached. She had curly red hair pulled back in clips and freckles on her nose and cheeks kind of like Little Orphan Annie.

"Can I pet your dog?" she asked.

"Sure. Her name is Georgie."

The girl squatted down, held her hand out for Georgie to sniff, then sat on the pavement to pet her.

"My name is Susie," she said. "I just moved here from Chicago. Do you live around here?"

And just like that, I had a new friend. She only lived a few blocks from me, but in a much nicer part of Nob Hill. We had a blast together because she loved exploring just as much as I did. I showed her all my favorite places—downtown, Union Square, the Embarcadero.

"My parents said I'm getting to know the city even better than they are," she joked. "Where to today?"

"Let's check out Chinatown," I said.

I took her through the tourist shops on Grant Street, then led her through the sights and smells of the *real* Chinatown on Stockton. We weaseled our way through hoards of people, passing produce markets, bakeries, and herb shops along the way.

"Hungry?" I pointed to some barbecued ducks hanging by their feet in a nearby window.

"Nope. I think I'm okay."

The next shop had baskets of dried goods sitting out front on the sidewalk. Roots and plums, and all sorts of dried fish—from tiniest minnows to the really big fish, all flat as a pancake and crispy. Under the Chinese writing, there were English labels like squid, shrimp, cuttlefish, and things like that.

"Pee-U!" Susie plugged her nose between her fingers. "What's that awful smell?"

"Shhhh!" I whispered. "Don't let anybody hear you. It's probably this dried squid." I picked up a piece and put it to her face. "Here, try some!"

"Ewww!" She pushed my hand away. "That's disgusting! How does anybody eat that stuff?"

"Shhh! Come on. I wanna show you some frogs. We're almost there. We're headed to that store with the huge tanks out front." I pointed down the street, then skipped through the crowds with Susie following close behind.

"I have to warn you before we go in, whatever you do, don't watch if someone buys a fish."

"What? Why?"

"Just don't. Trust me. The guy will take a hammer and bang it on the fish's head to kill it. Then he takes a knife and cuts it open while the fish is still squirming all over the place. Then he takes out its guts."

"Eww! Okay. That's enough."

"I know. It's so sad! Come on. Let's go in."

A row of plastic bins lined the floor of the shop, all alive with movement. Susie's eyes were as round as bottle caps as she moved from one container to the next. She covered her hand over her mouth as she moved from fish to tanks of eels, to bins of snakes. The snakes were arranged according to their size, small snakes, medium snakes, and large snakes all piled on top of each other, moving and squirming.

"I bet the tourists never see anything like this," she said.

"I know. Come look over here. This is what I wanna show you." I pulled her by the sleeve toward a container near the back wall. "Aren't they adorable?" I asked.

"Uh, I guess?"

"They remind me of the big frogs I used to play with when I lived in Florida. But those weren't even half this size."

"What do you think they do with 'em?" she asked.

"I think people might eat 'em. I'm not sure, though. And I'm not sure about the turtles and snakes, either. Maybe you can get 'em for a pet or somethin'."

I ran my finger along the cool, bumpy skin of one of the toads, gently petting its head. "I wish I could take all the frogs and turtles out of here and set them free. It would be so cool. I could stuff 'em in my jacket and bring 'em to that mountain by my apartment to let 'em loose."

"Yeah. That would be nice," she fanned her face and scrunched nose. "This place smells really disgusting. Can we go now?"

"Yeah, I should be gettin' back home now, anyway."

"No. I don't mean go home. Just somewhere else. I still wanna hang out."

We had spent a few hours exploring, and the evening fog was already beginning to roll in—a clear sign for me to head home to get supper ready.

"I don't think I can. I kind of have a lot to do tonight."

"Please. It's Friday. There's no school tomorrow. I'm allowed to stay out later. Please! My place is so boring!"

"I dunno. Let's just do something tomorrow."

"I know. What if I have dinner with you guys?"

Shit! I had already slept over her place a few nights since we met. I knew the day would come sooner or later when it was my turn to host.

"I can phone my mom to see if it's okay, but I'm sure it'll be fine," she said.

Shoot! No! What do I say? I don't even know what the apartment

looks like right now. I should clean it and have her come tomor-
row. Maybe, then, I could bribe Rachael into cooking supper for me.

"That would be fun. How 'bout tomorrow? I really have a lot
to do tonight."

"No. Please! I can help with whatever you have to do."

Ugh! She hated being the only child and always told me how
lucky I was to have brothers and a sister, since her life was so boring.

"My parents are having friends over tonight and I'm gonna be
stuck in my room while they're all out there drinking wine and
laughing," she said.

"Oh. Okay. I guess?"

I've heard many stories of Susie's parents' friends, and how she liked
to stay hidden in her room, so they wouldn't ask her all the same stupid questions over and over again. "How are you liking it here? How's
school? Did you meet a lot of new friends? Any boyfriends? Hahaha!"

My stomach shriveled into a tight ball of rubber bands as
we headed up the hill toward my apartment. *Crap! Now what?*
Why in the heck did I say yes? Now she's gonna know that I have
to cook supper. What can I tell her? Maybe, Mama just had sur-
gery and I have to help out? Oh, no! What if Mama's in one
of her moods? Please let Primus be there. Please, please, please!

I don't think I'd ever seen Mama happier than when Primus came
into her life. He was her new boyfriend, a handsome cable car gripman, like Pete. Only he had green eyes, was tall and slender with
light brown skin. Yep, you heard right. Light brown skin. Primus
was black. I never thought I'd see the day when Mama dated a black
man, much less, be head over heels for him. These last four and
a half years had changed her. She said San Francisco washed her
clean of the prejudiced filth she learned in Louisiana and Florida.

Please, dear God. Don't let her be in a bad mood. Let Primus be there.
Please, let Primus be there.

Susie had never been inside our apartment before. I'd have her
meet me outside, on the corner, in front of the Chinese restaurant.

She hasn't even met Mama yet. I had always hoped she'd think our place was humongous like hers, but now she was about to see how crammed it really is. At least Jon Eric wasn't still there with his sleeping bag on the floor.

I walked up the stairs as slow as I could in hopes that Susie might change her mind. Maybe she'd remember that her parents' friends were going out to dinner with them instead of heading to their flat. No such luck, though. I put my key in the door and pushed it open. There wasn't a sound inside. No laughter. No chit chat. Primus must not have been there. I remembered Rachael said she was going to a friend's house after school, and the twins must've been out back. I peeked around the corner of the hallway as Susie followed me in.

Crap! Mama's sleeping. There couldn't have been anything worse than that. I hated when she took naps, because I never knew if she'd wake up normal or as a monster, and trust me, it was usually the monster.

"Can I use your phone," Susie asked.

Crap! "Sure. The telephone's over there." I whispered, then held my finger over my lips and pointed to the phone next to Mama's bed. "Try not to talk too loud, or you'll wake up my mom."

She nodded and began dialing her number. "Hi, Mom, it's me," she whispered. "Susie. Susie," she whispered a little louder. "I have to whisper so I don't wake up Teresa's mom."

Crap! How embarrassing!

"Teresa's Mom! I can't talk louder!"

Mama rolled over, then sat up, stretched her arms wide, and made a loud, exaggerated yawning noise.

"Can Susie eat supper with us?" I asked.

Susie crossed her fingers and held them behind her back for me to see.

"I don't see why not," Mama said.

Susie hung up the phone and gave me a thumbs up.

"Hi," she said to Mama with a smile. *Thank God Susie's smiling and thank God she's the one who said something first.*

"Mama, this is the girl I've been telling you about. Susie. She lives up near Grace Cathedral."

"Hi, Susie," Mama said. *Thank-you-God! Thanks for letting her be nice!*

"Come on, Susie," I held onto her arm to lead her to the kitchen. "Let's see what I can make for supper." I opened the freezer and began shuffling around inside.

"You have to make dinner?" Susie whispered.

"Yeah. Shhhh!" I mouthed to her, covering my lips with my finger again.

"Whatcha gonna make?"

"Not sure yet," I said as I continued rummaging. "Ah-ha! I'll make these!" I pulled out packets of sliced beef with gravy. *Yes! Thank God I don't have to make anything from scratch.* "I'll just have to make some potatoes to go with 'em, but that shouldn't take too long." I pulled out the frozen packs of meat, then grabbed a can of green beans out of the cabinet. "Here, would you mind opening these for me?" I tossed her the can opener as I started peeling potatoes.

"How do you know how to cook that? It sounds complicated."

"Nah. Easy peasy. These are already made." I opened one of the packages and pulled out a sealed plastic bag of the beef with gravy. "They're just frozen. All I have to do is throw this bag in boiling water for a few minutes and they're done."

"That's cool!"

Susie stood by my side as I got the three pots going, then she helped set plates on the table. To her, it was fun. She smashed the potatoes as I threw in a dollop of margarine and some milk, and was amazed that I knew how much salt and pepper to add. To be honest, I was having fun, too. I liked having her in the kitchen with me. It made me feel like a teacher. Or, maybe, one of those grandmothers you'd see in movies, showing their granddaughters how to cook. Instead of being ashamed, I felt proud that I knew how to do it, even though I chose such a simple meal.

Rachael came home and walked in the kitchen to see what we were cooking. "Smells yummy," she said.

When we were done, I held up my hand and gave Susie a high-five. "Teamwork!" I said as I served the food on the plates. "We rocked this! Thanks for your help."

By then, the twins were inside playing Batman and Superman with some cloth capes Mama found at a garage sale. I circled my hands around my mouth like a megaphone and shouted, "Dinner's ready!"

The twins ran in with Rache following behind them, but Mama wasn't with them. She must have fallen back asleep. I called again, then heard her heavy footsteps stomp toward the kitchen.

"You never did the dishes today," she said as she walked in. "You said you'd have them done when you got home. But here they all are."

I loathed dishwashing more than any other chore, and it was the one job that got me in the most trouble. The last thing I wanted to do after spending so much time cooking was to have to stay behind to clean up the mess. It was bad enough that I had to wipe down the table and pack the leftovers away. I needed a break after all that. Usually, I'd go play with Georgie, then come back to clean up, but sometimes I'd forget.

Then, either I'd be extra late for school by doing them in the morning, or I'd do them as soon as I got home. Either way meant trouble for me, but especially the latter, since Mama would have to stare at dirty dishes all day.

I was so excited to show Susie the frogs that I completely forgot. It didn't even faze me when I dumped the boiling water from the potatoes on them either. My hatred for that job made them invisible to me. Even if I did notice, I wasn't about to wash them in front of Susie. No way would I want her to know I had to do more than just cook supper.

Please don't start, Mom. Maybe I shouldn't say anything. I wasn't sure which would be better—to keep quiet and act like a little coward while she trampled me, or to be strong in front of my friend. There was no denying Mama woke in one of her moods.

I figured she wouldn't do anything in front of Susie, especially after the missionaries sent those men to my school. And since she always tried so hard to fit in with the other mothers, I became even more confident that she would remain peaceful.

"You and your filth are the reasons we have roaches in here."

Seriously? Shut up! The tension was thick. Susie hadn't even picked up her fork yet. *Come on!* But Mom didn't shift her cold stare from me. Her eyes stayed glued, waiting for a response, a fight.

I cleared my throat. *Please let this end.* "I thought maybe somebody else could do them since I had a friend over today." I tried my hardest to sound sincere and not antagonizing.

"I thought somebody else could do them since I had a friend over today," she mocked.

No! Please! Don't say another word, Teresa. Mom took a forkful of potatoes and began smacking her lips. I swear it was louder than usual, probably doing it on purpose to get to me. *That's so embarrassing.*

Each bite sounded like cymbals crashing in my ears. I tried to focus on the radio in the background to tune her out, but no song could penetrate that noise. Nothing. It might as well have been broadcast on a loudspeaker. Mom pushed her chair out and stood up. *Merde!* "Get those damn dishes washed, now!" she pointed to the sink. "You know I can't sit here and enjoy my meal while looking at that filth. How many times do I have to tell you that?"

I started to push my chair out, then stopped. "Can't I just do 'em after Susie leaves? Please?" Her face didn't shift. Cold as ice, her beady eyes stared right through me. I couldn't back down, though. Not in front of Susie. "Or can't somebody else do 'em for once?" *Okay, I didn't have to say that. Shut up! Just wash the stupid dishes before she makes a scene.*

"How dare you talk to me like that, you little crumb. Yeah, that's right! You're nothing but a little crumb, just like your father!"

No! Please don't start! I bit on the inside of my cheeks to stop the tears.

"I didn't talk to you in a bad way! I just asked why nobody else can wash them since I have a friend over, that's all." My voice quivered as I tried to backpedal my way out.

Mom held her plate off the table. *Please take it to the other room. Don't throw it at me. Please, please. Don't throw it. God!* She lifted it a little higher, *please,* then flailed it across the table at my face. I didn't believe she'd do it. Not in front of Susie. My guard was down. I didn't have time to deflect the plate.

I wished it could've been funny like when someone gets a cream pie to the face in the movies. Then I could laugh. *Ha, ha, Susie. Isn't this hilarious?* But it wasn't funny at all. No humor could ever come from that.

Mom sat back down with her squinted eyes still glaring at me. *Don't cry. Don't cry. Don't let the witch see me cry.* I sucked in a deep, quivering breath and felt for the lump on my lip with my tongue. *Don't cry.* Without lifting my head, I looked over to Susie. Brown gravy had splattered the side of her yellow shirt. *Don't cry.* Susie's face said it all. Tears mixed with terror. Her eyes were even wider than when she looked in the snake bin earlier that day. I had to look away. That's not the way I wanted to remember her face, since I'd probably never see her again.

The potatoes Susie and I had so much fun making together sat in a big glob on my lap. *Susie. I can't believe she did this in front of my friend! I can't believe it!*

"What are you still sitting there for? You want some more? You better get those dishes washed before I have to get up from here."

My fists clenched into two tight balls. She ruined everything for me. I finally had a best friend to do things with after school.

"I hate you!" I screamed. "I hate your guts! I wish you were dead!"

Mom leaned across the table to smack me, but I scooted back, just out of her reach. She was trapped between the table and the wall, flanked on both sides by the twins. She couldn't reach me. *Run before she gets out! Run! What about Susie? I can't leave her. Do something! Hurry!*

"Let's go, Susie." I pushed my chair out, but wasn't fast enough. Mom lifted her side of the table off the floor, sending everyone's plates sliding right toward me and my friend. Most slid by my side, not touching me or Susie at all, which made Mom even more infuriated. She stumbled over Jonas and charged toward me.

I should've run, but I couldn't think fast enough. Instead, I clenched my eyes shut and covered my head so she couldn't grab my hair.

"Ow!" I screamed as she began stabbing my wrist with her fork. I jerked my arms down and cradled them in front of my body for protection. She didn't stop though. The fork kept coming, jabbing the side of my face. "Ow! Stop!"

She was out of control. The switch in her head had clicked allowing the monster to take over.

"Stop it!" I yelled. "Stop! I'll wash the dishes!"

I reached for her wrist as the stainless steel prongs continued to pound the side of my face. She grabbed hold of my hair and yanked so hard my chair tumbled from under me, leaving me sprawled on the floor.

"Look at this mess! Look what you made me do, you filthy whore!" she screamed at the top of her lungs.

"I didn't make you do anything! You did it yourself. You're a crazy witch!" I didn't care that I was screaming at her. What could be worse, anyway? Susie had already witnessed everything.

"You. Little. Tramp," Mom said through clenched teeth, then pounded me in the ribs with her foot.

"Stop it, Mama!" Josh shouted.

"Ouch!" I hugged my knees into my chest while Georgie licked gravy from my face.

"Get that fucking mutt out of here before he eats all that food." Georgie squealed as he went sailing across the room from her kick.

"Georgie!" I screamed. Jonas grabbed him and ran out of the kitchen.

Susie backed into the corner and slumped against the wall. The sound of her whimpering hurt more than anything Mom could ever do to me.

"You're lucky I don't wash that filthy mouth out with soap," she said. "I should make you eat soap for dinner. That's what I should do." She grabbed the oven handle so she wouldn't slip and kicked me again.

"Stop!" I screamed.

She didn't stop, though. She couldn't snap out of it. Kick after kick pounded my side.

This is it! She's gonna kill me this time! I hope she does. Kill me! Please. "You should just kill me." I screamed. "That's what you wanna do, anyway."

Another kick. This time even harder. I pictured my ribs snapping in half, and my body filling with blood. *I'm gonna die.* Blood flowed from my eyes and from my nose, painting my face red. *Can't she see she's killing me?*

All of a sudden, out of nowhere, she stopped. It was Josh. Standing next to her with a screwdriver in his hand, trembling and shaking. *What just happened?* His little body went crashing to the wall next to Susie.

I clenched my eyes and tried taking a deep breath, but my ribs hurt too much. I had to block out Susie and Josh's crying. Music. I barely heard it, but I finally found the music. Billy Joel's "Just the Way You Are" played in the other room.

The one song that always made me cry when no one else was around. The very song that made me wonder why Mom could never love me, now played on the radio to save me from the screams.

"Stop! Stop it! You're hurting him!" Rachael's voice rose above Billy Joel.

"You're gonna help your sister clean this fucking mess!" Mom shouted to Josh.

The room went quiet, except for Susie's whimpering. *What's happening?* Footsteps pounded down the hall, then the front door slammed shut. Rachael had broken the curse. I wiped my face with my hand, then checked for blood. Nothing but tears and snot.

Susie leaned against the wall in the corner, eyes stained pink.

"Here's a towel so you can clean off your clothes," Rachel said. "Do you need to call your mother to come and get you?"

"No. It's fine. I can walk home from here." Susie took the towel and wiped her shirt. Then she squatted next to me and placed her hand on my shoulder.

"That was the scariest thing I've ever seen, Teresa. Now I know why you never wanted me to come here. I'm so sorry! I hope you're okay." Her eyes filled with tears again.

"Please don't tell your mother," I whimpered. "Or anybody else. Please. Could you just say we got in a food fight or somethin'?" I tried getting up, but the pain stopped me. Instead, I forced a smile so she wouldn't know how much I hurt.

"Okay."

"Pinky promise?"

Her pinky latched onto mine. "Next time just come to my house." She smiled, then used the towel to wipe her nose and eyes before heading out.

Next time? After she left, the twins came to my side.

"I think Mama broke my ribs," I said. "It hurts to breathe!"

"Go lay down," Jonas said. "We'll clean this for you."

"I can't believe she did that in front of Susie. I can't believe it! I wish she would have just killed me," I whispered. "I really thought she was going to."

Jonas held his hand out to me, then he and Josh each took an arm and walked me to my room.

"You okay, Josh?"

"Yeah, she didn't get me nearly as bad as you."

"Would you mind bringing me a mirror?"

"Sure." He came back a few minutes later with one of Mom's small compacts in his hands. "Here you go," he said.

"Thanks for helping me."

"It's okay."

I reached out, took the mirror in my trembling hands, and closed my eyes as I held it to my face. I was too scared to look, though. I pictured the blood again as a tear dripped down my cheek. Tears of blood.

"It doesn't look that bad, Treedy," Josh said in a soft, fragile voice. "No one'll probably notice."

I squinted my eyes open to take a look. No blood. A clear tear dripped from my eye. Clear. Not the thick red gore as I had imagined. My cheek was red and swollen from the fork with welts of bluish purple bruises—but no blood. An unbroken stream of tears poured down my face as I looked at my reflection.

"I can't believe Susie saw this." I tried swallowing the pain. "I can't believe she was here."

As I drifted to sleep, I pictured the scene in my mind, the same scene I had imagined so many times before. One that starts off with me excited and happy, watching as Mom's hands get cuffed behind her back.

A police officer pushes her forward, then turns and winks at me. It's Officer Mike. It's always him. The one I imagine coming to take her away. My excitement turns to sadness as I watch her get into the police car, and I wish she could change and be nice like other mothers.

I stayed in bed all weekend, and Mama didn't make me cook or do anything. On Monday, she used some sort of skin colored lipstick on my cheek to cover the bruises so I wouldn't be embarrassed at school.

By Tuesday, Susie called to see how I was doing. I didn't think I'd ever hear from her again, but she invited me to spend the night at her house the following weekend. I couldn't believe it! She never broke her promise, either. Not another word was ever spoken of the night she had supper at our apartment.

* * *

At the end of that summer, Mama gave in and bought Jon Eric a bus ticket back home to Florida.

Part Three

–

Dixieland

Loosened lug nuts . . .

were a really bad idea.

– 29 –

Graduation

Life is a journey, not a destination.
— *Ralph Waldo Emerson*

Summer of '81

I was excited to graduate eighth grade from NDV. Not that I
didn't like it, I really did enjoy my time there. From my earliest
years with Trez and Lori, to the French choir, and all the fancy places
we sang, all the way to my last three years with Teresa and Adrienne.
Things at school had become better after Mama quit showing up
for yard duty.

When her ominous black cloud left the schoolyard once and
for all, I was able to let my guard down and figure out how to be
myself. An awkward, goofy kind of girl, but at least I made some
of the kids laugh.

In religion class, Father Mike taught us the seven deadly sins:
anger, lust, envy, gluttony, pride, wrath, and greed. They weren't as

bad as some of the other sins, but they got in the way of spiritual growth, so that's why they were considered sinful.

"We all get a little angry or proud at times," he said. "It's just a matter of staying in control of those feelings that keep them from becoming a sin."

It made me wonder, is it a sin every time Mama loses control over her anger? According to Father Mike, it would have to be. So Mama sins every day. How about when it comes to her beating us? Why wouldn't that be considered a sin? And what about the way she talks about gluttony only as an excuse to ridicule people? Who's more sinful there? It didn't make any sense that the overweight person would be more sinful than the one who constantly judges them. I wasn't about to ask Father Mike those questions, so I asked God instead.

Dear God, am I a sinner because I'm envious of the kids who have money? I never really do anything else bad. Well, I do have bad thoughts, sometimes, especially about Mama, and I do steal toilet paper, but that's not my fault. Does that mean I'm a sinner, too? I don't wanna sin. And I try not to be too envious. I just wanna have a good life when I'm older, that's all.

I figured being envious of the lives of others was my stepping stone from poverty to comfort and from abuse to gentleness. I eventually came to the conclusion that if I had remained envious of others but never did anything about it, that's when it would have been sinful. Because, really, what's the point in having a strong opinion about something if you never take action.

* * *

My excitement for graduation grew even more when I passed the entrance exam and interview to Mercy High, especially since Teresa and Adrienne were also going there. My life was about to get a whole lot better.

A fresh start where I could be myself, away from any taint Mama left on me at NDV. Hardly anyone would know her at

Mercy, and since I'd be wearing a uniform, all I had to do was fix my hair nice, and no one would ever know how poor I was.

* * *

Mama was sitting on the bed with a map spread out in front of her when the twins and I walked in from school. She looked deep in thought as a yellow highlighter pen flicked back-and-forth between her fingers.

"Come here, y'all." she said. "Rachel!" she called into the other room. "I have something I wanna tell ya." She tidied up some papers on the bed as we waited for Rachael.

"Grandmama called today," she said, pausing to look at us, one at a time.

I had no idea what this was about. She rarely spoke to her mother.

"Aunt Velma died last week," she said in a flat voice, then looked down at the marker in her hand as we waited for her to tell us more.

"Oh. That's sad," I said to break the awkward silence.

Mama cleared her throat. "She left us her home."

"Huh?"

I looked at the highlighted route on the map in front of her and followed the bright yellow mark from San Francisco to the boot shaped state of Louisiana where most of Mama's relatives lived.

"Really? A house?" Josh jumped up and down with his eyes sparkling like the smile on his face. "Yay!" He and Jonas grabbed hands and spun in a circle.

"Where is it?" I asked, afraid to hear the answer. I didn't know of any relatives near the San Francisco area.

"It's in West Monroe. Louzi-ana."

"Louisiana?"

The words knocked the air out of me like a kick to the stomach. Thoughts of all the times we visited relatives throughout the years clouded my head. The big grassy yards, the sweltering days and even hotter nights, the small towns... I held onto my belly while I tried taking a deep breath. *Aunt Velma, Grandmama's sister. Which one was her house?*

"Well, what did ya tell her?" My words came out barely louder than a whisper.

"I said, of course we'll take it! Are you kidding me? It's a three-bedroom house. I'd be crazy to pass that up."

Rachael stared into space, deep in thought. I wish I knew what she was thinking, but as usual, I couldn't read the look on her face.

"I've been on the phone all day," Mama said. "Billy's giving me a great deal on his truck, so between that and the camper, we'll be able to move most all our stuff."

"When are we movin'?" Rachael asked.

"Well, Jon Eric's comin' in two weeks, so he can help with the driving. I'd like to have everything packed and ready by the time he gets here."

I didn't know what to feel. I'd always dreamt of having a house, instead of an apartment, and now my wish was coming true. I wouldn't have to pretend I didn't live in a studio anymore. No more stinking garbage chutes. No more hiding from landlords in the closet or worrying if the neighbors could hear Mom each time she yelled at us. The twins could have their own room, too, away from the sickening clutches of Mama.

But I loved San Francisco. I didn't know much about Louisiana at all, other than stories of the Ku Klux Klan who still burned crosses in people's yards. The thought of men with the pointed white hoods caused me to shudder. And they use the N-word there like Mama always used to. Other than swimming to keep cool, there wasn't much to do at all unless we were in New Orleans.

"The timing couldn't have been more perfect since you and Rache just graduated. There's a high school called St. Frederick's in Monroe for you, Teresa. And Rachael, if you want to go to college, you can go to NLU. Like I said, I've been on the phone all day sortin' things out."

Rache looked as if she had just seen a ghost even though she didn't say anything. I wished she'd open her mouth and shout out what she was thinking. I stormed to my room and threw myself onto my bed.

"Make a pile of stuff you wanna get rid of, and we'll bring it to the Salvation Army tomorrow," Mama shouted.

"Double, double, toil and trouble; fire burn, and caldron bubble," I whispered. My belly was on fire.

* * *

Just like that, my time in San Francisco came to an end. I know it's weird for a kid to like a place so much—well, unless it's Disneyland or something—but I loved living there. Every day a new adventure awaited as I escaped from the craziness of my home. The smell of eucalyptus trees, the colorful sight of nasturtiums, the cooing of pigeons, and rattling of cable cars—those sensations would stay with me forever.

* * *

I'd like to say our move to the deep South went smoothly, but then I'd be a liar. First of all, the green Chevy truck Mama bought from Billy had a stick shift, and no one knew how to drive it. Well, Mama claimed she knew, but she wasn't very good at it.

She lined both sides of the truck bed with large sheets of plywood so we could pile it high with all of our stuff. Just about everything we owned went in that truck, and it didn't stop at the top of the plywood, either. No siree! That truck was stacked like a three-tiered hillbilly wedding cake. So, not only did Jon Eric have to learn to drive a stick shift, but he had to learn in a jalopy straight from Sanford and Sons on the big hills of San Francisco.

To make matters worse, Mama came up with one of her not so brilliant ideas. To keep ahead of the game, she loosened all the lug nuts on the tires of both vehicles so it wouldn't take the Bionic Man to change them if they went flat.

I rode with Jon Eric through the jerking, stalling, honking, and cursing as we made our way out of the city. Once we were further down the freeway, the stress eased as his driving got a little smoother. We passed the time by switching back and forth between the "Dixieland" song and "Yankee Doodle Dandy," then reminisced about our time in San Francisco.

Everything from when we had first arrived, going up and down the big hills, singing the Rice-a-Roni song at the top of our lungs, to all the ways we tried to make money when we were all together.

We laughed at how Brother and Petesy made up words to the song, *Alla en el Rancho Grande* while standing in front of Woolworth's on Powell and Market with marionette puppets they got in Tijuana dancing by their side.

We talked about the times we dressed as clowns and went to Fisherman's Wharf to put on magic shows, then laughed at how we always ended up with no money, since we spent every cent we made buying more tricks for the show.

And how there were such stupid things like magic smoke and snap gum. We spoke of the times we dressed up like Mary and Joseph with towels on our heads to sing Christmas carols outside the Fairmont Hotel.

"Remember New Hampshire?" Jon Eric asked. "That was so crazy. I'm glad we made a detour to the New England States that summer.

"How could I forget? That was the coolest thing ever. I was halfway down the block when I heard you shouting Deborah's name."

A wave of chills ran through me as I thought of the scene. Mama, Rache, and I were coming out of a store when we heard Jon Eric squeal.

"She looked so different. I hardly recognized her," I said.

"Yeah, that's when I learned the word serendipity," Jon Eric said. "It was crazy!"

Deborah was working on a big ship that happened to be docked in Boston and was visiting Hampton Beach for the day when she saw the camper. She told her friend, "hey, that looks just like the camper my mother has," and sure enough, it was.

"You should've seen the twin's faces when Deborah ran up to hug them," Jon Eric said.

"I know. Well, they hadn't seen her since they were three. I don't think I would have even recognized her with that dark tan and permed hair!"

"Yeah, and wasn't that cool she let us check out the ship when we got to Boston?"

"Yep, the Brig Unicorn. I'll never forget it. I still can't believe Deborah had to climb up those high masts. That would've been so scary."

"You know that was the same boat they used in the movie, "Roots", huh?"

"Yeah."

Jon Eric let out a loud yawn. "I'm getting sleepy."

We had been following the camper south down Interstate 5, then turned east onto I-10 as we told our stories. Jon Eric punched the gas to pull alongside Mama while I shouted out the window for her to pull over. That was our only method of communication between the two vehicles.

We stopped at the side of the road, got out to stretch our legs a bit, then Jon Eric went in the camper to sleep. Rachael refused to drive the stick shift, so she took over the camper while Mama drove the green truck. I hopped in to keep Rachie company.

* * *

What the heck is that noise?" Rachael asked once we made it out of the chaos of the Los Angeles area. "Do you hear that?"

Before I could respond, there was a loud clanking sound.

"I'm gonna pull over and check," Rachael said.

She pulled to the side of the freeway, and we both got out to search for the source.

"I don't see anything. Do you?" she asked.

"No."

"Great, Mama's nowhere in sight now, we better get going." She looked in the side-view mirror as she pulled onto the freeway.

"Oh, my gosh! The back tire is wobbling like crazy," she shouted.

She quickly turned the camper back to the side of the road and slammed her foot on the brake. The truck jerked and dropped low on one side as the rear tire rolled right past us down the freeway.

"What the heck? That's our tire!" Rachael jumped out and took off like a rocket chasing it to the center divide. Luckily there weren't many cars on the road.

"Now what are we gonna do?" she asked after she rolled the tire back to the camper. "We don't even have a jack in here to change this. I saw Mama pack it in the truck."

It didn't take too long for Mama to realize we weren't behind her anymore, so she circled around at the next exit, then parked the truck behind us, and dug for the jack. All the lug nuts were missing from the tire, every single one of them, so, Mama, being the genius that she was, borrowed one from each of the tires of the green truck.

* * *

Jon Eric and I were back in the Chevy, reminiscing of the first time we drove through Arizona on the way to San Francisco.

"Holy crap!" he said as the truck began to wobble. He laid on the horn to get Mom's attention, then pulled to the side of the road. Mama circled the camper around, parked behind us, and came to check out the tire.

"What in the hell?" she asked. "The damn studs are sheared all the way in half. That's just great! Didn't you feel anything while you were driving? Why did you wait so long to stop?"

Jon Eric didn't answer.

"Now I have to go find a damn tow truck."

"It's not my fault," Jon Eric whispered.

We stayed behind while Mama, Rache, and the twins drove to

the next town. When they came back, Mama was even more huffy than before, yelling at Rachael about something, so I did my best to keep out of sight.

A man with greased-back hair and dark, wet circles under his armpits arrived shortly after them. We stood around watching as he attached the Chevy to the back of his tow truck.

"Get away from that truck!" Mama screamed as he pulled it onto the road. The whole thing began to tilt. "Stop!"

The driver must not have heard her. He pressed his foot harder on the accelerator to enter the freeway, causing the green truck to topple, then crash onto its side. Splinters of wood shot all over the place, as boxes, loose clothing and furniture spilled out.

The color drained from Mama's face. She grabbed two fistfuls of her hair and stood in complete silence as the driver unhitched the Chevy. She was still in shock when he told her he'd come back with a different type of tow truck.

I backed toward the camper as her shock turned to rage. She began rustling through the heap, throwing things all over the place, then ripped open a black garbage bag and began screaming.

"This is all your fault! I told you to get rid of some of your shit before we moved."

She looked Rache straight in the eyes, then grabbed an armful of her clothes from the bag, and heaved them onto the cracked dry earth.

"I'll show you how to lighten your load," Mama said.

She scooped more clothes, then stormed further away from the road. Rachael stood frozen as a statue with her lower lip between her teeth as Mama tossed her stuff all over the place. Mama went back and forth, carrying loads of Rachael's clothes, spreading them through the desert like a maniac. When she was done, she sat on top of the big pile of clutter next to the fallen truck, buried her head in her hands, and began to cry.

Jon Eric, age 14.

– 30 –

Natchitoches Street

You have brains in your head. You have feet in your shoes.
You can steer yourself any direction you choose. — Dr. Seuss

Cicadas buzzed around the lamp post, filling the night air with their southern song as we pulled up to the small white house in West Monroe. Memories of catching frogs, climbing trees, and playing London Bridge under a running hose swept through my mind, but that all seemed so long ago now. That sweet innocence was stolen in the blink of an eye from the very person who was supposed to be protecting it. Seven years had passed since I last chased those frogs into the night. Seven long, miserable years, and a new house could never bring them back.

The door to the screened-in porch screeched as Mom pulled it open, causing the hairs on the back of my neck to stand. I backed closer to Jon Eric.

"Nothin' a little WD-40 couldn't fix," she said.

"I bet Aunt Velma died here," Jon Eric whispered. He had the flashlight under his chin, lighting his face with shadows, while moving his eyes side to side.

"Stop it!" I swiped the light from his hand, sending it tumbling to the ground.

"Gosh darnit, Jon Eric," Mama said.

"Is that true, Mama? Did Aunt Velma die here?" Jonas asked.

"Honey, I don't know where she died. I think Grandmama said she died in the back bedroom."

"What if she's still in here?" My body shivered at the thought.

"Don't be foolish. Nobody's anywhere. Let's bring in the sleeping bags, and we can just stay here on the floor tonight till we figure things out. Tomorrow we can check out the place in the daylight."

The next morning, a loud rumbling noise woke us from our sleep. The floor began to vibrate as it got louder.

"We're having an earthquake!" I shouted.

Mama sat up just as an obnoxious horn sounded throughout the house. "What the heck? That's not an earthquake. That's a train," she shouted above the noise. "I forgot about the railroad tracks behind the fence in the backyard. What the hell time is it?" She squinted her eyes to see her watch. "Sheesh. It's only 6:25. I sure as hell hope that thing doesn't come by this early every morning." She stretched her arms and let out a big yawn. "Well, since we're all up now, we might as well start unpacking."

With a lot of moaning and grumbling, we got up and followed Mom around for a quick tour of the place. Then she sat on a couch that was left behind from Aunt Velma and went over the move-in.

"I'll take that front bedroom. The twins'll have the middle one, and you two'll be in the back."

Her words caused my chest to tighten. "You mean the room where Aunt Velma died?"

"When y'all unload, drop everything off where it should be. Kitchen stuff in the kitchen, my stuff in my room, and so on," she said, while ignoring my question completely. "Let's try and get all this done before your father comes."

"What?" My jaw dropped open.

"Daddy's coming?" Jonas asked.

"Yeah. He's bringing me my dresser. No way I'm lettin' that wife of his use stuff that I bought with my own money. He's gonna bring Jon Eric back home with 'im, too."

Rachael bit on her bottom lip to hide her smile, then stared out the window, tapping on her chin, as if she were deep in thought as Mom continued. As for me, my emotions were all over the place. Excited about the house, and even more excited that we'd get to see Daddy, but sad Jon Eric was leaving, and scared about being in the back bedroom.

We spent most of the day unloading the green truck, then Mom let the twins take a break to check out the neighborhood. There was only one other house on Natchitoches Street, so the twins hopped on their bikes and headed to the other side of the railroad tracks.

I figured they'd take advantage of their freedom and not return until everything was out of the truck and put away, but not even an hour had passed when they came speeding back, running in the house shouting for Mom. Josh's shorts were covered in mud with a trail of blood running down his leg.

"What in hell's tarnation happened to you?" Mom asked.

"Some boys called us faggots since we told 'em we're from San Francisco," Jonas whimpered. "One of 'em pushed Josh over on his bike, and he fell in a ditch. They said they don't want fuggots in their neighborhood."

"Sum' bitch," Mom said. "Welcome to the trash talkin' shithole of the South. If I ever hear anybody say somethin' like that, I'll kill 'em. Hold on." She walked out of the room, rummaged through some boxes in the bathroom, then came back empty-handed.

"I can't find a damn washrag anywhere. Here, let me see your leg." She bent down to get a closer look at Josh's knee. "It's not that bad, but you better go rinse it off in the shower. Meanwhile, let's finish unpackin' these boxes here. We're almost done."

After loading the last dish in the kitchen cabinet, I went to look for everyone else. Rache was outside, sitting in the shade of a large oak tree, so caught up in her own thoughts that she didn't even notice me standing next to her.

"Can you believe Daddy's coming?" I asked. "I'm so excited!"

"Yeah. I know. Mom told me on the way here. I…"

A deafening shrill from inside the house stopped her from continuing. We hoofed it toward the front door just as Josh came running outside with a towel around his waist.

"What's wrong?" I asked.

Jonas and Jon Eric ran out after him.

"Something hit me! It shot out of the shower at me," he screeched. "It was huge." He swiped one of his hands across his body. "As soon as I turned on the faucet it landed on my chest."

Mom came out with a broom still in her hands. "No worries. No worries. I killed it," she said. "It was just a cockroach."

"No it wasn't!" Josh sniffled. "It was huge."

"Well, that's something else we're gonna have to get used to here," she said. "The cockroaches are as big as one of those cicadas. And they fly."

* * *

The next day, Rachael and I kept our eyes peeled out the window, waiting for Daddy to arrive, and by late afternoon, a silver car with a small trailer hitched to the back pulled in front of the house.

Mama waited patiently while we hugged him and showed him around the place, then she handed over a long to-do list she had jotted down for him. Things like building shelves, fixing the door on the closet, and stuff like that. He agreed to help as much as he could during the two days he planned to stay in West Monroe.

Mama cooked supper that night so we could spend more time with him, and that's what we did. We followed his every move. Every tap of the hammer, every pull of the measuring tape, and trip to the hardware store, we were right by his side. The only time I wasn't near him was when Mom sent me to the grocery store.

To my surprise, his visit with us went smoothly. I guess because Mom was in control and he stayed busy checking things off the list she gave him. By the time he was ready to go back to Jacksonville, most of the items were completed.

"Well, I guess it's time for us to head back," he said as we were finishing dinner.

The thought of him leaving that day weighed heavily on me since the moment I woke up. Even though I knew it was time, his words still hit hard—especially to Rachael. The color drained from her face, making her look as pale as grits. She leaned into Daddy and mumbled something under her breath, but I couldn't quite make it out.

Daddy cleared his throat. Something looked wrong with his face, like he was scared, or something. He cleared his throat again, like Mr. Bergez, but without the Adam's apple.

"Rachael's comin' back to Florida with us, too." His words sounded weak, different than they had been the past day and a half.

It took a few seconds for his words to register in my head. *What did he just say?*

"The hell she is," Mom said. Her fork dropped to her plate as her eyes spewed hatred toward him.

"I'm eighteen now. You can't make me stay," Rachael's words came out loud and clear.

The room began to spin as I fought to make sense of everything.

"Sorry, Mom," Rache continued. She held her head down and wiped her tears on a napkin.

No! No wonder she's been so weird. How the heck did she ask Dad? She never says anything. No wonder why she never unpacked her things.

"Rachael, please!" Mom begged.

"Don't move away, Rachael," Jonas said.

"Yeah, don't leave us." My words were no more than a strained whisper. *How dare her! Who does she think she is?*

"Come on. I want to hit the road before it gets dark," Daddy said.

"You louse! You came here to take my daughter away? You stinkin', fuckin' bastard."

"I did nothing of the sort. She asked if she could come back with me yesterday." He raised his voice back to her.

"It's true, Mom," Rache said without looking up. "Daddy didn't have anything to do with it. I'm the one who asked him."

Mom slammed her hand onto the table. "How could you leave me after all I've done for you?"

"Come on, Rachael, Jon Eric. We gotta get goin'. Give your mother a hug goodbye," Dad said.

My body went numb as Mom dropped to the floor, crying, and cursing, and punching at the ground. Too much was happening at once. First moving far from San Francisco, then the neighbors calling the twins faggots, and now this?

I was always more scared of Mom when Rachael wasn't around. I don't know why. Rachael never really did anything to protect me. But whenever she stayed at a friend's house or something, for some reason, Mom seemed to be a lot meaner, so in a way, I guess she did protect me.

As the fighting and yelling went on between Mom and Dad, I felt stuck in the middle of a battle, not knowing whose side to take. I guess, in some sort of weird way, I wanted to be on Mom's side. As strange as that seems, she's all I knew, and I felt bad for her. Especially after seeing her crumble to the ground. I wanted to comfort her and help get rid of her pain. I couldn't believe Rachael was leaving. How could she do that? I felt betrayed by both her and Daddy.

After they drove off, Mom stormed to her room and slammed the door shut. Her wailing and sniffling could be heard all through the night, into the next day. It reminded me of the story Deborah told me—about when Mom was pregnant with me and didn't come out of her room during the whole time I was in her belly. As the afternoon turned to night, I hoped that wouldn't be the case this time. Deborah said she changed into a monster while she was locked up. What if that happened again and she got even worse?

To my surprise, she came out when I called her for dinner. Her eyes were red and swollen from all the crying when she entered the dining room. I wanted to look at her. Not only to check for changes, but to see her in the way she normally saw me, hurt and sad. But I couldn't. No way would I risk letting the monster out if she caught me staring.

She took a seat but didn't do anything. She didn't pick up her fork or say grace. She just stared at the homemade lasagne I prepared. I had hoped her favorite meal would brighten her mood, but she didn't even seem to notice it at all. The plate might as well have been empty. The silence in the room was deafening, louder than the freight trains that ran behind our house.

Mom finally brought a small forkful to her mouth. I strained my eyes to the side while looking down at my plate in order to see her expression. She didn't smile or say anything, but I could tell she liked it anyway through her lip smacking.

My ninth grade class picture at St. Fredericks in Monroe, Louisiana, age 16.

– 31 –

Saint Fredericks

The way to get started is to quit talking and begin doing.
— Walt Disney

St. Frederick's High school meant a brand new start, a new beginning, just as it was going to be in San Francisco—and boy was it ever. Unlike the kids in our neighborhood, the ones from Monroe loved the fact that I was from California. It was easy to tell I was different, too, but not by my appearance. My long hair and uniform made me look like a prepster just like them. They knew it by the way I talked. I could barely understand a word anyone said, and had to keep saying, huh? over and over again. Even so, they thought I was cool because I came from California. And I'm not talking about just anyone, either. I'm talking about the rich kids. They snatched me up right away, and for the first time in my life I became part of a group, a popular group.

I ran for student council and won. I guess that's what popularity does for you. High school was the best. Unlike grammar school, I didn't only have one class, I had six, which meant a lot of new friends. Even the upperclassmen liked me.

Football games and team spirit were a huge part of life in Louisiana, and at our pep rallies I cheered loud as part of the pep squad team. The girls adorned themselves with carnations and ribbons. They had ribbons in their hair, ribbons pinned to their shirts, and blue and white laces on their shoes representing our school colors. I was having a blast, but there was no way I could keep up with those kids. Every home game meant free dress, a day we didn't have to wear our uniform, and the last thing I wanted was to be stuck wearing floods or an old stained t-shirt. I needed a job, so my quest for money began in those first few weeks.

Each day, I'd get on my bike to search for someone to hire me, but no one wanted an inexperienced fourteen-year-old. Door after door closed in my face, but I wasn't about to give up. I couldn't. I came across a hair salon called Cutter's Corner, parked my bike, wiped the sweat from my brow, and peeked my head in the door.

"Welcome in!" the lady behind the reception counter said. She had a warm smile and a soft, gentle voice.

I had never stepped foot into a salon like that before. As a matter of fact, I'd never been in any type of hair cutting place. Sure, I used to see some in San Francisco when I'd ride my bike around, but they were only for the rich people. I'm the one who trimmed my hair. Mama used to, but she'd cut my bangs so short that I had to beg her to let me do it myself.

The place smelled sweet, kind of like coconut, or something you could eat. From the second I walked in, I knew it's where I wanted to work. I bit on my lower lip and looked down at my feet as I spoke.

"Hi. Do you have an application I could fill out?" I asked.

"An application?" The lady's drawn-out southern accent was even stronger than the kids at school.

Unlike a lot of the people in West Monroe who were either preppy or more country-like, this lady had the New Wave type of look. Colorful. She had short hair cut above her ears, and long bangs that reached to her chin, and wore sparkling purple eye-shadow with blue eyeliner and mascara.

"What is it you're asking for, honey?"

I cleared my throat and asked again. "Do you have an application I could fill out? I'm looking for a job."

"A job?" she snickered. "These are all licensed beauticians who work here, sweetie."

My face blushed, and I thought it probably looked as pink as the rouge on the lady's cheeks. I had no idea what a licensed beautician was, but I knew I wanted to work in a place like Cutter's Corner.

I bit the side of my lip as the lady stared me down. *She probably thinks I'm gross cuz I'm so sweaty.* "Oh. Okay," I said, then turned to leave. I reached for the door then hesitated for a moment.

"Is there anything else I could do? I can do just about anything. I'm a really fast learner." A smile forced its way upon my face.

"Well, honey, I'm sorry. We don't have anything. I wish I could help you out."

I figured a place like that was too good to be true, but at least I tried. I hung my head low and said, "Thanks anyway."

"You might try back some other time, sweetie," she said.

"Really? Thanks!"

Those words filled me with energy. I ran out the door, hopped on my Schwinn five-speed, and pedaled home, singing a medley of every single Billy Joel song I knew.

"I think I have a chance at a job!" I squealed as I ran in the front door of the house.

The twins were in Mom's room watching television. Well, it wasn't exactly Mom's room. Not anymore. The twins slept on the bottom mattress of her trundle, just as they had in our apart-ment in San Francisco, which was kinda weird since they were in the fifth grade. But, of course, Mom made it more tantaliz-ing for them by keeping the one and only television set in there. Even though I wanted the twins to have their own room, at the same time, I was glad they didn't. It meant I didn't have to sleep in the scary back bedroom, and the middle room became mine.

"This lady at a hair salon told me I could come back again," I said as I pirouetted in front of the TV.

"Move," Josh said.

"I wonder how long I should wait? Next week will be too soon, right? Maybe I'll go back in a couple of weeks."

The twins kept watching TV, so I went to my room and paced back-and-forth while trying to decide when I should return. *A couple of weeks will be too long. I need a job now.*

I wanted that job so badly, and the wait was torture, so after only one week, I hopped on my bike and headed back. The lady walked behind her booth as I entered. She looked just as colorful and glamorous as she did the last time, wearing a black jumpsuit with a rhinestone belt that shimmered a rainbow all the way to the wall. Her eyes were painted with pink and purple shadow this time.

"Hi!" I said, smiling from ear-to-ear. I held onto the counter, gripping its edge next to some bottles of shampoo.

"Hi, sweetie. Do you have an appointment?"

"Huh? No." *Crap!* "I'm here to fill out an application for the job."

"The job?"

"Yes." I looked down at the black and white tiled floor. "Uh, last time I was here, you said I could try back another time, so I thought I'd give it another try. I was just wondering if maybe any jobs opened up?"

"Ah, yes. Well, you sure didn't waste any time, did you?"

"No, Ma'am," I said proudly.

"Well, honey," she looked down at her long pink fingernails. "I'm not sure of anything you could do here. We really aren't looking to hire anyone right now."

"You're not?"

My body slumped, as if she had stuck a pin into it to deflate all my hope and excitement. That lady held the key to my carnations and ribbons, to my new clothes, and tickets to the football games. She was the key to hiding my secret—my secret of poverty. The bottles of shampoo and conditioner on the counter now seemed to separate us like bars on a cage. Bars to keep me out, to keep me trapped.

"Do you think maybe you might have something in the future?" I managed to mumble.

"Well, I can never say never. There's always a possibility, sweetie."

Those words echoed through my mind for the next couple of weeks. *There's always a possibility, sweetie.* They gave me a glimpse of hope and freedom. I had to go back. Besides, I hit up just about every other place in West Monroe for a job already. After three weeks, I climbed back on my bike and headed to the salon.

As soon as I got there, I wanted to turn around and go back home. *What if she laughs at me? I should've worn something else. I look so plain. Shoot, I think this is the same thing I had on last time.* I reached for the door and slowly walked toward the counter.

"Hi," I said. I kept my eyes down, too scared to make eye contact.

"Boy, you don't give up easily, do you, kiddo?"

"No, Ma'am."

"Give me just a sec."

She held up a finger painted with an iridescent purple polish, then walked to the back of the salon. Her purple jumpsuit swayed with each step. It looked so elegant and comfortable, something I could wear if only I had a job. I heard her voice, then a man's, so I strained my ears to listen to what they were saying.

"But she keeps coming back," she said. "I don't have the heart to turn her away again."

No matter how hard I tried, I couldn't make out what the guy said.

"I'm sure we could come up with somethin'," she said.

After a little more back-and-forth, she headed to the front of the salon with the man following behind her. I pretended to be reading the label on a bottle of shampoo as they approached.

The man held out his hand to me. "Hi, I'm Mike."

He was a good looking man, tall like the lady, and dressed equally as nice.

"How would you like to be our new shampoo girl?" he asked as I shook his hand.

"Yes! I'd love it!" I said, probably a little too enthusiastically. My heart raced in my chest. I wanted to jump up and down, but shifted from foot to foot instead. "What's a shampoo girl?" I asked.

"It's a position we made up just for you," the lady said. "My name is Nancy, but everyone here calls me Fancy Nancy." She shook my hand. "It's your persistence that got you this job, you know. As a shampoo girl, you'll wash our client's hair before we cut it."

"And you'll wash the towels and sweep hair from the floor, too," Mike added.

"Thank you so much!" My eyes welled with tears. "You won't regret hiring me. I promise."

"You want a haircut?" Mike asked. "It comes with the job." He winked at me and smiled.

"Seriously?" I wanted to do a backflip right there in the lobby.

"Yeah, and I can show you how we like to shampoo hair here."

I followed him to a small room with funny-looking, mauve colored sinks lined up against the wall. Each had a black leather reclining chair in front of it. He told me to take a seat in one of the chairs, then explained each of the different types of shampoo as he scrubbed my scalp. It felt so good. I could have fallen asleep right there. I had to fight to focus on what he was saying. No one had ever washed my hair before. Well, except for Deborah when I was little, but I couldn't remember what it felt like. I left the salon smelling like coconuts, like a virgin pina colada one of the Kurs (or coeurs) bought me one time at the Hyatt Regency Hotel.

I couldn't quit running my fingers through my hair on the way home. No tangles, and it felt so light and soft. Mike had given me some layers and I absolutely loved it.

* * *

Even though I had earned enough money to buy ribbons and carnations for the pep rallies, and I had new clothes for free dress days, it didn't stop my novelty from wearing off at St. Fredericks. Don't get me wrong, I still had a lot of friends, just not the super rich, popular ones any more. You see, clothes weren't the only things I needed to hide how poor I was. I needed transportation. Those kids lived on the other side of the river, and for me to do anything with them, they'd have to come pick me up. Living in West Monroe wasn't the issue, either. It was Mom... and our small house. As long as I lived with her, I couldn't pretend to be someone different.

That's where the irony came in. All those years living in San Francisco, I always thought that having a house instead of a tiny apartment would make all the difference in the world. But that still wasn't good enough for the rich kids. They didn't care who I was as a person. All they cared about was that I came from a poor family.

It didn't stop me from loving my job as a shampoo girl, though. That was the best job I could have ever imagined, and having my own money gave me a sense of power. I could buy just about anything I wanted, and didn't have to rely on Mom for much at all. Well, except for food and a roof over my head, of course, but it was good to know that I could make it on my own one day.

Me, Mom and the twins in West Monroe.

– 32 –

Who's In Charge?

A true leader is always led. — *Carl Jung*

*M*om despised Louisiana, and with each passing day, things only got worse. No more big hotels with all their fancy dances, no more flirting until the wee hours of the night, no more Folk Song Club, and worst of all, no more Rachael. Mom's face rarely had a smile on it anymore, and a day didn't go by where she wasn't complaining about the heat.

"I can't stand this fucking heat! That's why I moved from Florida in the first place," she'd scowl. "It's miserable here!"

A sense of evil lurked through our home as Mom's fits became more rampant. Any fear I had ever experienced in our San Francisco apartment was more like a Disney movie compared to what I felt in West Monroe. Walking up to the house was like entering a scene from a horror film. Black smoke could be seen seeping through the cracks and windows from the creature that awaited me inside. That's what I saw, at least. My heart pounded each time I reached for the front door, not knowing what would jump out at me when I entered.

Mom attacked me relentlessly, as if it were my fault we ended up in West Monroe, and my fault that she couldn't be happy anymore. Her monster never retreated back inside her like it used to. It took up permanent residence, making itself known throughout the house.

Adrenaline became a part of my everyday life. It's what nourished my body and kept me on edge. I was scared of everything in that house and was prepared to duck and dodge whatever came flying at me in any given moment. The way Mom treated me in Louisiana made her look like Snow White in San Francisco, and everything I wrote up to this point could be rewritten as sunshine and lollipops compared to this.

My only escape was school and work. I joined just about every club the school had to offer. It was my chance to pretend to be normal, to pretend my life was just as wonderful as everyone else's. My chance to put Mom out of my mind...to erase her as if she didn't exist at all.

Mom had so much hatred and anger inside her that it didn't just stop with me. During my absence, Josh became more of a target. He took on my role while I tried my hardest to stay away—and Jonas took on Rachael's.

You'd think Jonas had it good, being the king of the house and all, but he despised it, especially since the tension between him and Josh grew even stronger. As Josh would scream and fight back at Mom, Jonas would cower in the corner and cry just as hard. Mom tortured him in a different way. He endured a different kind of pain, one that Josh and I could have never understood.

* * *

Toward the end of my sophomore year, since I had money, I decided to paint my room. With each stroke of the brush, my bedroom transformed from dingy and boring to vibrant and exciting. Tiny specks of lavender paint showered on me like fairy dust, but I didn't mind. It smelled so good, fresh, and clean.

Just as I painted the last stroke, the phone began to ring. No one answered as it kept ringing and ringing.

"Can't someone get that?" I shouted. "Sheesh!"

I guess I couldn't blame them since I was the one who got most of the calls, but still, they all knew I was busy painting. I wiped the paint from my hands onto my shorts and wiped the bottoms of my feet onto my legs so I wouldn't track anything out of the room, then ran out to pick up the phone.

"Hello?"

"Hi. This is Sue Sampson from University Health Hospital. Is this Teresa?"

"Yeah." I scraped dried paint from my fingernails as the lady spoke.

"Hi, Teresa. I'm calling to let you know that we have your mother and brother Josh here. They've been in an accident. No need to worry. They're both okay. Your mother has a laceration on her leg, but she'll be fine.

"What? What happened?"

"They were struck by a car while they were on their moped."

My heart stopped. I couldn't hear another word. All I could see was an image of Josh lying across the pavement covered in blood.

"Don't worry. Your brother's fine, too." The lady must have read my mind. "We're just going to keep 'em here a little while for observation."

It took two attempts to place the receiver back on the phone when she finished talking. *Keep them there for observation? A laceration? What the heck does that mean?*

"Jonas! Are you here?" I shouted. "Jonas!"

I ran to the back door where he was outside, sitting on the trampoline, playing with a car he got for his birthday.

"Come in!" My hands were shaking, so I squeezed onto the handle of the screen door to stop them. "Mom and Josh were in an accident! We have to go to the hospital!"

"What?"

"The hospital just called. They said Mom and Josh are there. Let's go!"

The hospital was in Monroe, but I knew how to get there since I passed near it on the way to school each day. We hopped on our bikes to make the long journey over the Ouachita River.

Please be okay. God, let them be okay. Please, God.

I couldn't shake the vision of Josh out of my mind, but even with that haunting thought pumping through me, it still took a lot longer to get there than I had expected. It felt as if the streets were being stretched like taffy, or like one of those dreams where you try to run, but your feet can't make contact with the sidewalk. That's what it felt like. And the heat blazing down on us didn't help one bit either.

"I hope they're okay," I panted as we rushed toward the hospital entrance.

As I reached for the door, I caught a glimpse of my reflection in the glass. I had forgotten all about the little specks of lavender paint on my arms and face, the splatter in my hair, and the smear marks on my legs. I looked horrible, but at least I was at a hospital, because if anyone I knew saw me, I would have died right there from embarrassment.

I used my hand as a shield to hide behind as a candy-striper led us down the long hallway.

"Here you go." She pulled the curtains aside for us to go into the room.

Josh was alone, sitting in a chair next to an empty bed. Both his knees and one elbow were wrapped in a gauze bandage, and a large goose egg on his forehead caused one of his eyes to squint half-way shut.

"What's going on, Josh? You okay?"

As bad as he looked, I was still relieved to see him sitting upright and not covered in blood, half-dead as I had imagined.

"Yeah, I'm okay, I think. Just got all scraped up, that's all."

"Where's Mom?"

"She had a huge gash on her leg that they had to stitch up. It was so gross. I could see all the way through to her muscle."

His face scrunched in disgust. "Ouch!" He brought his hand to the large lump on his forehead. "I think I even saw her bone."

"Eww!" Jonas said.

"Yeah. So scary. They took her to get x-rays now to make sure nothin's broken."

* * *

At home, Mom followed everything the doctor told her to do. She kept the bandages clean and dry and elevated her leg as much as possible. She might not listen to what most people tell her, but when it comes to doctors and priests, their words are like gold.

One of her friends drove us to the clinic the following week for her checkup. I wasn't sure what her leg was supposed to look like, but after seeing the nurse's face as she unwrapped it, I knew it couldn't be good. Part of the gauze stuck to the wound, and every time the nurse pulled on it, Mom let out a scream.

Her leg was red and swollen, and some of the stitches had popped open. Josh was right. I could see the red flesh of her muscle right through the gap. The nurse excused herself, then returned a few minutes later with a doctor and some students. They stood around Mom's bed, talking about what might be happening with her leg.

"An infection," one of them said. He wrote something on his clipboard, then straightened the stethoscope around his neck.

"What else?" the doctor asked.

They went back-and-forth, discussing all possibilities of what could have gone wrong.

"Is she diabetic?"

"No."

"Is there gangrene?"

"No."

"Is there an odor?"

"No."

"Could she have had a reaction to the sutures?"

"Possibly. I like how you're thinking. What labs should we order?"

"CBC?"

"Yes."

"Culture?"

"Yes."

"Sed rate?"

"Yes. What about a Homan's sign?"

One of the students held onto Mom's foot and pushed it forward.

"Ouch!" Mom shrieked. She grimaced, showing both pain and agitation.

Please, God, don't let her do anything embarrassing. I kept my eyes on her, waiting for the explosion to happen, then noticed her fidgeting with the blanket. She wasn't about to explode. She was scared.

Someone came in to draw blood from her arm. Someone else jabbed a long Q-tip into the open wound on her leg, then the nurse wheeled her away for an ultrasound. The twins and I waited close to an hour for her to come back, and a few more hours for the doctor and his entourage to return.

"Well, I have good news and bad news," the doctor said. "The good news is you don't have an infection." He nodded his head to Mom.

"Yeah, and what's the bad news?" she asked.

"The bad news is you have a large blood clot in your leg."

Mom's jaw dropped.

"It runs all the way from your ankle to your thigh. We're going to have to keep you here 'til we get it dissolved."

The room went silent. *A blood clot? What does that mean?* Josh climbed onto the bed next to Mom and held her earlobe between his fingers.

"Is she gonna be okay?" Jonas asked. His face looked white as the bed sheet.

"Yes, son. We'll give her medicine to make it go away. It'll just take a little while, that's all." The doctor picked up his clipboard. "No need to worry," he said before closing the door.

It took a few minutes for the shock to wear off before Mom could say anything.

"A blood clot. How the hell did I get a blood clot?" she sniffled, then wiped a tear from her eye. "Well, I guess I won't be here for too long. You think y'all can manage on your own at home?"

"Yeah, we'll be fine," I said.

And that was the truth. We really didn't rely on Mom for much at all. The twins walked to school every day, and I got a ride from a friend. Other than that, I did all the cooking and shopping, and Josh helped with the dishes and cleaning now. We'd be fine on our own.

* * *

Every couple of days, the twins and I rode our bikes to the hospital to see her. She didn't seem too upset about the clot anymore. In fact, it was just the opposite. Mom enjoyed all the attention she was getting.

"For the first time in my life, I have people waiting on me," she said. "It's like being at a fancy hotel, gettin' all the room service I want."

What's she talkin' about? That's all we do is wait on her. I scrunched my face into a frown. *How could she say that? I do everything for her. She doesn't have to do a single thing at home. I wish I was in a hospital. Maybe one day she'll hurt me bad enough that I'll get to be here. Or maybe a car will hit me when I'm riding my bike. That would be cool. I could sleep all day and not have to lift a finger like her.*

As one week turned to two, my anger and jealousy toward her began to fade, and I started feeling sorry for her again. She was right. It *was* nice for her to be waited on. She never got over how she was treated as a child, and re-lived her nightmare every time she spoke of it. I wished she could forget about it so she could be happy, but for some reason, she just couldn't. She let her past eat away at her almost every single day.

I liked being home alone with the twins. Without Mom's screaming, fighting, and cussing, it was nice and peaceful.

"When I go to school, I forget all about her," I said one morning at breakfast. "I have fun, and don't even think about her until I'm on my way home again. It's like she doesn't even exist at all." I swept my hand back and forth in the air above my face to dismiss her. "I wish she could do the same. She doesn't even know that the more she gets mad about Grandmama, the more she acts just like her."

"I know," Jonas said. "That's so true."

"That's what we have to do," I continued. "I know it sounds mean, but we have to forget about her when she's not around. Otherwise she'll haunt us every day. Really. It's our only escape. I know *I* never want to be like her when I grow up."

"I wonder why we ended up with a mother like her in the first place?" Josh asked.

"I know. We could've been born into another family," Jonas said.

"Yeah. That's the weird thing about other kids, too. They could've had a mother like ours just as easily. It wasn't our fault."

"They could be just as poor, too," Josh added.

"Yep. I think about that sometimes." I said. "Especially when they're so snobby. But there's nothing we can do about it now. We're stuck with her. All we can do is change how we live our lives once we're old enough to leave her."

* * *

The twins and I hurried down the hall of the hospital, doing one of those crazy speed-walking things people did for exercise, arms and all. We raced to claim one of the two chairs so we wouldn't be the one to get stuck standing. I don't know why no one ever brought in a third chair for us. It's not like they didn't know we'd be coming, or anything.

"I told 'em about all the headaches I've been gettin'," Mom said once we got settled in the room.

She had been getting headaches for quite a while, but never as bad as the last few months in West Monroe. She always said it was Louisiana that made her head hurt, but I thought it probably had to do more with Rachael leaving than anything else. That's when they really started getting bad. More and more often, Mom would hold the sides of her head to make the pain go away, especially after one of her screaming fits.

"So yesterday they did an MRI to see what's goin' on," she continued. "The doctor came in this morning and told me I have a brain tumor."

I wasn't fully listening as she spoke because I hated going there to visit. The smells, her greasy hair, the IV needle in her wrist... I hated all of that. I only went so she could see the twins. But the words "brain tumor" stood out as if she had screamed them into a microphone. The twins were busy elbowing each other, fighting over the chair, so I don't think they heard a word she said, either.

"What? What did you say?" The alarm in my voice got the twins' attention.

"A brain tumor," she said. "It's about the size of a golf ball. That's why I've been getting all those damn headaches."

"What does that mean?" I asked.

For the first time in all our visits, I scooted my chair closer to the bed. Mom looked out the window as her lips began to tremble. I reached my hand to her, to comfort her, but then quickly pulled it back. I couldn't bring myself to touch her, no matter how much I wanted to.

"They said they're gonna have to do an operation to cut it out," she mumbled.

Her voice sounded flat, almost lifeless. I couldn't see her face, but drops of tears began to form a small wet circle on the blanket. Not a sound came from the room other than an occasional beeping from one of the machines. The twins sat motionless in their chair, as if Mom's words had the same power as Medusa's eyes. Josh held Jonas' earlobe in his fingers for comfort, then brought his fist to his mouth and bit on his knuckle. The room became stuffy. I wanted to get out. I needed fresh air.

"They're gonna be keeping me here for a while now," she said. "Teresa, you're going to be in charge. You take good care of your little brothers for me, okay?" her voice shook, and I barely noticed that she called me by my name.

"What do you mean?" Jonas asked. "Why do you have to stay longer? I thought they said you'd be coming home soon." He wiped the tears from his cheeks.

"I'll be okay, sweetie. They'll be scheduling surgery in a few days. Said they'll have to shave my head first, so I guess I'm gonna be bald." She ran her fingers through her long black hair, and shrugged. "Come over here and sit with me."

As she patted the side of her bed, I noticed a big bruise around the IV needle in her wrist and another one higher up her arm.

"Those are from the blood thinners they put me on," she said when she caught me staring. "I was gonna go home, Jonas, but now they have to do an operation to remove the tumor. They have to wait until my blood gets thicker, though." She pushed a button to raise the head of her bed as the twins climbed on.

"So, you're having... brain surgery?" I sputtered. The tightness in my throat made it difficult to speak.

"Yeah. Don't worry. I'm gonna be fine." She reached out and tucked Josh's hair behind his ear as a continuous river of tears flowed down his face. She turned toward me. "You gonna be okay watchin' the boys by yourself? Maybe I could get somebody from the church to help y'all while I'm in here."

I sucked my lips close to my teeth to stop them from shaking, then wiped my face with the back of my hand.

"No. We'll be okay."

"I know you will," she said. "I raised y'all to be strong, independent children. Just don't forget to keep going to Mass on Sundays."

High school toga dance with Kay and
Kim Marley, 1982.

– 33 –

The Marleys

About the time we can make the ends meet,
somebody moves the ends. — Herbert Hoover

I had never seen anything scarier than what Mom looked like following her surgery. I'm not sure which was worse either—the day after, or several days later. The first time the twins and I went to visit her she had a gauze bandage wrapped around her head like a turban with a large reddish-brown stain of dried blood on one side of it. I couldn't even recognize her. She looked like Rocky Balboa from the boxing movie with all the swelling and bruising.

The next time we visited, the bandages were off, but she looked even worse. Not only was she bald, but she had a half-circle of staples in her head. Staples! Instead of Rocky, she looked more like Frankenstein's monster.

* * *

After Mom missed the parent/teacher conference at the twin's school, it didn't take long for word to get out that we were home alone.

Sunday, during the announcements at the end of Mass, I sunk low in the pew as the priest spoke of our situation. Whispers filled the church.

I wish he'd shut his stupid mouth. We've been doing fine. We don't need to go anywhere.

"Let's get the heck out of here," I whispered to the twins as the priest did his final blessing. "This is so embarrassing. Nobody better say anything to us."

We slid to the end of the pew and started making a beeline toward the exit.

"Teresa?" a woman called out behind us.

"Keep walking," I whispered.

"Teresa!" This time louder. A hand grasped my shoulder.

"Yeah?"

"Hi, my name is Mrs. Marley. Dottie Marley." She extended her hand for me to shake.

"Uh, hi." I bit on my lower lip and kept my eyes to the ground, pretending not to notice the hand.

"Teresa, your mother's in the hospital, right?"

Shit! Leave me alone. "Uh-huh," I mumbled.

"Well, we'd love for you to come stay with us until she gets home."

Where in the heck did the twins go?

My eyes darted around the church, but they had already made their way outside.

"How old are you, Teresa?"

"Sixteen." *Why didn't they wait for me?*

"That's what I thought! My daughters are almost sixteen, too! Do you know them? Kim and Kay Marley?"

"Uh, no." I cleared my throat and looked at her for the first time. "It's really nice of you to offer, but we're doing okay on our own. Really. We're fine. My mom won't be in the hospital that much longer, anyway."

"Yeah, but you and your brothers are too young to be staying alone. Don't worry, the church council already set up a place for the boys to stay as well."

"We're getting along just fine!" I snapped.

I folded my arms over my chest. I didn't expect my voice to sound as mean as it did. The lady seemed nice and all, but I liked being alone with the twins.

"You know, if Child Protective Services found out, they could take you away from your mother." She stared down at me. "Forever."

I thought back to the two men who came to NDV when I was in the sixth grade, and the same fears I had back then resurfaced right there in St. Paschal's Catholic Church. *Would they really take us away? Would they separate us? Would Mom go to jail?*

"Really?" I asked.

"Really!" She nodded her head up and down. "That's the truth. So let's swing by your house and grab some of your things, then I'll take you back to our house. You can stay with us the whole time. The family we set up for your brothers can only keep them a few days, so we'll keep looking around for them, too."

* * *

I gathered some clothes from home, then sat in the back seat of the Marley's car, between Kim and Kay, and didn't say a word. The girls made small talk and did goofy things to try to make me laugh, but it didn't work. I kept my eyes forward, looking out the front window as Mr. Marley drove through the countryside. We passed houses with yards big enough to have cows and horses, then pulled up to a beautiful home in a part of West Monroe I didn't even know existed.

"You'll share my room," Kay said. She pulled a strand of her soft curls from her face, and held it back with her hand. Her smile caused her light blue eyes to sparkle. "Come on. I'll show you."

"Okay, let me just grab my stuff first."

"Oh, don't worry about that," Mr. Marley said. "I'll get it for you. Just go inside and make yourself at home."

"Come on!" Kay tugged at the sleeve of my dress.

She showed me around, with Kim following behind us, pointing out different rooms along the way. Apparently, they had been planning my stay for the past couple of days and already had a place all set up for me.

Kay rambled on about her neighborhood, and how she and her sister were twins, just like my brothers, and stuff like that while I checked out my new bed. The comforter was so plush, my hand sank deep when I touched it. I ran my fingers along the little pink roses embroidered in the fabric. If I were alone, or with the twins, I'd twirl around and dance, and I'd jump on the bed, squealing with joy. But there was no way I could do that now. I couldn't let them know how excited I was just to have such a soft blanket and a nice house.

"Wanna go for a walk around the neighborhood?" Kay asked.

"We can introduce you to some of our friends. They can't wait to meet you," Kim added.

Kim and Kay weren't identical twins, but you could definitely tell they were sisters. Like Jonas and Josh, they weren't the same height either. Kim was at least a few inches taller. They had the same shoulder length, feathered haircuts, and pretty much the same smile.

"Okay. Cool," I said.

From that very first day, Kim and Kay became my very best friends. They acted as if we had known each other for years. Their parents were the same, treating me like I was part of the family.

I was in paradise, and for the first time, I got a glimpse of the way the other half lived—a beautiful home, a loving family, no screaming, and no beatings. Meals were cooked for me, and we laughed and talked as we ate. I never wanted it to end but couldn't help feeling guilty for enjoying it so much. Guilt because the longer I stayed meant the longer Mom was in the hospital. Two weeks at their house turned to three weeks, three weeks to a month, and one month to two months as Mom went through rehab.

I wish I could say the twins time away was as good as mine,

but then I'd be lying. No one wanted to host two rambunctious eleven year olds, especially when they were together. They ended up being separated and only stayed a few days with each family, until eventually the State took over and put them into foster care. I'd see them on Sundays at church, and afterwards the Marleys would take us all to visit Mom in the hospital.

Mrs. Marley tried to cheer me up by saying how good Mom looked and how she'd be out in no time, but her encouraging words were more like a knife in my belly. Don't get me wrong, I wanted Mama to get better. I really did. But how could I wish her a speedy recovery when it meant my life would turn to shit again? She had no idea the real reason the visits got me down. How could she? As close as I was to Kim and Kay, I'd never let them know how things really were for me at home. No way. I wasn't about to risk losing them as friends. I hoped and prayed the tumor was the reason Mom turned into such a crazy witch in the first place.

Maybe it showed up while I was in her belly, but nobody knew about it. I cringed at the thought. *I hope surgery took away all the meanness from her so she could be normal like Deborah said she used to be.*

I felt sick when the day arrived for Mom to come home, but I had to pretend to be happy. Spending the summer with the Marleys was like being at camp. Now I was about to go back to prison. I tried my best not to sulk on the drive home by putting on a fake, excited smile, but it was too difficult to include myself in their conversation. As distracted as I was, I couldn't hear a word anyone said, anyway.

Mr. Marley parked the car in front of my house, then everyone got out with me.

"Thank you so much for everything," I said. "Y'all have been so nice to me."

"You're welcome," Mrs. Marley said. Her eyes turned to two crescent moons as she smiled. "You can come back to our place anytime." She began walking to the screened porch as I lingered by the car.

"Yes," Kay agreed. She wrapped her arms around me and gave

a big squeeze. "Maybe you could come over for a little while after church on Sunday."

"That'll be great," I said.

"Come on, you two," Mrs. Marley called from the porch.

I bit on the corner of my lip as I slowly made my way up the steps. "Thanks again," I said.

* * *

The wooden platform of the trundle bed creaked from inside Mom's room, causing my body to tense even more.

"Little girl, is that you?" her voice sounded weak.

I gulped. *Maybe she's nicer.*

"Hi Mom. Yes, I'm home!" I shouted, then turned back to the Marleys. "Okay, thanks again so much for letting me stay with y'all." *Please leave.*

I pushed the door open just as Mama entered the living room. The ruffled fringe on her pink negligee moved side-to-side as she hobbled toward me.

How embarrassing. Why does she have to wear that?

"It's about time you blessed us with your presence. I've been home since early this morning."

Oh, my gosh! Please don't start. I pulled the door to close it behind me, but Mrs. Marley still had her hand on it.

Why aren't they leaving? Please go home. Leave now!

Mama looked just as frightening as before the staples were removed. Her hair had grown about an inch since the last time I saw her, but the half-moon shaped scar stood out like pink puff-paint. Another scar ran up her hairy leg all the way from her ankle to her knee.

Mrs. Marley pushed the door open behind me.

"Hi, Mom. Welcome home," I managed to smile, then cleared my throat. "These are the Marleys. Mr. Marley, Mrs. Marley, Kim, and Kay." I pointed to each as I introduced them.

"Hi, I'm Dottie!" Mrs. Marley extended her hand.

"Hello, I'm Helen," Mama said, using her fake syrupy voice.
Thank God! She's being nice.

"And I'm Stan!"

Okay, please leave now.

"Teresa was a delight to have at our house," Mrs. Marley said. "She's a very sweet and polite girl."

"Well, she better be. That's how I taught her to be."
Leave. Now! My heart began racing. *Why are they still here?*

"Okay, well, I guess I'll see you at church on Sunday." Mrs. Marley winked at me, then headed toward the screen door, followed by Mr. Marley, then after one last hug, Kim and Kay. Tears rolled down my cheek as I watched them get into their car.

"You could have let me know that they were coming so I could have put on something more presentable to wear," Mom said.

"Sorry, Mama. I didn't mean to embarrass you," I said. "I didn't know they were gonna come up. How are you doing? Are all the headaches gone now?"

"Yeah, they're better. Still some throbbing every now and again, but I don't know if that's from the surgery or the tumor." She rubbed the scar on the side of her head. "I'm gonna go back and get some rest now." She limped back to her room. "Meanwhile, go to the store and get some food in this house."

My first Communion, Jacksonville, Florida, one year before the family separation.

– 34 –

Home Sweet Home

When you stop expecting to have problems,
you take a big step in letting go. — Hale Dwoskin

I couldn't wait to get the spaghetti mess cleaned up after supper so I could make Mom the surprise I had planned for her. Since she and the twins were watching an episode of *Fantasy Island*, the timing couldn't have been more perfect. I put bananas and milk into the blender, added some ice and honey, then slowly poured in a packet of banana milkshake powder, and blended it all together.

With a dish towel folded over my arm, I carried the shake to her room on a fancy platter left behind by Aunt Velma.

"I made something for you, Mom!"

Knowing how happy she'd be caused my insides to burst with joy. Sunshine flooded my heart. Mom pushed herself up to sitting and propped a pillow behind her back.

"Oh, what is it, sweetie?"

Sweetie! My heart was about to explode.

"It's a banana milkshake." I stumbled over a stuffed animal as

I carried it toward her bed, but grabbed a hold of the cup before it fell from the tray.

"Here you go."

I held it out to her, and without hesitation, she put her lips to the straw and took a long, slow sip.

"This is delicious! Mmmm! My favorite!"

A warm sensation washed over me as she took another sip, and then another. I knew she would love it.

"I want some," Jonas said.

"No. It's for Mom."

Holding the shake close to her chest, Mom cradled it like a baby, the same way she snuggled the Little LuLu paper doll Jon Eric and I had given her eight years ago. She never liked sharing her sweets and always had a stash of chocolate and other candies hidden somewhere just for herself.

"Can I try some?" Josh asked.

"No, just let Mom have it. Leave her alone," I said.

"Can't you just get one for them, too?" Mom asked.

"No. I only made enough for us."

"But I want some. It's not fair," Jonas said.

"Yes, it is! I bought it with my own money!"

"Get them a milkshake and quit being so selfish for once," Mom said.

She pulled the straw out, held the cup to her mouth for another swallow, then licked the thick banana moustache from her upper lip.

"No. If they want some, they can buy it with their own money, like I did."

When the twins wouldn't stop with their whining and begging, Mom let out a loud sigh, and handed the cup to Jonas.

"Just a tiny sip," I said. "I made it for Mom."

Jonas kept the cup to his mouth until his cheeks puffed out like a chipmunk. My jaw clenched tight as my excitement fizzled to anger.

"Give me that," I snatched it from his hands and gave it back to Mom. "That wasn't a tiny sip."

"I want some, too," Josh said as I turned to go back to the kitchen. I spun toward him and shouted, "It's Mom's. Go make your own!"

"Gosh dammit!" Without a second thought, Mom hurled the cup at me, hitting me square in the jaw. The cold liquid doused my face and hair, splattering the wall behind me, while the cup landed on the white carpet and rolled next to the stuffed animal I almost tripped on. It was so unexpected.

Staring back at Mom, I clenched my fists by my side, and imagined myself looking like Carrie from the Stephen King movie, covered in pig's blood.

"I hate you," I screamed. "I hate your guts!"

I wanted to use my mind to throw something back at her, or even better, to shatter her precious television set like Carrie could. My hands trembled at my sides as I tried to concentrate, but I couldn't make anything happen.

"You little tramp. Clean up this fucking mess before I throw you outside for the night."

"It's all y'all's fault," I shouted at the twins, then picked up the cup and pelted it in their direction.

Shit. Why did I do that? I quickly squatted down and began wiping the mess with the towel I had draped over my arm.

"You goddamn little shit," Mom said.

She yanked the covers off, stormed toward me, and kicked so hard, I tumbled to my side.

"Dammit!" she screamed. "So help me God, if I hurt my leg, I'm gonna kill you."

Josh scooted closer to Jonas and held his earlobe between his fingers. The twins looked at me with their big, round eyes. Eyes full of fear and sadness. Eyes that screamed, "We're sorry!"

Just as Mom limped back to her bed, the doorbell rang. I wiped my face with my arm and looked from Mom to the twins.

No one moved. Another ring, then knocking on the side window of Mom's bedroom that looked onto the screen porch.

"Teresa?" Mrs. Marley asked.

What's she doing here?

"She's looking right at us through the window," Josh whispered.

More knocking, and then Kim and Kay's faces appeared next to hers.

"Teresa, we forgot to bring your bike when we dropped you off earlier," Mrs. Marley said. She tapped on the window again. "I have it here for you."

What did they see? How long have they been there? What can I say happened?

Mom sat at the edge of her bed with her face buried in her hands.

"Thank you. You can just leave it on the front porch for me," my voice came out high-pitched and shaky.

"Teresa, can you please come here?" Mrs. Marley demanded.

Shit! What am I gonna say?

"They're not going to leave until I go to the door," I mumbled.

"Yes, they will. Don't look at 'em," Mom said.

"Teresa!" Mrs. Marley said again, this time raising her voice louder. She rattled the handle to the front door, but thank God it was locked. "Stan! Get out of the car and come here."

She must have seen more than just the shake in my hair.

"I'm coming!" I shouted.

I ran to my room, grabbed a t-shirt from the floor, and quickly wiped as much of the sticky mess off of me as I could before heading to the door.

"Hi." I put on a fake smile. "Thanks so much for bringing my bike."

"What's going on, Teresa? What's all over you?"

"What? Oh, nothin'. I tried making a shake but didn't put the lid on all the way, so it blew up all over the place."

She raised an eyebrow. *How much did they see?*

"Are you, uh, is everything okay here? I thought I heard shouting when we pulled up."

Oh good. Maybe she didn't see anything. "Yeah. Everything's fine."

My heart pounded so hard I could feel it all the way in my ears. I could barely breathe. "I was just upset about the shake, that's all. I really wanted to surprise my Mom with it. It's her favorite. But I just ended up making a big mess instead."

"Okay, Teresa." Mrs. Marley hesitated, then looked me up and down. I gripped onto the bottom of my shirt so she couldn't see my hands shaking.

"Please call us anytime if you need anything." She glanced back in the window of Mom's bedroom. "And I mean... anything."

"Okay. Thanks again for bringing my bike."

"I'd give you another hug," Kay said, "but you're a mess!"

I forced a laugh. "I know! Those darn lids!"

Their walk back to the curb took a painfully long time. Mrs. Marley stopped by the open car door, looked at the house, then took a few steps back toward our front porch.

Don't come back. Please, don't come back.

She paused, then turned around to join everyone else in the car.

Thank God they believed me!

Jonas and Josh were busy cleaning the mess for me, so I went in my room and threw myself on my bed. My body felt as if it were covered in white school glue, but as much as I wanted to wash the stickiness off, I'd never take a shower when Mom was in one of her moods. No way. Bad things always happened in the bathroom.

I cried myself to sleep until the telephone woke me up.

Mrs. Marley!

I sprung out of bed to grab it before she had a chance to speak to anyone else. "Hello?"

"Hey, Treedy! It's Rachael! How's everything going?"

Rachael? "It's okay."

She caught me off guard. I hadn't spoken to Rachael ever

since she left us almost two years ago. I spread my fingers wide, peeling them apart from each other. "How's it there?"

"Great! I have a boyfriend! We've been dating over a year now." She sounded different. Happy and excited. Alive. "He works at the same place as a friend of mine, so she introduced us."

"Oh, wow! That's cool!"

I didn't really know how I felt. Happy for her, for sure. But I was still a little angry and envious that she got away. She was one of the only things that could have brought Mom even a tiny glimpse of happiness in West Monroe.

"Guess what? I got to go to prom last year," I said. "A junior asked me! It was so fun!" I don't know why I even told her that. I didn't have to compete with her anymore. It was a game I always lost anyway.

"That's nice! Don't say anything out loud because I want to be the one to tell Mom, but I'm calling to tell y'all that I'm getting married and I want you to be a bridesmaid."

If it weren't for the sticky milkshake residue on my hands, the phone would have dropped to the floor. "No way!"

"Yes! And I know it's short notice, but we're getting married in two months. I hope y'all can come!"

"That's so cool, Rache! I'm happy for you. What's his name?"

"David. Okay, lemme talk to Mom now."

* * *

Things got weird during the next few weeks when I'd see the Marleys at church. Not with Kim and Kay, but with Mrs. Marley. As subtle as she tried to be, it still felt as if she were watching me under a microscope.

"Teresa, what happened to your arm?" she whispered in my ear while we were in line to get doughnuts after Mass.

Bluish-green bruises peeked from under the hairs on my forearm. "Oh, nothing," I covered them with my hand. "I was just horse-playing with the twins."

I always had to be on top of my game. Always ready with an excuse at the tip of my tongue.

"Teresa, why are you wearing a sweater today? It's over a hundred degrees outside."

"Because it matches my dress."

"Teresa, have you been crying?"

"No. I've just been rubbing my eyes. Allergies, I think."

Each time she'd frown and shake her head. I'm not sure if she didn't believe me, or if she just thought I was too careless and clumsy. Whatever the case, she never seemed happy with any of my answers. She didn't push it, though, not with Mom standing an earshot away in the church hall.

Family Reunion in Alaska for Mom's 89th birthday, 2019. Left back: Jonas, Gregory, Brother (Leigh), Josh, Jon Eric, Petesy (David); middle row: me; front: Deborah, Mom (Rachael is missing)

– 35 –

The Talk

If you reveal your secrets to the wind, you should not blame the wind for revealing them to the trees. — Khalil Gibran

Kay put sleeping bags on the trampoline for us to have a sleep-over. We held hands while jumping, took turns doing flips, and laughed hysterically when we'd miss our feet and land on our bottoms. That's the thing with Kay, she brought out the silliness in me and allowed me to forget about my real-life.

After we wore ourselves out, we lay head-to-head, looking up at the stars, talking about boys, and school, and stuff like that.

"I wish I was still staying here with y'all," I told her.

"I know. Me too. That was so much fun."

"I mean, I hate it at my place. My mom is seriously so mean to me. She hates me."

"Oh, that's not true, Teresa. She's your mother. She has to love you."

"No, Kay. She's a crazy witch."

I don't know what happened, but once I started, I couldn't stop.

I figured I could trust Kay and didn't think she was the type who would quit being my friend if she knew the truth about Mom.

"She beats me almost every day." The muscles trembled in my chin like a small child, as tears began to pour down my face. I pushed myself up and sat crossed-legged facing her. "And I'm not talking about just spankings, either." I paused to recover my breath before continuing. "Last night, she threw an iron at me." My hands trembled as I lifted my shirt. "See this? Thank God it wasn't hot." I showed her the reddish-blue mark on my side. "She's so mean, Kay. I think she might kill me one day."

Kay sat up, wrapped her arms around me, and rocked slowly. I buried my head on her shoulder, soaking her shirt with my tears.

"Oh, Teresa. I'm sorry! We knew something was wrong, but had no idea it was anything like this," she said as she wiped the mist from her own eyes.

"It's so bad, Kay. I wanna run away."

I spent the rest of the night spilling my guts through sobs and trembling, but didn't feel relieved like I thought I would. The secret I had held onto so tightly for the past eight years erupted like a molten lava volcano. A somber feeling of guilt weighed on me like a pile of cinder blocks. I had betrayed Mom, the very one I had tried to protect all my life, and now I risked losing my best friend over it. My stomach burned inside. I wanted to throw up. *Why did I say all that?*

"Please don't say anything to anybody," I said. "Please. I don't want anything bad to happen to my mother."

"Okay." She rubbed her hand up and down my back. "I'm so sorry this has been going on, Teresa."

* * *

The next morning, Mrs. Marley called out to me. "Teresa, can you come here?"

Kay's sleeping bag lay balled up and empty next to me. *Shoot. What time is it? How long did I sleep?* When I went into the house, Mr. Marley and Kay were sitting on the couch with expressionless looks on their faces. Kim sat across from them in an overstuffed chair.

"Teresa, have a seat over here," Mr. Marley said, patting the cushion on the other side of him. I looked from Mr. Marley, to Kay, then to Kim before taking a seat.

"Teresa," he began. "How have things been at home with your Mom?"

I tried swallowing, but my mouth was dry as pork cracklings.

"She's doing a little better. She doesn't have headaches anymore. And all her surgery sites healed up nicely." My throat tightened a little more with each word.

"That's great, darlin'. I'm glad she's doing better. But that's not what I'm talking about."

Crap! I knew it.

"What do you mean?" I asked.

"You know, Teresa, we can't help but notice the bruises and the scratch marks you sometimes have," he said.

"And I know Helen did something to you that day we brought back your bike. We know she hurts you," Mrs. Marley added.

My stomach tangled into a tight ball. I leaned over and glanced at Kay, but her head was hung down, looking at the floor as she twirled her thumbs.

"Teresa, it's not right for anyone to hurt you," Mr. Marley said. He reached over and handed me a tissue.

My chest felt as if it was wrapped in a tight cocoon, preventing my lungs from expanding. I wanted to run out of the room and bury my head in the soft pillow with the embroidered roses on the slip, but I couldn't. I was trapped with nowhere to go.

"We've been talking, and think it's best that you call your father to see if you could live with him in Florida," Mr. Marley continued.

Beads of sweat covered my forehead like raindrops on a window. I wiped them off, then kept my hand over my eyebrows to hide my tears.

"It's not that bad at home. Really. I'm okay." I paused to stop my voice from cracking, then took a deep breath, and whispered. "I promise."

"No. It's not okay. How can you say it's okay for someone to hurt you? No matter how much you try to tell yourself that it is. It's just not okay," Mrs. Marley said.

"Teresa, we're not going to let you go back home. We're serious about this," Mr. Marley looked over to Kay, whose eyes were still glued to the floor, then stood up to face me. "You have two choices. Either you can stay here and live with us..."

My shoulders shuddered up and down while I tried to stop my sobbing.

"Or you can get on the phone and call your father to see if you can live with him in Florida." Mr. Marley's blue eyes softened when I looked up at him. "The choice is yours, sweetie. Whatever you decide is fine with us, but we're not going to let you go back home. I hope you understand. We just want what's best for you."

"And don't worry, we'll arrange everything with Child Protective Services if you decide to stay with us," Mrs. Marley said. Her eyes stabbed through me as she spoke. Eyes that pierced my heart and shouted that they weren't about to budge with their decision.

Mrs. Marley left the room and came back with more tissues and a glass of iced tea for me.

"We'll leave you alone to think about it. You can go to Kay's room while I finish up supper, but we'd like for you to make your decision by tonight," she said.

* * *

I went into Kay's room, sat on the edge of the bed with my forehead buried in my hands and broke down. I cried thinking about Mom's bald head after her surgery and cried about the banana shake that she had tossed all over me. I cried about her excitement when she took us on trips and cried about the iron she recently threw at me. I cried about how she always tried to fit in with the other mothers and cried over the friends I had lost because of her. I cried over the way she showed me off for dancing the Charleston and for all the times she threw me out naked. I cried until my voice was hoarse and my shirt sopped with tears. I could have cried for days, but felt bad that I had locked Kay out of her room. I wiped my face on my damp shirt and headed back to the living room.

My voice cracked, barely audible. "I'll call my father.".

Thompson Family Reunion, 2014. From left: Joye, Dad, then in order of age Deborah, Brother (Leigh) Rachael, Petesy (David), Gregory, Jon Eric, me, Jonas, Josh, and then Mom.

– 36 –

The Letter

Between every two pine trees is a door
leading to a new way of life. — John Muir

I dragged my heels to the kitchen and leaned next to the phone that hung on the wall. That same phone I had used so many times to call Mom while she was in the hospital now gave me a sense of foreboding. I took a few deep breaths to get up my nerve, then picked up the receiver. Grief poured from me in a flood of uncontrollable tears as I listened to the ominous sound of the dial tone. A sound that usually went unnoticed now filled me with dread. Another breath, this time shallow as my heart began to race faster.

I brought my fingers to the dial, then pulled them back. As often as I had dreamt of living with my father all those years, I just couldn't make the call. He'd probably say no, anyway. If he wanted me there, he would have invited me long ago.

Sliding down the wall, I buried my head in my knees while more tears flowed. I didn't know what to do. Mr. and Mrs. Marley meant what they said. They weren't about to let me go back home to Mama, and as much as I would have liked to, there was no way I could stay there with them.

A loud beeping from the phone caused me to jump. I pushed the switch-hook to reset the dial tone, then held it back to my ear. My finger trembled as I brought it to the first number, making it difficult to fit in the hole of the rotary, but somehow I managed to dial all the numbers.

It's ringing. I'm calling Florida. I can't! My heart cartwheeled as my body seized in a fit of shivering. Between the air conditioning and my nerves, it felt freezing in their kitchen. *I can't do it.* I slung the phone back on the wall, then ran into Kay's room to grab a blanket. Squeezing the blanket tight around my shoulders, I went back into the kitchen, and dialed the number again. *Maybe he won't be home.*

"Hello?" a man's voice came on after the first ring.

"Daddy?" I coiled the phone cord around one of my fingers as my throat began to tighten.

"Yes?"

I couldn't open my mouth. Nothing else could come out.

"Teresa? Is that you?"

"Yeah." My voice choked on my sobs. I repeated myself, but it wasn't any louder than a whisper. "Yeah."

"Hi, darling! It's so good to hear from you. Is everything okay?"

"Yeah, Daddy." I held the phone away from my mouth so he couldn't hear my teeth chattering on the other end.

"Baby? Are you okay?"

"Daddy, I wanted to see…" I took a deep breath, the kind that makes my whole body shudder. "I wanted to see if I could come and live with you?" I closed my eyes tight as if waiting for a blow before continuing. "I only have two more years of high school left, so it wouldn't have to be for that long."

"Oh," he said, then let out a sigh. "Well, I'm sure that'll be fine. I'll have to talk it over with Joye first, though."

With each word, the chill left the room. Heat spread from my cheeks to my chest and stomach. The blanket fell from my shoulders, landing by my feet in a soft clump of cotton. I wanted to hang up. My stepmother would never say yes, and he probably didn't even want me there, either. At least that's what I always told myself. I peeked around the corner into the living room where the Marleys pretended not to be listening.

"Okay. Well, I'm staying with a family here in West Monroe. They're not gonna let me go back home to Mama." Heavy sobbing stole the rest of my words.

"What?"

"They said..." more shuddering breaths, "that I can either move to Florida with you, or they're gonna try to adopt me." My crying became louder. I couldn't hold it back anymore. "They might get Mom arrested or something," I bawled.

"That's probably a good thing. She deserves to be in jail after all she's done."

"What?"

"After stealing my children away from me. I'm sorry. You don't need to hear that. You can come here to stay with us. It's fine. I'll tell Joye."

His words left me feeling sick and relieved at the same time. *How can I leave the twins?*

"I don't know how we'll come up with the money to get you here, but we'll work something out," he said.

"No. It's okay. You don't have to pay for it. I have a job now, and I've been saving up a lot of money. I can buy my own ticket."

"Okay, well, we'll have to get you registered for school. What grade did you say you're in?"

"I'm going into eleventh. I'll be a junior."

"Okay, I'll have Joye call Wolfson High tomorrow to set everything up."

I knew about Wolfson. Jon Eric told me all about it on our cross-country drive in the green Chevy. He liked it there, but it was a public school. Deborah and Brother were the only two who graduated from Bishop Kenny.

"Wolfson?" I bit on my lower lip. "Can I go to Bishop Kenny, instead?"

"No, honey. We can't afford Bishop Kenny. Wolfson's a good school. You'll see."

I felt empty inside as I hung up the phone and slid back down the wall to sit on the floor. To Mom, sending us to a Catholic school all these years was everything. She fought hard to get me into NDV and put up the same fight for St. Fredericks. All that work to make sure we had a good, Catholic education was being flushed down the drain with one phone call. I was ruining everything. I pulled my knees to my chest to rest my chin on while trying to figure out what to do.

I only have two years left. I don't wanna spend 'em at a public school.

Mrs. Marley peeked into the room. "You okay in here, Teresa?"

"Yeah," I sniffed and wiped my face on my shirt. "I called my dad. He said it's okay for me to go to Florida. I'm just thinking about something right now." I twirled the end of my hair around my finger and brought it over my face to hide my puffy eyes from her.

"Is it okay if I call information?" I asked.

"Sure, whatever you need, sweetie."

"Thanks!"

I stretched the phone cord to reach a small built-in desk, picked up a pencil and a piece of paper, then dialed 411.

"Information, may I help you?"

"Yes, the number for Bishop Kenny High School in Jacksonville, Florida, please."

I wrote the number down and tapped the pencil eraser on the desk while thinking of a plan.

Rachael's wedding! Oh, my gosh! I can't believe it. It's perfect! Mama said she couldn't go to the wedding because of her surgery. That can be my excuse! I'll tell her I'm going to Rachael's wedding, and that I'll buy my own ticket to get there. I just won't tell her I'm not coming back, that's all.

My belly churned with both pain and excitement. *Mama*

*would have a conniption if she knew I wasn't coming back. She'd
never let me go. I just have to leave. I can't even tell the twins.* Tears
filled my eyes again. *I can't believe I'm gonna live with Daddy.*

I barely slept a wink that night. One minute my heart raced with
excitement, while the next was weighed down with sadness. The ups
and downs went on for hours until I finally fell asleep. The following
morning, I asked Mr. Marley if I could make another call to Florida.

"I can pay you back if you want," I said.

"Of course you can, Teresa. Don't be silly."

I went into the kitchen and unfolded the little piece of paper I
had crumpled into a ball, then dialed the number.

"Bishop Kenny High School. May I help you?"

Crap! I wasn't sure if anyone would answer since we were on
summer break.

"Uh, hi," I looked into the living room to make sure no one
was listening, then explained my situation to the lady on the
other end of the line. I didn't say anything about Mom, just that
I wanted to finish my high school years at a Catholic school.

"I recommend that you write a letter to the Monsignor.
He's the one who would be able to help you," the lady said.

I wrote his name and address down, then pulled up a chair,
grabbed a fresh sheet of paper, and began writing.

July 13, 1983

Dear Monsignor Logan,

*Hi. My name is Teresa Thompson. I live in West Monroe, Louisiana
where I've been attending St Frederick's High School. During this
next school year, I'll be moving to Jacksonville to live with my father.*

*You may remember my sister and brother, Deborah and Leigh
Thompson since they both graduated from Bishop Kenny. We come
from a large family, so money is always tight. That's why the rest of
my siblings had to go to a public school.*

I've gone to Catholic schools ever since kindergarten and really value the type of education I've been exposed to. I'm an excellent student and a very fast learner.

In order for me to go to Bishop Kenny, I would have to pay my own tuition, and I know the cost is more than I can afford on my own. I'll get a job as soon as I move there, but I was wondering if there's a chance I could get some financial aid or discounted tuition? I'm asking that you please take my desire to graduate from a Catholic high school into consideration.

Thank you in advance.

Yours in Christ,
Teresa Thompson

I wrote both the Marley's and my father's phone numbers under my name, jotted the school address on an envelope, put a stamp on it, and slipped in the letter.

Am I sure I wanna do this? I flicked the edge of the envelope back and forth between my fingers as I thought more about it. *Yes. I wanna go to a Catholic school. I'm not gonna ruin everything Mama did for me by finishing my last two years at a public school.*

Mama's words rang through my head, "I'm sending y'all to the best school in San Francisco. I'm not gonna raise a bunch of dummies."

Kim and Kay are happy at their school, and they're not dummies. And Jon Eric said he liked Wolfson.

I thought about our school assemblies and how the teachers spoke about preparing us for college. "This is a college prep school," they'd say, and I wondered if they talked about college at a public school? I paced back and forth in the kitchen.

They definitely don't teach religion at a public school. It would be weird not having a Religion class, especially after St. Francis watched over me all those years in San Francisco.

And without the nuns pushing college in my face every day, what if I changed my mind about it? None of the other kids in the family went to a four-year college. How will I ever be able to help people if I don't have a college education? Shoot! What would Jesus do? That's a stupid question.

The thoughts buzzed through my mind as I paced the floor. *Yes. I have to do it. I have to go to a Catholic school.* I didn't know anything about Wolfson, or any other public school for that matter. I only knew what Mama had preached about a good Catholic education, and if I could help it, I wasn't about to ruin the one good thing she did for me. I licked the seal on the envelope and kept my fingers crossed as I skipped out to the mailbox.

"Teresa, your father's on the phone," Kay called out to me.

My stomach tightened as I ran back to the house. *Shoot. Did he change his mind?*

"Hello?" my voice cracked.

"Hi baby. We got a bus ticket for you. You'll be coming here the end of the week. Friday."

Holy crap! I let out a deep sigh. *It's really happening. I can't believe it.* I put my hand on my forehead and looked down at my feet as he continued. *Catholic school or not, looks like I'm going to Florida.* I jotted down the details of the bus schedule, then hung up the phone, and sat back down at the desk. *I can't believe it!*

I felt light headed and numb until sadness took over completely, causing a deep ache to fill my chest—the kind that made it hard to breathe.

What am I doing? All the good things Mama had ever done for us over the years swirled through my mind. *I'm a horrible person to leave her and the twins.*

I walked out the side door of the kitchen, so I could be alone to map out my plan. *I'll have to leave most of my stuff behind so Mama doesn't get suspicious. Man, I wish I could tell the twins. Maybe I could. No. I can't. What if they tell on me?* I sat in the front yard and leaned against a pine tree. *The poor twins.* My hands shook as I broke a dried-up pine needle into tiny pieces.

Since the plan was set into action, the Marleys drove me back home the next day to begin packing.

"We'll swing by on Friday to take you to the bus station," Mrs. Marley said as she dropped me off at home.

"Oh, that's okay. You don't have to. I'm sure my mom'll take me," I said.

But that wasn't going to happen.

No one was home when I entered our small house. A note on my bed, scribbled in Mom's writing, read, "I have to go back to University. The twins are with me. See you soon, Love, Mama."

The paper slipped from my fingers. *University? She's back at the hospital? Why?* I dialed the number and waited for the receptionist to connect me to her room.

"Hello?"

"Mama, what's going on?"

"Hi, sweetie. Well, I started getting those damn headaches again, so they had me come in to run more tests. They're gonna keep me here while they figure out what's going on.

"What? How's that possible?"

Shit! I'll never be able to leave now.

My family: my husband Lance, me and my three daughters, Dyllan, Jolie and Jayden, 2019.

– 37 –

The Plan

Truth is like the sun. You can shut it out for a time,
but it ain't going away. -Evis Presley

*M*y stomach churned, a cauldron of bubbling acid as I pedaled my bike toward the hospital. *What's gonna happen now? No way Mama's gonna let me go while she's in the hospital. No way.* The nausea in my belly grew with each scenario that flooded my brain. *If she doesn't let me go to Florida, the Marleys are gonna take me from her.* Between the pedaling, the heat, and the nauseous feeling, I could barely catch a full breath. *I can't even imagine what would happen next. It would be awful. Mom'll fight tooth and nail to keep me.*

I veered off the sidewalk and pedaled along a path in an empty field. *If the courts find out how she treats us, they'll probably take the twins, too. The twins hated foster care. Mama would never forgive me. No one would. The whole family'll hate me.* I jumped off my bike, ran to an elderberry bush and threw up everything the Marleys had fed me that morning. A large tree stood motionless next to the bush. No cool breeze to rustle its leaves, or to change them to the brilliant red, yellow, and orange colors like they do in the fall. Its sprawling branches cast a shadow over me, but didn't do anything to lessen the heat. I hated the hot summer days as much as Mom did. I snatched one of the dangling leaves and blew my nose on it before getting back on my bike to cross the bridge.

If I do leave, I could have a better life. Daddy would never beat me the way Mama does. And they live in such a nice house, I could pretend I'm rich to the kids at school. No one in Florida would ever have to know about Mama. They don't have to know about anything. I could be normal like all of them. What's done is done with Mom. I can't change anything that already happened to me, but I can change what happens from here on out. It could be like a new day, a new start, a second chance at life. Yeah. I'll never tell anybody anything.

I wiped my nose on my arm as the nausea began to build again. *What can I say to Mom?* My stomach churned some more. *I just won't tell her. It's the only way. I just have to leave. I'm not gonna say anything to her.*

As I pedaled on and planned my escape, the thought of leaving the twins behind left a burning hole in my gut. Especially Josh. *How can I leave him?* But I knew I couldn't stay. I wouldn't be living with them anyway if I did. I went back over everything I had already thought about over and over that day. *I can't stay. I have to go. Maybe if I talked to Dad and Joye, they'd let the twins come stay in Florida, too. Yeah, I'll tell them everything.*

At the hospital I didn't have to wait for the candy-striper to show me to Mama's room, since I already knew the number from the telephone call. I ran past the information desk, straight to the restroom and threw up again before heading up the elevator

* * *

I had never felt God's love shower over me as much as I did during that last week in West Monroe. Throughout my life, I had always questioned Him. Why was I born to such a hateful mother? What did I do that was so wrong that He decided to place me with *her?* Did God even do this to me, or was it just random? I never understood. And to this day, I still don't. And never will. How could anyone ever make sense of something like this? You just can't.

But during that one week, everything fell into place for me. The doctor said he wanted Mama to stay in the hospital until Saturday to make sure everything was okay with her head after the surgery. They wanted to keep an eye on her, but weren't concerned about anything too serious.

Those three days in the hospital gave me plenty of time to sort through my things and pack what I could fit into two large trash bags. It also gave me alone time to be with the twins. We held each other and cried as I told them my plan of never returning home again.

I read and re-read the note I had written to Mom before finally placing it on her nightstand.

Dear Mom,

I hope everything's okay with the tumor they removed... The doctor said he thinks you'll be fine, so I don't think there's anything to worry about.

I'm sorry I'm writing this to you instead of telling you in person, but I was scared you'd say no. I'm going to Florida for Rachael's wedding because she asked me to be one of her bridesmaids. I have enough money saved for my bus ticket, so you don't have to worry about paying my way, or anything. The twins have supper already made for tonight, so they'll be fine until you get home tomorrow. See you soon.

I love you,
Teresa

I felt bad for not telling her that Dad was paying for my ticket, but then she'd wonder why he didn't buy one for Jonas and Josh as well. The twins carried my black trash bags to the front porch and sat with me while I waited for the Marleys to pick me up.

"Y'all can't tell Mom I'm not comin' back," I said. "She'll be mad if she finds out that y'all knew."

Just then, the phone rang. Probably a friend from school calling for one last goodbye. It wasn't a friend, though. It was Monsignor Logan from Bishop Kenny. The Marleys gave him my home number so he could give me the news himself. He told me he was so impressed by my letter, that, not only did he accept me into the school, but he, himself was going to make sure I'm placed in an advanced English class. After we talked about how much I would pay for my monthly tuition, I asked if he could please keep it a secret from the other students.

"No one will ever know," he reassured in a strong Irish accent. "I'm proud to have someone like you in our school. And I have high hopes for your future, young lady. Someone with as much drive and determination as you will undoubtedly go far in life. I look forward to meeting you in person," he said before hanging up the phone.

"The Marleys are here," Jonas said. He and Josh walked into the room and sat on each side of me.

I looked at the clock radio. One o'clock. Right on time. Tears ran down my cheeks as I gave the twins one last hug.

"I sure am going to miss y'all. I wish y'all could come with me," I said, then turned to Josh. "Josh, please don't let Mama bring you down, or hurt you. Remember that you're everything better than what she says you are. Don't believe anything bad she ever tells you."

I stood up, gave them each another big hug, and walked out the door.

⌒

Teresa graduates
with honors from the
California College of
Podiatric Medicine,
San Francisco, 1996.

Epilogue

"Success is to be measured not so much by the position that one has reached in life as by the obstacle which he has overcome."
— *Booker T. Washington*

Coming from a family of nine kids with a mentally unstable and abusive mother, we all have stories to tell. It doesn't matter if we were one of the favorites or one that received most of the abuse; growing up in that type of environment was difficult for all of us. Wildflower is my story. I hope one day my siblings will share in the catharsis by writing their own.

When I didn't return to Louisiana after Rachael's wedding, the incessant hate mail began to pour in on Patsy Ann Drive. Day after day, letter after letter, Mom wrote things like, "You'll never amount to anything, you piece of trash, whore." and "You're gonna rot in hell." The letters were eventually intercepted once my stepmother Joye caught wind of the hatred that spewed from them.

I promised myself that I'd never let my mother interfere with my new life in Jacksonville. Even though she could still weasel her way under my skin, I wasn't about to let her poison infiltrate any new friendships I had at Bishop Kenny. My mother was my secret, and so was my past. No one would ever have to know I was different.

Later that year, Dad paid for a bus ticket for Josh to come to Florida as well, but after being there for only a couple of weeks, Josh decided he wanted to go back to Louisiana. He liked the freedom he had with Mom and didn't want to conform to the strict rules that Joye laid out for him in Florida.

Rachael accepted me as if we had been best friends all our lives, and even though I couldn't understand it, I certainly welcomed it. I guess I was some sort of comfort blanket for her, something familiar from the past as she navigated her way into the unknown.

Rachael invited me to go with her and her husband David on a road trip to the Grand Canyon the following summer, which of course, I gladly accepted. On the way, we stopped in Louisiana to see Mom and the twins.

Mom ran out, swooped Rachael from her feet, spun her around, hugged her, and filled her face with kisses. She then turned to David, whom she had never met, and called him by name. "David, so nice to finally meet you," then wrapped her arms around him as she did to Rachael.

Afterward, she turned in my direction. The smile left her face as she asked, "Who's that?"

When Rachael said, "Mom, that's Teresa," she replied, "No way that's my little girl. That girl is way too fat to be Teresa. I don't have kids who are fat slobs like that." I had gained a total of five pounds that year.

I worked two jobs to pay my way through Bishop Kenny, one at a veterinary office, and the other as a cashier at the local grocery store, Winn Dixie. On the months I was too careless with my spending, Jon Eric helped cover my tuition.

I fit in well at Bishop Kenny with my new set of friends, but as always, people with money intimidated me. I couldn't trust that they'd still hang if ever they found out how poor I really was, and especially if they knew anything about Mom. I had been down that road way too many times.

In high school, I got a lot of attention from boys at parties my friends would take me to. The question they most frequently asked me was, "so what does your father do?" I couldn't believe it! I was in a much better place than before, but as an insurance salesman, Dad certainly did not make a lot of money, and there was no escaping the snobbery of the wealthy. I wanted to say, Why do you ask what he does? Why don't you ask what I'm going to do? But I was way too shy and insecure to assert myself like that.

I kept the mantra going throughout my adulthood that I would never be hateful like my mother. There are many qualities I took from her though: the importance of a good education, my strong faith in God, the love of nature and travel, and a great sense of adventure.

I had always wanted to become a veterinarian, but that desire changed after working with a disgruntled doctor at the animal hospital. Even so, my empathy and need to help others in pain never ceased. I knew I wanted to become a doctor, and podiatry seemed to be a good fit. From what I saw when visiting various medical specialties, patients who limped into the podiatrist's office, usually left feeling at least a little better.

I paid my way through my pre-med courses at the University of Central Florida by bartending at night and working in the biology lab at school during the day. After graduation, I went back to San Francisco to study at the California College of Podiatric Medicine where I met my husband and graduated with honors.

I'm still happily married after almost 25 years and have the home I've always dreamt of in the quaint little town of Benicia, California. I have three beautiful daughters, and my oldest is following in my husband's and my own footsteps as a pre-med/biology major at Boise State.

My siblings and I are all very close and try to get together for reunions as much as we can. One such reunion was at my dad's funeral in 2014. He was 83. Last year, while in Alaska for my mother's 89th birthday, even through her dementia, she still remembered how much she hated me. This time, instead of being fat, she said to Petesy, "Who's that?" When he explained that I was her daughter, Teresa, her response was, "That's not Teresa! That's a boy!" Never mind the fact I was wearing a dress and had long hair.

* * *

I have several hopes for the outcome of my book, and the first goes to the teachers. Teachers have the ability to make a huge difference in a child's life, and all it takes is a little kindness. Wouldn't it be great if you were the one whose name came up when someone was asked, who was your real-life role model as a child? Teachers have that power.

My second hope is that my readers teach their children to treat others with respect, and that can only be done by example. Teach them to see the world through their hearts, not just their eyes. Not only can they make a difference in a child's life, but it also builds strong character for years to come.

Lastly, for those of you who have been dealt a life like mine, know that there is a way out. You don't have to repeat patterns, and you certainly don't have to be stuck. You may have to work five or even ten times harder than your peers, but in the long run, it's worth it. Stay in school and study hard. Keep your eyes on the future. Decide right now how you'd like your life to be, and never lose sight of those goals and dreams. The future is what you make it. Even if you're not doing so hot in school, your hard work and determination will pay off in the end. You may not be able to change the life you have now, but your future is completely up to you.

Prove everyone wrong, if no one believes in you. You have to believe in yourself, because if your life is anything like mine was, then YOU are all you have.

End

Acknowledgements

There are many people I'd like to thank for helping me through my writing process.

Dr. David Ross for encouraging me to write and convincing me I had a story worth sharing. Thank you for your positive words and for your unfaltering belief in me.

My brothers and sisters who met with me weekly on the phone. Thank you for your stories, love, and encouragement.

My friends whom I wrote about in the book—who listened and reminisced with both tears and laughter as I read them *their* chapter. You guys were always my light in the darkness. Trez Gregorian, Courtney Murphy, and Kim and Kay Marley.

My husband, Lance and my three daughters, Dyllan, Jolie and Jayden for the countless times y'all listened when asked, "How does this paragraph sound?"

Benicia Outlaws Read and Critique group. Without you guys, my book would never make it on a bookstore shelf. I learned and grew so much as an author from this amazing group of writers. They've been with me from the very first page–through my tears and misplaced commas, to taking over the reading for me when the pain was just too much.

Benicia Library Critique Group. Also there through my tears. Thank you for all your wonderful insights and critiques.

Janene Biggs who graciously took on the role as line editor to correct those misplaced commas and Nicky Ruxton for content editing.

My three Beta readers: Deb Bezanson, Tiffany Rendon, and Teri Bailey who proofread my manuscript before it left my hands completely.

Jan Malin, book designer and publisher, Canyon Rose Press. Thank you for believing in my book enough to take on this project — and for all the hard work you put into formatting my words into a beautiful book.

And finally, thank you to my dog Suki, who always found a way to snuggle on my lap as I wrote. Also thanks to my dog Bodhi, who remained close by my side and to my two cats Shanti and Santosh, who sat on the table behind me. Animals have always brought peace and love to my life and still do to this day.

Chapter titles, numbers and initial caps were set in Winsome, designed by Laura Worthington of Washington State. Laura's type designs are based on her own writing and calligraphy.

The text was set in Adobe Caslon, a renewal of the originals developed by William Caslon between 1734 and 1770. Carol Twombly is the type designer.

Made in the USA
Columbia, SC
08 June 2021